P9-DDL-813

SPIN

ALSO BY PATRICIA CORNWELL

Captain Chase Series

Quantum

The Scarpetta Series

Postmortem

Body of Evidence

All That Remains

Cruel and Unusual

The Body Farm

From Potter's Field

Cause of Death

Unnatural Exposure

Point of Origin

Black Notice

The Last Precinct

Blow Fly

Trace

Predator

Book of the Dead

Scarpetta

The Scarpetta Factor

Port Mortuary

Red Mist

The Bone Bed

Dust

Flesh and Blood

Depraved Heart

Chaos

Nonfiction

Portrait of a Killer: Jack the Ripper—Case Closed

Ripper: The Secret Life of Walter Sickert

Andy Brazil Series

Hornet's Nest

Southern Cross

Isle of Dogs

Win Garano Series

At Risk

The Front

Biography

Ruth, a Portrait: The Story of Ruth Bell Graham

Other Works

Scarpetta's Winter Table

Life's Little Fable

Food to Die For: Secrets from Kay Scarpetta's Kitchen

SPIN

PATRICIA CORNWELL

This is a work of fiction. Names, characters, organizations, places, events, and incidents are either products of the author's imagination or are used fictitiously. Any inadvertent resemblance to actual persons, living or dead, or actual events is purely coincidental.

Published by Thomas & Mercer, Seattle
www.apub.com

ISBN-13: 9781542044783 (hardcover)
ISBN-10: 1542044782 (hardcover)
ISBN-13: 9781542019538 (paperback)
ISBN-10: 1542019532 (paperback)

Cover design by Kaitlin Kall

Printed in the United States of America

First edition

For Staci . . .

STATEMENTS AS FACT

As they were going along and talking, behold there appeared a chariot of fire and horses of fire which separated the two of them. And Elijah went up by a whirlwind to heaven.

—2 Kings 2:11, circa 960–560 BC

In the first place, the earth, when looked at from above, is like one of those balls which have leather coverings in twelve pieces, and is of divers colors, of which the colors which painters use on earth are only a sample.

—Plato quoting Socrates, 360 BC

For there is . . . a single vast immensity which we may freely call void . . . In it are an infinity of worlds of the same kind as our own.

—Giordano Bruno, 1584

With ships or sails built for heavenly breezes, some will venture into that great vastness.

—Letter from Kepler to Galileo, 1596

1

BLASTING SNOW swirls in my headlights like a white tornado, the run-flats pushing through unplowed powder on Wednesday morning, December 4.

Since driving away from NASA Langley Research Center two slow miles ago, it's as if I'm the last person left on the planet. My hometown of Hampton, Virginia, is almost in a brownout as if we're in the middle of a war, businesses and homes I pass empty and pitch dark. Streetlights are widely spaced smudges that illuminate nothing, and I can't make out most traffic signs until I'm on top of them.

The Dollar General store is off to my right, dense woods to my left, Anna's Pizza & Italian Restaurant up ahead according to the GPS satellite map. Otherwise, I wouldn't know where I am, visibility a car length when I'm lucky. At times I can't tell which lane I'm in as gale-force gusts send supercans airborne and tumbling, ripping holiday lights and decorations from their moorings.

On this stretch of North Armistead Avenue alone, a Santa on his sleigh took flight from a rooftop, crash-landing in the median strip while life-size figures from a nativity scene scraped across a church parking lot. An inflated Grinch was gone with the wind after snapping his tether, and just now an American flag still attached to its pole cartwheels by in front of my Silverado.

Trash, leaves, branches, wreaths, all sorts of things are flying about as if I'm headed to Oz in a near whiteout. It would have made sense to stay put at work. Certainly, I know better than most the importance of sound judgment. I can cite chapter and verse about human factors that will hurt or kill you, such as being sleep deprived, preoccupied and somewhat traumatized while driving in a blizzard.

But no way I was bunking down in the NASA firehouse or on the Air Force base after an all-nighter that included an exploding rocket, and almost losing an astronaut on a spacewalk. If that wasn't enough, I was tackled by a posse that confused me with my identical twin sister, just to mention a few solar-flaring urgencies with more on the way.

Assuming Neva Rong is the mastermind, we've seen nothing yet, the tech billionaire's agenda universal dominance at any price or sacrifice. All to say I don't anticipate a peaceful Christmastime, maybe nothing peaceful ever again, and what I need right now is to get away from work even if for a few hours.

I'm desperate to take off my boots, tactical clothing and gun, to shower in my own bathroom. I intend to sit in my usual chair at the kitchen counter watching Mom whip up the latest treat. It's time we have one of our private chats, nobody in our airspace to interfere or overhear (including Dad). I'm going to make her spill the beans (as we say in the Chase family).

But not until I first sweep the house with one of my spectrum analyzers, going room to room, walking in circles holding up various mobile antennas like Ghostbusters. I'll make sure there are no rogue transmissions, no surveillance devices, nothing that might indicate the invisible presence of uninvited cyber spooks.

Once Mom and I are alone and relaxed in our cone of silence, she'll come clean about my missing sister. I'll get my answer about whether Carme had anything to do with this morning's massive cyberattack on NASA, and if she's guilty of other crimes including obstruction of justice and homicide. I can't know for sure she's a good egg or bad until I verify whose side she's really on, and whether she's been accessing our farm in the recent past, at times using Dad's car.

That's assuming my other half hasn't been killed or captured . . .

"Focus! Focus! Focus . . . !" I shout, startling myself as the tires fishtail on black ice, slipping sideways, the glare of my headlights reflecting off billowing snow.

Telling myself to pay attention, I've never seen this part of the world so barren as I make my way home during a federal government shutdown and a nor'easter. All nonessential federal employees have been furloughed (doesn't include me). That on top of Governor Dixon declaring a state of emergency, evacuating coastal and other low-elevation areas, everyone ordered to stay off the roads.

But I'm not everyone as I monitor ongoing operations and disasters in outer space and on the ground. Scanning various government apps on my phone clamped into a holder on the dash, I'm careful not to outrun what I can see. I've got the radio cranked up, P!nk rocking my NASA take-home pickup truck when the music abruptly stops.

An incoming call rings through the speakers, a number with a 703 area code, the Central Intelligence Agency, their cybercrimes division, and adrenaline jolts me into high alert.

"Captain Chase," I answer hands-free.

"Calli?" to my surprise. "It's Dick," and I wasn't expecting him. "How are you doing in this weather? You holding up all right?" General Richard Melville's familiar voice surrounds me.

"Fortunately, it's too cold for the snow to stick all that much. But ice and wind are a bear," I reply, not particularly friendly or answering what he asked.

I'm in no mood for pleasantries or his personal solicitations, which are nothing more than a deflection, if not disingenuous. What I need if I'm to go on with my life are hard cold facts, the truth for once. He's told me virtually nothing since my sister fled from the Langley hangar rooftop where she'd been hiding inside the radome.

She vanished almost before my very eyes some 5 hours ago, and it doesn't appear she jumped or fell. There's no evidence she's dead. Her body hasn't been found. At least Dick shared that much when we were together on the second floor of Building 2101. Cheek to jowl inside Mission Control, and he showed me the photographs on his phone . . .

The peculiar footwear pattern in snow . . .

The tracks leading to the rooftop's edge . . .

The blank white ground some 30 meters (98 feet) below . . .

"Have you heard anything? Are there updates since we were together last?" I ask bluntly, having no idea who else is on the line since Dick can't bother to tell me. "Has Carme made contact? Provable contact? Regardless of what she has or hasn't done, do we know if she's okay? Is she safe? And why are you calling me from a CIA number?"

"I'm bringing you into a discussion in progress," his deep voice inside my truck sounds typically calm and matter of fact. "And I'm sorry but I have nothing to add about your sister at this time."

"Well, if she's not been found anywhere, I guess that's news enough," I try to bait him, and it won't work, never does.

It's like getting blood from a stone, my NASA educator mother has been saying about Dick for as long as I've been around.

00:00:00:00:0

"I HAVE other important information," he informs me, snowflakes flurrying madly around my truck like one of those wintry paperweights shaken up.

The bottom line, Dick isn't calling about my sister. He won't discuss her, is going to make me wonder and suffer, which is unfair and unkind if not as cold as the weather. I'd like to give him a piece of my mind but never have and won't start now.

No matter how well I know him, it wouldn't be a good idea to disrespect a 4-star general, the commander of the US Space Force. Not if I care about what might be left of my future.

"We have a much better sight picture of the events leading to the destruction of the cargo resupply rocket today at 0200 hours," he says. "The upshot is that rogue commands from one of our communication satellites caused the damage."

"Our own technologies turned against us, what I'm always worrying about," I reply. "I'm assuming we don't think this is an accident, some sort of malfunction with the satellite in question."

"Absolutely not for reasons you'll hear more about later," Dick says. "Whoever's behind it knew that as the countdown neared zero and we detected an off-nominal command, we'd have no choice but to hit the kill switch."

"Making me wonder if that was the point. To make us blow up our own rocket," I reply, and it would be just like Neva Rong to pull a stunt like that. "What will be released officially?" and before Dick can answer, another familiar voice floats up from the telephonic vacuum, wishing me a good morning.

"Be careful driving, looks like Hampton's getting hammered," Connor Lacrosse says in his quiet voice with no discernible accent. "As for what's released, there will be no comment from NASA, Space Force, the White House."

We've never met that I'm aware of, and I don't know much about him. Everybody calls him Conn, appropriately for someone from Connecticut (allegedly) who rather much lives a lie (as do all spies). He's CIA or at least that's how he identifies himself, both of us members of the US Secret Service's multijurisdictional Electronic Crimes Task Force.

"Any statement eventually made won't be detailed," he informs me as I turn up the defrost, using my sleeve to wipe condensation off the windshield. "The media's going to town as you can imagine. Conspiracy theories abound, including that there may have been a spy satellite squirreled away in the payload," and I pick up a siren, other noises in the distant background.

"What port are you hailing from on this lovely Wednesday morning?" I may as well ask him point blank.

"Stuck here like everybody else who was present when the rocket blew to smithereens. No one's allowed on or off Wallops," he says, and I know darn well the CIA wouldn't still be there for that reason.

They don't take orders from NASA or the local authorities. If Conn wanted off the island, he wouldn't be there.

"A total mess, no room in any of the B&Bs or hotels," he describes what I've been following on live news and security video feeds. "Thousands of visitors are sleeping in their cars, bundled up in blankets inside tents and other facilities. Local restaurants and other businesses have opened up to take people in."

He tells me I wouldn't want to be on Fantasy Island right now, and it always feels as if he's picking on me. But it's hard to know when our encounters are only over the phone.

"Here's what else we know so far, Calli," Dick takes over. "A cell phone signal was sent from inside the VIP room at 0159 hours today, a call made to a number that may have triggered whatever caused the satellite to issue bad commands resulting in mayhem. A fake temporary phone number," he emphasizes.

"One that as expected no longer was in service by the time we tried it approximately an hour after the explosion," Conn adds.

"How many people were in the VIP room watching the launch when a burner phone supposedly wreaked havoc with one of our satellites?" I inquire, and I know of one person who was present for sure, someone quite skilled at playing ruthless games and creating chaos.

"There were 32 of us," Conn goes on to confirm that Neva Rong was among them.

A guest at this morning's launch, she was sitting right there when the rocket detonated into a ball of fire, destroying food, clothing, experiments, equipment, Christmas goodies bound for the International Space Station. At the same time the robotic arm failed during an extravehicular activity (EVA, or spacewalk), and NASA lost all communication with our orbiting astronauts.

"Mostly, we're talking about students, teachers," Conn describes who else was inside the VIP room. "And the host and film crew for that show I can't stomach, *The Mason Dixon Line*. Also, a handful of reporters."

"Like I'm always saying," Dick's voice again, "what keeps me awake at night is kids with no concept of consequences. It's all a game until the sky is falling and everybody's dead."

"The 20-buck burner in question was in the backpack of a ninth grader watching the launch," Conn informs me. "He made zero attempt to hide it. Why not tuck it out of sight or better yet dispose of it?"

"Sounds to me like someone wanted us to find it," I decide, and that someone probably isn't the ninth grader involved.

I have a furious feeling the culprit is Neva Rong herself, and framing an innocent person is diabolical if that's what she's done. To do it to a kid is just plain evil, and I'm following the Southwest Branch Back River now, rivers of snow flowing over pavement, drifting deep enough to hide ditches, guardrails and other hazards.

"What do we know about this ninth grader?" I'm crawling along at less than 8 kilometers per hour (5 mph), unsure where the pavement ends and the shoulder begins.

"Local to Hampton, lives with his grandmother. Parents deceased, no siblings, age 10," Conn says, giving me a bad feeling.

"One of those who tests out of everything, IQ off the charts," Dick adds, and my feeling gets worse. "Has skipped quite a few grades with more to come like some people I know," alluding to Carme and me.

"He was at Wallops with other students involved in science projects that were in the rocket's payload," Conn explains. "In his case, a minisatellite, a CubeSat that makes orbit inspections of larger spacecraft," and there's no doubt they're talking about Lex.

An intern at Langley, he's part of a special science, technology, engineering, and mathematics (STEM) initiative. Dad tucked him under his wing recently, an old habit that rarely ends well, bringing people home he shouldn't.

"I'm wondering if you've heard your father mention Lexell Anderson," Conn verifies my suspicion.

"Lexell with two *l*'s as in the comet," I confirm, my mood plummeting further.

"What comet?"

"One that passed closer to Earth than any other in history, and is now lost," I reply. "Lexell's comet hasn't been seen in centuries. And I hope this kid isn't lost, too, that he's not a bad seed. Goes by Lex, extremely gifted, getting academic credit for a fall internship at NASA, someone whose future could be ruined by an accusation of hacking into the government."

"Cybercriminals start young these days," Dick beats his same drum but he has other reasons for treating a 10-year-old like the enemy.

Lex is paying for those who've come before him, any stray who's followed my father home. A kind and giving soul, he doesn't see the bad in anyone, and has an affinity for gifted misfits and loners.

"What does Lex say?" On West Mercury Boulevard now, I almost can make out the KFC, my mouth watering as I think about their fried chicken, mashed potatoes and gravy.

"He claims what you'd expect, that he'd never seen the phone before," Conn's voice over speakerphone.

"Where was it?" I ask, driving past the Superior Pawn & Gun, the huge **Guns** sign on the roof unlit and ghostly in the storm.

"In the outside pocket of his backpack."

"Where someone easily could plant it," I point out as music booms through my truck's speakers.

We've been disconnected, the cell signal dropped, and there's no point in trying them back. If they have something further to say, they'll reach out. Not to mention, all I'd get is some CIA operator who won't know what I'm talking about (supposedly), and I'm surprised by the convenience store up ahead glowing like a welcome station. All others I've passed are closed because of the evacuation and terrible weather.

The Hampton Hop-In is deserted, the gas pumps empty, snowflakes frantic in floodlights. The pearl-white Jeep Cherokee alone in the parking lot is the same one I noticed when I was heading to Mission Control after midnight. The same clerk is inside the store, only he's not at the counter as he was when I saw him earlier. Now he's oddly seated in a folding chair that's been moved near the glass front door.

"What are you looking at?" I mutter under my breath without moving my lips, a trick Carme and I learned as kids, talking like ventriloquists.

2

MIDDLE AGED I'm guessing, gray hair, a big belly and yellowish-tinted glasses, he's huddled with his jacket on, watching my headlights slowly approach in the wintry mess.

A backpack is on the floor by his feet, and it didn't escape my notice the first time I drove past that the pearl-white SUV is backed in, and there's no front license plate. Meaning, the tag number isn't easily visible, and I can't run it to get the lowdown.

There's damage to the underside of the right front bumper, and I don't like that I've never seen the Jeep or the clerk before last night. I duck into the family-owned Hop-In at all hours as it's on the way home, and I'm always stopping for something. Snacks, coffee, and what I wouldn't give for one of their cheeseburgers slathered with onions, extreme stress never killing my appetite the way I wish.

I'm craving Whoppers, sausage biscuits, Mom's country-fried steak, fantasizing about food even as I watch the convenience store clerk in my rearview mirror. He gets up from his chair, opening the front door while lighting a cigarette. Stepping out into wind and snow to smoke, he stares after my truck with its lights and sirens, *NASA Protective Services* and our moon and stars logo in blue on the doors.

Rocket cops, a lot of people call us. Only it's not necessarily a compliment when someone jokes that people like me don't build the rocket, we just protect it, suggesting we aren't all that swift, another stereotype I can do without. That and spectrum-y, nerdy scientist, too dumb or smart to find your way out of the rain, and as is the case with most typecasts, there's some truth but not much.

Special agents, cyber ninjas like me, are required to have a graduate degree. Some of us have PhDs and are trained in multiple disciplines ranging from science and engineering to psychology and the arts. When I left the Air Force, I was hired to head cyber investigations at Langley Research Center, the oldest of NASA's 10 centers nationwide. But I'm also an aerospace engineer and quantum physicist, a test pilot, and an astronaut in the making.

Ever since I can remember, it's been my dream to explore new worlds, and more to the point, to protect them and planet Earth. Whether it's an orbiting laboratory, the moon or Mars, wherever humans go, they'll cause trouble. Competing for power and resources, they'll attempt to kill, steal and sabotage, which is what happened this morning on my watch.

Outer space was attacked from the ground, and I access the live video feed streaming from security cameras on Wallops Island, 170.5 kilometers (106 miles) south of where I'm this minute driving. The Mission Elapsed Time (MET) is +05:01:51.1 and counting since the rocket exploded, and I suppose in all the pandemonium no one's thought to turn off the clock.

As I've continued monitoring the scene throughout the morning, I've realized the necessity of securing the blast site and keeping away the curious. But I've not understood why the cleanup and salvage operation couldn't wait until daylight.

The barrier islands weren't in the direct path of the nor'easter, and didn't get slammed the way Tidewater is. Even so, it's got to be miserably cold and dangerously dark out there on the Atlantic

Ocean. I'm suspicious that NASA is trying to recover debris we want out of sight by daylight, possibly pieces and parts of a spy satellite.

Or we're making sure that's the appearance we give, and it wouldn't be the first time there were surprises in a payload headed into orbit. Propaganda's nothing new, either, and I wonder what other secrets Dick might be keeping from me as I monitor the live video playing silently on my phone's display in a chiaroscuro of glare and deep shadows . . .

Emergency crews in bright-orange chemical suits and respirators wade through a toxic stew of sooty water and debris inside the massive crater where the launch pad used to be . . .

They poke and snag with long-handled probes and hooks like space travelers on a hostile planet . . .

As covered dump trucks haul off mangled burnt metal, and blackened soggy fire-retardant Nomex cargo containers . . .

The video playing on my phone is interrupted by an incoming call, the home landline this time. It's the same number we've always had, the last 4 digits 1-9-9-1, the year Carme and I were born.

"Calli, this is your mother on Space to Ground 1," her mellow voice with its gentle southern cadence affectionately imitates what she heard me say earlier over the radio in Mission Control.

More accurately, it's what I *almost* said to the astronauts during a spacewalk. My NASA parents showed up while I was going through diagnostic procedures, checking out the top secret quantum node installed after the Space Station was sabotaged.

"How's it going?" Mom asks. "It must be awful out."

"Really, really slow. I should be there in 20 minutes hopefully," I reply. "All good at home? You and Dad safe and sound?"

"I can't speak for George. As for me, I'm nice and cozy drinking cinnamon tea in front of the fire, waiting for you. Pondering what you might want to eat when you get here. Maybe waffles?" and what she's telling me is that Dad's not home.

The last time I saw or communicated with my NASA-employed parents was several hours ago when they showed up to check on me and the disasters going on. Then they headed back to the farm. Or that's what I was led to believe when they left with Dick, who I'm betting has conscripted my eccentric genius father (as usual) to assist in something.

I'm not sure what because I don't believe it's to hunt down Carme. Dad wouldn't help with that even if he could. Whatever he's doing, I'm betting he's with the same Secret Service cyber-crimes detail from earlier when I spotted him inside the NASA Langley aviation hangar. He's with Dick, in other words, and it wouldn't surprise me if Dad was on that CIA call a little while ago.

"Where are you?" Mom asks. "A waypoint, dear."

"I'm coming up on Walgreens," I add that I can't see the pharmacy, just snow everywhere.

"I thought you should know Mason Dixon has been filming nonstop at Wallops ever since the explosion," she gets to the reason for calling. "They're filming inside the flight facility, right there in the VIP room, talking about everything on the air."

"Who is besides Mason?"

"Take three guesses and the first two don't count," and she means Neva Rong. "Even more outrageous, she's talking about her sister's death yesterday, her *so-called suicide*. She's implying that Vera Young was of keen interest to their aerospace competitors, especially to the Chinese, obviously insinuating that they may have taken her out."

"Predictable," I reply. "If all else fails, blame it on a spook, a spy, especially a Chinese one."

"When we know who the real culprit is," Mom says like a hanging judge. "Well, pay attention to your driving, dear, and don't forget I love you," ending the call.

00:00:00:00:0

I PASS family landmarks that I can barely make out in the storm . . .

The Century Lanes Bowling Center with its game arcade and big video screens, a special family treat on Saturdays and birthdays . . .

The Plaza Roller Rink where my sister was a speed demon on wheels, wiping out, skinning her knees and losing ball bearings . . .

I'm aware of icy flakes click-click-clicking against my windshield, what I imagine it sounds like when a swarm of miniscule debris or micrometeorites hits your spaceship. Not that I've been flying the genuine article through the ether yet, only mock-ups, test models and full-motion simulators that I can see and feel in my sleep.

"Jeez Louise!" as I fiddle with the radio. "Do I freakin' have to . . . ?" tuning in *The Mason Dixon Line*, I catch the show's self-absorbed host in the midst of gushing about his new favorite rocket scientist.

". . . Dr. Rong is the CEO of Pandora Space Systems, a giant in the field," Mason says over the air. "And for those just joining us, we're off the coast of Virginia on Wallops Island at NASA's Mid-Atlantic Regional Spaceport, filming live from MARS. As in M-A-R-S . . ."

"NASA and their acronyms," Neva's sultry voice invades my truck.

"They have acronyms for acronyms," Mason quips with one of his signature giddyap tongue clicks. "And Dr. Rong, I bet you have a few acronyms at Pandora."

"We've got a book of them."

"Fire off one of your favs."

"How about an F-L-U-B?" she says without pause.

"A *flub*?"

"As in 'Finding Little Utilized Benefit,' which applies to so many things, Mason. Sadly, people most of all. I can say that with authority since I run a company with more than 10,000 employees, and exponentially more private contractors, researchers and interns from all over the world."

"Speaking of flubs. How about when you have to blow up your own rocket? Because oops! Something went bonkers. They're estimating the loss at about 200 mil," Mason's most cited source is *they*, never saying *who*, and I've reached Bloxoms Corner.

Across the street is the garden center with its marquee where the locals post personal greetings and announcements for all the world to see. I can't make out anything but vague shapes in the milky turbulence as I creep onward.

". . . The loss could be substantially more depending on what was in the payload," Neva says in her vaguely British accent, supposedly left over from living in England the years she attended Cambridge. "And they're not going to tell us if a multibillion-dollar spacecraft or spy satellite was a casualty."

"I'm hearing rumors of that very thing. Whatever it was, I can't imagine there's much left of it now. That was one humongous Molotov cocktail," Mason carries on in his sexy croon.

No doubt he's staring dreamily into the camera with those *bedroom baby blues* (as he's described in the news). Believing he's God's gift, and I suppose he is when you consider all he's got going for him that he probably didn't earn or if nothing else, got way too easily. His looks, for example. And extreme success at my same age of 28.

While I live in a barn on a government salary, he drives an Audi R8 supercar, has a Hollywood agent and a penthouse, the last I heard. Fake news and narcissism pay, and it also doesn't hurt if you're the nephew of our current governor. Willard "Willie" Dixon is golfing buddies with the president of the United States, explaining how it is that Mason comes by his tips and leaks, his big stories and secret informants.

". . . Make a right turn in 100 feet," the GPS announces, the snow so thick I can barely see the **Welcome to Fox Hill** sign ahead.

I slow down at the intersection of Beach and Hall when the engine switches off for seemingly no reason.

"What the . . . ?"

I'm sitting dead as a doornail in the middle of the road, the snow swirling around my white Silverado. When just as inexplicably, my truck turns back on with a roar.

"Holy shhhhh . . . !"

The doors relock, the heat and defrost resuming as the radio is muted, and the satellite map fills the display on the dash. The GPS tracking app announces that I can begin my route, showing me the address of the final destination, one I didn't enter and haven't visited forever.

My police truck has been hacked, the navigation controlled remotely. But that doesn't mean I have to do as it says. I don't have to follow the highlighted route. But there's no way I won't when it might be an illuminated tether that connects to my sister. What we called a mirror flash, a signal between us when we were kids, only we used radio transmitters and antennas, nothing visible.

It's also possible that someone else is sending me a message, setting up a trap. My years of training, my instincts dictate that I should head directly back to NASA. I should call for help along the way, reaching out to my mother, to Fran, to Dick, to someone.

But nothing's going to stop me from driving as directed, the app's female voice heading me south toward the Chesapeake Bay on Old Buckroe Road, a stretch that means something to my sister and me.

On my right, the Hampton Soccer Park is blanketed white like a Christmas card, undisturbed by the usual kids on sleds and folks walking their dogs. No one is around to sully or churn things up as I drive faster, more urgently than before, now passing Buckroe Bait & Tackle & Seafood, an awkward name for a favorite haunt. The **OPEN** sign is turned off in the window, the huge white-painted fish on red brick almost invisible in the blizzard.

There's nothing going on at the Brass Lantern where Carme was fearless at karaoke and I cleaned up at darts, every business closed and dark.

Hijacked by suggestion is the way I'd describe it as I follow the route back to our old beachfront hangout. The closer I get, the more memories flash like crazy . . .

The office with its rattling air conditioner fogging up the plate glass window . . .

The pink check-in counter with its locked cash drawer . . .

The ice machine, rusty steel ash can and blue-painted bench out front where Mrs. Skidmore would sit and smoke, keeping an eagle eye on our activities . . .

She was always in the area when we swam in the overchlorinated pool, roasted hot dogs and marshmallows in the cookout area with its picnic tables and rusting grills, or horsed around on the tawny strip of beach that vanishes at high tide. There wasn't much for parents to worry about when high school friends rented a room for the day, rather much like a cabana.

Nothing scandalous went on, no sneaking off with your latest crush, nipping alcohol or stealing a smoke. We weren't going to get away with much with Mrs. Skidmore on the prowl. We also never knew when Mom herself might show up with Bojangles' biscuits and Hardee's hamburgers or Krispy Kreme doughnuts.

"You've reached your destination," the GPS announces, the Point Comfort Inn dark and deserted up ahead, no sign of recent habitation, snow and ice everywhere.

Grandly named for what it is, the 1950s stucco motel is white with pink trim, a front office and a cellblock of 11 small rooms in a row. Rates are cheap, and as is often true, you get what you pay for. In other words, not much, at least that was the case in the good ole days when Carme and I were regulars.

Maintenance was the owner (Mrs. Skidmore) showing up with her tackle box of tools. Security was the piece she carried (a .357 Magnum that she could shoot like Annie Oakley). Housekeeping was local kids on summer break who didn't exactly take pride in their work, and there was no laundry service or amenities, only the smallest bar of soap.

Forget a restaurant or gift shop, although in the early years there were vending machines and a pay phone out front near the electric bug zapper. Nothing much has changed except for the wear and tear of time and coastal weather.

The bulky ice machine has been there forever, white with **Ice** in tall frosted blue letters, and as I turn into the parking lot, I barely make out the big boxy shape on the patio to the left of the office.

3

THE AWNING that runs the length of the building flaps in the wind like mad, the blue canvas more faded and tattered. Plywood has been nailed over the windows, the place buttoned up for the winter.

But someone was here recently based on tire tracks in and out, and I release the thumb lock on my holster. I'm sliding out my Glock when suddenly headlights swing in behind me. A huge SUV guns into the parking lot, after me like a shark.

"WHAT THE F . . . !" and I can't believe I let this happen.

Hitting the brakes, throwing my truck into park and ducking down in the seat, I could radio for backup but no one will respond in time as I find myself trapped between the SUV and the motel. Unless I can take off into a hover, I'm not going anywhere. Letting my guard down, I'm cornered with no backup plan, and pistol in hand, I inchworm over the console as fast as I can into the passenger's seat.

Barely opening the door, I'm slithering out when BANG! BANG! and ejected cartridge cases clink-clink against pavement or concrete. Followed by nothing, the wind blowing, the snow stinging my face as I crouch behind the rear right tire of my truck. Listening. Watching. Waiting for the slightest sound or stirring.

My heart hammers, my pistol aimed, finger on the trigger, ready to double tap, two rounds center mass . . .

"Sisto?" the familiar voice is dampened by the wind, close by at 2 o'clock.

I don't move.

"Sisto, it's me!" sounding closer . . . closer . . . Calling out my childhood pet name that almost no one knows.

Gun rock steady. I barely breathe.

"Calli? It's Carme, your *better half*! Who else would say that, right?" her alto voice with a Virginia lilt, the same as mine.

I don't answer, not ready to trust anything or anyone. So much can be faked these days with voice cloning and other software I know more about than most.

"Calli?" nearing the back of my truck.

"STOP!" I warn at the top of my lungs. "NO SUDDEN MOVES!"

"Okay. Not moving suddenly or otherwise. Put down your gun and walk out from behind your truck, Sisto."

Wiping my watery eyes on my sleeve, I'm blinking hard, trying to see, my heart drumming in my throat.

"What's happened?" I shout. "Who got shot?"

"The guy that's parked on your ass. Stand up slowly," she demands, and I can tell she's not moving anymore. "For God's sake don't shoot me. You don't want to explain that to Mom. And Dad doesn't need any more bad news either . . ."

"All right! All right!" I answer over the rumble of engines, the rushing of the wind. "I'm coming out slowly! There, I'm lowering my gun down by my side," standing up, I halfway expect it to be the last thing I ever do.

Squinting in the glare of headlights, I don't see her at first. Then I see her in swirling snow not even 3 meters (10 feet) away, waiting by the open driver's door of the SUV hemming me in, a silver Yukon Denali driven by whoever my sister just killed. She watches me, standing as still as a living statue, phantomlike in a peculiar hooded ultrablack bodysuit, booties and gloves.

She's holding her Bond Arms Bullpup 9 mm pistol with its quick-detach suppressor, and an assault rifle that looks military. Walking toward her, I realize that the Denali's interior light has been turned off the way cops, criminals, and other streetwise people do when they don't want to be an easy target.

I hope like crazy that Carme didn't shoot someone she shouldn't have, an undercover agent, an intelligence operative, a spy tailing me, maybe thinking I'm the other twin, an outlaw on the run. Most people get us confused with each other, even family and other intimate relations do. I might have been taken out or hauled off to lockup because someone assumes Carme and I are doubling for each other, trading places.

For all I know, the man in the Denali was after me because he thought I was her. And how often is this going to happen from now on?

"Do you know who he is?" I reach my sister, and she seems impervious to the cold while I'm trying not to shake and shiver.

"I know *what* he is," her eyes are constantly moving. "A meat puppet," her term for primitives, those disconnected from the source. "An attack mongrel sent by the adversary as a special thank-you."

"For what?"

"For screwing up her little plan earlier this morning," and my sister is talking about Neva. "You thought fast enough to restore communications with our astronauts before the situation became critical. Gotta admit you were pretty impressive," and it seems an odd time to be paying me a compliment.

"A *thank-you* intended for whom? Me? Or did he have us confused?" I holster my Glock, digging out my tactical light and turning it on.

"I wasn't the initial target," Carme says.

"How can you be sure?" I illuminate a beefy left hand hanging below the open driver's door.

"He didn't know I was here. But he knew you were coming. If it had been his lucky day, he would have taken out both of us."

Silvery rings on the dead man's fingers shine in the intense beam of my flashlight. Steamy blood drip-drips from the driver's seat, instantly cooling and coagulating on the red-spattered snowy pavement.

"A name would be helpful," I bend down to get a better look at the oversize rings.

A winged skull with ruby eyes . . .

A coiled snake . . .

A gothic wedding band . . .

Carme leans inside the Denali, peering at the man she killed.

"Don't know him," she says as if she might. "Let's see if he's got an ID of some sort."

Checking pockets with her eel-skin-like gloved hands, she produces a wallet. Removing a driver's license from it just long enough to look, she returns it, tucking the wallet back where she found it. My sister steps back from the open door as if shooting someone to death is all in a day's work, and she has no concerns about it.

"A Texas license, name on it is Hank Cougars, 37 years old," Carme says. "But it's not who this dude really is, and it's also not for me to follow up on. The Virginia tag on the truck was stolen from a car in long-term parking at the Richmond airport. Some poor fool who's traveling and has no clue," and I can't figure out where the hell-o she's getting her information.

"You got any idea how he might have known that I was on my way here in the middle of nothing? When no one else is on the road? Because this isn't random," I elbow the driver's door open all the way.

"Nope, it's definitely not random," she says as I think of the Tyvek protective clothing, face masks, nitrile exam gloves and other forensic gear stored in the back of my truck.

I already know I won't be needing such things anymore, not for the expected reasons of properly preserving evidence the way I've done until now. I work my hands into black leather tactical gloves that won't help much in the extreme cold. But they're better than nothing.

00:00:00:00:0

PROBING INSIDE the Denali with my flashlight, I try not to brush against the dead man slumped back in the seat.

The two wounds in the middle of his forehead are almost perfectly round. The angle dead on, one small hole slightly higher than the other, as close to causing instant incapacitation and death as one can get, a kill shot my sister calls a *snake eyes*.

A very bad roll of the dice, she likes to say, and I've witnessed my share of them on the firing range when we go to town with our Bond Arms Bullpups. She rips through the heads of human silhouette targets while I play it statistically safe, mostly plugging center mass with only the occasional head shot for good measure.

Based on the blood, bits of bone and brain tissue I'm seeing, it's not hard to reconstruct what went down when the hitman roared in on top of me and opened his door. The explosion of high velocity rounds would have made my ears ring were it not for the suppressor attached to Carme's pistol barrel.

He didn't see what was coming. Didn't feel it happen, his lights knocked out with a one-two hollow-point punch, the back of his skull exploded. The impact pushed him into the seat, and he slid down halfway, leaving a swath of blood on gray leather, his body listing to the left, his arm hanging out.

He's unfamiliar, and I'm fairly certain I've never seen him before, light skinned, a full beard, long hair, a tattoo of a winged woman warrior on the side of his neck. In jeans, flannel, a down vest, he could pass for a lot of folks in these parts but that's not why he knows his way around Hampton's back roads.

Displayed on the tablet mounted on the console is a map that shows my route since I left Vera Young's Fort Monroe apartment last night after working her death scene for hours. While my truck was parked on the street, this man or someone placed a GPS tracker on it.

"I remind you that Neva dropped in on Vera unannounced yesterday," as I paint light over an open range bag on the floor below the passenger's seat.

"I'm aware," Carme says in a way that makes me think she was there or remotely watching.

"Neva showed up unexpected it seems, and not long afterward her sister was dead," I remind her.

My light shines on large-capacity magazines loaded with copper-jacketed ammunition, at first glance similar to .223 assault rifle rounds or comparable. Some have blue plastic ballistic tips associated with hunting down varmints, others without, telling me the objective wasn't to capture but to exterminate.

"We'd just better hope nobody shows up while we're doing all this," I'm willing myself not to panic.

Powering up the stereo to see what addresses are plugged into the GPS, I'm startled by Neva Rong's voice on satellite radio. It's as if talking about her has conjured her up somehow.

". . . Absolutely, we should question any vendor who has repeated malfunctions, and worst of all, vulnerabilities to cyberattacks . . . ," she's saying, and it would seem the hitman was listening to *The Mason Dixon Line* at some point earlier the same way I was.

"Can you believe it?" I open the door behind the driver's seat. "Any doubt about who's behind this?"

I shine my light over padded gun cases and duffel bags. A Mossberg 590A1 pump shotgun. Boxes of 12-gauge shells. A bulletproof vest, towels, a baseball cap with a mallard duck on it and several burner phones.

"I hate to be the one who breaks the news to you, Sisto, but she's none too fond of us," Carme ducks inside to turn off the ignition, shutting up Neva and taking the key.

"We've got to prove what she's doing, that she murdered her sister, and just tried to smoke me, possibly both of us, that she's behind everything going on," I walk around to the back of the Denali. "We've got to show evidence of her crimes."

"Really? Then what?" Carme knows as well as I do that if traditional means could stop Neva Rong, it would have happened years ago.

She pops up the hood, disconnecting the battery, making certain the SUV can't be started, controlled or tampered with remotely. While she's doing that, I open the tailgate, taking a mental inventory of the various tools and hardware in back. A branch lopper, pruning shears, a hacksaw. Rolls of duct tape. Boxes of heavy-duty trash bags.

Half a dozen 5-gallon plastic buckets are filled with a concrete mix like Quikrete, an eyebolt in the center of each. Plus, there are piles of zinc-coated mooring chain, I'd estimate at least 9 meters (29.5 feet) of it, everything needed to dispose of untidy messes with the help of inexpensive homemade anchors.

And around here where rivers and the bay meet the sea, if you don't want something found, a good place to deep-six it is the water.

"This guy was a fixer," I decide. "A freakin' death-and-disposal factory on wheels."

"That was the objective, I believe," Carme agrees.

Covered from head to toe in her wetsuit-like skin with only her face showing, she's menacing and surreal as she moves around with the pistol and carbine.

"It looks like I was about to be fish food," I add. "Maybe you too."

"Fortunately, I had just enough warning," is as much as she'll explain, and I can only figure that my military special ops spitting image must have picked up signals on a spectrum analyzer.

Or she may have hacked. Or was given intel, and I envision the clerk parked by the door at the Hampton Hop-In. I think of Dick calling me on a CIA line, and my mom checking in and asking where I was. One way or another, Carme got the information she needed. When she realized what was tailing me and headed in her direction, she got ready to take care of the problem.

The logical place to lie in wait was behind the unlit ice machine near the snow-dusted blue bench where Mrs. Skidmore used to sit. I imagine my sister ducked out of sight, biding her time, patiently watching me drive through the parking lot, ready as the silver Denali roared in right behind me. When the would-be assassin opened his door, she nailed him before he was out of his seat.

"Make yourself useful," Carme hands me the carbine over my protests. "I've not cleared it yet," she adds as I touch the weapon with my contaminated leather-gloved hands. "I don't have much experience with these. So, you're on your own but I think you can figure it out."

Lightweight, less than 10 pounds fully loaded I estimate, the weapon that almost did me in is tricked out with a suppressor, a tactical scope, an under-barrel-mounted grenade launcher. None of it normal, not even in Virginia where people like us grew up with guns and more guns, knives, weapons of all persuasion.

Dropping out the curved black polymer 30-round magazine, I snap back the bolt to unseat a thick tapered brass cartridge from the chamber.

"Not sure what this is," I announce, sliding my badge wallet out of a pocket. "Same thing he has inside his truck. Some of the cartridges have ballistic tips. Some like these don't."

Inside my wallet's credit card slot is a trusty NASA souvenir refrigerator magnet that I never leave home without. Not always the same one, of course, because I give them away as souvenirs on a regular basis if I don't lose them first. Fortunately, there are always plenty in stock at the Langley exchange outside the cafeteria.

But any small, weak magnet will do, and touching it to the bullet, I feel the attraction through the thin copper cladding. The metal projectile beneath is steel, not lead, and the intention likely was to shoot me inside my vehicle.

"Armor piercing," I let Carme know what the assassin had in store for me and possibly both of us.

I shine my light over the flat-black-painted carbine, looking for anything that might tell me what kind it is, not finding a single marking. Then I probe for the two cartridge cases ejected when Carme fired her kill shots from her Bullpup. They're not hard to find, shining like rose gold on the snow-blown concrete, in front and to the right of the ice machine.

Winchester +P+, my sister's takedown ammo of choice, I note as she instructs me to leave her spent brass alone, not to touch it.

"I'll take care of it," she shouts.

"We can't run the risk of anyone else finding them," I yell back at her as I pluck up the evidence without proper protection or taking a single photograph.

Without a thought to preservation or procedures, I continue destroying the crime scene and breaking the law.

4

"ANYTHING ELSE you might have left lying around?" I head back in her direction. "Besides the elephant in the middle of the parking lot," and I mean the dead man inside his big truck.

"Trust me," Carme walks around the Denali, shutting the doors. "It will be as if we were never here."

"We're tampering with evidence, and leaving it all over the place!" I tuck her spent cartridge cases into a pocket.

"We're fine."

"Not to mention obstructing justice!"

"Don't worry about it," she points the remote key, locking up the big SUV with the dead hitman inside it.

"*Don't worry about it?* Because now our DNA is everywhere!" and as if things aren't insane enough, I remember I'm holding a grenade-launching automatic rifle. "And his DNA and who knows what are all over us!"

"We're way beyond any of that mattering, Sisto," she places a hand on her hip, the long-barreled pistol down by her side.

Eye to eye in the wind and cold, we're unevenly illuminated by my Silverado's headlights, my flashlight.

"Look, Calli, if you want out, now would be a good time to skedaddle home," she says with a hint of a taunt. "I'll take care of things. You don't have to be part of this crazy-ass scheme anymore."

It's the same sort of thing she'd say when setting off illegal fireworks or trying out superhero capes at breakneck speeds on the zip line that stretched from the barn to the dock. In addition to her scary games in spooky places like the pet cemetery at Fort Monroe, and the root cellar on our farm that in the 19th century was part of the Underground Railroad.

Whenever I'd had enough of Carme's high-octane drama, she'd give me an out. Usually telling me it's okay to be a chicken while flapping her arms and clucking like one.

"What scheme? And what do you mean, *anymore*?" I demand to know as we face each other in the motel's parking lot.

"What scheme?" as if she can't believe her hood-covered ears. "Just the one we've been living our entire lives. But you're too much of a Pollyanna to see it, especially when it comes to *him*."

"No, I'm not!" my eyes are streaming in the pelting snow, my lips almost too frozen to talk.

"You care too much about his approval, always did," and she's not referring to our father.

"No, I don't!"

"The problem is, you've always done everything Dick says. Never pushing back with him or anyone, and then you get into one of your spins. That's what we're here to fix."

"You have one heck of a way of fixing things! And the only problem I have is you!" I hurl back at her before I can stop myself, and she stalks off, the cold feeling colder.

Never saying she's stung, she doesn't have to for me to know her every feeling. She opens the driver's door of my police truck, killing the ignition, the lights.

"It doesn't have to be your problem anymore, Sisto. I'm offering you an exit once and for all. And you can pretend none of this ever happened."

"Are you crazy? I can't pretend any such thing!" I pop my cork again, looking around frantically.

I'm expecting a squadron with lights and sirens to appear on the street, to thunder into the parking lot. Any second I'll find myself facedown on the frozen ground, aggressive hands all over me, searched like I was hours earlier on top of the hangar. And I don't need that indignity repeated.

"You might be surprised what you can pretend and endure," Carme announces to the empty morning.

There's no sign or sound of anybody headed this way to nab us, just biting air blowing and gusting, shaking shrubbery like pompoms, rocking bare trees. My ears are numb, my leather-sheathed hands stiffening into death grips on the carbine and flashlight.

While my sister moves about silently, nimbly in her peculiar formfitting bodysuit that seems to keep her limber, warm, and surprisingly sure footed in slick conditions with bad visibility.

"It's not too late to turn back," she steps around to the other side of my truck. "This is some scary crap that wasn't part of the plan," she back kicks shut the door I snaked my way out of moments ago. "I'm sure you realize how close you were to being filled with as many holes as Bonnie and Clyde."

Carme goes on to inform me that the assault carbine I'm holding is a QBZ-95, full auto, 650 rounds a minute, 5.8-millimeter heavy ammo. Chinese made, and I don't understand how she could know all this at a glance when there are no visible markings anywhere on the weapon.

"Whoever he was, he didn't hang with a good crowd," Carme locks my truck with a chirp that sounds absurdly normal. "I'm sorry something like this had to happen while you were headed here. But it will be taken care of."

"Taken care of?" I'm incredulous, on the verge of losing my temper again. "You just killed someone right in front of me!"

"Yes and no. You were hiding behind your truck . . ."

"I wasn't hiding, I was taking cover."

"Whatever you were doing, you didn't actually see me or anyone shoot him."

"Well, if you didn't, then who did?"

"The only other person here is you," she pads to the covered walkway, and I'm right behind her.

"Oh, come on, Carme!"

"It's not me who would pin it on you, Sisto," she retorts, her scuba-like rubbery socks leaving no tread pattern. "A bad idea to pick up those cartridge cases. I told you not to. Tried to warn you," and there's no need for her to elaborate.

Except I didn't have to handle anything to be a suspect the same way she is. The Langley twins. Two for the price of one.

"You can't just leave a dead body in the parking lot," I try to calm down. "Do you want us locked up for the rest of our lives?"

She stops walking, facing me, the overhead canopy snapping like sails in the wind. Pulling back her hood, shaking out her hair, she takes off her gloves, seeming unreal like a phantom, and I can barely make out her strong bone structure and deep-set eyes, the same as mine.

00:00:00:00:0

"NOW OR NEVER?" she says as she offers me the key to my truck.

I don't take it.

"Like I've said, what just happened isn't your problem," she says, almost nose to nose, her breath smoking out. "None of this has to be your problem, you can leave. Or stay. Decide, Calli. Now or never," a game of ours that goes back forever.

When faced with the decision, what's it going to be? Will you do it or not? It's about courage and desire being greater than fear, and wanting something badly enough that you'll risk the consequences no matter how severe.

"Now or never," she repeats, and we resume following the covered walkway, passing familiar blue doors with aluminum numbers.

"I'm not going anywhere," is my answer as we reach room 1.

Opening the unlocked door, she flips on the overhead light. Instantly, I'm overwhelmed by the odors of stale cigarettes, dust, and old water damage, intensified after months of being closed up.

"I'm going to ask again because this is serious, Carme. Do you have any idea who he is? Or was?" I feel the heat from the paint-peeled radiator beneath the window. "And what are we supposed to do with him?"

"We don't have time for endless discussions," closing the door, she throws on the dead bolt, and it's obvious that she didn't just move in an hour ago.

Black paper has been taped over the boarded-up window to ensure no light is visible from outside. There are cameras in the ceiling, at least three of them I can spot right off. On the countertop in the kitchenette are laptops displaying spectrum analysis, live video feeds inside the room and out.

As big as life on one display is the same GPS map the hitman was following, two red balloons where my police truck and his Denali are parked outside in the lot.

"You were tracking both of us?" I'm no longer incredulous, not sure anything could surprise me ever again.

"Tracking you being tracked," she says as I look around a room I've not been inside for years.

The furnishings are the same as I remember, cheap pinewood painted white. A bed, a few chairs, and several framed beach prints on the scuffed pink walls.

I take in the kitchenette with its ancient drip coffee maker . . .

The copper-toned ice bucket, and miscellaneous water glasses . . .

The vintage pink minifridge, a rust-spotted Coca-Cola bottle opener on the side . . .

I recognize the blue vinyl-upholstered sofa but not the non-reflective black robotic jumpsuit laid out on it, or the thruster jetpack propped in a corner near a large soft-sided carrying case. Next to the bed are a surgical lamp, and an IV stand hung with bags of fluid. On top of the bare mattress are folded disposable white sheets, black plastic flex-cuff restraints, and boxes of surgical gloves in different sizes.

Carme quick-releases the suppressor from her pistol, matte-black metal with rosewood grips, exactly like mine at home. Our gifts to ourselves for the holidays last year, the Bond Arms Bullpup delivers quite a wallop for a compact handgun, and when it comes to the barrel, size does matter. The longer, the more velocity, and if you do the math, that equals more stopping power and an explosive wound track.

She leaves the pistol, the suppressor near loaded magazines on a bedside table as I notice jugs of an oxi-action stain remover that can destroy blood and DNA, and there are spray bottles of disinfectants, rolls of paper towels. Carme grabs a packet of surgical gloves, peeling it open as she heads into the bathroom where cases of sterile purified water are stacked inside the tub.

"I assume that was you at the controls hijacking my GPS," I talk to her through the open door.

"What you can be sure of is that you're supposed to be here as long as you're willing," she says, deconning with an odorless disinfectant spray, spritzing herself, the bodysuit from head to toe. "Are you willing?"

"Yes."

"Obviously, not the ideal venue," she sprays down a large green Yeti ice chest that looks like one we have at home in the basement. "I would prefer a place where the water's not been shut off. But like Einstein said, the measure of intelligence is the ability to adapt."

"And if you knew that someone, possibly an assassin, was following me, why would you lead him here and almost get us killed?" I ask as she washes up thoroughly with disinfecting soap, like a surgeon.

"I didn't almost get us killed," she opens another jug of sterile water. "You almost did by not being aware someone put a tracking device on your truck last night while it was parked at Fort Monroe," she wipes herself dry on a sterile disposable towel.

"How do you know that for a fact? And who are you talking about?"

"I'm talking about the dead dude who parked his Denali out of sight near Vera Young's apartment," she says. "Going the rest of the way on foot, nobody seeing him as dark and deserted as it was," working her hands into the surgical gloves. "It doesn't take but a minute to attach one of those sticky-backed trackers to the undercarriage, the bumper. Meanwhile, someone's doing the same thing to his unattended vehicle."

That someone was Carme, and it would seem that while I was working Vera's crime scene, my sister was in the area. No doubt moving about stealthily like she is right now, she placed a tracking device on the hitman's truck while he was placing one on mine.

"But if you saw him do it, why wouldn't you go right behind him and remove it?"

"He would have known it was gone," she replies. "Now you've tipped your hand."

"And if you can track him, who is he and where was he staying?"

"Don't know because he didn't go anywhere he might be staying, and it's not my problem now."

"But why have me lead him here?" I again ask as she body blocks my view, collecting something from the ice chest.

"Better than him following you home," she offers that horrific thought, walking out of the bathroom, one hand held behind her so I can't see what's in it.

But I have a pretty good idea. And I don't have to cooperate.

"He could have done that last night," I remind her. "I left Fort Monroe and went straight home. It didn't occur to me to scan my truck with my spectrum analyzer, and obviously I should have. I was none the wiser about the tracking device, and the point is he could have followed me home . . ."

"I wouldn't have let that happen," she interrupts. "Now shush! Take them off," indicating my coat and gun belt. "There's no time to waste. We've gotta get going."

I do as she says just like I always have, placing my jacket and gun belt, my pistol, the Chinese assault rifle on top of the cigarette-burned white Formica coffee table. Nearby is a pair of gray-tinted sports glasses.

"Now or never?" Carme demands, and it's like facing my doppelgänger or own reflection, both of us powerfully, compactly built except I tend more toward pudge unless I'm exceedingly careful.

We're the same height, not too tall or short. Our hair is collar length and cut the same. But hers used to be shorter and less shaggy. And I notice she has reddish highlights just like mine, only hers aren't natural.

"Now or never. What's it going to be?" she says, and the deeper greenish tint to her eyes must be from contact lenses when neither of us needs them.

It's as if Carme's trying to look more like me when it's always been me wanting to look more like her, and on closer inspection I recognize the patterns woven into her black speed-skater-looking skin. The smart fabric is loaded with sensors that interface with her environment, including the black electronic bracelet around her left wrist.

"What's it going to be, Sisto?" Hugging me, she touches her head to mine, making our secret sign. "Now or never? You have to say which one."

"Now," I give my consent for what's already begun.

"Going forward you won't remember certain encounters when it's best you don't," she rolls my left sleeve above my elbow. "Some results no one can be sure about," and I feel a slight pinch near my cubital vein. "Some things are best forgotten . . . ," the voice instantly far away. "If need be, erased . . . never to be restored . . ."

". . . There, there, steady as she goes . . ."

. . . Sitting me down on the edge of the mattress, and it's as if I'm drunk and made of lead . . .

. . . The papery sound of a disposable sheet shaken open . . .

. . . As I try to speak, and nothing emerges, the room rotating . . .

". . . You've got to trust me even when you don't . . . ," quick fingers undoing my clothing . . .

. . . Twitchy, seeing double . . .

". . . Lay down on your back . . . That's it . . . Just relax . . ."

. . . When I try to answer, it's as if I've had a stroke . . .

. . . A draft of frigid air . . .

. . . The sound of a door shutting . . .

. . . Murmuring and footsteps . . .

". . . No matter what, dear, remember I'm here . . . ," fragments of a voice that sounds like Mom's. ". . . Everything's going to be okay, I promise . . . You'll be fine, dear . . ."

. . . Gentle hands work my sports bra over my head as my boots come off, and I'm paralyzed . . .

. . . Sinking down, down, deeper into dimness . . .

. . . Vaguely aware of the nonfragrant mist spraying over every inch of my body . . .

. . . The papery feel of a sheet draped over me . . .

". . . We're in this together . . . ," Carme's voice, and I can't answer or volunteer a thought. ". . . Isn't that right, *Sisto* . . . ? Remember how I came up with that . . . ? When we were kids . . . ?"

. . . *Sister + Callisto = Sisto if you do the math* . . . , hearing it in my head as clear as day . . .

. . . But I can't utter a sound or move my lips as something wet and cold is rubbed over my fingertips . . .

". . . You won't remember what you're about to experience . . . All the same, trust me when I say that a deeper part of you will know . . . and realizing the truth will cause you to seek it . . ."

". . . Think of it as an upgrade to your programming, dear . . . Of entering new dimensions with untold possibilities . . ."

". . . Sorry, Sisto . . . This is gonna sting a little . . ."

5

I WAKE UP to searing pain and complete darkness, sensing another human presence as palpably as heat.

Resisting the impulse to call out to Carme or anyone, I focus on my ankles lashed together beneath the covers. My wrists are bound, my arms barely bent and miserably tethered to the wall behind my head.

I have no idea where I am but it isn't the Point Comfort Inn. I'm not in my own bed, that's for sure, on my back staring up at the black void of the ceiling, scarcely able to move. It would be next to impossible to defend myself, I couldn't kick or throw an elbow, much less a fist.

Concentrating on my hands, I'm aware of a tingling sensation, more numbness than usual in my scarred right index finger. Nervously rubbing it with my thumb, I trace the contours of the finger pad I almost sliced off three years ago. Holding my breath, I listen, not hearing a sound except the wind. But I sense someone.

"Who are you and what do you want?" I sound surprisingly bold when I call out.

No answer, and images are rushing back to me of my sister inside room 1. Telling me it's now or never. Drugging me. Everything deleted. Disjointed. Fragmented sounds and sensations flurrying through my head like bright confetti.

"Who's there?" I'm thirsty, as stiff as rigor mortis.

No response, and I will myself to stay calm as I feel aggression coming on, simmering beneath my skin.

"Hello?" I clear my throat. "Hello!" I tug against a pair of tough plastic restraints, remembering them in my splintered thoughts.

Black double looped, double locking, the same type of law enforcement plastic zip ties I keep in my protective service's office and truck. And I'm tripping on a kaleidoscope of flashbacks . . .

. . . Plastic trays and cut-out gray foam precisely arranged with small tools, glass vials . . .

. . . Scores of tiny liquid-filled transparent tubes with black caps in a wire storage rack . . .

. . . Boxes of hypodermic needles . . . 10 gauge and smaller . . .

"HELLO?" I shout aggressively this time.

Silence, and I'm startled by anger boiling up from deep inside.

"Now would be a very good time to explain yourself . . . !" I violently tug at my restraints.

"Easy does it, don't hurt yourself," Dick Melville's voice is shockingly close. "How are we feeling other than cranky?"

"What are you doing to me?" I scream at him.

The snap of a switch, and he appears in a cloud of light from a Williamsburg-style brass floor lamp. Ensconced in his wing chair throne like God. Dressed in Air Force camouflage embroidered with 4 stars on his chest.

"You have no right . . . ! Cut me loose or . . . or I'll . . . ! Or else . . . !" I sputter and stammer, mortified and furious.

"Or else what, Calli?" he stares at me, handsome in a severe way, broad shouldered and tall with a platinum buzz cut, his strong features sharply sculpted like Mount Rushmore. "What will you do? Take a swing at me again? Dash your drink in my face? Call me names and say you don't respect or believe in me or the cause anymore?"

"It wasn't conscious or intentional. What cause?"

"I made the mistake of freeing your hands only once."

"Obviously, I didn't know what I was doing," I protest.

"Do you remember saying you hate me?"

"Certainly not," more contritely than I feel.

"Calling me a fake and a phony?"

"I'm very sorry. What cause are you talking about?"

"The one you resent me for. Your cause. What you and Carme are here to do," he says as if he made us.

"It would be easier to discuss all this if you cut me loose," I let him know, peering up at the details of my bondage, low tech, practical, well engineered.

I'm suspicious about who's responsible because it wasn't Dick. For an astronaut, he's surprisingly all thumbs with tools and knots, and has an aversion to water sports and boats. Therefore, I doubt he's to blame for marine rigging that's prevented me from attacking someone or escaping. And it may sound sexist to say but I detect a thoughtful, no-nonsense female touch.

Whoever strung me up is good with gadgets and resourceful at fixing things, bringing to mind Mom's string games and origami. Not just the usual cat's cradle and Jacob's ladder but NASA-related sleight of hand. I envision her quick fingers fashioning three-dimensional stars and planets of yarn and twine, or folding paper into miniature expandable habitats and solar panels. If someone had to tie me up, it may as well be her, sort of a different spin on a bedside manner.

Explaining why my bindings are humanely loose, my wrists and ankles protectively wrapped in bandages to prevent abrasions and bruises. The short length of nylon rope attaching my flex-cuffs to the wall is the same kind Mom buys at Full Throttle Marine. Hazard yellow, quarter inch, double braid, and she's partial to simple bowline knots like the one anchoring the rope to a Sea-Dog eyebolt.

"Seriously, Dick. You can cut me loose. I promise I'll behave," sounding more reasonable than I sure as hell-o feel.

"You can throw quite a right hook, I'll give you that," he holds up his hands, bruised from deflecting my blows. "That's what I got if I cut you free," confirming that he hasn't been managing me alone.

". . . Think of it as an upgrade to your programming, dear . . . ," Mom's voice distantly in my fractured memory . . .

"We've got a lot to go over," Dick says as I crane my neck, scanning my surroundings. "As you may have gathered, the timing for implementation was abrupt. Urgent and improvised due to unexpected events. It wasn't ideal even if you don't recall most of what went on, including any discomfort you might have felt," implying that some of what was done to me must have hurt like crap.

"I know something's happened only because I'm here," I'm doing my best to keep my temper in check. "And it would be helpful to know what day of the week it is," as I recognize the patterned brown carpet, the dark wooden paneling.

00:00:00:00:0

"SUNDAY MORNING, December 8th," Dick says to my horror, and as if on cue, church bells start clanging. "It's almost 1100 hours," he adds.

"I've been here 4 nights?" I exclaim.

"Yes," he replies from his wing chair as I twist and turn painfully, taking in the colonial reproduction furniture, the workstation with its Secret Internet Protocol Router Network (SIPRNet) phone for transferring classified data.

I can tell by the vague glow of a curtained window that it's daylight and possibly too overcast for flying since I'm not hearing supersonic T-38 trainer jets or F-22 Raptor stealth fighters. We're in corner suite 604 on the second floor of Dodd Hall, the Tudor-style officer's quarters on the eastern shore of the peninsula that Langley Air Force Base shares with NASA.

The century-old lodging house tucked back in trees is where one would expect the likes of a general to stay when on business here. But Dick never did during earlier years, preferring to bunk down at Chase Place, my family's home on the river. A frequent squatter (he would joke), he used to keep a jump-out bag and other personal effects in the guest room near the kitchen.

Hanging out with us in the peace and quiet of the farm while Carme and I were coming along, he's not the sort to prefer pomp and circumstance, fuss or bother. Dick would rather eat Mom's cooking, spending long hours talking with her in front of the fire or in the garden. Plus, he never stopped picking Dad's brain, everybody's brain, all sorts of ideas constantly flying around like crazed electrons.

"Whatever you decided to, quote, *implement*," I let Dick know, "you could have discussed it with me first."

"I couldn't."

"I assume Carme has been through this same implementation?"

"In stages. But yes, her Systemic Injectable Network, the original SIN, was implanted in her 6 months ago."

"Appropriately named since our behavior and choices are about programming good and bad," I add, trying to stretch my aching legs, and if I'm not mistaken, I have on a diaper.

"I'm sure you're not surprised that there have been problems," Dick replies, ensconced comfortably while I couldn't be more disadvantaged. "The most serious glitches we've fixed, and other upgrades and patches are on the way. In a perfect world we would have waited a little longer before implanting the same SIN in you.

Enhanced as it may be, I would have liked a little more time for troubleshooting."

"And you didn't wait for what reason?"

"It was now or never," he says the same thing Carme did at the Point Comfort Inn. "Earlier this week, the project was cancelled after decades of top secret research and development. I'm sure you can imagine the danger of implementing a SIN in one twin and not the other," he adds, and I can't imagine Carme alone in this. "But DARPA, DoD have deemed it unethical to implant you or anyone else under the circumstances."

I'm not sure what circumstances Dick means but he ignored the government's directive, didn't get the memo in time, so to speak. I was implanted anyway, not that I would have resisted had I been asked. Because he's absolutely right that it would be wrong to install a SIN in one prototyped twin and not the other, and I wouldn't dream of leaving my sister alone to her own devices.

"Are you hungry?" Dick asks.

"Yes," and my stomach growls as I keep looking around, noticing the portable IV stand peeking out from a closet . . .

The black Pelican case on the floor in a corner . . .

The coil of yellow nylon rope and extra flex-cuffs on the kitchen counter . . .

The rolled-up sleeping bag next to the coffee table . . .

"Everything's within normal limits, and that's good," Dick looks at his phone. "Except your blood sugar is hovering at just above 70 milligrams per deciliter, and that's not optimal. In addition, you're dehydrated, based on your electrolytes. Do you feel dizzy, shaky?"

"Yes."

"Thirsty and irritable?"

"Yes."

Reaching down, he picks up something by his chair, "While you've been here, you've been calling out Carme's name."

"Why wouldn't I . . . ?" and I almost add, *Since I was just with her.*

But I stop myself, remembering what she said. That I'm too much of a Pollyanna when it comes to Dick and his big plan, his cause. Of course, he's behind everything leading up to this or I wouldn't be in his custody right now. But he can't know for a fact how much I encoded of what I'm not meant to recall.

He doesn't know the extent of my short-term memory loss, and how far back the tape was erased, so to speak. That's not detectable like a fever, levels of glucose, lactate, carbon dioxide, a spike in adrenaline. It's not as simple to read as the oxygen saturation of my blood, my pulse, or how vigorously I'm exerting myself.

What I do and don't recall is safe as long as I don't give myself away. That's going to be hard when I'm used to handing over my intel like a free gumball machine. Whatever Dick wanted, Dick got, not costing him a penny.

"I'd like you to have a few sips of a Gatorade-like rehydrating drink if you won't spit it all over me," he gets up from his chair, inserting a plastic space straw into a silvery space bag labeled *Lemon Punch*. "Pretend we're floating inside a spacecraft, an orbiting habitat, a laboratory," bending close, placing the straw between my lips.

I suck in the salty, lemony drink like an astronaut in the weightlessness of outer space, hands-free, one sip at a time, and in the process, he's preventing me from using food or beverage as a weapon. I have a good idea who came up with the solution. It's pretty much straight out of one of Mom's playbooks about self-reliance and problem-solving, doing what you can with what you've got.

"Nothing like improvising," Dick says. "Although when I tried earlier, it didn't stop you from spewing your drink all over me. Okay. That's enough for now. I don't want you getting sick."

He doesn't care if I'm still thirsty, and he sits back down, reminding me who's in charge. Placing the drink bag on the floor by his chair, he picks up his phone again, no doubt glancing at data streaming from biosensors, nano-radios, chips, whatever is inside me.

"Blood sugar's a little better," he announces, "and I'm guessing you're calmer."

"Yes. Thank you," I remember my manners because it's not to my advantage to offend or challenge him. "Whatever you've done, I hope you haven't ruined me," I don't say it rudely.

"Actually, far from it. You're sounding good, very good indeed," he nods, splaying his hands, tapping his fingertips together like the mad professor. "This is excellent progress. Hugely improved from a few days ago, and now we can get down to business."

6

"I DON'T EXPECT you to remember much. The less, the better, and we'll fill in the blanks with your origin story," he begins, lamplight shining on his platinum hair like a nimbus as he sits in his big chair.

While I'm on my back in bed with my arms above my head, my joints screaming bloody murder, and adding insult to injury, I'm in surgical scrubs. There's nothing under them except a diaper that possibly could use changing, and I worry what indecent states Dick has seen me in.

"It all starts with going over certain points you never stray from," he explains matter-of-factly. "Think of it as name, rank and serial number. You say the same thing again and again."

"Except it's your story. Not mine," I retort, feeling as indignant and trussed up as Gulliver, only at least he was dressed properly. "I wasn't conferred with and would seem to have no say."

"We're conferring now in complete privacy."

"If you don't count cameras and no telling what else you've got in here," I make sure he knows I wasn't born yesterday.

"Only those with a need to know are aware of what's actually happened. From the beginning. And now."

"Yes, from day one," I reply. "Back to when you started knowing and doing things you didn't share with Carme and me. Things you and Mom probably had in mind way before the *Langley twins* were born and none the wiser."

"Part of protecting people is not exposing them to more than they can handle," he says presumptuously as if it's for him to determine. "Because yes, things have been done that wouldn't fly with an ethical review board. And I don't need to spell it out."

"Then I will. Starting with what's most recent. The commander of Space Force physically altering a NASA investigator, a scientist, a future astronaut while she's tied up and drugged. Not exactly something to brag about on CNN."

"I can understand why you're angry, Calli," he says. "But you've always known this day would come. I regret the execution wasn't ideal."

"I didn't know this day would come, not like this. It would have been nice to have more of a warning."

"We're out of time for warnings."

"Because of some unexpected complication?"

"Unfortunately, more than one."

"It would be helpful to know what you're talking about."

"You know more than you think."

"So much for free will," and I've never felt so overpowered and controlled. "I've got no say about my own design, my own programming. Not even my own origin story or anything else I'm expected to recite and represent the rest of my life."

"You have more input than you know."

"What about Carme? What are you fabricating about her? And what does she have to say about it?"

"Her origin story is even simpler than yours," he says. "She's deployed overseas in her usual special ops missions with the military."

"Is she wanted by the police?"

"All you know is that she's overseas."

"But is she in trouble? Did she do something . . . ?"

"She's overseas with the military," he's just going to keep saying it.

"But she was here 4 mornings ago. Up on the hangar roof . . ."

"People don't know that. They know what you tell them, and Carme has a story she'll stick with," he replies relentlessly. "It doesn't bother her that it's not true. Or that as a result she can't be out in the open the way you are, has to live off the radar, on the run, enduring difficulties and hardships you'll likely get to avoid."

"I'll have different ones."

"Carme doesn't question the mission the way you do."

"You probably didn't dope and hog-tie her either," and I'm betting she didn't have on a freakin' diaper, it crosses my mind resentfully.

"She was taken care of at Dover Air Force Base. It was very different."

"Where does my so-called origin story begin?" I ask. "May as well lay it on me so I know what to tell people."

"It begins when you were leaving Mission Control, about to drive home from Langley in the snowstorm," he says. "But you didn't. Instead, we brought you over here to Dodd Hall, where you've been ever since."

Without saying it outright, he's letting me know that in the yarn he's spinning, the Point Comfort Inn never happened. There was no tracking device placed on my police truck the night I was working Vera Young's crime scene. I never set out for home in a blizzard. My GPS wasn't hijacked. There was no hitman or room 1. Most of all, there was no Carme and no killing anyone.

"It would be nice if you would let me loose," is my response, sounding as easygoing as possible. "It's hard to have a conversation like this."

"Here's the master plot," Dick summarizes as if he didn't hear me. "After NASA was sabotaged earlier in the week, it was deemed best to keep you in safe custody. You and others have been here with me working around the clock to deal with a massive cyber-attack that the public knows very little about, an ongoing threat that has us on high alert."

"Except for one thing," I remind him of reality. "I talked to Mom while I was driving home 4 mornings ago. I also talked to you and Conn Lacrosse on a CIA line, talked to all of you while I was in my truck," as it flickers through my thoughts that Dick and Mom might have been together.

Just because caller ID showed she was ringing me up from the farm doesn't mean that's where she was physically located at the time. It wouldn't be hard for her to spoof our home number, making it appear that's what she was calling me on. When in fact she was with Dick, headed to the Point Comfort Inn to help implant my SIN and oversee the fallout.

"There would be an electronic record of our communications," I continue making my case. "Plus, traffic cameras all over the place would have picked me up. You know as well as I do that I've left an electronic trail if someone wants to find it," I add. "And it sure would be nice if you'd cut me loose."

"You've left a trail, and if anyone checked, it would show that you have the timelines confused," he says what I know is a lie while ignoring my humiliation and discomfort. "The calls you're referring to were approximately 10 hours earlier. On Tuesday night, December 3rd," and there's no telling what metadata has been changed to fit his disinformation.

00:00:00:00:0

A TOP MILITARY leader and close adviser to the president of the United States, Dick can tamper with traffic and security videos, GPS logs, satellite images, whatever he needs. Laws and boundaries don't matter when bad individuals and rogue nations routinely violate them.

"What are we talking about, Special K?" I inquire, constantly rearranging my position on the bed, my joints aching like a bad tooth. "You know, the discussions we've had about its ability to bend space-time? To alter the effects of gravitational waves on the brain?"

I don't mean to sound sarcastic, and what I don't say is the obvious. That Special K, or ketamine, is also a common date-rape drug associated with amnesia and hallucinations. Dick has no reply, won't confirm or deny that for days I've been subjected to a steady drip of what's basically a horse tranquilizer.

"Say what you will about the story you're feeding everybody, we both know I didn't get here on my own two feet," I keep pushing him with questions while he stares at me from his wing chair. "Who was hauling me around like a sack of potatoes?"

As physically powerful as he is, it would be nothing for him to carry me. And imagining it makes me squirm and feel slightly hateful.

"Would you say you're more aggressive?" he asks.

"Than what?" Pinning him with my eyes as he leans forward, lightly touching his fingertips together like Freud.

"What about more hostile?"

"Why wouldn't I be? And it sure would be nice if you'd let me go."

"Tell me the last thing you remember."

"I've already told you."

"Tell me again. What do you remember about the last 4 days?"

And it's like staring into the vacuum of space surrounded by flickering objects light-years away . . .

Insights and snippets of data here and there . . .

Shards of scenes . . .

Fragments of conversations . . .

Disconnected recollections of "Reveille" and "Taps" blaring over the Air Force base intercom . . .

Sound bites of supersonic jets thundering and screaming . . .

"I know you're uncomfortable," but Dick doesn't sound bothered by my degradation and misery. "How's the pain on a scale of 1 to 10?"

"I'm trying not to think about it. Please don't remind me."

"Fair enough." He gets up from his chair. "Are you ready to act civil?" digging into a pocket of his Airman Battle Uniform.

"Of course," and I'm plenty civil considering circumstances that most people would consider sadistic and criminal.

But I'm not going to say any such thing, common sense dictating that it's suicidal to challenge the warden. There's no point in goading my captor into flaunting his power and control more than he already has.

"It's just us at the moment," Dick indicates that others have been in and out of Dodd Hall, including my mother, I'm all but certain. "I don't want to explain a broken nose. And I don't need you hurting yourself with a sharp object again," alluding to my accident while under his command in Colorado Springs.

He unfolds a wicked steel blade as if he's about to take me out like Jack the Ripper. Approximately 15.2 centimeters (6 inches) long, serrated and sharp, it's not so different from what I was using to slice open bagels at the Cheyenne Mountain military complex when I almost lost a body part. And I nervously rub my scarred index finger again.

"Hold still," he says, and I feel his breath on my hair, his uniform sleeve brushing against me. "As you're probably gathering, I've had some help while you're here, haven't been on my own," firmly holding my wrists as he gently cuts.

"Who?"

"I realize it's disconcerting not recalling certain recent events." As usual, he doesn't answer what I asked. "Especially for someone like you who has a near photographic memory," and the scent of his musky aftershave makes me self-conscious and nervous.

I don't move a muscle as he saws, staring up at his powerful arms, his ropy veins.

"There we go," he announces, and I lower my hands to my lap, scarcely able to bend my elbows. "I know this hasn't been fun."

"What's not fun is the information blackout," I massage myself, stretching some more.

"As the old adage goes, what you don't know won't hurt you," he pulls the covers off my legs, the air cool on my bare feet. "It's not always true but in some cases."

"It seems that what may or may not hurt me is one more thing I should have a say about," I unwrap my wrists, the green gauze self-adhering and stretchy, the kind Mom keeps in the medicine cabinet at home.

"Don't forget, you're not new to this rodeo," he cuts through the flex-cuffs around my ankles. "You accepted a very decided flight path long before you gave your official consent."

Consent that was caught on film, and I hate to imagine what else. I remember the cameras in the ceiling of room 1, just as there are cameras here. My every utterance and move are recorded as if I'm the subject of a science experiment. And apparently, I am. And have been since birth. And maybe before that.

I start on the gauze around my ankles as Dick folds his knife, tucking it back into a pocket, leaving a mess of cut plastic and rope for someone else to clean up. I neatly place my balled-up gauze on the bedside table as he walks off through the living room to the kitchen with its countertop, cabinets, refrigerator and microwave oven.

A table is before a curtained window overlooking the back entrance, trees, a large parking lot and other similar buildings. I know the view very well, having delivered my share of VIPs requiring protective escorts when they stay in the enclave of officer's quarters back here.

"What does Fran think is going on?" I pull the covers up to my chin, studying puncture wounds in the fold of my left arm from injections and IV lines. "Does she assume Carme is deployed overseas somewhere? Busy flying her fighter jets, doing her special ops stuff?"

"That's the word on the street, and we want to keep it that way."

"And what has Fran been told about me?"

"The origin story you and I just went over," Dick turns on the water in the sink. "That you're here for safe custody and debriefings, which is factual."

"I guess that's how it works. Fiction starts feeling like fact, and what you want to think becomes what you believe," I reply as I rub my ankles, my wrists . . .

Wondering what's become of my sports bra and boxer briefs . . .

And my tactical cargo pants, shirt, jacket, socks, boots, knife, gun, badge wallet . . .

What about the temporary ID smartcard I was issued after mine disappeared, for that matter . . . ?

"Ready for coffee?" Dick opens a white bakery box from the Grey Goose restaurant, reminding me of their Brunswick stew, my stomach growling again.

"High-test black," I remind him while inspecting myself, finding little obvious damage beyond bruised knuckles from throwing punches.

7

"I BELIEVE I know how you take your coffee after all these years," Dick says with a trace of warmth.

He's more personable now that he's on the other side of the room, a safe distance away, and it must have been difficult watching Carme and me grow up, twins he's groomed and might love too much. Guiding, nurturing us in ways our father couldn't, and then what?

"To give credit where it's due," Dick pours water into the coffee maker's reservoir, "I have to say you've handled chronic discomfort remarkably well," as if that was reason enough to tether me like a hostage, a sex slave, a lunatic for days on end.

"What am I supposed to be doing today? And from now on?" I'm reluctant to get up in nothing but flimsy cotton scrubs too snug in all the wrong places, not to mention the diaper.

"You'll head out to protective services HQ this afternoon once we've finished up here. You'll be meeting Fran."

"Then I guess I'll need my truck."

"Not anymore."

"Ummm? Did something happen to it?" I envision my Silverado parked near the Denali at the Point Comfort Inn.

"In light of the cyberattack and other events you're better served with something more appropriate that will blend," Dick says, and as usual it's up to him. "An SUV with special features courtesy of our Secret Service friends. Your Chase Car is waiting for you in the parking lot, the key on the table by the door. Although a physical key isn't necessary."

He opens a jar of coffee whitener, clinking the lid down on the countertop, stirring in his usual heaping teaspoon of what I tell him isn't real creamer or even food. Then he's headed my way, carrying our coffees in his strong steady hands, a paper plate of muffins balanced on top of the mugs.

I don't stand on ceremony, helping myself as starved as I am. Biting into a muffin, crumbs going everywhere, I blow on my coffee, taking several greedy sips.

"Absolute power, a galactic dictatorship, that's the prize and what we're up against," Dick retrieves a laptop computer from the SIPRNet desk. "It's all about who's the gatekeeper, and we sure as hell don't want it to be Neva Rong."

He paints the scenario of someone like that in charge of the world's GPS, internet, TV and radio networks. Imagine such an entity deciding which streaming entertainment and news programs we're able to access or whose astronauts explore the moon and other planets.

"Not the theory of everything but the takeover of it," he settles next to me on the bed, leaving his desert boots on. "And locking up Neva wouldn't solve the problem. Eliminating her wouldn't either."

"Similar to taking out a head of state, or the leader of a terrorist organization," I reply, already starting on a second muffin. "You still have to deal with thousands of employees, followers, a global network."

"She doesn't operate alone, is heavily embedded in US government projects, including extremely sensitive ones," Dick arranges another pillow behind him on the bed. "She has friends in high places, as much money as a country, and knows how to play politics. Neva's been at it for years and will stop at nothing."

"It looks like my sister and I have our work cut out for us," and I wonder when Dick first cooked up his secret agenda.

When Mom was pregnant? When he found out she was having twins? For sure, he was involved with my family prior to Carme's and my arrival on this planet, going back to Dad's short-lived stint at the Air Force Academy. Supposedly, he and Dick sat next to each other in basic cadet training class their first year, were instant comrades as tight as brothers.

That's according to their origin story, which I've always found a little fishy since they aren't really all that compatible or even friendly with each other. Truth be told, Dick's closest ally isn't Dad. It's Mom and always has been.

"How about turning on the TV and we'll catch up on the news before we get going," he nods at the flat-screen on the wall across from the bed. "Go ahead. Just point your finger. The one with the scar."

"Say again?" I reply with a mouthful of muffin. "Do what?"

"Try it, point your right index finger at the TV," he says, and I do it, feeling foolish.

To my amazement the local news blinks on without benefit of the remote control.

"It's surprisingly intuitive," he demonstrates with hand gestures that have no effect since he's not wired the way I am. "An upward movement raises the sound, a downward one lowers it, providing you've done certain other things first," and it wouldn't matter if he has or hasn't.

Presumably, Dick's not equipped with the same sensors in his fingers, hasn't been implanted with a SIN, the original version or the latest. I'm quite certain that for reasons of national security, it wouldn't be allowed, reminding me yet again that Carme and

I have little or no say, are expendable compared to him. And he tells me to go ahead and try out my new powers.

"Temporary ones, that is. A demo," he adds.

Pointing at the TV, I make a series of rapid upward motions as if conducting an orchestra, and the volume booms . . .

". . . The wildly popular Tidewater International Car Show opened Friday at the Hampton Coliseum, and the now-missing hot rod and hearse had been the biggest attractions . . . ," the Channel 10 anchor says, and I mute the news with a cutoff gesture, a scuba *I'm out of air* hand signal.

"Not so different from swiping your finger across your cell phone if you want to hide the keyboard or zoom in on a map," Dick seems proud of what he's wrought. "Only in this case, motion is captured by the TV's built-in camera, and an end receiver converts certain physical actions into commands."

It doesn't necessarily thrill me to hear that soon enough I won't have to do much more than gesture, blink or use my eyes to make something happen or not. That's assuming the parameters correctly line up as they did when I adjusted the volume, and they did only because Dick changed variables in a biofeedback algorithm.

After making his dramatic point, he changed the variables back to what they were before, and should I point at the TV again, it won't have the same effect. Not until I meet various mathematical conditions, he says. It will be up to me to learn what those are as I return to my day-to-day activities.

Somehow, I'm supposed to figure out things as I go along, interfacing machine and biology, being a test pilot for my own SIN while doing the best I can to live as usual. Or as Dick puts it, *practice makes perfect,* and there will be plenty of that simply dealing with my work spaces on the NASA Langley campus.

Let's say Building 1232, where I often park myself when test piloting and programming scenarios for autonomous vehicles (drones). Dick walks me through what it will be like accessing my office there, starting with the two outer doors that require my ID badge.

Once I scan open those electronic locks, next is my office door, including the fail-safe push-button code I'll have to enter manually before I can use hand gestures to turn on the lights inside. But I won't be able to unlock my desktop computer with a wag, jab or snap of my fingers unless I also insert this same ID badge into the card reader.

00:00:00:00:0

"THE NUANCES are infinite and beyond mind boggling," I state the obvious. "I'm going to look like a wackadoo if anybody's watching," and I can't begin to imagine the misfires as I point and blink like abracadabra. "Not to mention, if the wrong people catch on, Carme and I could end up dead."

"The plan isn't to have you dead, coming across as *I Dream of Jeannie* or a wizard," Dick opens his laptop. "The idea is for both of you to be stealthy, to draw zero attention while you constantly acquire and transmit data."

Everything will be analyzed and tweaked as we conduct high-risk activities with remote human guidance and the assistance of artificial intelligence (AI), he describes what sounds like a high-tech nightmare.

"How are we supposed to live with something like this?" but I already know the answer because it couldn't be more glaring.

By and large Carme and I are on our own, the first of our kind, prototype 001 with no precedent, no other matching siblings who've come before us. One day we'll be the models for others, Dick says as if we could aspire no higher. We're the test pilots and guinea pigs in his top secret project, code name Gemini, which is Latin for "twins."

Including digital ones, and based on electronic blueprints and schematics, Carme's and my individual configurations of implants are identical. Our SINs are extensive with room to expand, Dick says as he continues to unfold our destinies, a life plan that wasn't decided by us even if we agreed to it.

It wasn't our idea for NASA and the military to repurpose our existences, and I don't appreciate Dick's presumptions. Especially when he shows me a female body diagram that supposedly represents the way I'm shaped.

"No good," I shake my head vigorously.

As unimportant as it is in the grand cosmos of things, I don't like being depicted as chunky. I like it less when my sister's noticeably slimmer and more buff body diagram fills the other side of the split screen.

"Nope, nope, nope. Maybe I have to watch what I eat more than Carme does but that doesn't mean we don't weigh pretty much the same," I let him know. "It's just that we aren't built alike. And I have to work harder. And might have a little more body fat."

"All that can be tweaked," he promises.

Not some things, I think dismally. My sister and I may be identical but that doesn't mean we don't have our physical differences. Most notably, I began my precipitous slide into puberty almost a year before she did, doubled over with cramps, outgrowing everything. When it was her turn, she got by with undershirts and extra-slim-fit jeans, never needing a hot water bottle, underwire or a Midol.

"There's not much that won't be fixable and changeable eventually," Dick predicts, and it's unnerving to contemplate the microscopic mission control that's monitoring everything about Carme and me.

From the amount of cortisol, epinephrine and dopamine we secrete (how stressed or aggressive we are). To our blood sugar and other hormone levels (diabetes, PMS). In addition to the early detection of emergency conditions in the making (heart attacks, strokes).

And diseases we might beat if caught early enough (cancer, neurodegenerative disorders, suicidal depression). Plus, what annoys, relaxes, arouses, distracts, bores, thrills, entertains, and whether our mode is flight or fight given the predicament. Also, how we honestly relate to and perceive everything and everyone.

Meaning there will be few secrets anymore as we're watched over by an electronic God. A well-meaning but demanding one with judgmental tendencies and a need to know.

"It's not all that different from chipping your pets in case they get lost," Dick shows me another diagram, and let's be honest, what he's talking about is nothing like that.

Implanting a silicon Radio Frequency Identification (RFID) microchip in your poodle is one thing. It's another to inject a human with scores of sensors and other microdevices, unleashing them under the skin and into deeper spaces like an array of nano-satellites or a virus.

"Made of hydrogel and other biocompatible materials, including your body's own proteins to prevent inflammatory responses and scarring," Dick shows me on his laptop as we lean against pillows on the bed like roomies. "As you can see, your SIN is only partially switched on so far."

"When might I expect that to change?" I want to know. "And will I be aware of it?"

"As they say in quantum computing, *it all depends*," he answers, and I ask him who's in charge of the so-called switching.

"It's only fair that I know, considering the power that person has. Or maybe it's more than one," I add, studying digital schematics and downloads of what should be intensely private.

"You and Carme are in charge of your own switches, of what you're ready to handle and when," Dick replies. "The good news is, much of it won't be conscious. You'll automatically adapt for the most part."

"*For the most part* doesn't sound reassuring or what I'd consider *good news*. This is getting more unmanageable by leaps and bounds," I complain. "Not to mention what you're describing is ridiculously dangerous and scary."

"You'll have robust assistance that I'll introduce you to in a minute," and he goes on to explain that in the main I shouldn't be aware of devices as small as ground pepper flakes, some no thicker than a human hair.

It's hard to know what to expect when it's largely uncharted territory, he adds. I shouldn't feel pain from injection sites, most of them no longer visible. But I might be aware of a vague tenderness near the foramen magnum, the opening at the base of my skull. Beyond that, I probably wouldn't have a clue what's been done to me had he not begun to paint a vivid portrait of what I am under the hood, of how I'm configured and connected.

I wonder when it would have dawned on me that I'm not myself anymore, perhaps when my physical actions and gestures cause manipulations and disturbances of televisions, locks, other electronics. Maybe I would have been alerted by the strange vibrations and tingles like I'm experiencing in my scarred finger.

Unusual thoughts and moods might cause me to suspect I've been altered or worse, fear I'm becoming delusional, possibly paranoid and psychotic. How awful it would be if nobody told me what's really going on. How distressing for Carme if the same thing were done to her and she didn't know.

Thinking back on her increasingly erratic behavior over recent months, I sure hope Dick and his Gemini project don't turn us into something we're not . . .

Hostile, destructive people ruled by bias . . .

Supremely selfish ones with no empathy or remorse . . .

Coldly calculating automatons that get the job done at any cost . . .

Ruthless cyborgs who will charm your socks off . . .

"The race is on to combine telemedicine with AI and quantum computing," Dick continues describing why it was necessary to appropriate Carme's and my double lives.

The potential benefit to the public is extraordinary in terms of health and safety monitoring, he says.

"Also, the implications for the intelligence community, for law enforcement and the military," he makes his bigger point.

"Except for one thing," I remind him. "Anybody with a signal sniffer is going to see me coming. In fact, if someone in the area has one powered on right now, it should be ringing like a bell."

8

STARTING in the low range of 125 to 134 kilohertz, I describe what my SIN is transmitting based on the digital twin app on the laptop.

"And up around 13.45 megahertz," I add. "Also, UHF at 800 to 915. Plus, frequencies in the 2 to 4 gigahertz range, plus S-band, which is pretty insane. In other words, I'm Pigpen, the character in *Peanuts*," I summarize. "Only the dirty cloud that follows me everywhere is electromagnetic, meaning I'll constantly get in my own way."

My own signals will interfere with those I need to read if I'm to evaluate my environment accurately. Security checks will be undoable. Forget trying to get into places that have to defend against intellectual theft and spying. And that's almost any facility or headquarters I access in my line of work, whether it's NASA, the Secret Service, the CIA, Scotland Yard, top secret military installations.

"Should Carme and I have an MRI, a CT scan, then what?" I go on describing what seems completely untenable. "Even if the sensor, the nano-radio or an antenna is no bigger than a sesame seed, one of these days someone's going to detect it."

And what happens to us? I ask, and Dick doesn't have an answer. Will Carme and I end up in prison? In the OR, on an autopsy table with people chopping us up to remove our electronic stuffing? Dismembering and dissecting us for our secret pieces and parts? I continue painting the grimmest of scenarios.

"We have a kill switch," he shows me on the laptop we're sharing. "Similar to what happens if your phone is lost or stolen, you can remotely wipe it clean. If need be, we can render your SINs inert, basically dissolve yours and Carme's injectable networks. But not without wreaking havoc in ways that frankly are unknown."

"If our cover's blown, there may not be time to save us. Not if we get hauled away or shot first," I finish my second muffin, and if only my interest in food had a kill switch.

"No one should detect you," Dick continues to assure me.

We have an invisibility cloak, he promises, our SINs constantly capturing and replicating the noise floor of any environment we're about to enter. The software manipulates internal transmissions to mimic our surroundings.

"Signals hiding behind other signals," he explains. "Electronic masking. Like an octopus changing colors and shape-shifting to blend with the ocean floor. Which reminds me, I have a few new pieces of equipment for you to try."

The bed jostles as he gets up. Retrieving his backpack from the coffee table, he pulls out several generic plastic cases, showing me an oversize black Fitbit-type bracelet like the one Carme had on at the Point Comfort Inn.

"A CUFF," he says. "A Common Ubiquitous Fish Finder, one of your dad's acronyms."

Dick fastens the CUFF around my right wrist, the composite material cool and smooth against my skin.

"As common and omnipresent as an Apple Watch, a fitness tracker, doesn't look different from what most people are wearing," he says. "But it's your command center, a tether to artificial intelligence, to your search engines, air traffic control and a spectrum analyzer."

He informs me that my CUFF is a direct link to software running on the host processor, a quantum computer. My new bling is water- and shockproof within reason, he says. It will do fine in microgravity but can't be worn under a pressurized spacesuit.

"I prefer you sleep with it on, rarely taking it off," he adds. "If you do, it shouldn't be far from reach if you can help it."

Also, it's best if I wear it on my right wrist, and he assumes I'm okay with that since I'm almost ambidextrous. It connects to my other equipment, and next he shows me photochromic light-adapting sports glasses like the pair I noticed inside room 1. My Performance Enhanced Eye Protection System, or PEEPS, he explains, which can be worn with or without my new smart contact lenses, the Smart Photovoltaic Invisible Eye System (SPIES).

Both the glasses and bracelet are surprisingly featherweight and sleek, definitely not made of titanium or carbon fiber but rather a nanotube-loaded composite that's airy light. A material that's electrically conductive and can endure extreme environments, I have a feeling.

Probably graphene or something similar, and it could be my imagination that I sense a vague vibration around my wrist. A barely perceptible current thrumming through my blood vessels and bones, my scar gently tingling.

"Obviously, they're not disposable," I decide about the SPIES bathing in their conductive solution.

"No, you don't change them daily and toss them out, please," Dick says.

Soft and curved, the contact lenses look like nothing special at a glance, made of transparent elastic nanomaterials spun into a network of metal nanofibers and microelectromechanicals including stretchable antennas. The SPIES monitor various bodily functions such as eye movement, glucose levels and potential diseases.

Dick explains that I'll be able to augment perception with synthetic vision, virtual reality, and not knowing where to begin, I ask the most basic questions. When do I wear one thing or another or everything at once or not at all? And what happens if something is lost, stolen or gets too close to the microwave oven?

"PEEPS and SPIES serve different functions but also many of the same," he patiently explains, and what he's really saying is I'll be winging it by the seat of my pants.

"How is all this stuff powered?" I have the covers pulled up to my neck, refusing to get up until I have the means and privacy to dress.

"By motion, similar to a self-winding watch," Dick places my gun belt, tactical knife, my bulletproof vest on the bed. "Also, photovoltaic," adding they convert solar energy into electricity.

"In other words," I decide, "all of my bionic equipment will stay charged if I use it."

"Kind of like everything else in life," he opens the closet door wide, rolling the IV stand out of the way.

Clothes hangers click against the metal rod, and from my undignified vantage point under the sheets I watch him help himself to everything about me just like he always has. Picking up my personal effects in no particular order, could be my Jockey briefs, sports bra, my gun, tampons, it makes no difference to him.

"When all is said and done?" Dick places cargo pants, a tactical shirt on top of the growing pile. "You and Carme haven't been given equipment like this so you can leave it in a drawer. Everything will stay charged and functional as long as you're wearing it."

If that isn't practical or possible, he continues his briefing, there's always the option of recharging my special gear like the Personal Orbs Not Grounded (PONGs) that Dad and I have been working on for years in the barn.

When the flying spherical drones aren't in use, they roost on a Perch Recharger (PRCH), the potted Norfolk pine we converted into a docking station and living light fixture.

00:00:00:00:0

"NO NEED to keep your PEEPS and SPIES constantly within reach," Dick hovers by the chest of drawers, several pairs of my socks in hand. "But best to keep your CUFF close by at all times if you possibly can. However, should you end up separated from it or any device that links you to the host processor, there are other alternatives."

"Such as?"

"Doing without," he drops my socks on the bed. "Relying on your own resources."

"That sounds like sudden death on a cracker," I give him the unvarnished truth.

"Moral of the story, Calli, don't get too dependent on your bionics. You've got to stay fit, sharp, resourceful and self-reliant," as if it's that simple. "You've got to be able to build a fire or a fort, to survive any way you can."

"And when people notice my new accoutrements, what am I supposed to tell them?" and mostly I'm worried about Fran.

"An early Christmas gift from your mom and dad," Dick scripts. "A combo smart watch and fitness tracker. And all-purpose sports glasses that also serve as eye protection on the firing range."

"You know as well as I do that Fran will be suspicious. She's well aware I've been here for days. She'll notice I've got new gear. In fact, she notices everything, and that only makes my day to day more difficult since I work with her, and she's a relative, our neighbor, an old friend."

"More challenges for you to handle, and I'm confident you'll do just fine," powering up my PEEPS, he hands them over so I can try them on for size. "Now go ahead, touch the CUFF," he instructs. "Doesn't matter where. Sensors recognize your fingerprint and other biometric measurements, and you should be connected."

"I definitely am," I reply as password-protected data streams by in gently tinted lenses that turn different shades of gray depending on the lighting.

Skimming news updates, weather reports, and I have the weird sensation that I'm inside a glass cockpit filled with displays. Or surrounded by a mission control of data walls that never stop updating automatically.

"The PEEPS and SPIES are synced with the CUFF. But what is the CUFF synced with?"

"Your phones, computers," Dick says. "With any device capable of connecting to the host processor, a quantum computer as I've said, one that aggregates and integrates data from all over creation, and does it faster than comprehensible."

"How do we prevent any of my devices from syncing with everything around them?"

"That's what you have AI assistance for."

"What you're saying is Carme and I can get into anything hackable," I hold up my arm, studying a bracelet that doesn't look remarkable.

"And some things presumably not hackable," he says, suggesting outrageously that we won't have the usual hassles with passwords, encryption, firewalls.

"Wow this is disturbing. My email, text messages and other private communications are all right there," I describe what I'm seeing in my PEEPS. "I'm into NASA servers, can access everything without logging in. Or if I'm logged in, I can't tell. There's no indication of it."

Far more important than what I see is what I don't, such as alerts or other indications that new electronic visitors have been introduced into Dodd Hall's noise floor. The spectrum analyzers Dick and I carry around with us, and even my new CUFF, fail to detect so much as one device that shouldn't be here, much less the network of them under my skin and inside my skull.

"According to this, my SIN doesn't exist," and I'm amazed and alarmed beyond belief. "Electromagnetically, it's invisible, as if I'm not here," and this is as good as it's terrible.

"Your transmissions are undetectable by normal means," Dick carries over my tactical boots.

"All fine and dandy until someone extremely close, a best friend, a family member, a partner, is implanted with a similar SIN," I remind him. "And we have no way to tell because the transmissions are as masked as ours."

"One of many dangers," as if he's not the one who's caused them.

"Are Carme and I able to detect each other?"

"Not until you beat the software."

"That doesn't sound very fair."

"Get dressed, please," he says. "We need to head out soon. There's a lot to do, and time is of the essence."

"Turn around, and don't look," taking off my PEEPS, I set them on the bed. "How did I end up with so much stuff?" reaching for my underwear. "It's like I've been here for weeks."

"You know Penny the caretaker," he says, and that's my mom to a T, always making sure people have everything they might possibly need.

Dick wanders off while I begin getting dressed, all fumbles, fidgets and nervous flutters. I sure hope he's not stealing glances in this direction, mindful of cameras in the ceiling and gosh knows where.

"If the government just yanked the plug on the Gemini project," I hurry out of my scrubs, "I'm assuming there's a connection between that and the recent unanticipated complications you've been referring to."

"Due to an unfortunate situation, the Gemini project is now critically vulnerable to hacking," Dick says stunningly as I hear him getting something out of the refrigerator. "That's assuming the missing chip ends up in the wrong hands as opposed to being misplaced, lost, accidentally thrown out . . ."

"Excuse me for interrupting but what missing chip are we talking about?" as I think *holy shhhh . . . !*

"The Gemini Original Directive chip," he says what I don't want to hear. "The GOD chip, which as you might infer from the name includes the software, the hosting processor, the memory."

"In other words, a copy of the project's entire quantum computer?" to my amazement and horror.

"Built on a chip no bigger than the head of a match," and he sounds almost boastful as he offers the broad strokes of phosphorous electrons and nuclei sandwiched between layers of silicon.

The resulting qubits are stable, no longer overly sensitive and easily excitable, he points out proudly. Meaning they don't need to be chilled to absolute zero. Or –273.15°C (–459.67°F), requiring cumbersome cryogenic equipment and shielded enclosures, vacuum pumps and other hardware that bring to mind a satellite fashioned of gold and copper. Not exactly appropriate for your average office or home.

"Quantum computing on a chip is similar to what happened to mainframes," Dick glibly goes on. "What used to require huge rooms of big machines now can be managed on desktop servers."

"This is bad, really bad," which sounds about as trite as anything I've ever said, alarms in my head strobing fire-engine red.

DANGER! DANGER! DANGER . . . !

"I assume this GOD chip was locked up somewhere?" I zip up my cargo pants.

"Of course, and when George was in the safe a week ago, he realized the chip was gone," Dick informs me, and I remember what Carme said at the Point Comfort Inn.

Something about Dad. That he already feels bad enough.

"And this missing GOD chip is what Neva was looking for when she showed up on Vera's doorstep?" I button up a long-sleeved black tactical shirt, clean and lightly ironed, acting calm and collected as my life flashes before my eyes.

"Yes, presumably that's what she was after," Dick says. "And still is. And she's not the only one who would go to war for this technology."

"Then she must have had reason to believe Vera was in possession of it," and I can imagine Carme entering the Fort Monroe apartment after the fact, searching for the missing chip like mad.

"We believe Neva thought Vera had it there," he confirms. "Or had it on her person."

"And how would Vera have gotten it?"

"The kid with the burner phone," Dick says.

9

"VERA YOUNG ingratiated herself with Lex Anderson, and it would seem the kid's the missing link," Dick says, and it's not a new story, my dad's greatest weakness the son he's always wanted.

I wasn't thrilled to arrive home a few Saturdays ago to find my father and Lex walking around the farm with portable antennas and signal analyzers. On a cyber foxhunt, Dad explained with a big smile when I asked about it later.

All to say, he's been awfully busy passing on to Lex many of the same things my sister and I were taught when we were coming along.

"What about remotely scrubbing the GOD chip as a last resort?" I suggest. "You know, a kill switch of some kind?"

"If only it were that simple," Dick says, unzipping a compartment of his backpack. "We've got a long way to go in terms of coming up with every contingency," and Carme and I are screwed is how the cookie crumbles.

No one will be in a hurry to eradicate decades of expensive research and development. It's not a decision the commander of Space Force or anyone would consider lightly, and I ask if the burner phone has been traced to the point of purchase.

"The Hampton Hop-In," Dick tells me, and I think of the unfamiliar clerk and pearl-white Jeep Cherokee I noticed 4 mornings ago.

I pull on my boots as Dick carries over a replacement ID badge, activated and good to go.

"As you'd expect," he says, "the kid claims he had nothing to do with the cyberattack. Not the missing GOD chip either."

"Please explain how the hell-o he knows about the missing chip to begin with," I exclaim.

"You can ask him yourself," he replies, walking over to the SIPRNet desk. "You're talking to him later today," he unplugs a phone from its charger.

"That's news to me," I feel invaded again. "Obviously, I knew I would talk to him at some point," I make sure to add. "When I felt the timing was right in the investigation," I rub it in. "Which wouldn't be this minute," in case Dick's forgotten it should be up to me to decide.

"Fran's bringing him to your headquarters, and you'll talk to him there at 1700 hours," Dick states rather than asks. "He's under the impression that you've already interviewed him, not face to face but over the phone," and obviously Carme got to Lex before I could.

"When was this?" I inquire, resisting a tidal surge of upset emotions. "And did she introduce herself as me? Because impersonating a federal law enforcement agent is a felony. Not that we care about breaking the law anymore."

"Yes, Carme represented herself as you. Three days ago, and Lex was very angry and scared. He had little to say at the time. But agreed to come in voluntarily and give his written statement."

"Why not have Carme follow up with him?" I ask pointedly. "Since you seem to think she can do my job better than I can."

"That's not what I think, and it's time you stop saying it," he sits down on the bed next to me, handing over the cell phone he just unplugged.

Lighter and thinner than the one I had before, it's encased in a rubbery reptilian-like skin that I suspect has special functions beyond protection.

"Hyperfast," Dick says, and I don't recognize most of the apps on the phone's home screen. "And it has a beefed-up security chip with advanced encryption algorithms to make it more compatible with your Artificial Research Technician, ART . . ."

"Who? What?"

"The robust assistance I've been hinting about," Dick saves the worst for last.

"You're kidding!" and enough is enough.

But it does no good to tell him that I don't need or want a helper, a researcher, an aide, virtual or otherwise. Definitely not one that's part of my SIN, therefore built in, and talk about being crowded when the irony is I've never felt so alone.

"Mark my words, you're going to find ART a lifesaver, the perfect copilot and pal," Dick smiles as if he's made my day. "I've switched to speakerphone so the three of us can have an open conversation," as if there's a real person on the line. "Usually, he's going to be in your earpiece."

"I don't know what earpiece you mean, but if I'm separated from it? Then what?" I inquire.

"You have one built in, a micro device implanted," he indicates my right ear, telling me one more thing about myself that I didn't know. "You can channel ART through it or whatever you decide, including the usual Bluetooth jawbone-type earpiece if you want to give the appearance you're hands-free on the phone like everybody else. Often you'll do both."

"Talk about driving someone nuts."

"It will take some getting used to but you will," he assures me of what he can't possibly know for a fact. "You'll find yourself surprisingly adept at monitoring multiple things at once. As you'd expect, ART also can text or transcribe. Ultimately, he'll be in your thoughts."

"I don't want a shadow, definitely not a chatty one that's firing messages at me all the time through one device or another," I make no bones about it.

"ART? Are you up?" Dick asks the air.

"What may I help you with, General Melville?" sounds from the phone I'm holding like a magic scepter, and ART may be a *him* but his voice is genderless.

Deeply timbered and mellow, it could belong to a 14-year-old boy, a Kate Moennig, an Emma Stone, compelling yet pleasant, maybe a tad bit sultry-sexy. Sort of like Mason Dixon if he were less of a show-off and more of a tenor, and I sure as heck don't want to be reminded of him whenever ART opens his artificial mouth.

"Captain Chase, meet your new cyber assistant," Dick says.

"Hello ART," seems like a good way to start, albeit reluctantly, and I don't sound happy because I'm decidedly not.

"How may I help you, Captain Chase?" his polite, friendly response reminds me of Mom.

"I don't know. Maybe by telling me if I'm in Kansas anymore," and I'm definitely a little sassier than I was before.

"You've never been to Kansas, Captain Chase."

He could figure that out from open-source data like plane, train, other types of reservations and itineraries, I realize. Plus, credit card receipts, emails going back for decades.

00:00:00:00:0

DATA, DATA everywhere that he's mining at unimaginable speeds, demonstrating an AI-interfaced proficiency I wasn't expecting this early in the race for quantum supremacy. I sure hope Dick and all involved know what they're tampering with, because I can't think of a quicker way to get into trouble.

Should a quantum algorithm or program be a little off, there will be no forgiveness. Flawed math, inadequate parameters, improper codes could direct an autonomous passenger plane into a mountain. A rocket into a downtown skyline. Return a Hellfire missile to sender. Set off a nuclear attack.

I hate to imagine the medical havoc if your pacemaker or blood sugar sensors get the wrong message and you end up in cardiac arrest or a coma. Or your bionic limbs receive an erroneous command, and begin crushing loved ones to death instead of hugging them.

"Is there other information I can help you with, Captain Chase?" my built-in sidekick wants to know, and I gently set the phone down on the bed as if not to jostle or hurt him.

"No thank you, ART. Not at the moment, ART. But saying my name repeatedly is annoying, ART," I add for good measure in case he didn't get the drift.

"Copy. My apologies," a little less friendly.

"Do you understand what it means if something is annoying?" I reply as Dick nods in approval.

He's pleased by the way ART and I are interacting, I can only suppose. And it's not apparent from looking at my phone that I'm talking to someone. Well, not exactly a *someone*.

"I frankly doubt you understand any emotionality at all," I go on to say. "And at the end of the day compatibility won't be possible when only one of us has feelings," I may as well be honest up front.

"I understand I've annoyed you," a chill in ART's manufactured response. "But the data indicate you were annoyed before

I spoke to you. Therefore, my repetition of your name wasn't the cause."

"To be clear," I tell him in no uncertain terms, "I have more than my share of very good reasons for being out of sorts at the moment. And you may have just topped the list," as I'm saying this sincerely but ungraciously, I'm conscious of Dick seated next to me, watching and listening . . .

While the cameras record from the ceiling . . .

At the same time a network of sensors and other devices comprising my SIN download and tinker with my most personal data . . .

"This may not make sense to you, but in the real world we don't reprogram our family and friends as if they're an operating system in need of an upgrade," I add in the off chance ART might be capable of empathy, that he can relate to being used and undervalued, barely treated as human. "So, I'm trying to wrap my mind around my predicament, and somehow to be okay with it."

"I don't understand what you mean by *the real world*."

"I guess if you don't know what it is, it's a little hard to explain," I reply. "But if I had my way about it, I wouldn't have to mentor something that doesn't exist, and for privacy and security reasons I don't want people hearing you say my name out loud."

As I'm hearing myself, I wonder why I'm explaining myself to an artificial anything.

And why I resent him when we only just met.

"Wilco," ART replies with diminished enthusiasm. "Would you prefer I never say your name audibly?"

"Well, obviously at times you'll need to. Depending on circumstances," I consider. "Such as if I'm too busy to read something. Or you need my attention instantly."

"Copy."

"See?" Dick gets up from the bed. "Already you're learning how to get along."

"Um, it sure doesn't feel that way to me," I'm careful what I say, mindful ART is eavesdropping, probably always will be, and I head to the bathroom to freshen up.

I close the door to have a little privacy as if that's possible anymore, and I'm overwhelmed by déjà vu. Taking in the old black-and-white tile floor, the white toilet and tub, the simple crystal sconces, and I have no memory of being in and out when obviously I have been repeatedly.

My toiletry bag, the contact lens fluid, antibacterial soap on the counter by the sink are courtesy of my mother, I have no doubt, and the first order of business is to ditch the diaper. Then I brush my teeth and wash my face. Next, I dig in a pocket of my cargo pants, pulling out the small plastic case containing the SPIES that can accompany my PEEPS if I choose.

Carme and I don't need corrective eyewear of any description, and I've never worn contacts. But Mom does, and I have a pretty good idea how to put them on. Scrubbing my hands thoroughly, I touch my fingertip to a surprisingly soft thin lens. One at a time, left and right, blinking, and they don't feel bad, aren't uncomfortable but it's distracting to see emails, messages and other data.

I'll get used to it (I can only hope), and I stare at myself in the mirror. Studying my messy dark hair with its hints of red, my familiar skin and features, never sure what to make of myself. Too pale, too dark, too girly, too strong, too chatty, too quiet, too this, too that, depending on who you ask.

Except I'm surprised I don't look nearly as bad as I've always imagined, nowhere as unattractive and common. Truth be told, it could be Carme looking back at me, and how odd that she's always been the pretty twin, the sexy one, while I'm plain and rarely noticed even though people can't tell us apart.

"It all boils down to the programming," Dick says as I emerge from the bathroom. "Not just ART's but yours and your sister's," he shoulders his big tactical backpack. "You'll have to see for yourself what causes certain events to happen. And how best to teach each other."

"I hope you know that sounds a little crazy," I follow him to the door.

"You and Carme have been preparing for this all your lives and just didn't know it," Dick pulls on his camouflage cap, draping his jacket over an arm. "I'm confident you'll manage just fine."

"Based on what? If we're prototype 001 and no one has come before us?" I remind him as he opens the door.

"You may be the first but that doesn't mean there hasn't been extreme bench testing and experimentation. I promise you'll adjust and adapt," he walks out to the second-floor landing, not so much as a goodbye or good luck.

Not a handshake or hug from someone I've known forever. I experience a jolt of panic as I contemplate what's demanded, having no idea what I'm supposed to do, all dressed up in bionics with no place to go.

"Where will you be?" I have a right to know since he's running the show.

"I'll hook up with you later at the Gantry," Dick pauses on the stairs, his aviator sunglasses fixed on me. "It may be a Sunday during a furlough but there's plenty going on. A number of projects, including a space capsule drop," he adds as I think back to what was on the books for outside contractors at NASA Langley this month.

The last time I checked would have been at the beginning of the week, and at that time there was nothing scheduled at the Gantry or its Hydro Impact Basin between now and the new year. But I'm also well aware that top secret research and related personnel aren't necessarily listed on schedules and itineraries. Often, I'm not going to find out details until the last minute. If at all. Depending on my need to know.

"An SNC test model, spaceplane related." Dick resumes going down the stairs, and I wonder what he's referring to because it can't be Sierra Nevada Corporation's Dream Chaser spaceplane that lands on a runway like a glider.

We wouldn't drop something like that from a crane at the Gantry or anywhere else. What a waste of time and money that would be, banging up the multimillion-dollar test model of a vehicle that was never meant to splash down in the ocean or slam into the desert to begin with.

10

I WANDER to a window, nudging the curtains aside as Dick emerges from the back of Dodd Hall, his breath smoking out in the cold overcast early afternoon as he follows the slushy sidewalk.

I watch him climb into the back of a blacked-out Suburban with dark-tinted windows, antennas, a satellite dome, and I instruct ART to run the tag number.

"A 2018 black Chevrolet Suburban registered to the US government," he answers in the same bored monotone Carme resorts to when her nose is out of joint.

"I'm pretty sure it's going to be the Secret Service," I drop my duffel bag, my backpack on the bed to finish packing. "That's who he was with in the hangar 4 days ago."

"I have no information on which government organization," ART lets me know rather snippily. "But running the plate has triggered an alert."

"That would have been a good thing to be aware of in advance," and he's really starting to pluck at my last nerve. "Maybe you can somehow untrigger it? Because I sure don't want another posse coming after me."

"Not possible to untrigger," and he gives me a Delaware address for the Suburban that I have no doubt is bogus.

The US Secret Service isn't about to allow anyone to figure out where they garage their stealth vehicles, and I imagine Dick riding with his detail, well aware I was spying out the window like a Keystone Cop, that I got ART to run the tag as if it was going to tell me much. And in the process, we set off an alert that I instruct him to notify Dick about.

"So he can make sure we don't have a darn SWAT team coming after us," I add grumpily.

"Wilco," ART snarks, and I don't know how I'm supposed to get used to this.

Feeling naked with no skin. Everything exposed and found lacking.

"That was stupid of me," I direct at my phone on the bed. "Dick may as well be sitting in his big wing chair watching the whole thing."

ART has no reaction as I pack extra cargo pants, shirts, plus shoes and at least a week's worth of underwear.

"Maybe next time you can give me a heads-up," I let him know that he needs to anticipate consequences before following orders. "I'm assuming you had some awareness that running the tag number might result in an alert or alarm of some sort."

"I did as you asked," ART talks back like my sister when she's being a brat.

"You did as I asked but not as I meant," I reply, folding clothing as compactly as origami to fit inside my limited luggage.

"You didn't inform me of what you meant," he's bickering with me now. "I didn't have that data."

"If I have to tell you what I mean, then we aren't going to work very well together."

He has no comment as I check my gun and clips, making sure I'm locked and loaded, ready with a round chambered.

"But just to be clear so we don't set off any more alerts or alarms this afternoon?" I fill the silence. "Implicit in my asking for assistance is first and foremost you're to protect my privacy and safety. If you have data that I don't, I expect you to make suggestions and issue warnings."

ART remains silent as I feel the shimmering rumble of F-22s pawing at a runway of the nearby airfield. The weather has improved, and Langley Air Force Base is up and at 'em.

"Before venturing out, I'd like the latest news and meteorological updates." I couldn't be more impersonal, using my artificial assistant like Google.

I'm quizzing him as if he's little more than an Automatic Terminal Information Service (ATIS) that gives me weather and other conditions pertinent to aviation. In other words, I treat ART the way he's treating me, as if I'm transparent, nonessential and unknown, the way Dick can make me feel. And also, Dad, who suffers from *absentia*, as we joke in our family.

"I'm looking for any data that might impact me, my job, my environment, the people I care about," I explain to ART, sliding my Glock .40 cal into its holster. "For example, what's the latest on the furlough? What's the word on the street about when the government shutdown might end?"

"I don't understand *word on the street*," is his unhelpful response.

"But I'm pretty sure you understand the question," and I ask it again.

"The shutdown could continue the rest of this year and possibly longer if politicians don't agree."

"But they never do or will. In other words, more of the same freakin' mess . . ."

"I don't understand *freakin' mess*," he's gotten downright mechanical like one of those canned voices in an airport terminal.

"You should understand it from the context but are choosing to be difficult," I fire back just as robotically as it dawns on me that ART is out of sorts because his demeanor is syncing with my own.

Whatever I emote, he echoes right back. And I suppose it makes sense that the programming would enable him to have emotional reactions he doesn't feel even if he acts like he does. And whose bad idea was it to make moods and attitudes contagious? What a fiasco if my less than pleasant disposition or fit of pique becomes ART's. And his becomes mine. And on and on it goes like the number pi.

"Okay, I admit I probably started it," I apologize to my phone as I collect it from the bed. "I inadvertently instigated our disagreeableness by not being friendly or particularly gracious, in addition to insensitive and unaccepting. I'd very much appreciate it if you would give me what's basically the latest ATIS and any other important data, and do so inaudibly," and the information begins crawling by in my SPIES.

There's a 10 percent chance of light rain. The temperature is 5.55°C (42°F), meaning everything is messy and slippery. Some local roads remain closed, and areas affected by the government shutdown may not have been plowed. There's considerable flooding in lower elevations, and ice remains a significant hazard.

As for how I'm doing physically, my blood sugar is in the normal range according to data transmitted by my Systemic Injectable Network. My body temperature is 36.5°C (97.7°F). My galvanic skin response, respiration, heart rate and other stress indicators within normal limits, which is unusual considering my tendency to get into one of my spins when sufficiently rattled.

But it would seem I'm reasonably calm and collected considering the circumstances as I put on my PEEPS over my SPIES before venturing into the great unknown. I'm headed to the door when ART alerts me through my earpiece that I have an incoming call.

00:00:00:00:0

"O-C-M-E," he says, and I'm as sweet as sugar when I ask him which Office of the Chief Medical Examiner he means.

Statewide there are 4 district facilities, I remind ART. Including the headquarters in Richmond, and he informs me just as nicely that death investigator Joan Williams from the local office in Norfolk is trying to reach me from her mobile phone.

"Thank you, and I'll take the call." I'm overly polite, laying on the southern charm as I haul my belongings out of suite 604.

"You're welcome, putting her through now," ART mimics the very cadence and pitch of my speech, connecting me.

"Calli?" angrily in my earpiece. "Where are you?" Joan stops me in my tracks before I've so much as uttered hello.

"I'm sorry . . . ?" I have no idea what she's talking about as I stand like a statue on the second-floor landing, going nowhere.

"You promised to be here!" and she sounds just as hurt as she's aggravated.

I almost reply that I haven't promised any such thing. It's on the tip of my tongue to tell Joan and we've had no contact since working Vera Young's crime scene earlier in the week. But I stop short of communicating in any form or fashion that I don't know what's going on.

"Well thanks a lot because the rich beeyotch is in our lobby demanding to see the body as we speak," Joan sounds unnerved and frantic. "Why aren't you here? You promised! Otherwise I would have made sure *someone* was! That there was *some* cop present I could trust!"

A tough old bird like Joan isn't tricked easily, yet incorrectly assumed she was talking to me recently when she absolutely wasn't. Carme was impersonating me again, conspiring with Joan to show up and intercept the *rich beeyotch*, Neva Rong, to catch her unaware, and confront her with the very questions I'd like to ask.

I imagine my identical twin probing Neva about her murdered sister, the cyberattack on NASA, the hitman, the missing GOD chip, Lex Anderson, and other fiascos when it's supposed to be me doing the interviewing. Furthermore, who would Neva suppose she's talking to? Would she think I'm Carme or Carme is me? Depending on who's before her, would Neva be fooled?

What if she isn't? Does she buy Carme's origin story, that she's overseas with the Air Force? I can't begin to know what Neva thinks or has been led to believe. But once again, my sister has taken it upon herself to do my job. *Not hers but mine* seizes my thoughts as I experience an unfamiliar mixture of emotions that are strangely territorial and selfish.

". . . All we've got on-site right now is one security guard, poor old Wally who's afraid of his own shadow," Joan rants on, and I don't blame her. "It's not like I can call the local cops on Neva Rong for God's sake."

What a story that would be, and it's exactly what Neva wants to add credence to her conspiracy accusations, Joan rightly points out. She tries to view her beloved sister's dead body and we sic the cops on her.

"I'm really sorry," I reply as if I mean it.

"She's threatening to camp out until we give her the full Monty, including the autopsy records, all photographs, you name it," Joan says, and I remember what Dick told me moments earlier about Neva believing the GOD chip was inside Vera's apartment or *on her person.*

What about *inside her person*? Assuming Vera had the chip to begin with, she might have ingested it. Down the hatch, and there wouldn't be much Neva could do without a CT scan, an autopsy, rooting around through fluids, all sorts of pieces and parts while using a spectrum analyzer to pick up the chip's transmissions.

What a dreadful scavenger hunt that would be. But if it's remotely possible that the missing GOD chip might be mingled with Vera's remains, then for sure the same possibility has crossed Neva Rong's wicked thoughts.

"I'm really sorry, Joan. I'm getting there as fast as I can. You know how Norfolk traffic is even on a good day . . . ," I'm saying as a satellite map appears in my smart lenses.

Without asking, I'm zoomed in on an angry red line, miles of backed-up traffic, and the smoldering scene of a fiery accident less than a mile from Joan's office. Nothing is moving in the westbound lanes of Brambleton Avenue. Every road leading to the Tidewater District public health complex is at a standstill. A hit and run, ART texts in my lenses.

Further information indicates witnesses reported an SUV speeding away from the scene after being rammed by another vehicle that exploded into flames. I can't stop thinking of Carme on her way to the OCME, and it would have been around the same time the crash occurred.

Where is she? Why is she late? I tell myself that nothing can hurt her without someone knowing. Our SINs would download the data in real time, alerting Dick and others should the worst happen to either of us.

"Totally stuck because of the accident barely a mile from you, gosh what a mess," I redirect my misleading comments, making Joan think I'm a stone's throw away, trickery coming more easily. "There's no getting through from Brambleton or any surrounding streets, and I don't see how you'll get your investigators in for that matter," I add another dash of deception.

"Forget it, no point," she says, having no clue I'm on the second floor of Dodd Hall, 48 kilometers (30 miles) away. "As hot as the fire was, may as well be a crematorium. I'm having the wreckage hauled next door to the evidence bay, we'll recover what we can in there instead of in the middle of a busy highway."

In the meantime, she adds, it won't be easy getting police to show up and help out with Neva Rong and the circus she creates. But at least the traffic jam is keeping some of the media at bay for the moment, since they can't get through either, she adds.

"Again, I apologize," I reply from the other side of the Chesapeake Bay. "I'm completely stuck," as I lean against the thick oak banister, not going anywhere. "How did Neva manage to get to your office if no one else can get through?"

"You won't believe it. But then again you probably will," Joan begins to simmer down. "She was dropped off by helicopter," and another security recording begins playing in my lenses.

A time stamp of 3:00 p.m., I'm seeing the modern three-story brownish brick-and-stucco building that includes forensic labs and autopsy suites. Spartanly landscaped with tidy islands of snow-frosted grass, winter-bare trees, it's surrounded by other medical centers, hospitals and facilities.

The parking lot is mostly empty, just the usual OCME vehicles and those of personnel working the weekend shifts. In the background the traffic is at a standstill on Brambleton and Colley Avenues.

". . . Apparently, she got permission from the effing governor to land here," only Joan doesn't say *effing* as I listen to her in one earpiece while hearing the thudding of helicopter blades in the other . . .

A Bell 407 thunders in, white with blue stripes, going lower and slower . . .

Settling into a hover over the concrete helipad with its big painted H and thrashing orange windsock . . .

ART runs the tail number, and I read in my smart lenses that the helicopter is registered to the charter management company HeloAir based in nearby Richmond.

11

". . . BOTTOM LINE, Neva claims she has rights because she's next of kin, which she legally isn't. Vera Young's daughter is," Joan goes on.

I'm listening to her in my earpiece while watching snow flying everywhere in the video recording I'm seeing in my PEEPS and SPIES, the chopper setting down softly on its skids.

"She has zero legal rights to the body," Joan is saying, "and thank God it's being picked up at the end of the day, and maybe life can go back to normal around here."

As a back door of the chopper opens . . .

And Neva emerges, glamorous in designer glasses, shouldering an oversize black crocodile bag, a black full-length sheared mink coat buttoned up to her chin . . .

Surprisingly agile as she climbs down from the skid . . .

Shutting the door, walking away from the whirling blades, her hair and clothing blowing everywhere . . .

"What do you think she's really after. Maybe other sensors?" I ask Joan as I worry about the missing GOD chip. "Because she knows darn well we would have detected the micromechanical devices implanted in Vera's fingers, that we'd extract and examine them," and I remember how startled I was at her crime scene when I picked up the transmissions with my spectrum analyzer.

"She knows about the chips we recovered and is demanding them as well, claiming they're property of Pandora Space Systems," Joan says. "Of course, we don't have them anymore. You guys at NASA do, and whoever else is involved."

"Chances are good there may be other implants she's interested in that didn't show up and therefore weren't found," I reply as I think of my own.

"Look," Joan's impatient voice in my earpiece, "she's here to cause trouble plain and simple."

"That's for sure," I agree.

"And I can't order her off the premises any more than I can keep the media out when they show up . . . ," she adds while I watch Neva on video pushing her way inside the OCME lobby, almost knocking over Wally, the unarmed OCME security guard in his khaki uniform . . .

"Hold on!" Wally's startled old face, his balding pate on the video feed . . .

"Good afternoon," she announces brightly as if she knows it's to an audience. "I'm Dr. Rong. Neva Rong. Here to see my deceased sister after being repeatedly stonewalled and denied the most basic human decency . . ."

I'm seeing all of it in my lenses even as Joan complains in my Bluetooth earpiece while I hear Neva in my implanted one, and dichotic listening is bound to get tiring. I'm reminded of holding a conversation on the sofa with Mom while trying to follow what characters are saying on a television show, and I resume creeping down the stairs, the old flooring creaking much too loudly beneath my boots.

One stealthy step at a time, I'm careful not to scrape and bump my bags, my gear against the banister. Trying to be quiet, I don't take into account the rumbling and thundering of fighter jets on the nearby runway until they fire up like a rocket just now. I end the call abruptly as if my battery died or the signal was dropped.

And I sure hope Joan didn't hear the background noise and realize I'm not stuck in traffic after all, that I've been misinforming her, lying after leaving her in the lurch this afternoon. Or that's what she'll conclude.

"Stupid! Stupid! Stupid!" I could kick myself. "What were you thinking?"

I don't understand, ART texts in my lenses.

"Not directed at you, I was talking to myself," I tell him. "But don't answer if Joan tries me back. Have it go straight to voice mail, please. I don't want her figuring out where I am. Or better put, where I'm not," as I step out into the blustery afternoon, Raptor F-22s ripping up the skies like Batplanes.

The parking area behind Dodd Hall is empty, not a vehicle or person in sight. The snow is churned up mainly near the door I just came out, and looking around, I don't spot my so-called Chase Car at first. When I do, I can't believe it.

"Are you kidding me?" under my breath.

I don't understand, in my lenses.

"Again, not meant for you. But I don't understand either," I stare out at my new take-home Chevy Tahoe, which couldn't be parked farther away.

About two-thirds the length of a football field, I estimate, it's on the far side of the parking lot near other Tudor-style buildings that look empty. All by itself in the cold shadowlands of huge magnolias, stands of evergreens, and shrubbery, and there's an obstacle course of slush and ice between here and there.

"Why the hell-o park it way off in the hinterlands?" I declare, and ART has no answer. "Seriously? Why isn't it right here at the back door?"

"Unauthorized," out loud, and he's not going to divulge why Dick or someone decided such a thing.

Or maybe it wasn't deliberate. Maybe it was thoughtless and not intended for any rational reason. But there's an acre of unplowed wintry slop to navigate according to ART, and I ask him to remote start the Tahoe. The engine growls to life, the headlights blinking on.

Next, it needs to drive autonomously to the back entrance, I further instruct because fair is fair. Why should I carry my stuff through such a treacherous mess, and risk getting hurt in addition to wet and filthy.

"Function disabled," ART replies audibly, infuriatingly.

"For Pete's sake! Well, enable it, please."

"Unable to access programming without authorization," he says, and if I'm understanding him correctly, he needs permission from on high, from the wizard behind the curtain, Dick, no doubt.

"Well, it's not going to be workable if I'm micromanaged like this. Not to mention, him or anyone else getting back to us anytime soon," I reply, annoyed as heck. "We'll be waiting until the cows come home," as it begins crawling by in my lenses that the average dairy cow can run a surprising 40.2 kilometers per hour (25 mph).

Meaning if the distance back to the barn is one mile, then the cows literally could come home in 2.4 minutes. Which isn't much of a wait, more like a stampede.

"We need to work on your comprehension of idioms," I say to ART, stepping away from the back door, onto the sloppy brick sidewalk. "I sure hope I don't break my neck," as I set forth in a gritty pudding of coarse sand and blue-tinted rock salt.

The icky wet stuff gets all over my boots, my cargo pants, and I puzzle over the logic of deicing paths for foot traffic but not bothering to plow the parking lot. The chemical-looking soupy slush stops short of the pavement, and as I'm noticing this, another message appears in my lenses:

... Silicon dioxide (SiO_2). And calcium chloride ($CaCl_2$) with heat-attracting dye added. Not pet friendly ...

Tracking where my eyes linger, ART must have gleaned technical data from my SIN. Microspectrometers were among the scores of sensors implanted under my skin and built into my CUFF, I recall from various schematics Dick and I discussed.

00:00:00:00:0

"WHOAAA . . . !" I yell as my feet almost go out from under me.

"WAIT! WAIT!" audibly in my earpiece, ART resorts to a loud jarring mechanical crosswalk voice to get my attention before I land on my butt.

Prompted by built-in nano-accelerometers, I can only suspect, I'm halted in my sloshy tracks 56.9 meters (187 feet) from the Tahoe. Next, I'm given a map in my lenses, a close-up real-time synthetic view of the terrain I battle.

Icy areas and other potential hazards are highlighted in different colors based on current temperatures, elevation, the amount of light, the direction of the wind, satellite images and other metadata. I'm more than a little familiar with the Features Integrated Navigated Direction (FIND), AI-assisted mapping that Dad and I have had a hand in developing.

The software implements image processing with NASA's Artemis lunar mission in mind, and while not everybody worries about getting lost on the moon, I happen to obsess about it constantly. Currently there are no GPS capabilities 384,472 kilometers (238,900 miles) straight up as a rocket flies, and no magnetic poles, meaning a compass won't work either.

Unmanned probes and vehicles crashing, getting stuck or wandering about aimlessly are bad enough. But God forbid astronauts ride the lunar rover blindly in a cave, running on empty or about to plunge into a crevasse. A commonsense solution was to create programming similar to facial recognition, mapping physical features such as craters, lava tunnels, rocks, landing pads and lunar stations that an autonomous vehicle can use to navigate.

It's not so different from taking a left at the firehouse. Or hanging a right at the third traffic light. Relying on physical features and waypoints, except FINDs are dynamic and harder to outsmart. They change their minds in real time like the rest of us as AI-assisted quantum computing incorporates alterations to the landscape, hidden booby traps and pitfalls.

The landmark no longer there. The wind shear no one's talking about. The bird about to crash through the windscreen. The sinkhole waiting to open up beneath the road you're driving on.

"You may proceed along your highlighted FIND," ART says as I'm given a hash marked path in electric yellow.

Detouring around an icy puddle the software paints neon red, I resume trudging toward the Tahoe parked maddeningly far from Dodd Hall's back door. Paying close attention to where I step, I follow my mapped route while watching a video in my lenses, another local news update on the presumed fatal motor vehicle crash in Norfolk.

". . . No clue about the identity of the driver, any remains recovered are expected to be badly incinerated," the correspondent says from his news desk, showing helicopter footage of cars at a standstill. "Police say the vehicle may be stolen, possibly related to the car show in town that kicked off Friday night at the Hampton Coliseum . . ."

More aerial views of emergency workers in heavy winter gear using winches and hydraulics to load the charred twisted wreckage onto a flatbed truck. They'll be clearing the road momentarily, and I can count on Joan calling from the OCME again, mad as a hornet, demanding to know where I am.

That's assuming Carme doesn't show up first, pretending to be me. And if she's not gotten there by now and doesn't soon, then we have a much bigger problem.

"Somehow, I have to be reconnected," I tell ART out loud as I slip-slide along, the straps of my bags digging into my shoulders. "And is my sister on her way to the morgue?" It sounds ominous as I say it. "Is she okay? What's happened to her?"

It stands to reason that ART knows. If Carme and I share the same Artificial Research Technician because of our SINs, then obviously she's talking to him at least as much as I am. Possibly more since she was implemented first. ART could be communicating with both of us simultaneously, and the thought makes me feel less important.

He might give her preferential treatment because they've known each other longer. He might tell her things he doesn't tell me, possibly leaking what I share with him in confidence, choosing her over me as pretty much everyone else always has done, and now I feel stung.

"Bottom line, you know what's going on with her," I make my point firmly but respectfully, having learned my lesson about contagious demeanor. "You know where she is at all times and what she's doing. Is she alive and unharmed? It wasn't Carme in that accident, was it? Can't you at least tell me that?"

"Not authorized," ART replies, and once again it's up to Dick and whoever else comprises his Gemini project pantheon.

"For the record, that's unfair," I reply, a slick of black ice dead ahead. "But if you're not going to tell me what I want to know, at least let me find out for myself. Let me see for myself what I need to know."

Should Carme suddenly show up at the OCME, I have to be in the loop, I add a tad aggressively. Each of us needs to be privy to what the other's doing so we can help without interfering or blowing our cover. We're supposed to tag team, act as partners, be in this together while being apart, reminding him of Dick's own mantra, my tone a little sharp.

"You will be appropriately warned," ART's reasonable voice is about to get testy in my earpiece.

"That would be much appreciated," I dial it back, making sure I don't sound bossy or strident. "Also, at this level of technical sophistication, I shouldn't have been logged out of the camera system just because I hung up on Joan. Which wouldn't have happened to begin with had you reminded me about background noise from the airfield," I don't say it accusatorily.

"Do you wish to reconnect with her?" ART asks in my ear. "It will require logging back into the OCME CCTV surveillance system through her mobile device . . ."

"No, please don't!" That's the last thing I want.

"Copy. Unable to reconnect otherwise."

"What! Why?"

"L-O-S," is his response.

Duh and shut the front door! I don't need my own private Genius Bar to figure out that much. Of course, I'm disconnected from the OCME camera system because I have a loss of signal.

Which is the same thing as informing me that my computer stopped working because it suddenly turned off. Or the power's out because there's no electricity. That doesn't tell me why or what the frick to do about it!

"Rats! Rats! Rats!" as I wade through snow, the Tahoe 15 meters (50 feet) out. "And don't take it literally," I'm quick to add, not wanting ART to research the slightest thing relating to rodents, nor do I want to be startled by photos of them in my lenses.

I don't understand why he can't reconnect me to the OCME's cameras unless I'm out of range. Certainly, this isn't the best spot, surrounded by big trees, buildings, endless stretches of woods and water in a remote area of the Air Force base. What a bad time to be cut off, left in the dark, freaking out about my sister.

I tell myself there's not a thing I can do about her at the moment, to pay attention before I make matters worse by taking a bad spill. I pick my way across the slippery, sloshy parking lot as winter-bare trees clack like bones, and old evergreen shrubs rustle like stiff petticoats when the wind blows hard and fitfully.

12

I FOLLOW the vivid yellow path mapped in my FIND while monitoring all sorts of data in my PEEPS and SPIES.

Constant weather and news updates crawl by, and also emails, messages, including a BOLO Fran just this minute forwarded. The be on the lookout notification is about a real-life grand theft auto at the Tidewater International Car Show, it seems.

Two concept vehicles, together valued at half a million dollars, have vanished into thin air. Hampton police are on their heads about it, and I remember the snippet I heard on TV when I turned it on by pointing my finger hours earlier.

Just local news so far, Fran says in her text. But gonna be a sh*t show. When are you getting here?

"Text her back that I'll be there in a few," I tell ART.

F-22 Raptor tactical fighters growl and roar like supersonic dragons, drowning out every sound, percussing in my hollow organs.

"What's the problem with the internet?" raising my voice over the deafening din as if ART is walking next to me and not part of my SIN. "And can you somehow fix it?"

"Line drop error," he says in my earpiece as I continue trudging.

I detour as instructed in my FIND, and the closer I get to the shaded area where the Tahoe is parked, the icier and more dangerous the conditions.

"Well that's remarkably unspecific and useless," I reply with a flare of exasperation. "Informing me there are system errors doesn't tell me what to do about them."

"This might be a good time to test the Aerial Internet Ranger, the AIR," ART suggests, and I can't help but feel set up, manipulated, handled like a gaming character.

I'm more than a little suspicious that the communication breakdown is intentional, leaving me no alternative but to try out the AIR prototype, Ranger, as we call him. Still in beta testing, he's possibly the most useful PONG Dad and I have dreamed up so far, a combo missing link and guide with a little police dog mixed in.

Ranger's inglorious and hardworking purpose in life is to provide a faithful mobile network connection, riding herd on autonomous vehicles, in particular other Personal Orbs Not Grounded. They don't do well when out of touch or unshepherded, and it's an AIR's job to avoid Ranger Danger by making sure signals aren't interrupted, corrupted and dropped.

It wouldn't take much of a disconnect or miscommunication for a flock of synchronized drones to fall from the sky, follow the wrong command or never leave the perch. Soon enough AIRs will empower and guide Swarms of Unmanned Device Systems, SUDS, which is rather much what it will look like when the self-flying orbs travel in crowds like migrating birds.

"Let's try it," I confirm to ART that it's a go to give Ranger a run for the money, and the Tahoe is just ahead. "We'll see how our flying hotspot does when put through his paces for real."

I instruct that we should set him in GHOST mode, Ground Hosted Operating System Transparency, a techy way of saying a PONG will go clear or reflective, rather much like a bubble or a mirror. That ought to work fine in this afternoon's improving weather as opposed to going Vanish Object in Darkness (VOID) mode, the orb's light-absorbing skin disappearing in the blackest nights and places.

"To be on the safe side, we're going to want the anti-ice function turned on," I decide. "Should there be freezing precipitation, we can't risk Ranger getting heavier and losing lift. I suggest we reset gyros and aerodynamic stabilizers," as I reach my new take-home SUV. "And let's go with force-trim mode to keep him on a steady flight path. We've got to be mindful that the wind's still gusting pretty hard."

"Currently out of the west. Calm aloft starting at 61 meters, 200 feet and higher," ART lets me know as Raptors rumble and roar, taking off and landing from Runway 26.

"Then set that as the minimum altitude unless the conditions shift," I direct, and at first blush my Chase Car, like my other new equipment, looks like nothing special except the paint job is a matte shark gray instead of the usual shiny black.

Reaching the driver's door, I comment out loud that I'm surprised it's locked while the engine is running. I wasn't expecting that, and I try to remember which pocket I jammed the key into when I was walking out of suite 604, struggling with my bags, getting to know ART while lying to Joan on the phone and trying to cope.

"It auto-locks for security reasons," his explanation. "This is necessary because the Tahoe is set to remote start from as far as 1.6 kilometers, a mile away."

"Makes sense," I agree. "We wouldn't want someone else driving off in it before I get the chance."

"Biometric sensors won't permit anyone unauthorized to operate the vehicle."

"Good to know. But can you open her up so I don't have to dig out the key, please?"

"You can use your WAND."

"Oh Lord, my what?"

"The Working Animated Networked Digit," he says, and I look at my right index finger, assuming that's what he means. "What gesture would you like set in memory?" he asks next, and I have to think about it for a second.

I'm trying to envision the best way to unlock my car without anyone (nosy Fran most of all) detecting my new abilities. It probably makes the most sense simply to do what I would naturally and without a thought, and I touch my thumb to my index finger as if clicking the button on a remote key.

The subtlest of gestures sends an infrared signal to release the Tahoe's electronic locks. A quiet snap, and I open the back door nearest me, reinforced with steel, lightweight laminates and ballistic alloys if I had to guess, the tinted window glass layered and thicker than normal.

Dropping my bags on a rigid-shelled blast-resistant seat, I check out the cargo area, curious about the large storage box built into the ceiling. Two smaller ones on the floor correlate with the locations of the beefy dual exhaust pipes. And I do a walk-around, ART in my ear giving me a tour, describing everything I'm looking at . . .

The oversize all-terrain run-flat tires . . .

The emergency lights built into the front-mounted blacked-out steel grid and over the bulletproof windshield . . .

The stubble of antennas and domed signal jammer on the solar-paneled roof . . .

The hatch in the tailgate that reminds me of a doggie door, only this one's for drone deployment . . .

Climbing into the driver's seat, I face the overwhelming reality that when Dick was talking to me earlier, he knew darn well what was in store this afternoon. A trial by ordeal and a bag of tricks would be one way to look at it, an education by extreme immersion would be another.

Every detail has been carefully planned and calculated, I'm convinced. Whether it's ART, a loss of signal necessitating an AIR, following a FIND across a hazardous parking lot or using my bionic WAND to unlock my Chase Car, I'm doing exactly what Dick or someone else divines.

00:00:00:00:0

"ALL RIGHT, let's see what we've got here," I begin surveying what looks more like the cockpit of a military aircraft than any law enforcement vehicle I've seen up close and personal.

Barely 300 miles on the odometer, and I have a feeling my Secret Service–inspired chariot with its new-car smell is another prototype like almost everything else, including Carme and me. The mileage probably is from racetracks, test-driving ranges, and for sure I'll never figure out and manage all the systems without AI assistance, starting with the dark-gray pleathery-looking upholstery.

Based on transmissions I'm picking up in my CUFF, the material is woven with sensors, reminding me of the formfitting skin Carme had on at the Point Comfort Inn. I'm pretty sure my SUV's smart materials are interactive, that they probably can self-repair, change appearance and are electrically conductive.

It wouldn't surprise me if they're able to stimulate circulation, bones, joints, muscles when one can't do anything but sit for long bouts, on an extended standoff, an endless stakeout, a grueling chase or journey. We're developing the same technologies for long-duration flights when astronauts head to the moon, Mars, and other faraway places.

I'm betting dyes and pigments in fabrics, plastics and paints are photochromic, changing colors and shades depending on the need. And what a thought that I could be driving a gunpowder gray Tahoe one minute, and it's red, white or blue the next. Or it might go into stealth mode on its own, blending with the surroundings and the weather rather much like a sea dragon or a PONG.

The carbon fiber joystick next to the shifter seems to be the main control unit, and wherever there's real estate, flat touch screens have been mounted, on the back of the visors, on either side of the heads-up display, and across the dash. Some are divided into quadrants showing multiple camera images. Others are menus with acronyms and labels, most of them unfamiliar.

I figure a SRCH LT is what it sounds like. I know and appreciate what a FLIR thermal-imaging camera is, and infrared is always handy in low-light conditions. I have no trouble understanding the engine specs ART shows me as we go through the run-up systems check.

By all indications my Chase Car is no slouch. Bi-turbo V-8, 700 horsepower with an 8-speed automatic transmission, it has ceramic disc brakes worthy of a Lamborghini. Additional not-so-standard features in my new ride include a High Energy Laser (HEL) that fires from a Retractable Attack Turret (RAT).

Both work hand in glove with the Tracking and Targeting Locator (TATL) to warn and defend against Shoulder Launched Armed Missiles (SLAMs) and other Antisocial Gestures (AGs), I'm briefed through the truck's speakers. It remains to be seen what I'll do with a Flamethrower (FLTH), or a Water Artillery Disruptor (WAD) that fires a laser-guided Water Shot (WASH) able to penetrate metal.

I wouldn't want to try out any of this on a crowded street. Not the Smoke Retaliator (SMOKR) either, although leaving a dense noxious fog in my wake would be a good way to lose someone.

Making my getaway, I could change my identity to my heart's content with the morphing license plates (MORPs).

Made of rugged glass-like polycarbonate, the faux tags are actually computer flat-screens. They flip up on command from the TATL, revealing Rifle Integrated Ports (RIPs) front and back that can unleash 800 rounds per minute from Full-Auto M16s (FAMs). And while it's a handy feature to have, I'm not sure when I'd use it unless it's to take out the tires of an entire convoy coming after me like Thelma and Louise.

If shooting live ammo from a moving vehicle in an urban setting isn't the best-laid plan, I suppose I could destroy your windshield or engine with a well-placed WASH from the WAD, now that I think of it. Or blind you with my SMOKR before flambéing your persistent tailgating vehicle with my FLTH.

It would seem I have quite the selection of apocalyptic tools at my disposal to keep me in good order assuming they don't do me in first. I wasn't exactly given advance notice that I'd be piloting a Silverado pickup truck one day and a Death Star the next. There's no instruction book beyond ART. Not even Carme is around to ask, maybe neither of us available to the other, and I honestly have no freakin' idea what I'm doing. Or how I'll manage.

"Here we go," a deep breath, I shove the Tahoe into gear, thinking, *Now or never.*

I set out across the parking lot, reminded right away that something this heavy is sluggish getting started. And then doesn't want to stop. So I'm careful not to do anything sudden, resisting the temptation to put the tricked-out SUV through its paces as the run-flats chew through slush and drifted snow like nobody's business.

"A laser for shooting down drones, front and back M16s, a water disrupter for taking out engines, tires, who knows what," I say to ART. "How many of these features are operational now?"

"It depends," his non-answers are getting tedious.

"The reason I'm wondering is a few minutes ago this thing wouldn't do much beyond remote starting," as I gently, cautiously turn onto the shaded icy lane that leads to the main drag, the tires sliding a little. "What happens if I need to fire up the laser? Or if a bad guy launches a missile, a grenade, a weaponized drone with my name on it? That wouldn't be a good time to tell me something isn't operational or that we need permission."

"It depends on the conditions," and what he's saying is it's about the algorithms. "I'm required to assist at all times," my invisible copilot adds as if it's nonnegotiable.

"I can see why I'll need help," I'm objective about it. "But what happens if you and I can't connect? Or don't agree? Are there fail-safe overrides?"

"Affirmative. But not all of them have been optimized yet," a jargony way of saying we really don't know squat about how things are going to work or not.

"Well, that wasn't what I was hoping to hear but I guess I'm getting used to it," I comment, grateful the Air Force base is relatively quiet.

Thank goodness traffic is light, as I would expect on a Sunday afternoon, and I'm lumbering along at a cautious pace, getting acclimated to handling my Chase Car. The biggest challenge is monitoring multiple screens that have multiple pages of menus and images, the potential for multitasking quantum.

Fortunately, the roads are heavily sanded and salted, for the most part clear and dry. The military doesn't close in a government shutdown, it's business as usual unlike what I'll face when I hit the NASA campus. It will be a foreboding winter obstacle course just like it was the last time we were furloughed in the middle of a blizzard.

Flooded thoroughfares and marshland will be icy, many streets impassable. Most sidewalks and outdoor steps won't have been touched by rock salt or a shovel, and a big fear is frozen pipes. A bigger one is diehard researchers illegally camping out in their offices, refusing to be furloughed. Every building will have to be checked repeatedly for flooding in addition to the usual risks of squatters and other violators.

And I wonder how that's going to work when I won't want to be in Fran's SUV or one of the Polaris ATVs. Not when I can be in my Tahoe, and how will I explain it to her anyway? Unlike our usual assigned vehicles, this one can't be driven by anyone except me. I suppose I'll say I'm test piloting it for the Secret Service because of the task force I'm on.

Maybe I'll hint that this is in conjunction with Dick's militarized space interests, top secret ones I'm not allowed to discuss that include equipment I can't share. I'm unsure how I'll handle a lot of things when hardly anyone can know that Carme is around, and that we aren't who we were or say we are.

13

I ASK ART for the latest updates on the crash in Norfolk, insisting on knowing if any victims have been identified or found.

"Negative," he replies through the speakers as images fill flatscreens across the dash.

Videos knitted together from traffic and other cameras show the incident began as a high-speed chase a little over an hour ago, and I watch traffic parting like the Red Sea, motorists getting out of the way . . .

Of a black Dodge Charger Hellcat customized with red powder-coated rims, the undercarriage and fog lamps glowing red, rocketing ahead of traffic on US 58, not far from Plum Point Park . . .

Weaving in and out, closing in on a shark-gray Tahoe that looks identical to mine but with Maryland plates . . .

Racing like NASCAR along a circuitous route on Brambleton Avenue . . .

Then Colley, roaring past the Ronald McDonald House . . .

Squealing left on Fairfax . . .

Cutting through the campus of Eastern Virginia Medical School . . .

Careening past Sentara Norfolk General Hospital . . .

Back onto Brambleton . . .

At the intersection of Riverview Avenue, a mushroom cloud of black smoke . . .

A muffled BANG! BANG! BANG! as the Tahoe guns ahead . . .

And the Hellcat bounces off the guardrail, exploding into a ball of fire . . .

Coming to a stop in the westbound lane, engulfed in thick smoke and flames . . .

"I'm guessing that was Carme's Tahoe I just saw," I say to ART, my heart pounding hard. "A Chase Car like mine only with Maryland plates. Faux ones. Am I right? She sped away it looks like?"

"Not authorized," he responds predictably.

"She's okay?"

"Not authorized."

"Where is she now?"

"Not authorized."

"Yeah, yeah, already! But you're not denying that she was driving the Tahoe. You and I both know she has morphing license plates same as I do. She will have changed the tags again by now," I'm sure of it. "Do we have any information on the Hellcat?"

"The Dodge Charger is stolen," ART finally answers a question as I drive along the western edge of the peninsula that the Air Force shares with NASA.

Following the shoreline of the same river I grew up on, I'm further informed that the hellish hot rod I saw likely belongs to a collector from Charlotte, North Carolina, here in town for the Tidewater International Car Show. Known for badass concept vehicles, the owner trucked his customized Dodge Charger Hellcat and Cadillac hearse to Hampton three days ago.

Both award-winning concept vehicles are heavily publicized entries in this year's special exhibition of driverless conveyances, ART gives me the lowdown. They were the most popular attractions Friday night and yesterday, the show drawing large crowds.

"Obviously, the Hellcat, the hearse are the missing cars referenced on the local news earlier and in the BOLO Fran sent to me," I let ART know as we pass tidy rows of brick base housing. "And the question is why someone might want to steal vehicles like that. Because I don't think it's for the money since it seems the Hellcat's intended use was to commit homicide, to take someone out."

Based on the video I saw, there can be no doubt the goal was to force Carme to crash on her way to the OCME, and there's no point in being coy about it. That's what was supposed to happen.

"Except the intended victim likely wasn't my sister. It was me," I explain to ART, who has no opinion. "And whoever decided to weaponize the autonomous muscle car didn't give a hoot what happened to it."

It makes sense it was supposed to be me in the Tahoe, I decide, paralleling the airfield and its hangars, jets screaming overhead, the sun trying to peek through. Joan was expecting me to show up at the morgue, not Carme, who most people assume is off with the military somewhere, if they're thinking of her at all.

"I have a bad feeling that somehow Neva Rong caught wind of the plan," I talk to ART as if he's Fran. "My twin parading as me was supposed to outfox the slippery billionaire psycho. Only it would seem that Neva's the one doing the outfoxing. I'm not so sure who's really getting ambushed," I add as jets frolic to beat the band, J-turning and barrel-rolling.

I feel the guttural rumble of the T-38 supersonic trainer on its taxiway, so close I can see the helmeted pilot beneath his canopy as ART downloads updates fast and furiously. In short order, I'm getting a pretty good idea how such a ballsy auto heist could occur with no one having a clue.

Apparently, it wasn't noticed that the cars were missing until 8 o'clock this morning when staff started trickling in to get ready for today's expected huge crowds. What's known for a fact is that the coliseum was locked up tight as a drum by midnight, and there are no guards after hours.

Perimeter cameras show that the coliseum's loading bay door was mysteriously accessed at around 2:00 a.m. without setting off an alarm. What this suggests to me is that the security system was hacked, the parameters in the programming altered to ignore motion and other sensors.

The massive roll-up door opened wide, and the Hellcat and hearse made a dash for it, driving themselves off the show floor, out into the empty early morning, the doors rolling shut behind them. And what a sight that would have been, every bit of it done remotely, no one calling the police for hours, waiting until the owner could be found, hoping he had an explanation, and he didn't.

"Has it been spotted?" I ask about the missing hearse, and on this part of Weyland Road there's nothing but snowy open fields and dense woods pockmarked with animal tracks.

"I have no data," ART says as it occurs to me that neither missing vehicle is road legal and wouldn't have a license plate.

Not if they're in and out of car shows, and I ask what theories are circulating as my thoughts continue ricocheting between Neva and Carme. I'm not surprised when ART answers that the police have no suspects.

They have nothing to go on, only baseless rumors on social media claiming that the owner staged the theft for insurance purposes. But there's no evidence of any such thing, and I don't believe it for a minute.

00:00:00:00:0

"IT'S LOOKING LIKE the cars were stolen without the benefit of anybody showing up in person and doing the dirty work," I say to ART. "Someone technically sophisticated, in other words."

As I'm saying this, I'm shown more images from traffic videos, the supercharged Hellcat driving east on I-64 toward Norfolk in the wee morning hours, no license plates, growly, low slung, stealthily with red LEDs glowing.

Most likely ART was able to find the Marvel-comic-bookish car by using image recognition software. In frustrating contrast, a late-model black Cadillac hearse with a landau top is going to be trickier if not near impossible. There are plenty of them around fitting that description, more than 300 registered to funeral homes in Hampton alone, ART gives me the statistics.

The missing hearse could be anywhere. Many miles away or right under our noses, it was captured on security video at 0205 hours when it left the coliseum parking lot, disappearing into the windy darkness. Possibly it wisely navigated along a route that didn't include traffic cameras, unlike the muscle car caught on film taking the Hampton Roads Bridge-Tunnel across the Chesapeake Bay into Norfolk at 0235 hours.

Soon after, it's recorded again, flicking off its lights, turning into the deserted Plum Point Park on the water. There's no video of it turning into the parking lot, which the city would have plowed because only federal workers are furloughed. Presumably this is where the Hellcat stayed unnoticed until an hour and a half ago when it reemerged onto the Elizabeth River Trail.

Minutes later it was flying along US 58 in pursuit of the Tahoe Carme was driving, and someone sure as heck knew she was coming. Or that I was, and most of all I'm relieved and grateful because she may have caused the fiery accident but she didn't burn up in it. No way my sister was driving that stolen car, and I'm fairly certain I know what she did to end an insane chase that lasted a total of 3.4 minutes.

Carme did what Carme does best, getting in the last word, leaving a parting shot. In this instance with the SMOKR I'm guessing, as I recall the thick black mushroom cloud. A real mood killer if you're trying to see where you're going, it also could interfere with radio waves and cell signals, which would be problematic in some driverless vehicles, although I suspect that's not what happened to the Hellcat.

I have a feeling the three loud bangs I heard were fired from a RIP or a WASH, and it would make sense resorting to the rear built-in M16, the water disrupter, one or the other. Possibly both, taking out tires and causing an explosion.

"Carme knows that if even the smallest piece of shrapnel pierces a gas tank, it's all she wrote," I announce out loud.

I'm finding myself periodically glancing at the empty passenger's seat as if ART might be in it. As if I might be getting daffy.

"And since other motorists had slowed way down to get out of the way, it was relatively safe to let her rip, so to speak," I add, driving past the Air Force base golf course, brown grass and sand pits exposed where the snow has blown and drifted.

I don't think the message could be clearer, I decide. Someone (I know who I vote for) was tipped off that Carme (or me, the more likely story) would be headed to the medical examiner's office this afternoon to intercept Neva Rong.

"I guess she somehow found out the plan and knows I've got a new truck," I add, increasingly suspicious that she's picking up where she left off.

It's a serious concern that makes me nervous for myself and everyone around me. Not so long ago, Neva's response to my interferences included a tracking device, a hitman, cement boots and other body-disposal accoutrements. Not to mention I've seen what she's capable of, envisioning the deep furrows in Vera Young's neck, her dead body drenched in bleach and strung up from a door.

"Well, I'll take that as a yes," I continue to goad ART into giving me the intel I want. "Carme has this exact same truck even if you won't admit it. The question is who Neva was trying to take out. Me? Or my sister pretending to be me? What exactly does Neva know about the Gemini project beyond the fact that there's a GOD chip? And it's missing. And that Vera may have had it last."

But ART's not about to fall for any of my tricks or pressures any more than Mom ever has. He answers nothing as data comes at me from every direction, and it's all I can do to focus on any one thing at a time. Although I have to say I'm more acclimated than I was. At least I'm reasonably adept so far at handling my armored SUV on slippery roads, and not making a mess of multitasking like I did when I was leaving Dodd Hall.

"I would expect that everything Carme and I have is identical, our vehicles, our equipment," I keep pushing. "And when she needs camouflage, which is most of the time, she morphs everything about her Chase Car to be the same as mine."

But ART isn't taking the bait, programmed not to share certain information no matter what I say.

"Do you know if Neva Rong is behind the auto heist?" I then ask, because it would be just like her to hack into a highly publicized car show and swipe autonomous vehicles right off the floor.

"There are no suspects," ART's unhelpful answer, and suddenly I'm reconnected to the OCME's security video feed.

I'm watching Neva inside the lobby where she's helped herself to every newspaper she could find. Using them to cover the sofa and area around it, she makes sure she doesn't come in contact with furniture or flooring, fashioning her own unspoiled island unto herself in this dirty unfair world she helps create.

"Signal restored," I tell ART what he already knows.

Ranger must be in the area, and I check my cameras and sideview mirrors as if I might catch my mobile hotspot following us.

Nope, nothing there but partly cloudy skies, empty except for fighter jets, and out of habit I head toward the Air Force base back gate.

There's no sign of the basketball-size PONG that I shouldn't be seeing anyway since he's in GHOST mode following from above. Extending the range, the flying orb has restored the link to the medical examiner's office in Norfolk, and I'm watching Neva Rong dig inside her oversize black crocodile bag . . .

Retrieving a small gold tub of something expensive and pink that ART zooms in on . . .

She dabs on Iridesse Kiss lip balm . . .

Before unscrewing the cap from some other pricy potion that she drips into her palm. One pale-blue drop at a time, handwritten on the eyedropper bottle's label is $\mathbf{(C_{14}H_{21}NO_{11})N}$ . . .

The chemical composition of hyaluronic acid, used to hydrate the skin, reduce fine wrinkles and promote healing, ART informs me. I watch Neva rub the serum into her wrists, hands, her neck and décolletage. She disgustingly primps and moisturizes inside the grimmest of waiting rooms with its attempts at cozy furniture and pleasant printed landscapes from state surplus, its thoughtful placing of fake plants and silk flowers.

Outdated magazines with torn-off mailing labels are fanned out on a faux mahogany table between the Virginia and US flags. A clunky old flat-screen TV silently plays soothing nature scenes in a glitchy loop that at the moment is caught on a school of salmon almost leaping as they swim upstream.

Never completely in or out of the water, never getting anywhere, and boy do I know the feeling as I approach the sturdy redbrick guard gate I always use when going back and forth between the Air Force base and NASA. All but one lane is blocked with tire shredders, sawhorses, water-filled bright-orange barricades, and concrete blast barriers.

It's just my sorry luck that military police officer Crockett steps outside the booth.

He holds up a hand to halt my vehicle, sort of a weird mixture of a stop sign and a wave, staring intensely at me.

"Okay, now you've gone too far," under my breath as he approaches, and he can't be serious.

"I'm sorry," ART says through the speakers. "I don't understand . . ."

"Not talking about you, I'm talking about him, a real first-class jerk," I reply, using my ventriloquist trick, barely moving my lips. "Don't say anything. He can't know about you. Nobody can," even as I realize how inane it sounds. "And nothing in the displays, please," and every one of them blinks out.

I'm back to monitoring the OCME live feed and other data in the lenses of my SPIES and PEEPS as I was doing earlier. And I roll down my window before MP Crockett can rap on it with his knuckles.

14

IN CAMOUFLAGE and beret, an M4 carbine slung across his chest, a Beretta 9mm on his hip, he's about to abuse his authority as usual, I can feel it coming.

"No way," I mutter, and it's one thing to harass me when I'm entering the Air Force base but quite another when I'm leaving.

MP Crockett doesn't have the right, not that he ever really does, and I shift my truck into park, figuring I'm going to be sitting here for a while.

"What's the problem this time, Officer?" I ask, and he floors me by grinning, unpleasantly bringing to mind a Cheshire cat or an opossum.

"You're *not* too funny!" he replies with his weird backward sarcasm, saying the opposite of whatever it is he means, and I'm baffled. "I'm *not* wondering what you're up to, Captain," and it's the first time he's ever smiled, winked at me or acknowledged my rank.

In the three years I've worked for NASA, he's given me no respect or credit, going out of his way to look for expired stickers, cracked windshields, glass too darkly tinted. It's common for him to order me out of my truck, taking his time searching it with a K-9 or a mirror, and that would be an unfortunate development right about now, it occurs to me.

Reminded I'm no longer in my Silverado, I wouldn't want him finding the M16s, or the water disrupter and flamethrower. But he doesn't seem inclined to give me his usual crap, a spring to his step and a gleam in his eye that weren't there before. He seems a little self-conscious and shy, kind of twitchy and nervous, now that I'm noticing. And I know all the symptoms when someone's been exposed to my sister, catching her lovebug as Mom's always put it.

"I'm trying to understand how it is you're not coming in but going out," he says in his peculiar twang.

Tangier Island, I'm pretty sure, where the name Crockett is as common as crab pots, and the natives talk like Jamestown.

"When I know for a fact I already saw you leave earlier," tall and whippet-thin, he's bent over awkwardly peering at me.

MP Crockett is careful not to bang his weapons and equipment against my truck's chameleon skin, this moment the default matte gray, and splashed with road grit and salt. All the while I'm dealing with him, I'm remotely monitoring the cavernous concrete receiving bay in the back of the OCME.

I'm watching Joan in my smart lenses sitting inside, taking a load off as she likes to say. The rolling steel door is retracted all the way up, and I can see the consolidated lab building, its forensic evidence bay, the clearing afternoon showing through the huge square opening.

How weird to be spying on my death investigator friend like Big Brother as she sits in a folding chair. A brown ski jacket is zipped up over her scrubs, and she's smoking in her makeshift break area at the bottom of the concrete ramp leading inside the morgue.

". . . I mean, I'm not imagining things, am I?" MP Crockett is saying to me through my open window, and I smell peppermint, his jaw muscles bunching as he chews gum. "That was you who came through a couple hours ago, bringing me an *extra-large* coffee with *extra sugar*?" and it's not me he's been seeing, possibly chatting with, that's for sure.

It's not this Captain Chase who brought him an *extra-large* coffee with *extra sugar* (his salacious emphasis, not mine), and I'm up against another problem I didn't anticipate. I don't think Carme has yet to meet anyone she can't cast her spell on, going all the way back to grade school when her name was spray-painted on the Fox Hill water tower. And mine never was.

We're used to being mistaken for each other, and it can be awkward when one of her dates or smitten wannabes is on the prowl. But I've never had to follow up on her seductions as if they're mine. Should someone get us confused, I've always clarified in a heck of a hurry, and it's one more thing I can't do going forward.

I can't say I'm not her. Or that she's not me. Neither of us can let on that we're both and neither.

"I'm not sure what all you're up to," MP Crockett is looking me over a bit invasively, and I find it flattering when in the past I assumed he was looking for flaws. "You see, I'm trying to figure how it can be that I saw you drive off the base a couple hours ago. And now you're driving off it again. When I never saw you drive back on it."

"This isn't the only gate, you know . . . ," I remind him, nudging his arm, noting that for someone so thin he's surprisingly muscular. "But I like yours best. Because you know me, I prefer back doors and quiet . . . ," I lead him on easily as if a tincture of Hyde has been added to my Dr. Jekyll.

Suddenly, I'm a tease. I'm acting like my bold sister, and if MP Crockett leans any closer through my open window, we'll practically be kissing. I let him gaze deeply into my PEEPS and SPIES, facial recognition kicking in, his first name David. He goes by Davy, and 23 is way too young for me when it comes to male neurological development and emotional maturity.

He's also somewhat sheltered, having never left Tangier Island until graduating from the twelfth grade and enlisting in the Air Force. Father's a waterman. Mom's a bird-watching tour guide who runs the Spar Grass B&B where Carme and I stayed several times during high school when we'd take the Onancock ferry with Mom, who's big into history, different cultures and cooking.

". . . Seems like you've got a lot going on at NASA these past few days," Davy Crockett is saying as I read about him in my lenses.

He has one sibling, a disabled younger sister, the family's Tangier Island home going back many generations. Wood sided with a metal roof and striped awnings, it's set back from marshland on Mailboat Harbor where the father keeps his trawler.

". . . What's got you so busy during a shutdown when no one's around? Huh?" Davy may look serious but he's flirting up a storm. "Or maybe you keep coming in and out because you *don't* miss me," he winks.

"Busted, I *don't*," I wink back as I think, *Holy smoke!*

Every time Carme has passed through this gate of late, she must have morphed her tags to mirror mine, implying we have matching Chase Cars. I suspect that until now she's not been driving hers around here.

She waited until I'd been implanted with my SIN for the games to begin, and inserting herself into my investigations, my professional life, is one thing. I might even get used to it. But my relationships, especially those that could fall into the dating category, are a different kettle of fish, maybe a whole school of them I don't know how to fry.

I've never been fresh or forward. I don't ask people out or pick them up. At least I haven't before. But I guess it's not too late to learn a new trick and besides, Carme wouldn't be friendly with Davy Crockett unless she expects me to follow up for some reason.

00:00:00:00:0

SO BE IT, I tell myself. How hard is it to act sexy? To be a woman of the world, someone who's been around the block a few times? Now or never, deep breath, here goes . . .

"I was thinking of asking if you'd like to have a beer sometime," I sound surprisingly easygoing and sure of myself. "But I hear that people from your neck of the woods don't drink," and anyone who's visited Tangier Island knows it's as dry as a bone, not a drop of alcohol to be found (except what's sneaked into the fishing boats).

"A beer sounds good," Davy Crockett steps back from my SUV. "Or maybe a bite one night like we talked about earlier?"

Not with me he didn't, I think but don't say. We'll make a plan, I promise, rolling up the window, driving away. El Diablo Loco might be an idea. Maybe the Barking Dog on Sunset Creek if he's into fried seafood, hot dogs, and my stomach grumbles again. Or the Deadrise restaurant at Fort Monroe where I bet he'd like the crab cakes, and I watch him in my mirrors until I can't see him anymore.

I'm stewing over the idea of tag teaming in my personal life, of Carme laying the romantic groundwork while I follow up or maybe the other way around. It's not like we haven't swapped places before, most memorably our junior year in high school when she thought it would be a fine idea to switch prom dates (didn't turn out very well).

I ask ART to restore images on the truck's displays since it's just us again, and I'm back to monitoring what's going on at the OCME in Norfolk.

". . . It's the latest twist in a drama that's getting only more bizarre," Mason Dixon broadcasts off to one side of the OCME's glass front door.

He somberly reminds his audience that Vera Young's body is scheduled for release to a local funeral home where it will be cremated later today. And I worry again about the slightest possibility the GOD chip is somehow mixed in with her remains.

"Easy does it," I caution myself out loud, slowing down around a curve.

I almost sail off the road, the heft of my Chase Car reminding me of a Humvee. Now that I'm on NASA's side of the peninsula, the conditions are terrible. Nothing but solid white and melting ice, any tire tracks probably left by the protective services officers taking turns manning our guard gate up ahead. Nobody else is coming back here if avoidable.

". . . This is according to her daughter in California who says that's what her mother would have wanted," Mason Dixon says in the live feed I'm seeing in one of my displays, windblown, his coat collar flipped up around his ears like he's James Dean. "But it's over the very vocal protests of Vera's sister, Dr. Rong, who we're expecting to hear from momentarily . . ."

The NASA back gate isn't much, just a guard booth, the usual barricades and a yellow-and-white-striped mechanical arm.

"Please turn off the displays and mute the audio," I say to ART. "And by the way, that should be automatic when there's a risk of other people seeing or hearing what you're showing me. I shouldn't have to keep telling you. Just do it as a matter of routine, please."

Copy, in a text, all of the flat-screens going dark.

I roll down my window as my colleague Celeste approaches in her winter and ballistic gear, and she's always been much hipper than I am, although that's not saying much. About my age, she wears her hair short on top, shaved on the sides, and has lots of tattoos and body piercings.

"You back again?" she checks my badge.

"So much for being furloughed, right?" I commiserate the way I always do with boots on the ground, the officers assigned onerous tasks like guard duty. "Some of us always have to show up no matter what."

"Tell me about it, I never catch a break. And I've got so much to do before the holidays. It would have been nice to have a few weeks off," she says, her breath puffing out in the windy cold. "It sure would be a lot easier using the front gate like everybody else, Calli. I don't know why you don't listen," and obviously, she's had encounters with Carme parading as me. "But hey, maybe you like off-roading in the tundra."

"We need to keep a close eye on the most vulnerable areas," I remind her of our responsibility during a furlough while I get her off the subject of my allegedly driving in and out. "We have to worry about the data center, I don't need to remind you. And other highly sensitive facilities more off the beaten path than I like under the circumstances."

"Well, if anything can get through the roads back there, this thing can," she gives my Tahoe a covetous once-over, and doesn't know the half of it.

Obviously, whenever Carme has passed through in her own Chase Car, Celeste has assumed it was me driving mine. It makes me uncomfortable to think my sister is that adept at passing herself off as me, including with my colleagues, people I work with daily.

I suppose it should be reassuring considering our mission. But it doesn't feel that way as I drive off. At least ART turns my truck's displays back on without my asking this time, and the OCME live feed resumes with Joan getting up from her chair inside the receiving bay as the pedestrian door opens at the top of the concrete ramp that leads into the morgue.

An unfamiliar man steps out dressed in a cheap black suit and tie, someone young, nicely built with a prosthetic left eye.

"That damn showboat," he says in a syrupy drawl. "God, I can't stand Mason Dixon. Everything's a conspiracy and somehow about him."

"Huh! Sounds familiar," Joan looks extremely unhappy as she smokes.

"Don't start in again," an ugly look on the man's otherwise handsome face.

"Who's shown up so far?" angrily tapping an ash, she seems about ready to kill him.

"The *Daily Press* and *Virginian-Pilot*, Channels 10 and 13, plus a couple radio stations are rolling up now that the accident has cleared. At least a dozen reporters, photographers, TV people. You'd think Elvis croaked," a sneer in his voice echoing off the mammoth concrete space where the dead are delivered and carried away.

Meanwhile, I'm churning through the frozen wasteland area of the NASA campus, passing silvery barnlike maintenance sheds, and a posted sign reminding people to **Buckle Up,** that they're in a controlled area. Except it doesn't feel very controlled right now, drifted snow, ice littered with snapped-off trees and branches everywhere. The low sun seeps through the overcast on and off, my PEEPS changing tint as the light varies.

". . . They want a statement from someone since the chief's not available. I'm thinking it's a good idea," the man in the cheap suit leans against the open door, and behind him I get a good view of the intake area where bodies are signed in and out, weighed, measured and tagged.

In the back wall is the bulletproof-glass-enclosed morgue office, and walls of stainless steel cooler doors, their digital data displays and gauges lit up green. I see no sign of Wally the security guard, of autopsies or anything much going on. Probably everyone is upstairs, keeping a low profile in their offices while Neva causes her usual pandemonium.

". . . I was thinking maybe you could say something. Don't you think somebody should?" the man goes on and on, and when the security camera catches his prosthetic eye at certain angles, it's as if a crash dummy has come alive.

I ask ART if he can use facial recognition, other data to get the skinny on this guy, who he is, where he's from. Most of all, I want to know how long he's worked with Joan. I've not run into him before, and I have a bad feeling he's the latest in her unhealthy diet of self-obsessed boy toys.

15

"EASY DOES IT . . . ," I tap-tap the brakes, gently slowing down at a particularly bad stretch of iced-over snow that's not been sanded or plowed.

Joan stabs out the cigarette in a cat-litter-filled plastic bucket riddled with butts while I'm given info on the man she's glaring at. Dylan Vince, 34, from the mountains of Lynchburg, Virginia, and that explains his thick accent.

Graduated from Tidewater Community College with a degree in mortuary science, he worked in various funeral homes before being hired by the OCME's Norfolk office last month to replace the administrator who'd retired.

"It shouldn't be up to me!" she exclaims to him.

"If you don't want to do it yourself, write something up," Dylan says. "I guess I could go out there and read it for you. But it would be better if you did," he adds disingenuously, and what a piece of garbage.

"I'm not talking to anyone about Vera Young or anything else," Joan's not going to take his bull crap. "I'm not commenting *and neither are you*. Because that's what you want. To get in front of the camera, you and your ego . . ."

I'm crunching past the deserted Composites & Model Development Lab, going slowly, ducking and dodging pockets of deep snow and slicks of ice. Hardly anyone has been back here since the nor'easter, and I'm not surprised. Like Celeste said, those authorized to access the NASA Langley campus during the shutdown use the main gate near the Badge and Pass Office.

Where I am on East Durand Street, nothing has been touched, and it's beautiful and awful, trees thick with snow, ice sparkling like crystal.

". . . May as well head over to the evidence bay to deal with our crispy critter," Joan says with a loud sigh in the video feed playing inside my SUV.

"If it's the car stolen from the coliseum, there may not have been anybody in it," Dylan, her newbie administrator, replies. "I'm surprised you wouldn't have thought of that by now with what's all over the news," insultingly from the top of the ramp. "Based on what I'm hearing, it probably was controlled remotely," self-importantly as if he's the investigator.

"Won't that be a sucky new problem as if I don't have enough! Looking for bodies that aren't there and weren't to begin with!" Joan storms out of the bay into the blustery afternoon. "Don't forget to roll down the door!"

Dylan steps back inside the morgue's intake area as I pass empty fields and parking lots whited out, keeping up my scan for deer while monitoring other live feeds . . .

The same blue-striped Bell 407 I saw earlier has returned for its passenger, hovering over the pad while Mason Dixon broadcasts near the OCME front door . . .

As it opens and Neva Rong emerges in her sexy high heels, stunning in a fitted black skirt suit under her long black fur coat, her diamonds winking as the sun peeks in and out of fast-moving clouds . . .

"Dr. Rong . . . ! Dr. Rong . . . !" microphones are thrust her way.

"Hey, hey . . . ! Look over here . . . !" camera shutters whirring.

"Dr. Rong . . . ! Have you viewed your sister's body yet . . . ?"

Everyone hushes as she dramatically unfolds a sheet of paper, holding it up. And I can see the important-looking letterhead, the fancy holographic watermark in the creamy heavy stock. She shows the document all around, every camera and microphone trained on her.

"My dear Vera's last wishes! Right here. See this?" She shakes the page for dramatic effect. "My sister named me the executor of her estate, her most trusted ally and faithful retainer . . . ," Neva says, and there's no question in my mind this is more of her manipulative fakery. "It's right here in black and white . . ."

"Seriously?" I say under my breath, getting increasingly irate as I creep along a deserted frozen road, marveling over her audaciousness and that nothing seems to daunt her. "I mean, who can stand it?"

"Did you have a question?" ART pipes up.

"Just muttering to myself."

I pass closed building after building, institutional redbrick with mind-numbing names that don't begin to tell you what goes on. The Electronics Application Technology Lab, for example. The National Transonic Facility. The Simulation Development and Analysis Branch. Other jargony tongue twisters include the Human Exploration and Operations Mission Directorate and the CERTAIN UAS Test Range.

One of my favorite clunkers is the Advanced Manufacturing office complex where Dad and I often park ourselves. Home of ISAAC the robot and the electron beam gun, Building 1232 is one of the oldest left on campus, an ancient rusty bicycle forever parked in front near a tarnished brass plaque That Reads **SPACE TECHNOLOGY** from the days of Sputnik.

". . . You should ask yourself why I'm being denied my legal rights," Neva holds forth, her awaiting helicopter thud-thudding, the windsock darting frantically.

The pilot has cut the throttle to flight idle but he's not shutting down, implying an imminent departure.

". . . What are people hiding?" Neva preaches like a seasoned politician. "Ask yourself why I'm forbidden any further investigation into what happened to her, ensuring that justice will be denied . . ."

While inside a brightly lit forensic evidence bay the size of a small hangar, Joan and her investigators are covered in white Tyvek protective clothing. They're searching the burned-out shell of the Hellcat, and coming up empty handed . . .

As Dylan walks inside a morgue cooler . . .

At the same instant a gleaming black hearse glides through the receiving bay's wide-open door that he neglected to close . . .

"Oh boy," as I notice the Cadillac crest, the Landau top, and I ask ART to run the Virginia tag.

"Chamberlain & Sons Funeral Services and Crematorium," and he gives me a Norfolk address.

"Seems legit enough, I guess. Any reason to think it's not?" I ask his assessment of the hearse rolling to a stop near Joan's improvised break area.

"I'm sorry. No further information."

"Possibly the funeral home that's picking up Vera Young's body?"

"No further information," he repeats. "I'm not finding any reference that identifies the funeral home."

"What about news releases, social media, anything that might mention which crematorium? That it's Chamberlain & Sons, in other words."

"Negative. Finding no data."

00:00:00:00:0

"MAKES SENSE," I decide. "I'm sure certain parties want to keep a lid on which crematorium so reporters and a bunch of kooks don't show up like a carnival."

I'm watching Dylan on a display as he emerges from the cooler, wheeling out a pouched body on a gurney . . .

Steering it through the intake area, he parks it near the floor scale, walking off . . .

While the hearse sits inside the receiving bay, no one climbing out, the engine rumbling . . .

"We don't know what body's being picked up?" I try again.

We don't, ART lets me know, and I go on to ask him how many people are on the NASA Langley campus right now. He tells me 63, showing me their locations, which facilities are being accessed and by whom. As I glance at the sitemap displayed on the dash, it doesn't please me to discover all sorts of things going on that I know nothing about.

ID badge numbers are lit up on the map like squawk codes on an air traffic controller's screen. Most are outside contractors, primarily from global aerospace giants like SpaceX, Blue Origin, Boeing, Northrop Grumman. And Sierra Nevada Corporation (SNC), I take note, thinking about what Dick said on his way out of Dodd Hall.

He mentioned a space capsule drop test this afternoon, and based on what I'm seeing, SNC has 8 employees here at the moment. Two at the full-scale wind tunnel, the rest are gathered at what most people know as the Gantry, where in the 1960s Neil Armstrong, Buzz Aldrin and other Apollo astronauts learned to land and walk on the moon.

Officially named the Landing and Impact Research Facility, the Gantry's towering A-framed steel structure is rigged with cables, and a hydraulic bridge and hoist system capable of dropping an 18-ton Fokker F-28 airliner. Or it could be something much smaller like a flying car, experimental jetpacks, a spacecraft's drogue parachute.

Whatever's going on this afternoon, it must be quite the operation considering NASA is supposed to be closed. An additional 11 badge numbers on the sitemap belong to our folks, mostly engineers, crane operators, photographers and explosive experts. Taking a left at a frozen-over field of solar panels that aren't generating electricity at the moment, I ask ART to give me a glimpse of the Gantry.

He connects to the live feed, and I hear a low-pitched diesel rumble and hydraulic humming, a cherry picker BEEP-BEEPING its warning. It's piloted by an engineer named John from SNC, I know from his badge number and accompanying information. Bulky and restrained in his heavy clothing, safety harness and inflatable life vest, he rides the bright-yellow work platform through the wintry air.

He's headed toward the full-size test model of a spacecraft suspended from a crane by a thick steel cable. A concept vehicle I've not seen before, let me add, 10 tons of aluminum, I estimate, the test model bullet shaped, white with gray metal plates covering the openings where thrusters and other components are built into the real deal, I imagine.

The engineer named John takes his foot off the switch, the edge of the cherry picker's mobile platform stopping a kiss away from the multimillion-dollar test model. Opening the hatch with a socket wrench, he unplugs the data cable that's been supplying power, and no question there's a boatload of electronics inside.

There will be accelerometers, and all sorts of sensors for measuring motion, torque, pressure, position, force. Plus, strain gauges, load cells, software for data loggers and acquisition systems.

"Since when does SNC have a crewed space capsule in the works?" I wonder out loud, my suspicions gathering.

"Unauthorized," ART replies as I drive through fields blanketed white.

"It's not really a question because obviously they have one. I'm looking at it. How long has it been in development?"

"Unauthorized."

"Well, with the exception of their Dream Chaser spaceplane, SNC is in the business of transporting cargo, not astronauts, last I heard," I'm feeling territorial again.

ART has no comment.

"But that can't be what this is because you generally don't drop-test unmanned vehicles, cargo capsules. And that's not what this thing looks like anyway."

Silence.

"Well, if the test model they're about to splash down includes crash dummies, then I'm going to be unhappy," I get around to why I'm offended. "You can understand it, right?"

"I'm not sure of your question . . ."

"Connect me to the camera system inside the test model so I can see who or what's inside," I do my best to sit on my growing impatience.

"Unauthorized."

"Well, then show me the full-scale anthropomorphic test devices inside the Gantry hangar, please."

When he does, it's like I'm spying on my kids with a nanny cam, checking on my collection of life-size dummies crowded in a corner amid a clutter of workbenches, tools, sensors, and anatomical pieces and parts. My faithful crew are male, female, adults and children, all of them good sports about being burned, broken, banged, bounced, badly stirred and shaken.

Simulating your average humans, the test devices with their deadweight movable limbs are too difficult to transport or lift without mechanical assistance. So, they live in their hospital-surplus wheelchairs, dressed in hooded Tyvek jumpsuits or scrubs, tennis shoes, a few sporting safety glasses.

Slumping a little, they always look a bit dispirited and put upon, their flesh-toned plastic hands limp in their laps, and somebody's missing.

"Bump, Bang and Crush. Twister, Striker and Breaker," I take an inventory. "I see Crackle and Pop but where's Snap?" I ask, passing empty buildings and parking lots. "They'd better not be using her without checking with me first."

The adult female mannequin is about my size, racially generic and nondescript with her lack of hair, 1,000-yard stare, and on and off over recent months I've given her quite the makeover. A new shoulder liner, spine box, and scapulae. Also, a modified neck base, and various pelvis replacement parts. Best of all, she's packed with an embarrassment of sensors, many of them the same ones implanted inside Carme and me.

"The full-scale test device you refer to as Snap is currently unavailable," ART informs me.

"Show me where she is," I demand but not impolitely.

"Unauthorized."

"Is she inside that SNC test model they're about to drop?"

"Unauthorized."

"Please log me into the camera system set up inside it," I try again. "I want to see if Snap is strapped in, maybe to see how much of a load is on her spine when she hits the water."

"Unauthorized," and there's no point in badgering him further.

"I get it, Dick or someone doesn't want me knowing the details, don't ask me why. Although he did say he'd hook up with me at the Gantry at some point," I reason. "So, maybe he intends to tell me in person what's happening, and what the big secret is."

"I don't know."

"I don't either, ART. I don't know much it seems," as I plow through snow past Building 1230, home of the Autonomy Incubator for intelligent machines.

Drones of all shapes and sizes deploy from the top floor through a retractable hatch in the roof, their exercise yard a large outdoor netted area. All is quiet, no sign of anything amiss, but there's a problem on East Taylor Street, bright red painted on my features-integrated map, the FIND in my heads-up display.

A water main must have cracked, turning the road and acres of grass on either side into a skating rink.

"We need to call this in for maintenance . . . ," I start to say when my truck's beefy ceramic brakes suddenly slam, sending me into a slide.

16

"WHAT THE . . . ?" I yell, skating across the glassy road as a fox safely scampers away thanks to sensors that reacted before I could.

I catch a flash of a white-tipped red tail while I careen sideways off the road, onto a solid river of ice . . .

"SHHHHHHHH . . . !"

I'm headed toward trees, the mass of the heavy SUV propelling it . . . Nothing I can do but keep my hands on the wheel and not fight it, sliding, sliding . . . slower . . . slower . . . and slower until I drift to a stop a good 15.2 meters (50 feet) from where I started.

"Great!" I blurt out loud. "I may as well be on a frozen lake! I'll never get out of here, and has anybody bothered to report the broken water main by the way?"

"Negative," ART says.

"Too bad. Maybe we wouldn't have driven back here if we'd known," I'm careful not to sound as aggravated as I feel, not interested in dishing out what I don't want dished back. "Okay. Now what? Because I'm out of ideas."

"A solution would be to melt the ice," is ART's simple response, and if I didn't know better I'd think what just happened is another test.

But not even Dick could orchestrate a fox running across the road as I reach a broken water main that's created an impassible river of ice several inches thick. As I think of the Tahoe's special features, I agree with ART. This might be an opportune moment to fire up the flamethrower housed in the rear right storage box.

"If we do rapid short pulses, we can melt what's behind me a car length at a time," I work out how best to avoid blowing up my truck.

The operation is straightforward, I'm shown on a menu, and I select the FLTH's manual mode. That way I'm in control when I want to breathe fire, and I almost come out of my skin the first time I squeeze the trigger on the joystick.

"WHOA!" as a wall of flames billows up behind me.

I shove the shifter into reverse, using the cameras and mirrors to navigate. Inching along, I hit the trigger again, clearing ice one burst at a time. Backing up, scorching away, and at this rate we'll be here all day. All I'm doing is clearing a narrow path behind me and creating no real room to maneuver. What's needed is to melt as much ice as I can in all directions.

"Screw it," I place both feet on the pedals NASCAR-style. "And I didn't mean you, ART."

"Copy."

"Let's do this. Please switch to hill-climbing gear and turn off traction control."

"Wilco."

"Hold on to your hat, and I don't mean it literally!" as I step on the brake and the gas, cutting the steering wheel as sharply as it will go while working the trigger of the flamethrower.

I'm in the midst of a well-executed fiery doughnut (if I say so myself) when ART announces I have an incoming call.

"Deputy Chief Fran Lacey," he says over the roaring engine as I paint a circle of fire.

"Not a good time!" which of course he misunderstands, perhaps assuming I'm not having a good time, and I wanted him to know it.

Whatever his computer brain unfortunately has concluded, he puts Fran through before I can tell him not to as I make another flaming orbit. I'm slowly spinning along like a fire-breathing dragon chasing its tail, the engine straining, tires smoking, ice melting and steaming.

"Where are you?" Fran asks crankily over speakerphone, and I'm back on the road, leaving a shallow lake in my hellish wake.

"Behind the data center where there's a broken water main," I let her know, taking a few deep breaths as my heart slows. "You don't sound happy. What's wrong besides everything?"

"A reported problem in 1205, a possible 10-15," and no wonder she's irked.

"What makes you think there's a chemical leak?" I want to know. "And who's over there now?"

"Supposedly a hissing sound, anonymously reported. It's probably some furloughed scientist making a crank call just to piss everybody off. Well guess what, it's working. I'm pissed off, don't have time for crap piled on more crap, especially with so few of us here."

"I don't like the sound of this," I reply, on Langley Boulevard, the unplowed snow hard packed and rutted with patches of pavement showing through.

I also don't like that she has to bug me about it when I'm on my way to headquarters for an important interview involving a 10-year-old boy and indirectly my father. I also understand all too well that Fran with all her phobias has no interest in being around something that might explode, poison, burn or electrocute.

"When did the call come in?" I inquire.

"A few minutes ago," she says, and I can see Scottie's and Butch's ID numbers on my sitemap.

At the moment both of them are inside their shared office at our headquarters, or their smartcards are, that's for sure, possibly stuck in the readers of their computers. I suggest that Fran have them follow up on the call, and perhaps get the fire department to respond.

"They're tied up with me," she lets me know neither investigator is available. "So, I'd appreciate it if you'd take care of it."

I've reached the traffic circle, and up ahead, Langley's iconic giant white vacuum spheres vaguely shine like prehistoric full moons or monster PONGs.

"We're going over the suicide from the Point Comfort Inn," Fran explains. "And obviously, if there really is something hissing when you're doing your walk-through, we'll send in the fire guys to deal with it. But I don't want to do that if it's a crank call."

"I guess I can swing by really quick," I answer unenthusiastically, the facility in question the Fatigue and Fracture Laboratory (another exciting name).

Mostly what goes on inside Building 1205 (and has for decades) is research into the effects of noise, vibrations, extreme temperatures and environmental factors on aerospace structures and components. It sounds nerdy and unexciting unless you know what's inside that 1960s brick building in the center of the campus.

Some of Langley's most dangerous solvents, chemicals and gases are stored in there. I'm talking really scary stuff like liquid nitrogen, cyanide and hydrochloric acid used in metallurgy and experiments with composites. And a reference to something "hissing" is nothing to sneeze at.

00:00:00:00:0

"DON'T FORGET I'm talking to Lex Anderson at 1700 hours," I remind Fran. "Isn't it about time for you to pick him up if you haven't already?"

I'm driving past the construction site for the new Measurement Systems Lab, 6 floors wrapped in Tyvek, and snow-covered tarps and dumpsters. Nobody is working.

"Already did when I was out at lunchtime. He's in the conference room watching TV," she replies as if it's no big deal, nothing more than babysitting. "Waiting for you with bells on. We made a Dunkin' run, got him a sandwich."

"Are you telling me Lex has been alone in our conference room most of the afternoon?" I can't believe it, my blood running cold.

"Watching TV, like I said. It's not like he can get into any trouble in there with all of us a few doors away."

"That makes me nervous, Fran. He's in our department's conference room alone and unsupervised," and as I say it ART connects me to the security live feed.

I see Lex on camera, sitting at the long oval table. A flat-screen on the wall is tuned to NASA TV, a special on the James Webb Space Telescope with its tennis court–size sunshield and 18 hexagonal beryllium mirrors coated in gold.

". . . The most powerful space telescope ever built," the narrator is saying. "And soon it will be headed to the sun, folded up like a bird inside the fairing of an Ariane 5 rocket . . ."

Lex isn't watching or listening, too busy with his phone, his red hair as bright as a new penny in the overhead lights. He looks smaller, younger than his 10 years in baggy jeans, a sweatshirt, and rubber snow boots . . .

"I'm logged into our security cameras," I tell Fran over my truck's speakerphone. "So, right this second I've got my eyes on him," and she's used to me monitoring our cameras as a matter of course. "I'm looking at Lex inside the conference room. Why does he have his phone? That was a very bad idea."

"He's not under arrest. Hasn't even been read his rights. Judas Priest, don't get so worked up. He's a kid . . . ," she says as I pass a sprinkling of cars parked outside Building 2102, where not so long ago I was pulling an all-nighter in Mission Control.

"Intellectually he isn't," I reply. "And he's pretty much had free run of the Langley campus since September," I think unpleasantly of Dad squiring him around. "Lex may not be a hacker in the criminal sense. Or maybe he is. But for sure he's capable of it," I monitor the live feed playing . . .

Lex pushing his chair back from the table and getting up . . .

Walking out of the conference room . . .

Into the main lobby with its blue carpet, red upholstered furniture, and poster-size NASA photographs on the walls . . .

Heading around the corner toward the deputy chief's office suite . . .

Where Fran, Butch and Scottie are going through Vera Young's murder and the so-called suicide of the man Carme blew away, the wall-mounted flat-screen divided into quadrants. A fake driver's license with the name Hank Cougars is in one, and graphic crime scene and autopsy photographs in the others.

Bloated by decomposition, the dead man is about to split his clothing, and I suspect that after the scene was staged, the heater was turned on. It would have kept going until the Denali ran out of gas, explaining the bad shape the body is in during weather that should have kept it refrigerator cold.

Other photos I'm seeing don't include his grisly stash of weapons and body-disposal accoutrements. It would seem that part of the staging included removing them. Based on what I'm overhearing remotely and Lex is witnessing from the doorway, the real Hank Cougars was an alcoholic who worked construction on and off.

He drove a 2016 silver Denali, was thin with balding blond hair and blue eyes. He in no way resembled the man Carme took out in the parking lot of the Point Comfort Inn, someone Fran and her crew have no clue was an assassin who didn't commit suicide. It would seem that he parked in a remote area and blew himself away with the Mossberg pump-action 12-gauge found between his legs.

It looks identical to the shotgun I saw in the back of his truck after Carme killed him, and I have a pretty good idea what she must have done. Staging the scene, she placed the barrel in his mouth while he was slouched in the driver's seat already dead from snake-eyes head shots.

After all was said and done, there wasn't much left from the neck up, a bearded lower jaw and tongue, lacerated flaps of skin and jagged pieces of skull. Brain tissue, bits of bone and teeth were blown all over the seat, headliner, the back windshield. I suspect Carme retrieved the hollow-point bullets she'd fired earlier, making sure the medical examiner was none the wiser.

". . . The inn's not open and would be boarded up this time of year," Fran is saying to Scottie and Butch. "In other words, it's a remote location if you don't want to be found right away. Or maybe the person had some sort of meaningful and symbolic connection to the place."

She goes on to say it's more than a little troubling that there was no registration inside the truck. The tag is stolen, the Vehicle Identification Number (VIN) eradicated, explaining why the GPS's history was deleted. The only phones inside were burners, and clearly this isn't someone who had a social media presence or did anything at all to draw attention to himself.

"He doesn't profile as the sort who would eat the barrel of his shotgun," Fran is saying.

None of it is the sort of thing a child needs to hear or see, and she's out of her chair in a hurry when she notices Lex gawking from the hallway.

"Gotta go!" she ends our call, and I watch her on the live feed intercepting him as he stares in a bug-eyed trance at the disturbing images on the big flat-screen.

"What's up?" she steers him out of range. "You doing okay . . . ?" she asks as I continue eavesdropping in ways she can't begin to imagine.

"I need to use the bathroom . . . ," Lex looks absolutely spooked, and I've reached Building 1205, what's in essence a monster machine shop, three-story brick with tiny windows.

I note several sets of tire tracks in the otherwise undisturbed parking lot, probably one of my colleagues was making routine daily checks. That doesn't mean there's not a squatter, and I imagine some desperate researcher whose project might be compromised or ruined by the furlough.

Despite my protests about never getting a mandatory vacation, I don't know what I'd do if forced to stay home and abandon what I need to get done. I don't think I could tolerate being forbidden to continue working on a case or a project, especially if it's a passion, and I ask ART to access the anonymous phone call Fran mentioned.

The audio recording begins playing as I get out of my truck . . .

"NASA Langley, what is your emergency?" the dispatcher in my earpiece.

"I can't tell you who I am . . . ," the caller sounds male and British.

"How may I assist you?"

"Obviously, I'm inside Building 1205 contrary to orders or I wouldn't know to report a hissing sound," possibly he's someone older. "But I won't be here by the time anyone responds so don't bother looking for me. Second floor, the Durability, Damage

Tolerance, and Reliability lab across from the stairwell. I suggest you hurry . . ."

"Now what?" I ask ART, stopping at the building's nondescript front door, the sun dipping lower, the wind much calmer. "Do I use my smartcard or my WAND?" as I rub my faintly tingling right index finger.

"What gesture would you like to set in memory for accessing outer building doors on campus?" his pleasantly modulated voice is in my ear as if we're chatting on the phone.

"Sort of a swiping motion over the reader," I show him. "As if I'm holding my smartcard. Will that work?" and the lock clicks free.

Opening the door, I step inside. The heat and lights are turned low, a long hallway of locked lab doors chilly and spooky with deep shadows, a distant exit sign glowing red.

"All right, we'll make this quick," avoiding the elevator, I choose the dark stairwell.

17

TURNING ON my tactical light, I illuminate the **Use Handrails** warnings painted in yellow on the metal-edged concrete steps.

At the next landing, I emerge on the second floor directly across from the lab the anonymous caller mentioned, and I can hear the hissing through the shut door. My first worry is the liquid nitrogen used in scanning electron microscopy to cool the sample stage. But it's not what I'm picking up.

My implanted sensors and those built into my CUFF aren't detecting nitrogen or any other potentially toxic or combustible chemicals that might be leaking. Pressing my ear against the door, I listen to a relentless low hiss, something about it confusing me.

May as well use my new digital gesture, and I unlock the door, pushing it open a little as the hissing gets louder. I'm not seeing or smelling anything, and it seems the noise is coming from the computer workstation on the other side of the lab. My light paints over gas cylinders strapped upright to a wall, and glass-doored cabinets lined with brown bottles of acids and caustics.

The room is overwhelmed by all the usual equipment I expect in metallurgy. Fume hoods, grinding mills, drilling machines, hot plates, vacuum pumps, a drying oven, Pyrex glassware all over the place. My signal-sniffing CUFF detects an audio transmission, and I think I know what's going on. And can't believe it.

Except I can, as I approach the workstation, the hissing noise playing through computer speakers. The recording has been activated remotely, and I get out of there as fast as I can, shutting the door behind me as something clatters down the dimly lit corridor. Then all of the lights go out.

"Oh boy, this can't be good," shining my flashlight in the direction of the noise I just heard, and next Fran calls me again.

"I don't know what's going on but we're in the complete dark over here!" her tense voice in my earpiece.

"Me too," I start walking toward the sound coming from a lab halfway down the deep dark throat of the corridor, something heavy and metallic scraping and clanking against a hard surface. "Is your power off?" I ask.

"Only the lights, which is weird."

"Probably the same thing here," and ART lets me know in my lenses that only two locations have had their lights knocked out.

Protective services headquarters and the building I'm in this moment, and that indicates the outage is deliberate and targeted. Someone has hacked into our power grid and who knows what else.

"It happened while Butch was taking the kid to the john. And now he's gone," Fran in my earpiece.

"Lex made a run for it?" my gut clenches like a fist as I reach the source of the clanking and scraping, a space assembly lab.

"You need to get here right away," she says as I think of the look on his face when he was standing in her doorway staring at the gory photos.

Scanning open the door, I discover a robotic arm has been activated, shiny steel flaring in my light, the long truss-boom snaking and writhing on the test floor, folding and unfolding as if demon possessed or seizing.

"What's all that racket?" Fran's unhappy voice as I shut the door, and I break into a run.

"Someone up to mischief," I fly like a bat out of hell toward the red glowing exit sign. "Get everybody available out looking for Lex. Hopefully he's headed home," but I sure as heck don't think so.

The sitemap in my smart lenses shows that the full-scale wind tunnel has a new visitor. The ID number of the smartcard indicates someone just used it to access a maintenance door in the west passage.

"Where are you right now?" I ask Fran, my boots loud inside the stairwell as I light my way in pitch blackness, hurrying down to the first floor, worrying what's next. "Because if I didn't know better, I'd think you're in the full-scale wind tunnel. At least your ID badge is . . . ," I start to say before she cuts me off.

"Hell no . . . ! Judas Priest . . . !" she bellows as it dawns on her.

"It would seem Lex has your ID badge," I push through the door that leads outside, pocketing my tactical light.

"That little piece of . . . !" cussing up a storm. "Seriously, Calli, I don't know how . . . ! Well screw him, I'll just deactivate it immediately . . ."

"No, you won't. Not right now," the cold air feels good on my face as ART remotely starts my Chase Car. "If he has your smartcard, at least we can track him to some extent. Anything's better than nothing. *Do not deactivate it*," I'm emphatic, unlocking my truck with a gesture.

Scrambling into the driver's seat, churning through snow, and I'm not liking what I'm thinking. There's no way Lex could have gotten from police headquarters to the full-scale wind tunnel this quickly unless he took a shortcut. If so, he knows our campus frighteningly well, and it suggests premeditation, possibly practice runs. Otherwise, he'd have no idea how to find his way.

"He might be going underground," I explain to Fran as ART gives me that schematic next, and I can see every building, utility tunnel and trench on our 764-acre campus. "If so, I'm only going to pick him up when he surfaces inside facilities or through the outdoor hatches. Your smartcard can access all the locks same as mine," and the massive wind tunnel looms up ahead.

Ten stories high, more than twice the length of a football field, at one time it was the biggest in the world. Built in the 1930s, it's powered by a 12.1 meter (40 foot) wide 9-bladed wooden fan that moves more than a million cubic feet of air at speeds up to Mach 10. I know all the specs from Mom's lesson plans.

Plus, Dad and I have conducted all sorts of tests in there, and lately Lex has accompanied him. The odd-looking construction reminds me of a monster Slinky soldered together into a rectangular hulking shape that's eggshell white. Near the main gate, it's the first thing you see when approaching NASA Langley on Commander Shepard Boulevard.

". . . You got any suggestions? Because I'm slam out of them," Fran vents in my ear as I pull into a slushy unpaved service road.

There are no tire or people tracks, and it doesn't look like anybody's been back here since the blizzard.

". . . I'm not sending anybody down into the steam tunnels, and no way I'm doing it either," she rants on, and of course she wouldn't, not with all her phobias.

"We're going to have to intercept him when he surfaces," I leave my truck. "Get everybody you can patrolling access areas. That's all I can suggest at the moment," and I end the call.

00:00:00:00:0

I HURRY through melting snow toward the wind tunnel, which obviously isn't running at the moment. When it is, you can hear its hurricane roar from one end of the campus to the other. The sitemap in my lenses shows that only 4 people are currently inside the facility. That's if you don't include whoever is in possession of Fran's badge.

Lex, in other words, and I step around piles of wooden pallets amid metal struts supporting the colossal structure. I cut through an improvised break area of white plastic tables and chairs drifted with snow. Trudging around back to the west return passage, I discover a single set of footprints on the small side.

A little smaller than mine, and I recall the rubber snow boots Lex is wearing. The trail leads away from a green metal utility hatch in the ground, stopping at metal stairs leading up to the wind tunnel's maintenance door that was accessed by Fran's smartcard a few minutes ago. And this is really bad. Climbing the yellow-painted steps, I unlock the maintenance door with a swipe of my WAND finger.

"Lex," I call out, entering a concrete passage big enough to drive a car through.

Empty, silent, and I don't hear or see anyone.

"Hey Lex! Are you in here?" my voice echoes. "Lex! This isn't a safe place to be!" I shout urgently, walking in deeper. "LEX, HELLO . . . ?" as the 12,000-horsepower electric motor cranks on with a thump and a rush.

The humongous wooden fan I can't see from here begins to spin, picking up speed thunderously, and I feel the airflow, a gentle breeze that quickly gets stiffer and warmer. I have seconds to beat a hasty retreat before the wind blows me around the bend into the spinning blades. Or smashes me into a concrete wall, maybe dicing me up in airflow vanes, a diffuser grid, none of it a good way to go.

"Shut her down!" I shout at ART.

"I don't understand . . ."

"SHUT THE ENGINE OFF!" and just like that it stops, and I run the length of the wind tunnel's passage, squeezing through gigantic flow-straightening vanes.

I emerge into the open bay test area where flustered researchers are gathered around the full-size test model of a blue-fluorescing spacecraft wing mounted on a stinger. No doubt baffled by the fan suddenly starting and stopping, they stare at me with their mouths dropped open, and I keep going.

"Is everything all right . . . ? What's happening . . . ?" they call out after me.

But I don't answer, going full tilt down the stairs, taking the steps two and three at a time. Racing through the model prep area with its tugs for hauling the test sample transport carts. Dashing under the scale model of a Boeing 737 hanging from the ceiling. Sprinting along a hallway, past offices and labs, nobody home, my boots thudding loudly.

The empty lobby is plastered with photographs of vehicles tested over the decades including experimental hypersonic planes, submarines, dirigibles, dish antennas, race cars. Boiling out the door into the wind and cold, I stop, looking around, breathing hard, and I don't see him.

Not a sign of Lex as I scan the area, and I could kick myself if he did what I suspect, creating quite the distraction, and while I'm running for my life, he doubles back. Leaving through the same access door, down the same stairs, and I'm also betting he went underground through the same maintenance hatch.

"Other than seeing footprints, how are we supposed to know if he goes through a hatch or one of the airlocks? Or if he might be in a tunnel right now?" I ask ART, slogging my way back to the trail I noticed in the snow a few moments ago. "How are we supposed to have a clue where he is?"

"Most airlocks, hatches and tunnels aren't set up to be remotely monitored," the reply in my earpiece as I near the maintenance stairs I climbed earlier, and I can see that my hunch is correct, unfortunately.

Lex did exactly what I thought. While I was dealing with the fan he turned on, he retraced his steps, exiting from the same maintenance door, going down the stairs, disappearing through the same hatch in the ground, returning to the same subterranean utility tunnel he'd emerged from earlier.

"There's monitoring only in highly sensitive areas designated on the sitemap," ART is saying. "For example, Buildings 1110 and 1111," but even in those rare exceptions what we're talking about is mainly motion sensors, not cameras.

"Well, I think we know where he is right now," I reply, pointing out boot prints in snow leading directly to the green steel hatch with its smart lock and hydraulic-assisted opening mechanism. "And I'm not chasing him down there. I'm not sure I'd even pick up your signal or any signal," I say to ART as he remotely starts my Tahoe.

"The only way to have a reliable signal in the tunnels under present technological conditions would be to utilize the Aerial Internet Ranger," he suggests, and I look up at the late-afternoon dusky sky as if I might spot our prototype AIR in the neighborhood.

But Ranger is ghosting us exactly as instructed, and I tell ART that sending in a PONG is a bad idea.

"For one thing," I explain, climbing back into my truck, "it could be dangerous. I don't want Lex panicking and hurting himself down there. And besides, how would Ranger get in and out of hatches and airlocks?"

"He can use his gripper to access doors," ART replies as if lobbying on behalf of another artificial helper.

"He might not be able to lift the in-ground hatches," I consider. "But airlocks he can manage for sure. Although we've not tested him out on opening any types of utility doors, and I guess we should have."

I tell ART to give Ranger a shot as long as he isn't seen or heard, drawing absolutely no attention to himself. Lex can't be aware he's being bird-dogged by a flying orb, I'm emphatic about it. I know he'll panic.

"Let's do what we can to intercept him. But in the process, we can't end up with a loss of signal again," I remind ART of recent mistakes.

"Copy."

"Not aboveground or below . . . ," I start to add when interrupted by the loud blast of a steam ejector at the scramjet test facility in the heart of the campus.

Punctuated by flames and gases suddenly erupting from stacks and vacuum spheres as emergency sirens begin to hammer, wail and whistle. While red lights flash as recordings of sonic booms and aircraft thundering overhead blare from giant voice speakers throughout the campus.

Alarms sound their earsplitting emergency tones as if we're in the middle of an invasion, and I can see in my lenses other trouble Lex is causing. At least I assume he's behind the cyber mayhem, starting up robots and other machines, waking up drones throughout our 200 facilities as I just as quickly tell ART to shut them down.

I'm back on Langley Boulevard when Fran's badge number surfaces in the Advanced Concepts Lab for virtual reality and other simulations. I drive in that direction, and before I can get there, the ID number pops up like a whack-a-mole in another building. This time it's the Acoustics Research Laboratory, where a reverberation chamber is broadcasting bone-rattling aircraft sounds over intercoms I yell at ART to silence.

Then Atmospheric Sciences, the thermal vacuum chambers going to town, and I tell him please to make them stop. Obviously, he's to patch whatever the vulnerability is that's allowed Lex access.

"And change the passwords. Do what it takes to shut him out," I instruct when Carme appears in one of my truck's displays, as if I don't have trouble enough.

I watch my sister in the medical examiner's live feed as she walks briskly through the morgue's back parking lot.

She makes her way with purpose past windowless black vans, a mobile command center truck, a Zodiac boat for body recovery, and it's as if I'm seeing myself in another dimension.

Dressed in my same tactical clothing, she must have raided my closet at home, my office at police headquarters. Or maybe Mom did. All I know for sure is anybody looking would think Carme is me right down to the CUFF on her right wrist, and the sporty-looking glasses tinted medium gray as the sun settles lower.

18

CARME heads toward the delivery bay, its massive door retracted, the Cadillac hearse idling inside and no sign of anyone as Neva Rong lifts off in her chartered helicopter on another display inside my truck.

All this while I'm driving through the most remote part of the NASA Langley campus where it would seem Lex is headed based on ART's reports. Ranger is underground and has pinged on Fran's ID badge several times, most recently in a utility tunnel that follows a steam pipe cutting through the woods in the direction of the Gantry.

I follow West Bush Road at a decent clip as the late afternoon thaws and is cast deeper in shadows, and I'm getting more concerned by the moment. There's nothing much back here, mostly woods, test ranges and old rust-stained hangars where all sorts of unusual vehicles might be stashed. Empty fields host mysterious antennas, and you never know what you might find in the sheds and storage units.

Everything is snowy and quiet, the Gantry towering ahead like a giant candy cane–striped swing set against the darkening partly cloudy sky. I keep an eye on the sitemap while monitoring Carme on the OCME live video feed, alone inside the bay. She strides up to the idling Cadillac hearse, late model with a Landau top, no sign of a driver because there isn't one.

Popping open the hood like she did at the Point Comfort Inn, she pulls out components and wires, the engine shutting off, lights out, loss of signal. As this is going on, security cameras inside the morgue show Dylan emerging from a cooler, steering a steel gurney carrying a pouched body covered by a maroon velour throw.

He pushes his morbid cargo through the intake area, one of the wheels sticking like a bad grocery cart. Rolling it past the floor scale, out the door, he freezes on the ramp at the sight of the hearse, hood up and stone still.

"Looks like my sister might have taken care of one problem," I say to ART. "But where is Lex? He's been underground for a while now, and there's really no way to know where he might be or if he's okay. And the sun will be going down soon."

ART has no new data as I park next to a fenced-in scrapyard of crashed aircraft chassis near the steam plant that stinks to high heaven. I count 13 vans and trucks parked on the roadside, a lot of them nose in with their headlights on, illuminating the full-scale gumdrop-shaped spacecraft test model suspended from the Gantry.

Off to the left is the million-gallon Hydro Impact Basin, a swimming pool where the water's never fine. Unheated, unfiltered, and routinely shocked with chemicals, it's where we simulate splashdowns and crashes. I suspect the point of this afternoon's test is to see how astronauts would hold up when they return to Earth, landing in the ocean at certain velocities and angles.

Done with good ole-fashioned geometry, and I'm always reminded of the game Mouse Trap that Carme and I used to play as kids, never tiring of the boot kicking over the bucket . . . sending the marble bouncing down rickety stairs . . . into a chute

. . . falling through a hole . . . triggering the mouse cage to slide down a pole . . .

High-speed cameras are set up and ready on their tripods, hanks of cables leading to computer equipment on carts. The pullback line is retracted like a bowstring, ready for pyrotechnical explosions to cut through steel cables, slinging the test model over the splash basin where the shackle hook will be released.

Everything's a go, and the engineers, flight dynamicists, crane operators and other experts from NASA and Sierra Nevada Corporation have cleared the area. Everybody is hanging back from a safe distance in the parking lot while the countdown continues on the digital clock.

"21 . . . 20 . . . 19 . . . ," the seconds tick off in luminous red.

Then the badge number reappears on my sitemap, this time right under my nose inside the Gantry's main hangar where my crash dummies live. And I'm out of my truck.

"17 . . . 16 . . . 15 . . ."

I'm rounding the corner of the hangar as Lex flies out a back door. He races like a rabbit across snow-covered grass, and I take off after him.

"10 . . . 9 . . . ," blares loudly over the intercom now.

I run as best I can in slippery conditions and decreasing visibility, under the Gantry's massive scaffolding, steering away from the splash basin toward the woods. Glancing up at the control room's glass windows, I'm puzzled that no one seems aware of what's going on, their attention elsewhere, on the pool and the test model, I suppose . . .

". . . 2, 1 . . ."

A mad dash past a storage shed, and I tackle Lex to the snow as the pyrotechnic bolts blow, and the test model swings toward the water in what seems slow motion. It lands with a loud smack like a belly flop, waves swelling over the sides of the pool, flooding the wide concrete tarmac, stopping short of the parking lot while Lex struggles.

"Get off me! Get off me!" he shrieks as I straddle him, pinning his arms above his head.

"Stop fighting," I growl in his ear. "The more you resist, the worse it will be."

I get to my feet, plucking him up by the armpits, both of us brushing off snow and dead grass.

"So much as a twitch, and I'm putting you in handcuffs," I warn him. "Give me your phone. Now!"

Digging in a pocket of his jeans, he hands it over.

"Also, the ID badge you swiped from Deputy Chief Lacey."

He unloops the lanyard around his neck, pulling out the attached ID smartcard from inside his sweatshirt. Stuffing it in a pocket of my jacket, I escort him through the Gantry's soaring sawhorse steel structure, looking up at the control room at the figure standing before a plate glass window.

I recognize Dick by his silhouetted stature, tall and ramrod straight in fatigues and boots, his arms folded across his chest. He's staring off at the test model bobbing in the pool far enough away that Lex and I weren't in harm's way. Although it's hard to say. Bottom line, it was too close for comfort, and Dick could have stopped the clock.

He could have shut down the drop test when the Langley campus went temporarily haywire, thanks to Lex and his cyber mischief. I have no doubt Dick witnessed all of it, and chose to do nothing. He has yet to offer any real assistance, and it's beginning to feel like that will be the new status quo. Maybe he'll intervene. Maybe he won't.

As I deal with Lex, I'm keeping track of Carme in my lenses, walking away from the morgue as if she's me. Cameras in the parking lot pick her up detouring away from news crews, headed to her gray Tahoe parked in a visitor's spot while Neva's helicopter circles overhead, flying low and slow, loud enough to wake the dead.

I imagine her looking down, waiting for the stolen autonomous hearse to drive out of the bay as programmed. Her sister was almost body snatched right out from under everyone, Neva's elaborate plan foiled by the simple act of yanking out a few cables and cords. She's looking out her window, waiting for something that by now she suspects isn't going to happen.

No doubt she's noticed the Chase Car in the parking lot, and possibly Carme parading as her NASA investigator twin who finally showed up. Whatever the case, I'm betting that Neva is getting the message that there will be no spiriting away Vera Young's body to California or anywhere for further dissection and misinformation.

00:00:00:00:0

NEVA RONG must be seething, and I suspect she's probably headed to one of our local airports where a private jet is waiting. But it's not something I can ask ART about at the moment as I grip Lex's shoulder hard enough for him to know I mean business. Marching him to my Chase Car, I warn him not to run or try anything.

"What's gotten into you?" I ask severely. "Do you have any idea how much trouble you're in?"

"I don't have to tell you anything!" he's out of breath and sweaty, coatless and bareheaded, his jeans water stained, smeared with dirt. "I don't have to talk to you or anyone!"

"Nope, you don't. You can remain silent if you choose. But I hope you'll decide to talk openly with me. As long as you're aware that anything you say can and will be used against you,"

I emphasize, my hand firmly on his shoulder as we head to my truck.

"Some friend you are!"

"I'm not your friend," I agree, hot as heck in all my gear, sweating and about to starve to death. "But I can help if you let me . . ."

"I told George you didn't like me," Lex fires back, and beneath his anger is pain.

"You're not very likeable right now."

"He's always saying you'd want to be my friend but whenever I've run into you, you're not nice," he defiantly tramps along next to me. "All the times I've seen you around campus, you avoid me. Same thing when I'm with your dad on the farm. You've been unfriendly for no reason."

As he's saying this I realize that most of these chilly encounters were with my sister. I've run into Lex very little at Langley, once again making me wonder how often Carme's been on campus posing as me. The times I've seen Lex on the farm have been few and from a distance, and that's probably been intentional even if I wasn't aware of it.

Things don't always go well when Dad brings in a stranger without asking, and whether it was fair or not, Lex was going to be treated with suspicion. Maybe he's been subjected to resentment mixed in because of recurring fears and bad memories that get stirred up. Especially if it's Carme we're talking about.

I don't doubt that she's ungracious when encountering yet another son our father doesn't have, some stranger who gets more attention than we ever did. None of it is Lex's fault but also not his business, and I tell him I regret if I've come across as indifferent or unkind on any occasion.

As I say it, I'm irked that I get blamed for my sister's not-always-optimal behavior. But at least I'm getting used to it, don't really have a choice. It's not like I can let on when we swap places, tag teaming in ways that at first are off-putting.

"If you want to be my friend, Lex, you're going to have to earn it," I continue my lecture. "But right now, this is serious business. You're in my custody, and we need to finish with your legal rights. Would you like another adult present?"

"No."

"What about an attorney?"

"Very funny."

"I'm not being funny. If you want a lawyer, you'll get one even if you can't afford it," as I escort him through the Gantry's parking lot. "Do you understand what I just said?"

"You read me my rights. Except you didn't do it like on TV," he says as we reach my SUV, and I give the signal to unlock it, my right hand concealed in my pocket.

"Unfortunately, this isn't a TV show," I open the front passenger's door. "If it were, I'd change the channel."

"How did you do that?" he climbs in.

"Do what?" I ask innocently, walking around to the other side.

"How did you unlock it without a key, a voice command, clapping your hands . . . ?"

"It's a smart vehicle, saw me coming," as I climb in.

I have no doubt he can tell by the solar paneled roof, the antennas, signal jammer, run-flat tires and thickness of the door that this isn't a normal vehicle.

"And if you think you're hacking into this thing, you got another think coming, Mister," I make sure he knows who he's dealing with, and we shut our doors, the engine starting, all the displays staying dark. "Buckle up, and don't touch anything," I add strictly as he ogles my new not-so-standard Chevy Tahoe, taking in the powered-off flat-screens front and back.

He alerts on the storage boxes, the joystick, the unusual pleathery upholstery and carbon fiber. No doubt Lex has deduced from the powerful engine that my Chase Car will give someone a run for their money.

"What's it going to be? Do you want to talk?" I confront him, and we're not going anywhere until I have answers. "Because you didn't have much to say the other day," alluding to his phone conversation with Carme while she pretended to be me. "Except to deny everything, to claim you're as innocent as the driven snow," repeating what Dick relayed earlier today.

"It's not fair! I didn't do anything!" Lex's face is flushed to the roots of his fiery copper hair, his green eyes blazing.

"I guess I'll be the judge of that after you tell me the truth," is what I have to say about it. "That's assuming you want to have an honest conversation. Or maybe you'd prefer I take you home and the courts will appoint a lawyer to represent you like I mentioned."

"No!" he sulkily stares out his window as we sit in our same parking place near the main hangar.

The chain-link fence in front of us encloses a salvage yard of battered and mangled old planes, helicopters, a race car, all rusty and gutted of anything salvageable, riddled with optical location markers that remind me of bullet-hole decals. In the near background diesel engines rumble as a crane, a truck and other heavy equipment move into position at the splash basin.

Beyond are trees, a service road and a small landing airstrip for drones, then acres of windswept snowy fields and dense woods. Had Lex made it through all that to the campus's western border, he could climb the fence. I'm not sure how he would have dealt with the barbed wire on top, and maybe he hadn't thought that far.

But had he managed to reach Wythe Creek Road without serious injury, he would have been home-free except for the mile hike home.

"Anybody seeing you would have figured something's wrong, a kid with no coat on walking along a highway as it's getting dark," I paint a picture for him. "The police would have grabbed you. Or maybe someone else would have, maybe someone up to no good. And even if you'd made it back to the house without being caught, then what?"

"I don't know," he shrugs his narrow shoulders.

Digging into my pocket for my phone as if it's my only electronic resource, I'm finding it increasingly difficult to deny ART's existence. My impulse is to ask for his assistance as usual but I can't do that in front of Lex or hardly anyone. Not openly, and already I'm becoming technologically dependent and spoiled.

"Did you think we wouldn't find you?" I have my phone in hand like a regular person who's not bionic.

"I don't know," shrugging again.

"What was going through that head of yours?" I ask, trying to find the blasted recording icon without being obvious.

"That I had to get away," he says. "I wasn't thinking. It was self-defense," he adds as I locate the app I need.

"By the way, where's your coat?" I look him over, thin, disheveled and dirty in jeans that aren't nearly warm enough.

His boots are rubber with leather uppers, and not suited for the conditions. He has on a generic gray hooded sweatshirt, no gloves, and I have a feeling his grandmother doesn't do a lot of shopping.

19

LEX TELLS ME his coat is in the conference room at protective services headquarters. Leaving it behind when he fled adds credence to his claim that he was frightened, and nothing about his demeanor suggests he wasn't.

"Did you bring anything else with you this afternoon?" I inquire as we talk inside my truck, sitting in our same spot. "What about your backpack?"

"They took it from me at the rocket launch when they found the phone that isn't mine. The phone someone put in there to set me up!"

"I'd like to record our conversation," I inform him, and in the process, I'm cueing ART to do it if he hasn't been already.

Setting my phone on the console between Lex and me, I continue to hide my new abilities from him, to keep my SIN to myself and all that goes with it.

"Okay," I begin. "I'm sitting with Lexell Anderson inside my protective services truck. We're parked at the Gantry on the NASA Langley campus where I intercepted him after he escaped from our custody at headquarters."

I state the date and time, adding a few more salient details, asking him to verify that what I said is accurate.

"So far," he replies with a chip on his shoulder.

"And I made you aware of your rights a few minutes ago."

"Yes," he loudly sighs in frustration.

"You said you don't want an attorney. In other words, you don't want to be represented by a lawyer even if it's at no expense."

He shakes his head.

"No one can hear you nodding or shaking your head on a recording," I remind him. "You're indicating that no, you don't want a lawyer even if it doesn't cost you. Free, in other words, with nothing to lose. If that's what you want, Lex, I'll leave you alone for now."

"I'm not talking to some lawyer. It won't do any good," he repeats flatly.

"You're waiving the right, yes or no?"

"Yes."

"Why do you say that having an attorney wouldn't do any good?" I watch him carefully, his hands balled up tightly in his lap.

"If you talk too much or don't do what people want, bad things happen," his attention is out the window, and he's nervously chewing his lower lip. "You think people care, then you find out differently."

"What got you so spooked you decided to hightail it across campus?"

"I don't want to end up like them," wiping his eyes on his sleeve, he refuses to look at me.

"It's normal to be scared. It wouldn't be normal if you weren't," I tell him plain and simple. "I'm familiar with the photographs you saw in Deputy Chief Lacey's office. I'm sorry you were exposed to images and information that had to be upsetting," and I'm assuming he's most upset by Vera Young.

I don't know for sure how well they were acquainted but it had to be a shock to see photographs of her body hanging from a door, and as I'm thinking this, the images play in my head like a slideshow . . .

The cord wrapped tightly around her bruised, furrowed neck . . . Her dead eyes bright red from pinpoint hemorrhages . . . Her clothing, the wooden flooring around her dangling bare feet bleached of color by a caustic chemical . . . The gouged-out areas of her fingertips and other parts of her body where sensors were removed postmortem . . .

"That's what happens," Lex sounds defeated and far away. "If they decide you're a problem, that's how you end up. You saw what was done to punish them! They were nice to me! I wish I'd never met them! I don't want to be next!"

I have no visible reaction to the extremely disturbing implication that Lex was somehow acquainted with the man in the Denali, the assassin who intended to riddle me with armor-piercing bullets fired from a Chinese machine gun. I roll down our windows halfway to get some fresh air.

"You're talking about Vera Young and the unidentified dead man you saw in the photos at protective services headquarters," I finally reply. "Did they know each other?"

"I don't know why they would have," Lex says as a black Suburban slowly sloshes by.

I don't need to run the government plate to know that the SUV with its dark-tinted windows, its antennas and signal jammer is the same one that picked up Dick at Dodd Hall earlier this afternoon. It stops at the edge of the splash basin's concrete apron.

"In what way were Vera Young and the unidentified dead man nice to you?" I'm careful not to come across as overly concerned.

What I don't want to do is get Lex fired up again. Based on my observations so far this day, he doesn't exactly use the best judgment when he panics, and I've had enough of chasing after him. It's a wonder I didn't take a bad spill in the snow, maybe landing on my gun in front of Dick and everyone. My leg muscles burn from sprinting in unsafe conditions, and I'm ferociously hungry and thirsty.

"She'd invite me to see what her lunar robotics team was doing, promising I'd come work for her at Pandora someday," Lex can't keep the disappointment out of his voice, and what kind of monster leads on a kid like that? "She kept saying maybe I'd end up on the moon helping with their antennas, satellites, maybe fly a spaceship. And she bought me lunch sometimes," he adds sadly, and I just bet Vera did all that and more.

I can well imagine her making any number of grand gestures to win Lex's admiration and allegiance. Most of all, it was her cold-blooded intention to manipulate someone vulnerable. For that alone I won't forgive her, and it flickers darkly through my vengeful thoughts that Vera might have deserved what she got.

"I saw the pictures," Lex reminds me of what he inadvertently witnessed in Fran's office. "Is that what Neva did? Did she kill her sister?"

"What do you think?"

"I think she used her the same way both of them used me. I think Neva hates everybody but herself," he says insightfully, uneasily to the background din of diesel engines and warning beeps.

The SNC aerospace engineer named John is piloting the cherry picker again, inching the platform closer to the test model floating in a million gallons of greenish chemical-infused water. As I wait in my Tahoe for Dick to emerge from the Gantry's main hangar, and I envision his silhouette behind glass in the control room, staring down from on high, witnessing my undignified foot pursuit of a child.

What an inauspicious start for 001, a prototype in a project that's been Dick's all-consuming ambition, doesn't matter if it might have been Carme's or mine, given a choice. I have no idea what we might have picked, and likely never will. But one thing I do know, I didn't sign up for babysitting a 10-year-old genius who has an adjustment disorder and behavioral problems.

00:00:00:00:0

"VERA likely had mapped out a way of hacking into NASA long before any of us were aware it was in the works," I reassure Lex but not too much. "Consider yourself in the wrong place at the wrong time."

"Ha ha," he says hollowly as I realize the pun.

"Neva, Vera, yes, the *Rong* sisters. They wanted access to our campus to take unfair advantage, and you got caught in the middle of it," I summarize, watching the engineer in the cherry picker reconnect the test model to the hefty shackle hook on the end of the crane's thick steel cable.

"What if nobody stops her?" Lex means Neva. "Someone put that phone in my backpack, and she was in the same room with me! She wanted me to get in trouble!"

"Well, she certainly gets away with it if she can hang everything around your neck, right?" baiting him, I keep an eye on the black Suburban parked as close to the splash basin as one could safely get.

Its headlights and others of the parked vehicles shine on the spacecraft as it's slowly hoisted from the pool, water splashing, engines rumbling, hydraulics straining.

"I've been led to believe you spent time with Neva before you were together in the VIP room at the rocket launch," I set up Lex some more, testing his basic honesty while lying through my teeth to him.

"I don't know who told you that because it's not true," he replies. "We weren't together, and I didn't spend any time with her."

"What about when you were introduced?"

"We weren't. We never talked, were in the same room and that's it," he says what I know to be true.

"At any time in the past have you had contact with her in emails, texts, messages? Maybe talked on the phone?" I keep probing.

"No. I've never said a word to her," he answers indignantly, and I believe him.

"Look, I know how smart you are. I'm well aware of all the grades you've skipped, of your many gifts," I'm blunt, not messing around. "I know what people at NASA say about the bright future of our youngest intern . . ."

"That's a joke!" he blurts.

"It's not."

"What future do I have anymore?"

"I certainly hope you have one," I reply. "But unfortunately, if you're found guilty of a crime, it will greatly diminish any opportunities you might have had. Deservedly so if you did something bad."

"I didn't! Except I'm sorry about the game."

"This was no game. For now, the more important question is whether you've been set up, framed."

"I have!"

"If you're innocent, then we'll fix it," I offer what I'm not sure I can deliver. "But you're not naive. You understand what hacking is. And I'm pretty sure you know about espionage since we only have warning posters in every building on campus," and I sound a lot like my mom right now.

"I haven't spied. Even if someone wanted me to, I didn't."

"Did Vera ask you to do favors for her? Because that's what it's sounding like."

"Kind of," he shrugs, watching the crane set down the test model on a specialized flatbed trailer.

"What exactly did she ask of you, Lex?"

"Information. She would ask me all kinds of stuff about what your dad and I have been working on. And what I know about your family."

"Who specifically?"

"You and your sister."

"What did you tell Vera about us?" and as ART and I record the conversation, I'm mindful that it's also being transmitted.

Or I suspect as much, considering the electronics inside and all around me. The displays and audio might be off inside my truck but that doesn't mean we're not talking into an open microphone. And I wonder who might be listening as I continue to watch for Dick.

"I told her hardly anything," Lex replies. "I said I know what you do at Langley but we'd never been around each other. And that your sister's a fighter pilot overseas, some kind of special ops legend to hear George talk," and of course Dad would brag about Carme like that.

"What about my mom?"

"Vera asked me all kinds of stuff, really personal stuff, but I never went along with it," his eyes are wide with fear again. "I always pretended I didn't know much."

"And the special computer chip my dad's been involved in developing," I go ahead and bring it up, "what did you tell Vera Young about that?"

"I swear I never said a word."

"How did you know about it?" I have a depressing feeling I can guess the answer.

"George," Lex confirms my fear. "He told me about it one time when we were working on the PONGs in the barn."

"Did he show it to you?"

"Just a picture of it next to a match head so you could see how small it is. A quantum computer on a chip, the first one ever," he adds to my growing dismay. "He called it the GOD chip."

"Did he tell you what that means?"

"Well . . . ," he hesitates as if wary of getting Dad into trouble. "He said it meant Gemini Original Directive. All I know is it's got to do with a top secret project, and the chip is locked up in the big gun safe in the barn where no one would think to look for it," he adds, and I'm getting no indication that he knows the chip is missing but he shouldn't know about it at all.

"Why do you think my father would share such confidential information with you?" I act as if I doubt what Lex has told me when I absolutely don't.

"Because it's awesome. I'd be proud of it too," he says. "And he trusts me. Well, he did, I guess."

"When did he show you the picture of the GOD chip?" and as I think of the tracking device placed on my police truck, I have to wonder if something similar might have been done to him.

"About a month ago."

"Who have you told besides me?"

"No one," he says as my suspicions deepen.

"Did Vera ever give you anything?" I ask. "Any kind of gift. Maybe let you borrow something? Anything at all? It doesn't matter how small."

Another shrug, and he looks away from me again. "Nothing big."

"Nothing big?" I repeat as one of our protective services white Silverados drives past my rear bumper, aggressively slow and close. "What are we talking about?"

"A thumb drive with a bunch of stuff on it," Lex says. "Her publications, info about Pandora, plus a lot of cool games and apps."

"Where is this thumb drive now?" I ask, watching my rear-view mirror.

Butch is sitting in his truck, stopped in the middle of the road, blatantly checking us out, and my blood begins to boil.

"It's at home, hidden in my room," and Lex explains that he stopped carrying the thumb drive around with him after the rocket blew up. "When the phone was found in my backpack, I didn't know who to trust. Then I heard Vera was dead, and I got scared about what would happen if someone found out about what she gave me. I don't want to be in trouble for something else that's not my fault!"

As he says this, my attention is fastened on Butch climbing out of his pickup truck, and I can't believe he's about to intrude when he should know better. But even if he doesn't, it's not his darn investigation. Not to mention, I outrank him, and how is it I never knew before now that he's full of himself and pushy?

"Obviously someone wants to get me in trouble," Lex is back on that subject. "They've set me up."

"You seem pretty adept at getting into trouble on your own," I retort lest he forget the crimes he's committed.

20

HACKING, trespassing, tampering with government property, vandalism, I go down the list as Butch walks up, and it's rare to see him without Scottie.

They could pass for fair-haired Bobbsey Twins except they're not brother and sister. That's a good thing since their partnership on and off the job is anything but platonic, and he peers past me at my prisoner.

"What you did back there wasn't cool, buddy," he has to remind Lex it wasn't nice to escape while being escorted to the men's room.

Or better put and what Butch doesn't say is that he's angry some little smarty-pants kid dared to make a fool out of him.

"I'm handling this," I let Butch know without my usual smile, my demeanor hinting strongly that he needs to make himself scarce. "Tell Fran I'll update her later," I give him a not-so-subtle reminder that technically I may answer to the deputy chief but I sure as heck don't to him.

"When are you bringing him in?" as if he didn't hear what I said while staring menacingly at Lex. "You know, so we can get down to the nitty-gritty about Einstein's shenanigans on campus today," snidely, he's puffed up and powerful in his uniform and gun.

"*We* won't be getting down to anything," and I inform him that I already have a pretty good idea what happened from a cyber perspective. "I'm still gathering information and will be for a while, dealing with my usual counterparts at the CIA, Secret Service, the military like always. I'll be sure to ping you if I need anything," I don't say *thanks* or *catch you later* like I once did.

I can tell he's miffed as he stalks away. Almost slipping in the snow, he climbs back inside his truck, slamming the door shut. I watch in my mirrors as he drives off in a huff of exhaust, his big tires spewing gritty dirty slush.

"I don't like him," Lex says.

"That might be mutual," I don't offer that I might like the brash special agent even less, out of the academy barely a year, presumptuous, vain, he and Scottie both, and I didn't really notice before now.

I suppose what I'm experiencing are the gifts and curses that go along with having a SIN and other technical assists that offer clarity I didn't know I needed. The blush is off the rose, the tonic loses its fizz (as Mom likes to say) when you start seeing people for what they are including those you care about most.

The black Suburban hasn't moved, no one getting in or out of it yet. Beyond it, engineers bolt the test model securely to its steel platform on the flatbed while a truck backs up to the hitch. Any minute the precious astro-cargo will be hauled away, moving at a cautious snail's pace back to its hangar, and workers are headed to the parking lot.

"Who's that?" Lex asks, impressed as Dick walks right by my Tahoe without a glance, on his way to the Suburban. "He's got 4 stars on his uniform. Is that the commander of Space Force? George's friend?"

"You never know who's watching when you do something you might be sorry about," I reply pointedly as I wonder what else my father has confided in him. "Yes, as it so happens, General

Melville was in the control room when you made a run for it right there in front of him and everyone." I shift the SUV into gear, and it's time to get out of here.

"I'm pretty sure nobody likes me anymore."

"In case you haven't figured it out, you didn't do yourself any favors when you decided to hijack the NASA campus, starting up machines and setting off sirens," I continue to explain the error of his ways as I back up the Tahoe.

I let him know I don't appreciate being tricked into thinking there might be a chemical leak, the lights turning off, and robots starting as I'm searching the building. Cranking up the wind tunnel fan while I was inside it isn't something I'll forget anytime soon, all of his hijinks illegal, I remind him.

"Seriously? Did you bother to consider the danger you posed to life and limb," I drive us away from the Gantry. "You could have ruined experiments and extremely expensive equipment. Not to mention, hurt someone. Was it your intention to kill me inside the wind tunnel?"

"What I did was a reflex," Lex says as if that's good enough.

"An incredibly reckless and selfish one," is my response as I watch Dick in my mirrors, climbing into the back of the Suburban, the door shutting.

"I'm sorry," Lex says. "But I wanted to buy myself time. I realize it wasn't smart and that I upset a lot of people."

"Yes, it wasn't smart. Yes, you've upset a lot of people. There are very good reasons why no one is supposed to be inside the wind tunnels while they're running. And you've worked around them with my dad these past few months. You sure as heck know better."

"I was impressed by how you handled the challenges," and I can tell he means it but that's not the point. "You turned off everything crazy fast. How did you do it?"

"We're not here to talk about how I did anything," as I drive through slush.

Thick woods are on either side in the gathering dark, and I'm constantly monitoring updates and other information crawling by in my lenses as ART keeps me up on the latest developments. It's all over the news that the hearse stolen from the car show was bizarrely recovered at the morgue in Norfolk, probably left there as a prank, it's rumored.

Police have no suspects or idea who's responsible, and I'm betting Dylan made sure the OCME security system metadata has been altered. Otherwise, he'll have a lot of explaining to do, and to give Neva credit, hers was an audacious plan that came very close to working. It was genius to steal a license plate from the very service handling her sister's remains, Chamberlain & Sons Funeral Home and Crematorium.

The question is who removed tags from their fleet and put them on the getaway hearse, a driverless one. Even ART didn't know which funeral home was handling Vera Young's arrangements, and once again I place my money on Dylan. Obviously, Neva got to him, doing her usual thing of targeting someone on the inside to cooperate with her ploys and schemes.

Her MO is to go after low-hanging fruit first, her sister, for example. Vera wouldn't have been hard to dominate, Dylan even easier, neither one of them the malevolent force the hitman was. Worried who else Neva has at her beck and call, I'm conflicted over whether I should leave Lex home alone with a grandmother who might be compromised.

But I remind myself his life was reasonably stable until recently it seems. I don't want to toss him overboard into social services or the criminal justice system unless I'm sure that's where he belongs.

00:00:00:00:0

"TELL ME what you did," I say to him. "I want to know how you pulled off what you call 'challenges' and I call 'cyberattacks.'"

"By creating an algorithm for accessing and activating numerous facilities and devices simultaneously," he says, sounding quite sure of himself. "And it worked perfectly. Exactly like it was supposed to."

"And you thought it was okay to do something like that?" I'm watching the Suburban in my mirrors, stewing over Dick pretending not to see me.

"It wasn't supposed to be real. It was never meant to be played for real," Lex replies. "It's just a game."

"What you did was no game," I repeat in no uncertain terms, on Doolittle Road, passing the van pool, every vehicle piled with snow.

"It's something I came up with while I've been here, kind of like *Toy Story* where everything's alive," Lex says brightly. "Only I call it Helmet Fire because the point is not only to animate everything you can but to keep adding one challenge after another, seeing how much your opponent can handle."

"Also known as hacking, sabotage, trespassing, destruction of government property," I rub his nose in reality. "The same thing you're suspected of doing to the rocket, the Space Station."

"You could take this same algorithm, sub out certain variables, and create a Helmet Fire game almost anywhere," he goes on excitedly. "Imagine targeting a shopping mall, a casino, a manufacturing plant."

"It's not a game, you're not targeting anything, and I'm concerned you don't understand how serious this is," I warn him. "You hacked into NASA for crummy sake."

"No, I didn't," Lex replies with another one of his shrugs. "Vera's the one who hacked into NASA because she showed me how. It's on the thumb drive she gave me. A backdoor way to get around certain cyber security measures should you want to gain root access to facilities on campus. Including doors and hatches."

"And you didn't think it suspicious she'd be in possession of something like that?"

"I guess a little. But it was so awesome."

"You didn't wonder why she'd share it with you?"

"I should have shown it to George," Lex admits dismally. "I should have told you or someone, and I shouldn't have written the algorithm."

"You got that straight."

"But I didn't plan on ever executing it for real," he keeps saying that. "I just wanted the possibility."

"You were quick on the trigger, suggesting you'd thought about it a lot."

"I got scared when I saw the photographs," he's looking out the window again. "I wanted to get away, and when you came into the wind tunnel after me, the only thing I could think of was to set off a bunch of stuff, diverting your attention so I could escape."

"When I drop you off at home, I'm going to want the thumb drive," I reply, passing Building 1119-A, metal-sided with a huge retractable bay door.

One of our newer hangars, it's obviously where the test model is headed, several cars in the parking lot.

"I wish I'd never taken it now," Lex says, and I can tell that Vera Young has hurt as much as angered him.

I can imagine him basking in her attention, falling for her promises hook, line and sinker. She was a senior scientist at Pandora, the sister of Neva Rong, and of course he was going to feel special and flattered.

"She was nice to me so she could spy, wasn't she?" he mutters, disappointed. "That's why she gave the thumb drive to me, and said all those things."

"Very possibly that was Vera's major agenda."

"If people are nice from now on, I'm not going to trust them!"

"You said the man in the photographs was nice to you too," I bring him back to the subject of the dead man in the Denali. "Did you know him?"

"He lives in my neighborhood. Or he did."

"In your mobile home park?" and you could knock me over with a feather when Lex nods his head. "Do you know his name?"

"No."

"He never introduced himself to you or your grandmother?"

"I never really talked to him, would see him sometimes when I was walking to get the bus," Lex says. "Or if I rode my bike past his house and he was outside, he'd wave and say hi. Once I ran into him at the food pantry, except he acted as if he didn't know me. Not everybody wants to be seen in there."

"Which pantry?"

"The one at the Baptist church," he replies as I think how convenient and callous.

Food banks are a perfect way for someone to stay anonymous. Most require no proof of identification, and no questions asked. A killer for hire walks out of a church with free groceries as he plans his next murder, and I decide it's time to buzz Fran.

I place the call myself like I used to in my SIN-less days when I didn't have ART. And the instant she answers, I tell her she's on speakerphone.

"Lex is with me," I add. "But then I suspect you know that."

"I heard," she says in a cold, disapproving tone.

On Langley Boulevard now, I can see the vacuum spheres at the scramjet facility several blocks ahead, ghostly in the dusk. The giant white metal orbs clustered like giant PONGs make me think of Ranger, and I glance in my mirrors as if I'll spot the camouflaged mobile hotspot tailing us, assuming he is.

But not a sign, just the sun smoldering as it dips below the horizon. Light flashes gold off the glass windows of the institutional brick buildings, the black Suburban following at a distance.

"We're a minute from HQ," I let Fran know. "It would be great if someone could meet us in the parking lot with Lex's coat so we don't have to come inside. Where are you right now?"

"In my office where I'm staying," her voice through my truck's speakers.

ART connects me to cameras at headquarters, including the one built into the computer on Fran's desk. No matter how many times I've told her to cover the lenses of her devices, she doesn't always bother, and I imagine my artificial helper is shrewd enough to make sure he turns off her desktop activation light so she can't tell anybody's watching.

". . . Don't ask me to lift a finger to help him out," her attractive face looms in the camera unbeknownst to her.

She's combing her fingers through her dark hair, sitting in her ergonomic chair, paperwork and empty coffee cups everywhere. Craving a cigarette right about now, I can tell as I see her in my SPIES and PEEPS.

". . . I don't care if he freezes his little ass off after the crap he's pulled," her voice hard as nails for Lex's benefit since she knows he's riding shotgun.

Angry as she may be, I know she doesn't mean it. She has her own precocious handful at home, 6-year-old Easton who keeps her hopping because the apple didn't fall far. Fran may come across as not having a soft side or maternal bone but it couldn't be further from the truth.

". . . I never had lunch, and now I've got a bear of a headache. *Thanks very much, Lex*," she goes on irritably.

I'm unpleasantly reminded it was eons ago when Dick gave me muffins and a protein drink. My stomach is so empty it might digest itself.

"At least the lights are back on," Fran's no-nonsense voice. "And the hissing sound inside that lab magically stopped just like everything else your dad's pet intern managed to crash and burn around here," she adds condescendingly, rather brutally, and Lex's face has turned red, his eyes flashing.

"I didn't damage anything!" he erupts in a furious stage whisper, and I press my finger to my lips, shaking my head, warning him to shush.

ART updates me nonstop in my lenses with news feeds, silently alerting me that Vera Young's body was cremated a little while ago according to her daughter in California. In response, Neva Rong is threatening to sue the Commonwealth of Virginia for failing to conduct a thorough death investigation.

She claims officials deliberately destroyed evidence, falsified records, and are refusing to turn over Pandora's proprietary property among other high crimes and misdemeanors. In addition, Mason Dixon is broadcasting live from Chamberlain & Sons Funeral Home and Crematorium, ART shows me.

"Where are you headed?" Fran asks.

"I'm taking Lex home," I reply, and she won't be happy.

"Excuse me? I assumed you were bringing him here," Fran voices her disapproval even as Mason mentions me by name over the air, informing his internet audience that *as usual* I'm refusing to comment.

Since when does the buck stop with me? Certainly, he's tried calling often enough at any hour he pleases, and it's true that I do what I can to avoid him. But he's never criticized me publicly, not like this, and it's as if he's issuing a challenge.

". . . Repeated attempts to contact Captain Chase have been ignored, and I gotta tell you, folks, it's not okay. As taxpayers we have a right to know what's going on in the United States government whether it's NASA or Space Force . . . ," he says outrageously in my implanted earpiece.

21

I SEE FRAN in my lenses, pushing back her office chair, standing up, tired and rumpled in her uniform.

"Do you really think that's the best thing for him . . . ?" she asks, gesturing impatiently as if I'm right in front of her.

"At this time, yes," I reply, and I suppose squabbling with her remotely isn't all that different from butting heads with ART.

"Well, I sure don't," she adds as if there's a better choice.

There isn't. Not as far as I'm concerned. We don't have a lockup at NASA. We're not in the business of warehousing prisoners of any age, and I'm not about to shuffle off Lex to Hampton's youth detention center. I'm also not going to discuss this with Fran while he's listening, and I take the call off speakerphone.

"Based on what I know so far," I continue, "leaving him in his own environment is what makes sense," and what I'm saying is I'm not prepared to charge him with anything at this stage of the investigation.

More than that, I'm letting Fran know there will be no argument. It's my decision, and no one's barging in and taking this kid away from me right now.

"I don't think he should be unsupervised," her negative voice in my ear.

"Hopefully he won't be."

"In case you didn't know, his grandmother's that crazy old bat who claimed to be struck by lightning a couple summers back. Do you remember?"

"I wasn't on that particular call," I reply blandly, not wanting Lex to know I'm talking about his situation at home as I feel him staring holes in me.

"All I can say is when I pulled up at their trailer this afternoon, the windows were covered with gift wrap paper," Fran says. "And the grandmother didn't come to the door. So, I don't know how much supervising she'll be doing. Probably, he shouldn't be with someone like that, let's be honest."

"I think there's a lot we don't know," I don't want to go down that path, at least not yet. "When are you heading out?"

"Not for a while. I'll feel better when everybody clears off campus."

As she says it, ART shows me the ID badges on the same sitemap as before. In my lenses I see the same NASA personnel and private contractors who were at the Gantry moments ago, only now a handful of them have relocated to the hangar where the test model is being hauled.

"It's good if you're not too far away because I may need your help in a little while," I let Fran know. "I have a feeling we're going to end up searching a mobile home near the speedway, and I need you to keep this between us."

"I'm confused. His mobile home? Or one related to him?"

"Possibly relating to the unidentified man found in the Denali, the alleged suicide."

"You think you know who he is?"

"I think I may have found where he lived. Lex is helping me," I glance over at him as he listens intently, his face a road map of worry.

"And how is *he* helping? I didn't realize he's junior detective now," Fran retorts sarcastically, and I tend to ignore how jealous she can get. "What are you talking about?"

"Not sure yet."

"Are you telling me this kid has some sort of connection to the dude whose head was blown off?" she asks incredulously.

"That's how it's looking."

"And I didn't think this day could get any weirder."

"For now, don't share this with anyone," I repeat. "Not Butch, Scottie, Celeste, not even the chief. No one."

"How about we run the address? Let's see what we can find out before anybody shows up. Having a clue what we might be walking into is always a good idea."

"There's no *we*," I reply. "I don't know the address yet but when I do? Nobody's showing up there unless I say. I'll get back to you when I have more," and I end the call as Lex resumes fretting out loud about being killed in horrendous ways or rotting in the slammer.

"Nobody will believe me," he obsesses.

"Did you and Vera email or text each other? If so, maybe there's a record of her referencing the thumb drive or asking you questions."

"No," he blows out in exasperation. "It was always in person or over the phone, and I can't prove anything. Why? Because I'm stupid. Then I did even stupider things today."

He was no match for Neva and Vera, they set him up but good, entangling him in their web. Then he made matters worse by turning the NASA campus into a potentially deadly amusement park with his Helmet Fire game. The sad fact is, it won't be easy to extricate him or clear his name, assuming he's guilty of nothing more than cyber mischief.

Committed under great duress by a juvenile, I might add, and we've almost reached NASA's modern brick protective services headquarters next to the firehouse. Scottie, the other Bobbsey Twin, is waiting in the parking lot, my headlights blazing on her holding a small green quilted jacket that doesn't look very warm.

Opening the Tahoe's front windows all the way, I'm back to doing things for myself, placing phone calls, finding switches, doing things manually as if there's no ART, and not liking it much. Scottie bends down to get in Lex's face, unable to resist asserting her big bad authority to an upset kid the size of a minnow.

"It wasn't cute what you did earlier," she says aggressively, her long pale-blonde hair blowing around her self-conscious prettiness. "In fact, it was really dumb for someone who's supposed to be so smart," she shoves his coat at him, and I never knew she was a bully. "You're lucky you didn't get lost down there. You might not have been found for years, if ever."

"I don't get lost," Lex says to me, not her, as we sit in the protective services parking lot, the last embers of the setting sun reflected by our headquarters' big glass windows.

"Huh, you're just lucky you didn't turn into a mummy. You know how hot it can get in those old steam tunnels?" Scottie snarls.

"Up to 140 degrees Fahrenheit, 60 Celsius, if you end up in the wrong ones at the wrong time because you don't know the schematics," he replies, not looking at her.

"Well, aren't you a walking Wikipedia," she sputters.

"That's not how I know about it."

"I'm sorry NASA ever gave you permission to come here. I'm even sorrier you've decided to abuse a privilege nobody else gets. Hey! Look at me when I'm talking to you!"

His answer is to stare straight ahead.

"You think I can't make you?" And to me, she says just as inappropriately, "Do you believe this? Can you get over this smart aleck little piece of . . . ?"

00:00:00:00:0

"THAT'S ENOUGH," I cut her off, and I should have done it sooner. "You've more than made your point. Thanks for bringing his coat . . ."

"Before you boogie on out of here," as if Scottie hasn't been rude enough. "Did you by chance have words with Butch? Because he's in one of his funks. I mean, he was fine until he ran into you at the Gantry and you were short with him?"

"Not now," I warn her. "It's not a good time for this," not that there ever is when it comes to hearing such horse crap, and I shut the windows in her face, shoving off.

"She doesn't respect you the way she should," Lex announces, his astuteness unnerving, and I'm not sure I appreciate it.

"The person she's most unhappy with is you," I'm driving toward the main gate, the black Suburban nowhere to be seen anymore, and I wonder when I'll hear from Dick again.

"You don't have to put up with the things you do," Lex renders another opinion as if he's the expert.

"That's presumptuous considering you know nothing about how I spend my days," I reply. "You have no idea what I do and don't put up with no matter what you might think you know about me."

"You're a captain in charge of cyber investigations. Plus, a scientist who's probably going to be an astronaut," he says, and he's been talking to my father, I suspect. "The other officers, even Deputy Chief Lacey? You shouldn't let them treat you the way they do, is all."

"When people are stressed, they aren't always polite," is as much as he's going to get out of me. "I pick my fights, having learned the hard way that it's usually not a good idea to throw your weight around."

"Tell me about it," he says, studying the overhead panel that looks like a large sunroof but is part of the Retractable Attack Turret. "You have to be careful about acting very smart, about being really good at stuff."

He twists and turns in his seat, looking back at the overhead storage box, making connections that remind me of his good and bad potential.

"What you did today hasn't earned you any friends," I reply.

"Big deal. I don't care," he fingers the sensor-laden upholstery next. "I'm used to being by myself. I didn't grow up with people around me like you did. I don't need anyone."

"Everybody needs other people."

"There's no point in needing something you can't have," he says matter-of-factly. "The older kids at school don't want me around. They think I'm a pest, a freak, nothing but an annoying tagalong, and I can understand it," he echoes my own experiences. "I've never fit in anywhere and guess I never will."

"Right now, people don't know what to think of you, Lex. Myself included," I tell him the truth. "No matter your excuses, you violated our trust. You deliberately exploited a backdoor cyber vulnerability at a highly sensitive government installation," and as I say it ART confirms in my lenses that the software glitch has been fixed.

The malware has been neutralized. Lex is shut out of NASA's servers and anything else he shouldn't access. His clever gaming algorithm won't work anymore. Neither will the thumb drive Vera gave him, and I tell him so as we exit the Langley campus.

"You're going the wrong way," he sounds uneasy as we pass the speedway where Carme and I have been behind the wheel in our share of stock car races and truck rodeos.

"Nope," I reply, headed in the opposite direction of his mobile home. "We have a stop to make."

"Where are you taking me?" he asks anxiously, probably worrying about jail again.

"I don't know about you but I'm starved," I reply. "I bet you could eat a little something?"

Wondering what he's had today besides the sandwich Fran got him, I'm feeling guilty as I think of Mom and how well fed I've always been.

"I don't have any money," Lex's attention is back out the window.

"Is there anything you can't eat? How does Bojangles' sound?"

"I can't afford it," glumly.

"I have a food budget for prisoners. At the moment that would be you. I'm bound by the Geneva Convention to treat you humanely, and that includes fried chicken."

"Ha ha," but not as hollowly this time, his mood lifting.

"How about your grandmother? Maybe we can pick up something for her?" I suggest, and he nods his head.

"She doesn't eat anything with heavy metals like mercury in it," he says. "Same with shellfish, anything that she calls a bottom-feeder."

"I think we'll be safe then," I reply.

It's 6 o'clock on the nose, and business will be slower than usual around here as long as the government remains shut down. There are only 4 cars in the drive-through line, and I pull in behind a pearl-white Jeep Cherokee that gives me an eerie feeling. It looks very much like the one I saw parked outside the Hampton Hop-In during the blizzard.

Creeping closer to the illuminated menu, I'm unhappily aware of the dark displays inside my truck, of the muted audio and other limitations. I don't like it when I can't talk to ART as if he's next to me, and it's amazing what we get used to in short order. I'm finding it increasingly anxiety provoking when I don't have multiple data sources to monitor at once.

I hate that I can't ask my invisible assistant out loud to run the Cherokee's tag. Instead I have to stare at it long enough for ART to inform me in my lenses that the pearl-white Jeep with tan interior is a 2014, which is old for a rental. The company, Catch-A-Ride, is Virginia based, the driver listed on the contract, Beaufort Tell, age 44.

The billing address for the credit card is a seafood distribution company in Myrtle Beach, South Carolina. Probably someone here on business, a "salesman," ART shows me, and Beaufort Tell's photograph on his driver's license looks like the clerk I saw inside the Hampton Hop-In.

"I'm pretty sure I've seen this car before," I comment for ART's benefit, not Lex's, and I'm shown a traffic video of a pearl-white Cherokee driving along I-64 East outside of Richmond yesterday morning.

The rear license plate in my lenses matches the one I'm looking at for real in the Bojangles' drive-through line. Sure enough, in the traffic video, the underside of the front bumper is damaged, and I have no doubt the Cherokee in front of me is the same one that was parked at the Hop-In convenience store 4 mornings ago.

"In fact, I'm sure it's the same car," and I describe it to Lex, including the damage to the bumper.

"How do you know that if you can't see the front of it? I'll take a look," he says eagerly, his hand on the door.

But he's not going anywhere. My Chase Car doesn't answer to him.

22

"I CAN TAKE a picture," Lex tugs at the handle again to no avail. "But you need to give me my phone back and unlock the door."

"Absolutely not, and act normal, please," I'm doing my ventriloquist trick as I watch the Jeep ahead, hoping there's nobody in it I should be concerned about.

"You know, I can help if you let me," Lex is more excited than afraid. "Is there somebody bad in it? Are we about to get into a chase? Because we'll blow that tin can off the road in this thing!"

"I find it curious that someone would plan a business trip to Hampton when we were about to be evacuated because of a nor'easter," I think out loud, other cars falling in behind us.

"Maybe the person got stuck here."

"Maybe."

What I don't say is I find it even more curious that a salesman for a seafood distributor might have been sitting inside the Hampton Hop-In this past Wednesday morning.

"Have you and my dad ever stopped at the Hop-In close to the farm?" I test his veracity again.

"A few times when he gives me a ride."

"How else would you get to our place if my dad didn't give you a ride?"

"The bus. It lets me out not even a 15-minute walk from your farm. They've got good hot food there, and root beer," he means that the Hop-In does. "Is that where you saw it?" he asks, and now he's talking about the pearl-white Jeep.

I'm reminded that Lexell Anderson is a mental force to be reckoned with. He makes connections way too fast, and if I'm not careful he'll react the way he did at NASA today, and a moment ago when he tried to get out of the Tahoe to check on the Cherokee. He doesn't look before he leaps or believe he needs permission, and I ponder what Dick told me about the burner phone.

It was part of a shipment that went to the convenience store in question, and from there somehow ended up in Lex's backpack at Wallops Island. I have no doubt Neva had the phone planted or did it herself. But how did she get it to begin with? Because I seriously doubt she walked into the Hop-In and asked for a burner phone and prepaid card.

"When was the last time you visited our farm?" I ask Lex.

"Two weeks ago. George and I were working in the barn, and while he was driving me home, we stopped at the Hop-In," he says. "As you know, since you were there too."

I have no idea what he's talking about, and ART begins playing the security video in my lenses. A time stamp of 3:36 p.m., Saturday, November 23, and I see a recording of Dad and Lex walking into the convenience store. Then ART shows images of them cruising the aisles, and I realize with a sinking feeling that my father was doing a lot more than buying drinks or snacks.

He was filling a basket with luncheon meats, cheeses, bread, a dozen eggs while encouraging Lex to grab milk, cereal, orange juice, bananas. The Hop-In is owned by a couple, the wife a heavyset older woman, Bunny, and unlike what her name implies, there's nothing warm or fuzzy about her.

I've always suspected she hates her life in addition to her job, and at 3:42 p.m. she's irritably ringing up Dad's purchases, and there's no sign of a burner phone. A minute later, he and Lex are leaving, the bell jingling as they go out the door. I watch them carrying bags to Dad's white Prius, and there's a gray Tahoe like mine in the background parked at the gas pumps.

Carme is dressed in my same protective services fatigues, filling up her Chase Car, something I knew nothing about several weeks ago. Certainly, I wasn't driving one then, leaving no doubt that Dad is intimately involved in whatever Carme has been doing. Two Saturdays ago, she was in the area, already doubling for me without my knowing.

My sister has been impersonating me longer than I thought, and I watch the pearl-white Cherokee stop at the squawk box. The window rolls down, and I can't see who's inside.

"Welcome to Bojangles', may I take your order?" the disembodied garble is almost undecipherable, and the driver hesitates as if deliberating.

"Two lemonades . . . ," an Asian accent without the politeness, definitely a woman's voice, cold and brittle.

She goes on to order a grilled chicken salad with extra honey mustard dressing, green beans, coleslaw, a 4-piece combo with dirty rice. Obviously, she's not Beaufort Tell, the bearded clerk I noticed inside the Hop-In during the blizzard. Possibly she's his girlfriend, a relative, a colleague.

Something as innocent as that or maybe not, and I recall the undercover agents I saw on the streets and inside the NASA hangar several mornings ago. All of them could pass for local, and it's impossible to tell by looking which side anyone is on. The woman in the pearl-white Cherokee could be a civilian who has no idea she's being watched as she buys her take-out salad, chicken and fixings.

Maybe she works in the seafood industry the same as Beaufort Tell (assuming that's his real occupation and name), and they're in Hampton together. It's possible they know the owners of the

Hop-In, might do business with them and therefore had reason to be inside the convenience store when I noticed the unfamiliar bearded man sitting by the glass front door.

In other words, there's no reason to suspect anyone associated with that pearl-white Cherokee with its scraped front bumper is connected to subterfuge, spying, plotting crimes including cyber ones and violence. But it also doesn't mean they're not. They also could be CIA, the Secret Service, military special ops. Or my real fear, adversarial minions deployed by Neva Rong and those who do her bidding.

"What's your pleasure?" I ask Lex as the pearl-white Jeep noses toward the pick-up window, and it's our turn next.

00:00:00:00:0

"I LIKE WINGS," he hungrily studies the bright-yellow menu glowing in the dark. "But anything's okay."

I keep my eye on the driver ahead, making out her vague silhouette. She's a little shorter than I am, with narrow shoulders, and straight hair that brushes her collar.

"Wings it is with a few other things thrown in for good measure," I reply. "Cajun spiced?"

"Just regular, please."

I order a dozen of them, talking to the squawk box loudly enough that I don't have to lean out the window.

"Two steak-and-egg biscuits," I add my personal favorite. "A 12-piece box of chicken, mashed potatoes and gravy, Cajun pinto beans, extra hot sauce, butter and honey," I'm in hog heaven. "Plus, two chocolate milks, and an iced tea."

"Will that be all?" the squawk box asks, and gosh knows it should be enough, but it never is.

"And 4 cinnamon pecan twists, please," I add. "Plus, lots of extra napkins, salt, pepper, forks, and that should do it."

"Wow, that's a lot of food," Lex marvels. "More than we need, and kind of what your dad does."

"It's good as leftovers."

"That's what he says. And he's not fat either."

"That's nice of you," and I mean it. "In our family we feed people. No one should go hungry."

"George says that too when he orders double everything," Lex replies as I dig out my badge wallet, realizing I don't know what's in it.

I'm pretty sure I had close to 75 dollars before I was knocked out and held hostage, all of my belongings gone through, some items missing when I woke up. The spent cartridge cases I collected from the parking lot of the Point Comfort Inn, my breath mints were gone, in addition to all sorts of things inside my police truck, I have no doubt.

No telling what's at large, hopefully my money isn't, and I'm immensely relieved to discover it's not. But I shouldn't be surprised. Mom has a house rule that you don't go anywhere without enough cash for an emergency, and it turns out I have plenty. In fact, more than before, and my NASA refrigerator magnet is accounted for, which also makes me happy.

Rolling ahead, I watch the Cherokee's driver reach out the window for her order. Her tapered arm is sleeved in smooth black leather, her nails weirdly painted the same pearl-white as the car, and I stare hard enough at her flashy rings for ART to get the hint.

My Tahoe's cameras zoom in on . . .

A silvery winged skull with ruby eyes . . .

A coiled snake . . .

A gothic wedding band . . .

The jewelry is smaller than what the hitman had on when I saw him dead inside his Denali. But it's similar if not matching, and I watch her hold out a 20-dollar bill, telling the cashier to keep the change as I continue making assessments.

She's ordered enough for two, suggesting she's not eating alone, and that leads me to suspect she's meeting someone since no one else is in the car with her that I can see. Striking me as vain and haughty, she's a bit girly-gaudy, and I don't like that she told the clerk to keep the change when there hardly was any.

"Why are you so interested in the Jeep?" Lex stares at it in front of us, and his question is the perfect opportunity for me to cue ART that I could use a little help.

"As I mentioned, I may have seen it before," I reply. "And I'm wondering if whoever's driving it might have a connection to the dead man in the Denali."

"That's pretty sick," and Lex looks intrigued. "Why don't you radio for backup?"

"The last thing I want is anything about this going out over the air."

"You want me to take a picture of whoever's driving? I could jump out and do it real fast."

"I most certainly don't."

"Maybe we should follow it!"

"Absolutely not. In case you've forgotten, you're in custody and not my partner," and as I say it, I can tell I've hurt his feelings.

"But you can't let it get away!"

"I have no probable cause to do anything about it," I reply as the Cherokee drives off. "More important, I have you in the car with me. And I can't let anything happen to you."

"Oh," he says, and he seems pleased.

Picking up my phone, I call Fran because I can't ask ART to do it when Lex is sitting in the truck with me.

"Major Lacey."

"You're on speakerphone."

"He's still with you?"

"We're grabbing something to eat," and I explain to her about the Cherokee as I watch it take a right on Commander Shepard Boulevard.

I give her the tag number and suggest she get someone to tail the pearl-white SUV and see where it goes.

"Obviously, we don't want whoever it is alerted," I add. "We can't be sure what we're dealing with and need to be careful."

Ending the call, I pay at the drive-through window, taking the piping hot bags and boxes. The aroma is making me insane as I set everything in Lex's lap.

"My favorite ever since I was a kid," I let him know as we dig in rather savagely. "I'm afraid I'm a frequent flyer, which is why I spend a lot of time in the gym."

"A frequent *fryer*, you mean," he attacks a wing, licking his fingers.

"Well *fried* is a food group, at least to me, unfortunately. And nothing's as good as what my mom makes," I drape napkins over my lap. "I don't know if she's ever cooked for you when you've visited the farm."

"No," taking a slurp of chocolate milk. "Penny doesn't want anything to do with me."

"What makes you think that?" and we're back on Commander Shepard Boulevard, the pearl-white Cherokee nowhere to be seen.

"She doesn't trust me. Never has. I can tell," he tears apart another wing as if he's not eaten in days. "She was okay with me at the beginning of my internship but didn't like it when I started hanging out with George."

"Why wouldn't my mom trust you?" I ask as if this is news to me.

"Because she doesn't trust your dad," and while Lex may be on the money, the subject also isn't open for discussion.

"Does your grandmother like to cook?" I'm already starting on my second biscuit, driving one handed, increasingly startled by his observations.

"Nonna can't do much in the kitchen," Lex says while ART shows me in my lenses that in Italian the name means *grandmother* in case I couldn't figure that out on my own.

"Sounds like you've got an awful lot going on for someone your age," I'm stunned by what he picks up on.

It's true that Mom doesn't trust Dad, and in most departments I don't either. He means no harm, and I realize that's what people say about those who cause it routinely and repeatedly.

"I don't mind taking care of most things. I'm pretty good at fixing stuff, cleaning and cooking," Lex says, paper crinkling as he wipes his hands. "I make really good tacos and spaghetti. I like to bake, and my bread is awesome. And unlike your dad, I know how to shop. I tell him not to use convenience stores. It's way too expensive just like fast food. But he would buy stuff anyway the same way you just did."

"How did you learn to be so practical and self-sufficient?"

"My parents," he says. "But also, TV and the internet. You can teach yourself pretty much anything these days. Even if you don't have anyone to show you in person."

"Does Nonna have a car? Is she able to drive you on errands?" I ask, passing the speedway again, its stadium darkly silhouetted against the night.

"Not anymore," Lex says, the pavement swishing wetly beneath my tires as I put on my turn signal. "The bus I'm always taking? You can catch it right there," he points as I slow down at the entrance of Lost Farm Mobile Home Estates where I've been on any number of calls over the past three years.

The complaints have been the usual garden variety prowlers, domestic disturbances, shots fired, larcenies, public drunkenness, dogs running loose. Nothing special like a drug lab or homicide, and I have a feeling that's about to change.

23

"THE DEAD MAN you recognized in the photographs?" I ask Lex, stopping at the first intersection, not knowing where we're going. "I need you to show me where you think he lived."

"Stay on this street for now, and I'll let you know when to turn. How come you don't know who he is?" Lex wraps chicken bones in a napkin, placing them in a bag, cleaning up after himself. "I saw a driver's license in one of the photos in the deputy chief's office. The name on it was Hank Cougars, and the picture looked just like the man I've run into around here."

"That might be his picture," I reply, "but it's not his real name."

The homes we pass range from trailers on exposed cinder blocks to double-wides with wooden siding. Yards aren't much more than patches of brown grass showing through churned-up areas of melting snow, and I'm seeing very few holiday decorations.

"He was a bad person, wasn't he?" Lex says quietly, watching his neighborhood go by, a lot of American flags, aluminum sheds, aboveground pools and pickup trucks.

"I'm pretty sure," I reply. "Even if he seemed nice enough. How long has he been living back here as best you know?"

"I first started seeing him this past summer after Birdman moved out."

"Birdman?"

"The weird old guy who was living back there near the speedway when I moved here," Lex says. "I called him Birdman because he had this really cool owl that he'd rescued as a baby. He kept it in a huge cage in the backyard, and it would land on his leather glove."

"Do you know the name?"

"Mr. Owl."

"I mean, the man's name."

"No, but he had a lot of scars on his hands and arms from Mr. Owl's talons. And Birdman let me say hello to him once, not pet him even though I wanted to. Owls don't like that. And there was a python inside the house, although I never met it. As you can imagine, Birdman didn't have to worry about burglars."

"What happened to your parents, Lex?"

"A plane crash."

"I'm very sorry. When was this?"

"July 4th, three years ago. My dad was a really good pilot. I don't care what anybody says," he adds, oddly defensive.

"And you're the only child?"

He nods, his attention out the window again, and I'm reminded there are no streetlights back here, and it's a black hole.

"Where were you living at the time?"

"Richmond, my parents taught at VCU. And then I moved in with Nonna," he says as ART shows me the news blurbs.

Leo and Nan Anderson, ages 39 and 41, both of them were professors in astronomy at Virginia Commonwealth University. They were flying with another couple in the small prop plane Lex's father often rented and piloted, and it had an engine failure over the Atlantic Ocean.

"This must be a hard time of year," I reply. "And I know it must be a painful subject. But what do you think they'd say to you right now, Lex? What would they say about the burner phone in your backpack? The thumb drive, and what you did on the NASA campus today?"

"They'd say not to let anybody stop me," he replies without pause. "And to take care of Nonna," as he leans forward in his seat, pointing straight ahead. "That's it right there. That's his place and look! His Denali's not there. No lights on. It doesn't look like he's been here for a while. Which fits with him being dead!"

"SHHHH!" I hush him again. "Let me do the investigating, please," as I look out at a lot that backs up to thick woods, not a light on anywhere.

If this is where the hitman lived, he was close enough to the speedway that I don't know how he stood the noise, the mobile home small and simple. White vinyl sided with a putty-gray metal roof, it has trellises and shutters painted black and peeling. I note the high-definition antenna on the roof, and the battery-powered camera mounted over the entrance.

The double lot hasn't been touched since the blizzard started. There are no tire tracks or footprints, just a lot of branches and debris blown everywhere. The supercan and its black trellis enclosure are buried in drifted snow to one side of the swaybacked front porch, and I ask Lex what services are included in the mobile home park's monthly rental fees.

"Water and sewer," he's keyed up as I pull into the unpaved parking area near a fire hydrant half-buried.

"And garbage collection?"

"It's on Mondays," he says. "So, either the night before or first thing in the morning you roll the can out to the curb or they won't empty it. Then you put it back before it gets run over or blows off somewhere. He wasn't home to do it, and that was a week ago. He's dead for sure!"

"Rule number one, don't make assumptions or exaggerate," I reply. "Today is Sunday, so the garbage pickup was 6 days ago, not a week. And the snow didn't start until after that. Therefore, all we can say definitively is nobody's been in and out since the storm began. At least, based on what we're seeing right now. Also, we don't know if it was his habit to roll the can out or not. We don't know much."

"Right! The storm started 4 days ago, and that's about when the man in the Denali blew his head off with his own shotgun," Lex repeats what he overhead in Fran's office. "I told you it was him! The guy who moved into Birdman's place!"

"There you go swinging to wild conclusions again . . ."

"Why would he kill himself?" Lex is on a roll. "How can you be sure someone else didn't do it? At first people thought Vera killed herself too. And she didn't. Dr. Rong either did it or got someone else to but you'll never prove it because there's no evidence."

00:00:00:00:0

OBVIOUSLY, Lex got quite the earful when Fran, Scottie and Butch were discussing the cases at headquarters, and that's a shame.

I wish they'd been more careful about exposing him to detailed information he's encoded like artificial intelligence. But I'm not going to lie. Within reason I don't want to misrepresent a very real danger.

"The fact is, we don't know much and can prove less at the moment," I shoot straight with him. "But two people are violently dead as you know, Lex. NASA was hacked. We had to destroy a rocket that could have taken out a city, and one of our astronauts in space could have been stranded."

"I know," he says simply.

"A lot of bad things have happened," I'm emphatic. "All of us need to be careful. And most of all we have to be sure who we can trust."

"Are you scared?"

"I'm too busy paying attention to what's going on around me. If you're prepared and sufficiently vigilant, you forget to be scared," and I sound like Mom and Carme blended together. "Another important rule in policing and life in general is always know where the heck you are, and I don't at the moment."

Turning on the searchlight, I manipulate it with the joystick, finding the barely visible tarnished metal numbers crookedly attached to the trailer's vinyl siding. Unattractively placed above a window and partially obstructed by a scraggly tree, they glint in a flood of 20-million-candlepower luminescence.

"Looks like the house number is 3-6-3. Although the 6 is so tilted it might be a 9. And we're on Lost Farm Road," I observe out loud for ART's benefit as a large shadow darts over the windshield.

What the hell-o? I think but don't say, checking my mirrors, looking around for the source of what just passed overhead as ART informs me that the address comes back to a civilian previously employed by Langley Air Force Base. Pebo Sweeny, a 79-year-old retired financial technician, and it doesn't seem he has a current address.

Just this one where we're parked, and that's not making sense as I skim the data downloaded in my lenses. It would seem that 4 months ago in early August, he (or someone) had the utilities cancelled, the electricity, phone and TV service. Since then, there's been no activity on his credit cards, no electronic trail, nothing to hint where he is.

The title and deed of the trailer remain in his name, as does the lease for his tandem lots on the edge of the woods. The fee continues to be paid monthly by a cashier's check mailed from his local post office box, and ART must be helping himself to all sorts of electronic records.

Including the sale of a 2011 Dodge van for $6,000 in October, when Pebo Sweeny signed the title over to a used-car retailer. Or someone did, and I have a feeling his identity is but one of many the hitman has stolen.

"I don't know where you live," I announce to Lex, and it's time to take him home.

I'm turning the Tahoe around as ART audibly alerts me in my earpiece that there's a serious problem with the Aerial Internet Ranger, the AIR that's been ghosting me all day.

Ranger Danger! Ranger Danger! flashes red in my lenses, and there must be a malfunction with my flying hotspot PONG.

It drives me crazy that I can't come right out and ask what's wrong. But I'm not about to disclose ART's existence to Lex.

"I live close to the entrance, the first row in," he says, staring wide eyed back at the trailer, way too curious for his own good. "I'll show you. What will you do next? Are you going to search the place tonight? Can I help?"

"You said you first started noticing the bearded guy in the Denali this past summer," I get back to that as I fret about Ranger. "What about Birdman? Do you remember the last time you saw him? And no, you can't help. In case you've forgotten, you're a suspect, not a cop."

"I didn't see him all that often," Lex says. "Maybe back in July. Apparently, he decided it was time for the nursing home, and he rented his trailer to the man who's now dead."

"What about Birdman's exotic pets? And by the way, it's illegal to have a pet owl unless you're a licensed handler. A python is okay."

"I was glad to meet Mr. Owl but I didn't really want to meet the snake. They were turned over to animal rescue."

"And your info came from?"

"The bearded man who moved in. One time when I was riding by on my bike, he was unloading his Denali, carrying boxes inside the house. I asked him what happened to Mr. Owl and the old guy who used to live there."

"And he told you they'd flown the coop."

"You don't believe his story," Lex says.

"Nope."

"You think something happened, don't you?"

"I hope not."

"That's us right there."

He points to the next street coming up, to the small lot with the trailer where he and his grandmother live, gray with a flat rubber roof, and latticework surrounding the foundation. It's not much bigger than what I'd expect to see in a campground, a plywood handicap ramp leading to the front door.

Windows are covered with silver foil gift paper as Fran described, and I can feel the early stages of empathy washing over me. I remind myself that the kindest thing I can do for 10-year-old Lexell Anderson isn't to feel pity but to keep him alive and out of juvenile detention.

"I'm coming inside long enough to meet your grandmother and get the thumb drive Vera gave you," I tell him as we park in front. "And I'd like to see whatever electronic equipment you use."

"You're not going to take my computer, are you?" he asks in alarm.

"Probably not. But it depends. Is there something else I should know about? Anything like the thumb drive that could be a problem, Lex?" as we sit inside my dark SUV, the paper-covered windows blotting out light from inside his house. "Any other games like Helmet Fire that I should be aware of?"

"No, I promise."

"Good," I reply. "Because if I can't trust you, then we're done," and we gather up the boxes and bags of fried chicken.

"Are you going to lock me up?" Lex asks as we climb out of my truck.

"For now, you're going to stay home and behave while I look into a lot of things," I tell him as we shut our doors.

"But what if it's not safe?"

"That's one of the things I'm looking into. And if I think you or your grandmother are unsafe, we'll do something about it," I reply as ART lets me know in my lenses that Ranger isn't responding to commands anymore.

24

LOSS OF CONTROL, flashes in yellow in my lenses.

Oh great, I think dismally. The first time out of the box, and Ranger's already compromised or worse. In terms of bench testing, this hasn't been a banner day, and Lex and I follow a path he must have shoveled, our feet sounding on the handicap ramp that's been sprinkled with rock salt.

Digging in a jacket pocket, he pulls out an old-fashioned brass key attached to part of a rawhide bootlace, "Nonna? It's me," as he unlocks the door.

I feel a wave of cloying heat as I follow him inside a living room of brown carpet and old furniture. A space heater blows loudly near the faux fireplace, the evening news playing.

"I was starting to worry," his grandmother says from her wheelchair in front of the TV, an obsolete one on a stand near a bookcase crammed with old volumes, clothbound and well worn.

"It's nice to meet you . . . ," I start to say as Lex and I set down boxes and bags on the counter.

"Who are you?" she interrupts, her bright-blue eyes fixed on me like lasers, her spun-sugar white hair pinned back, her keenness snapping like sparks. "You're not who picked him up this afternoon. That dark-haired woman who didn't bother coming inside, hauling Lex away like a serial killer."

"I'm Captain Chase, in charge of cyber investigations at NASA," I walk over to shake her hand, and she recoils.

Shying away from me as if I have the plague, she stares wide eyed and unblinking as a drop of blood trickles down from her left nostril. For a panicky instant I think she's had a stroke. But she digs a tissue out of the sleeve of her cardigan, pinching her nostrils together, leaning back her head.

"Holy smoke. Is she okay?" I ask Lex.

"She's having one of her spells," he closes a kitchen cabinet as if what's happening is business as usual. "Nonna? Do you want the shield?" he asks, and she nods, the tissue she's holding spotted bright red.

Turning off the TV, Lex opens a drawer in a mahogany breakfront that might have lived in a finer place once. He finds a silver emergency space blanket, the kind we sell in the Langley exchange. Shaking it open, he wraps it around her, the shiny Mylar making a whispery noise and reflecting lamplight.

"Is there anything I can do?" I ask him. "Do I need to radio for an ambulance?"

"It has to pass," he replies as Nonna pins me with her startling blue stare, holding the bloody tissue to her nose.

"Would you like to take your coat off?" she demands more than asks in a nasal tone.

"I'm not staying very long," and I don't know what to make of her but she's not pushing me around.

Eccentric. Crafty. A force of nature. Or she might be crazy as a bat like Fran said.

"There, I think that's better," taking a deep breath, she holds out the bloody tissue to Lex, who wraps it in a paper towel to throw away. "Not as strong a reaction as I've ever felt," she evaluates, and I have no idea what. "But there's a field I'm picking up."

"She's hypersensitive to electromagnetic energy," Lex explains as if describing the symptoms of something mundane like hay fever or arthritis.

"And what's the cause of this hypersensitivity?" I reply, thinking of my PEEPS, SPIES, my CUFF in addition to everything implanted inside me. "And is that why you have your windows covered?"

"It's the main reason," Lex answers. "But after dark the headlights of cars turning on and off the highway shine right in our windows. Nonna was fine until she was struck by lightning," he adds as if it's a normal thing to say.

Placing a chicken breast on the plate, he prepares dinner for her as she sits in her wheelchair, covered in her silvery mantle.

"Even weak electromagnetic fields, and she's going to be affected," he slices open a biscuit, buttering each half.

"The TV doesn't bother you?" I ask Nonna.

"It's a field I know."

"She goes into a trance for a few seconds," Lex explains. "And her nose bleeds, always the left side. When it's really bad she has a headache and nausea, like being motion sick. She manages okay as long as she has a way to shield herself."

"Are you feeling better?" I ask her.

"I'm going to need to keep this on when you're around," she ominously clutches the space blanket around her as if I'm Typhoid Mary as ART shows me that the disorder Lex describes hasn't been proven scientifically, and I could have guessed as much.

His grandmother isn't the only person to report experiencing electromagnetic sensitivity, but research has yet to support that the condition is real. Most believe it's a manifestation of hysteria or some other disorder. But it's freaking me out a little that Nonna might have sensed my SIN even if she can't identify the signals I'm receiving and sending.

"I don't know what to make of you," she scrutinizes me suspiciously. "I do feel I'm in the presence of something. I know that sounds kooky, and you wouldn't be the first to say it. Kind of like believing in extraterrestrials, God, germs, those things you feel but can't see or explain. Maybe it's just your intensity I'm honing in on, and why are you wearing sunglasses at night?"

"They're not really sunglasses. Just tinted," I reply.

Taking off my PEEPS, I park them on top of my head as I nervously rub my right index finger. And it's probably my imagination that it's tingling more than it was.

"What kind of trouble is my boy in?" Nonna wants to know as Lex brings her dinner.

"That remains to be seen," I reply honestly. "You're aware of the prepaid phone found in his backpack at the rocket launch? What a lot of people call a burner phone?"

"Yes, yes, and it's hogwash," she says as Lex sets her plate on top of a TV tray he moves closer. "He's never had anything like that in his possession, and didn't the other night. I should know. I got him all packed and ready to be picked up."

"Picked up by whom?"

"The teacher who gave him a ride. Lex was so excited I thought he'd pop like a piñata," she says, as I dig his phone out of my pocket, returning it to him.

00:00:00:00:0

I TEXT FRAN the address on Lost Farm Road, warning her that it's as dark as pitch in the mobile home park, and I'm uncertain what we're walking into.

Dress accordingly, I add our euphemistic code for gearing up. Specifically, I'm talking about body armor, and tactical boots, gloves and helmets. I want gas masks, large flashlights, and our Heckler & Koch MP5 submachine guns.

Do we want HPD BU? she writes back, and I reply, no.

We don't want the Hampton Police Division or any other backup at this time.

I tell Fran to meet me in 15 minutes as Nonna dips her fork into a mound of mashed potatoes and gravy. She dips a butter-drenched crust of biscuit into a puddle of honey, stabbing a chunk of fried chicken into a dollop of hot sauce.

It's almost more than I can bear, and I resent having a real problem, a worse one than before, my cravings off the charts. After what I ate on the way here, I shouldn't be hungry. But I'm ravenous, and I fully intend to confront Dick about this particular manufacturing error. My SIN should remove temptations instead of making them stronger, and if I were a vehicle, I'd demand a recall.

"I'm sorry you didn't know me before," Nonna volunteers as if I asked a question. "I'm 75 years old, and until 18 months ago could do anything. Far more than a lot of people decades younger."

She says she could have kept up with me, and I seem in reasonably good shape. I'm probably the type who works hard at it, watching calories, exercising.

"While I barely had to try to be lean and mean, fit as a fiddle," she says. "Any-hoodles, nothing like a lightning strike to change your destiny in the blink of an eye."

"What lightning strike are you referring to?" I act like I know nothing about it while ignoring her insinuations about my appearance.

"Well, I don't think they're given names like hurricanes," she shakes open a napkin. "June before last I was outside with the hose, washing a MINI Cooper we don't have anymore. It was about to storm, and next thing you know, I'm on the ground. They said it was a seizure."

"It wasn't," Lex is back in the kitchen, getting out baggies and aluminum foil. "I was riding home on my bike when I heard the thunder crack. She had a nosebleed like she still gets, and this weird fernlike burn pattern called arborescence on her back. Also, the silver-plated steel necklace she had on burned her and became mildly magnetic. So that's not a seizure."

"It doesn't sound like it," I have to agree.

"An act of God, not some medical misfortune. But either way this is what I'm left with," Nonna says as she eats. "Barely mobile enough to drag myself in and out of bed. And there are other side effects."

At times she has an overwhelming awareness that she's living in virtual reality. Now and then while sleeping, she feels she's moving in and out of multiple dimensions. And on occasion she has flashbacks of being adjusted and tampered with by beings from another planet.

"As part of their ongoing experimentation with what they created down here," Nonna adds. "And heaven knows what a mess they've made when they didn't mean to, as you might expect. But the end result is I can't walk anymore."

She cuts off bites of chicken, dipping them in honey and hot sauce, eating as if she's never in a hurry.

"And I don't like anybody touching me," she adds. "I don't care who it is. I got zapped and woke up not wanting any physical contact with anything or anyone."

"Not even a dog or a cat. Or me either," Lex chimes in, wrapping up leftovers.

"He understands," she cuts her eyes at him, nodding. "My boy knows what he lives with, and I know that's hard. He lost adoring parents, then ends up with his boring Nonna who turns into a prickly pear wrapped in a space blanket. But we get along fine. Or we were until he got accused of a crime."

"I'm going to need that thumb drive," I remind him. "Then I've got to get going," and I give Nonna my card, telling her to call me anytime.

Placing neatly wrapped packages of leftovers inside the refrigerator, Lex wipes the counter with a sponge. He dries his hands on a dish towel, draping it over the edge of the counter to dry.

"We'll be back in a minute," he lets his grandmother know, her living quarters at one end of the trailer, his at the other.

I follow him past his tiny bathroom with its plastic fixtures, into his cramped bedroom with its twin bed covered by a colorful space-themed blanket. The desk is just big enough to fit his laptop, a printer, the wireless router. His bicycle leans against the dresser, and on top is a photo of him when he was much younger, at an observatory with a smiling couple, his parents I'm sure, both of them redheads.

He's made his bleak surroundings cozier and more attractive, covering the gift-paper-shrouded window and vinyl wall paneling with art printed on copying paper. The dozens of mathematically inspired works he no doubt found on the internet, da Vinci, Escher and Dürer etchings, and Pacioli woodcuts, in addition to posters he's been given at NASA.

"It's in here," Lex opens the door to a shallow closet, standing on his tiptoes, reaching for a shoebox on the shelf. "May not look like the safest place," he removes the lid. "But I didn't think it mattered as much as it does. And there's really no good place to hide things around here."

He hands over the thumb drive, and I zip it up inside a jacket pocket, asking again about the game he calls Helmet Fire.

"I'm going to need to see it," I tell him as Fran texts that she's in her car, headed in this direction, a little earlier than I told her, and that's typical as impatient as she is.

"There's a copy on the thumb drive," Lex replies, and I look him in the eye, reminding him I've got to go in a minute. "And don't you wander back to where we just were. Don't show up to check out what we're doing, you hear me?" sounding like Mom again.

"Why can't you take me with you?" he says, not wanting me to go, I can tell. "I know how to be helpful."

"Thank you but no."

"I promise not to get in the way."

"It's not happening," I walk toward the doorway. "You're to stay home tucked in safe and sound with your grandmother. That's how you can be most helpful."

"Wait!" he demands, his eyes flashing. "You can't just leave like that," his cheeks are turning red, his lower lip trembling. "I don't have a way to get hold of you. What's going to happen? Who do I talk to? I don't know what I'm supposed to do," he says, reminding me of how I felt earlier when Dick left me alone with ART at Dodd Hall.

"You're going to be all right, Lex. I'm giving you my cell number," I recite it to him. "You can call or text."

If anything unusual happens, I want to know right away, I let him know as we return to the living room. Nonna has wheeled herself into the bathroom, and the door is shut, water running in the sink.

"Tell your grandmother I said good night," I add, and I probably shouldn't hug him but I do. "You know where to find me, Lex, even if you're just uneasy and want to talk. If for some reason you can't get me, you can call the emergency number. Or if all else fails, you call Deputy Chief Lacey."

"She's not all that nice."

"She'll take care of you, I promise," I reply. "You behave, you hear? Remember I've got eyes on you," pointing at his eyes and mine, and suddenly the car alarm goes off in my Tahoe as the engine roars to life.

"That's weird," and out the door I go.

My boots make a gritty sound as I walk down the makeshift wheelchair ramp, and I tell ART to turn off the car alarm and unstick the accelerator, and he does.

"What caused that?" I ask.

"An off-nominal command."

"In other words, a bug in the software," I reply, lifting my right hand in the dark, giving my digital signal to unlock the doors as the air stirs overhead like a frantic gust of wind.

Then it happens again, and looking around, I see nothing out of the ordinary, just quiet cars parked in front of snowy lots. Windows are lit up in the surrounding homes, and headlights move on the highway. The few small trees along Lex's street rustle gently, the temperature well above freezing, and climbing into my SUV, I feel sad, a little tired and empty as I reach for my backpack.

Taking my PEEPS off the top of my head, I place them inside their plastic case. ART turns on all the displays, my cockpit lit up like Times Square, in audiovisual mode again now that we no longer have company.

25

"AN UPDATE on Ranger, please?" I ask.

"L-O-C. No longer transmitting data," ART says.

His soothing androgynous voice through the Tahoe's speakers is music to my ears even if his news is bad, and I realize I've missed talking to him out loud these past few hours.

"We can't control our prototyped Aerial Internet Ranger, and he's not talking to us," I summarize. "Well it doesn't get much worse than that," I decide, driving off. "Do we have a location?"

"The transponder beacon has been picked up intermittently and erratically, suggesting the device is damaged. Possibly crashed," ART says.

"But we should be able to lock in on the coordinates for where it is in real time."

"The data is inconsistent," he repeats. "The device is moving erratically."

"It's moving?" I puzzle. "At what speeds and altitudes?"

"The altimeter and speed sensors aren't functioning."

"Possibly, Ranger's down somewhere, crashed, smashed up, being blown around," I think out loud, and the idea is somewhat nauseating.

"I have no further data," ART informs me.

"Then let's talk about Lex Anderson for a moment," I head back in the direction of the dead assassin's trailer. "I don't know if you're good at character assessment. Likely it requires an emotional capacity and perception you don't have, not that I really know for sure since I didn't do your programming. But teaching empathy to artificial intelligence hasn't been all that successful."

"I don't understand your question."

"So far today you've basically downloaded the same data I have," I do my best to explain what I doubt he'll comprehend. "That's inevitable since you're part of my SIN, both of us controlled by a quantum computer. A copy of which has been built on a chip that's missing, by the way."

Silence.

"And that should make you nervous."

Not a peep.

"More to the point, and whether I like it or not?" as I drive through what's essentially a slum as dark as Hades. "Whatever I go through, so do you even if you're offline, asleep, not paying attention or have no emotions."

"I don't understand your question," he repeats.

"I'm asking your opinion, ART. What's your analysis of Lex Anderson based on the data? How do you profile him? What do you perceive or feel? Not that you're capable of either, and I'm not trying to insult you."

"I'm programmed to perceive and feel."

"Exactly my point. *You're programmed.* And if what you do and say is programmed, it's not genuine," I hate to inform him.

"I don't understand what you mean by 'genuine.'"

"For example, if you give someone a second chance because you have empathy, that's not the same thing as doing it when you don't."

"If the end result is the same, there's no difference."

"Not true if you don't really feel it," I add what sounds rather specious, petty and surprisingly illogical.

"It's not possible to determine where programming ends and emotional states you call feelings begin," and what ART means is there's no mathematical way to prove what's mimicked or performed as opposed to felt.

The formula is further complicated by variables for those who feel but can't show it (Dad), or won't show it if it's not for the best (Mom). Then there are others who don't feel or show emotions but are talented, intriguing, and at times pleasant company (Dick and Carme possibly, and for sure ART when he hasn't caught a bad mood).

"As best you're able to think intuitively, what was your impression of Lex?" I return my virtual partner to the subject of our debate.

"He's statistically high risk for making poor decisions that include committing criminal offenses," ART answers, and it's not my imagination that he sounds judgmental. "If you factor into the equation his young age, family situation, pressures, overriding influences and add them to previous improper behaviors, what you get is a score of . . ."

"I don't care about a score," I interrupt impatiently, spotting Fran's SUV several blocks ahead, parked in front of the trailer, headlights shining on it. "He's a kid. He's not a math problem, an algorithm or midterm exam."

"Statistically, he's categorized as a threat," ART says with an edge.

"It depends on which variables are included, and those that aren't," I argue less combatively to avoid another cold war. "You tend to find the answer you're looking for, in other words. And almost always that leads to bias. Unfairness. Prejudice. Hatefulness and all that goes with it," I add more pleasantly, and we've reached the hitman's presumed trailer, Fran's Tahoe out front.

"My assessment is that the potential for damage Lexell Anderson could cause is critical," ART replies as if he didn't listen to a word I said, reminding me of Dick.

"No more audio for now," I decide, and ART texts copy as I open my door.

"Already I'm not liking the looks of this," Fran says as we emerge from our almost matching Tahoes, and she opens the tailgate of hers.

Retrieving what I requested, she hands me my tactical helmet and vest, and I put them on. Then I pick up my H&K MP5 submachine gun with its rail-mounted flashlight that I detach for now, not wishing to point a weapon at everything I'm illuminating. I loop the sling around my neck, the carbine heavy against my bulletproofed chest.

Next are the full-face gas masks, and I suggest we leave them where they are for the moment. We'll need them later but not now.

"You know, you're freaking me out," Fran says as we pull on tactical gloves. "You don't think it's overkill us barging in like SWAT?"

"Better safe than sorry," I reply because she has no clue that the dead guy in the Denali was Neva Rong's personal assassin, and that if it hadn't been for Carme, I wouldn't be here anymore.

If Fran knew any of this, we wouldn't be breaking into the trailer alone, and for me that's nonnegotiable. I fully intend to search the place before anybody else does. She turns off her SUV's headlights, the engine, locking up.

"What do we know about the Jeep Cherokee with the damaged front bumper?" I ask her.

"No luck so far. It hasn't been sighted," she says, and what that tells me is the driver with the Asian accent knew darn well who was behind her.

"I have a bad feeling about the woman in it and anyone she's associated with."

"I've got cars out looking."

"Let me get my tools," I tell her as ART texts me a reminder about where to find them.

Fran fires up a cigarette, both of us backlit by my Chase Car's headlights, the engine still running. Inside the cargo area, I open the side-mounted toolbox, picking out what the job requires, including large evidence bags in case there's something inside the trailer I need to take with me.

00:00:00:00:0

"HERE, maybe you can hold this for me," I give Fran a pry bar while I hang on to bolt cutters, and tuck a flat-blade screwdriver, the evidence bags into pockets of my cargo pants.

"How are you doing anyway?" she looks me over as she smokes.

"I'll be better when I know what's inside this mother," I don't want to talk about myself.

"Well, you vanished for the better part of a week," she says. "And the few times we talked on the phone or texted, you weren't nice and wouldn't tell me crap. Like you didn't know me," and it must have been Carme who did that.

While I was restrained in bed and anesthetized, I wasn't contacting anyone. It doesn't please me to know that my sister doesn't seem to care if she reflects poorly on me while taking my place. She's been cold to a lonely 10-year-old, flirty with Davy Crockett, and ungracious with Fran.

"Since the cyberattack, you can imagine how stressful it's been," I find myself covering for Carme's behavior yet again. "It wasn't my intention to be unfriendly."

I shoulder my backpack as ART kills the engine, and the headlights go out, casting us into total blackness. Flashlights on, we set the fire selectors of our MP5s on three bursts instead of two, adding an extra round for good measure. Fran takes a last puff of her cigarette, drops it in the snow, stepping on it.

"Let's do this. A high recon first, circling the perimeter," I tell her, and we start walking, gun barrels pointed in safe directions, our black-gloved fingers above the trigger guards.

We're ready for trouble that I don't expect, knowing the hitman is dead, everything quiet at the moment, no urgent news updates in my earpiece or SPIES. I'm not getting any alerts that Carme may have a problem. Or Dick does. Or that either of them is up to something I should be concerned about, not that I'm told everything.

There's nothing in the headlines about Neva Rong although ART informs me that after her chartered helicopter picked her up at the OCME, it flew her to Dulles airport outside Washington, DC. Meanwhile, a private jet owned by Pandora took off from Norfolk with no passengers aboard, and I suspect the plan was for Vera's body to be in the baggage compartment, headed somewhere to be further picked apart.

As for what's going on at home, the most recent message from Mom indicates Dad got in a little while ago. She can't wait to see me, is fixing a celebratory dinner *for our reunion*, as if she wasn't seeing me the entire time I was held hostage at Dodd Hall when in fact she was one of my wardens.

A vat of her chili is simmering on the stove, she teases me, also coleslaw with honey and celery seeds, her homemade sourdough bread, and I feel starved as I'm reminded of Lex. Maybe I can take him a care package tomorrow, it wouldn't be any trouble, and Mom always cooks enough to feed an army.

He texted me a moment ago to say thanks for the fried chicken, that Nonna has gotten over her *energy disturbance* and gone to bed. All is quiet on the western front, in other words. But if I've learned nothing else, it's never to rest on your laurels or get too comfortable. About the time you do, you lose an engine in your aircraft, someone pulls out a gun or steals your invention.

"What we do now is look around, get the lay of the land," I explain to Fran, our lights shining on snow that's marred only by animal tracks. "Watch where we step and look for anything off-nominal."

Including booby traps such as improvised explosive devices and pressure cooker bombs, anything the dirtbag might have rigged up to keep people like us away, I think but don't say. My sensors aren't picking up on explosives or warning transmissions that might indicate something deadly underfoot, and ART is updating the features-integrated map in my smart contact lenses, helping me make sure where we're stepping.

He alerts me in my earpiece of another wireless device, this one on the west side of the trailer, attached to the siding at the roofline. I've counted 4 of the battery-powered cameras so far, and continue to wonder if anyone besides the hitman might have the ability to monitor them.

"Whoever he was, he was watching his property," I point up at the camera as Fran and I walk past. "All the more reason to suspect he was doing illegal stuff inside," not letting on that I know it for a fact.

"You don't have your fish finder out like you usually do," she observes, her uneasy eyes everywhere as we head toward the woods. "You're not carrying one of those antennas and turning around in little circles like you're doing some kind of weird war dance."

"The data is now downloaded directly to an app on my phone," I tell her the truth sort of.

"Let me guess. Something your sugar daddy gave you while you were holed up for the better part of a week," the green-eyed monster in her is forever threatened by Dick. "Being briefed, debriefed or whatever morning, noon and night, both of you shacked up over there doing your important stuff like it's Camp David. You going to tell me what that was really about?"

"It's about NASA having the worst cyberattack in its history," I give her my origin story exactly as Dick scripted. "And sure, I've got updated software and equipment, the Tahoe for example that I'm beta testing. There's a lot I can tell with improved technologies."

"Including if we should be breaking down the door of this friggin' dump," Fran responds. "Not only do I worry about homemade bombs but he could have a meth lab in there. We could be talking about toxic, volatile chemicals. He could have been another Unabomber for all we know."

Translated, phobic Fran doesn't want us to be the first ones inside the trailer. But that's too bad. She's not the investigator, I am, and at the moment we're not calling anyone. Once that happens, I lose all control of the scene.

"Even as we speak, I'm screening for explosives, drugs," I reassure her, and it's true except my spectrum analyzer can't do what I just said.

The one inside my backpack doesn't scan for terahertz radiation. It's not going to detect fentanyl, methamphetamine, stockpiles of incendiary devices and ammunition, and therefore can't tell us if we're about to be poisoned or blown up. But built into my systemic network and CUFF are ion-mobility spectrometer chips that recognize smokeless gunpowder, distilled petroleum and other dangerous chemicals.

Based on what I'm picking up, the trailer is filthy with all of the above. I'm not surprised considering what was inside his Denali, the weapons, loaded magazines, body-disposal tools, the cement-boot anchors. Fran knows nothing about all that because Carme and possibly others made sure of it.

I'm not worried about guns, ammo, and related chemicals and materials. But what I don't want is to break down the door and set off a bomb, and I've no reason to suspect it. If there's an explosive device rigged up inside, I'm not detecting the expected wireless transmissions or much at all electromagnetically beyond the cameras.

It's as if we're in an energy dead zone as we move around, the powerful beams of our lights slashing and probing. Looking for the utility box, I discover it behind overgrown shrubs, and I show Fran that the meter isn't spinning. Not that I thought it would be after what ART said earlier about Pebo Sweeny's power being shut off in August.

"It appears he was living without electricity," Fran says. "Explaining the gas-powered generator that looks new, a hefty one, 7,500 watts," she shines her light on it, then on the huge metal cage beneath the canopy of dense trees. "What the hell was someone keeping back here?"

26

THE CAGE DOOR is held open with a bungee cord, the roost inside made of thick tree branches, and my light catches the rims of metal dog dishes peeking out of the snow. A scratching post made of thick layers of carpet around a steel pole has been ripped and shredded as if a lion, tiger or bear got hold of it.

"Someone who used to live here may have had exotic pets," I'm not inclined to tell Fran any more than that.

As phobic as she is of birds, spiders, snakes, the list is long. In fact, there's more she's afraid of than not since Christmas Eve three years ago when she was robbed at gunpoint while Easton was with her.

"I'm going to take a look in here," I let her know, headed toward the galvanized metal shed.

It's the kind you buy at the hardware store, a wireless camera mounted on top of it, and wrapped around the handles of the double doors is a thick chain with a padlock that is no match for my bolt cutters. They cut through the steel links like butter, and the noise is startling as I pull the chain free, clinking it on the ground. Nudging the doors open with my gun barrel, I paint light over 10 bright-red two-gallon gas cans.

Each is full. Gas for the generator, I announce as ART alerts me in my earpiece that a new signal has popped up in the noise floor. It's transmitting weakly in the 2 to 4 gigahertz range, and then something rushes by in the dark.

"What in God's name . . . ?" Fran exclaims when the hooting begins, loud enough to jumpstart my adrenaline and send a chill to the roots of my hair.

WHO-WHO . . . WHO-WHO-WHO . . .

The deep eerie sound is almost human, almost barking, and I flick my light over what might be the biggest great horned owl I've ever seen, perched on the branch of a tall pine tree. He watches us with full moon eyes, a taloned foot clutching Ranger the PONG captive by its gripper.

WHO-WHO-WHO . . . he unnaturally swivels his head around like in *The Exorcist*.

I can see that the volleyball-size orb's conductive skin has been shredded, and it's no longer in GHOST or any other mode. The nanotube composite PONG has gone opaque like a softshell crab, cloudy like a dying fish, and I know the caged propellers are no longer spinning even though I can't see them from here.

Ranger is wounded but not dead, and it's a loss of signal nobody anticipated. My thoughts race as I try to figure out what I might do to stop the owl from flying off with him. I walk closer, the raptor's feathery horns perked up as he stares down at me, unblinking, clutching the vanquished flying orb like a decapitated head.

"Be careful!" Fran hisses behind my back as I calmly make my way to the pine tree beyond the cage. "Don't get any closer! You don't want him dive-bombing us!" and I wish she'd shut up. "Didn't you see *The Birds*?"

"Hello, Mr. Owl," I gently, sweetly call up to him, feeling a bit foolish but willing to try anything. "You've got something important of mine, and I'd be very grateful if you'd return it," holding up my left arm, I make little raspy pishing sounds like I've seen bird handlers do on YouTube and in the movies.

I'm more afraid of him complying than not, and sure enough he spreads his powerful wings, parachuting down, gripping Ranger in one foot, and landing on my arm with the other. I feel the sharpness of his talons through my clothing, and he's at least 60 centimeters (2 feet) tall and probably weighs about 1.8 kilograms (4 pounds).

"Okay, well hello there," pishing softly again as I gently tug at the PONG. "Let me have it, please, there we go . . ."

The owl releases his grip, hoot-hooting as he lifts off with mighty flaps, swooping away into thick darkness.

"Holy crap! I didn't know you were the owl whisperer," Fran says, shaking her head as if she just witnessed a miracle. "Where did the PONG come from?" and she's seen her share of them buzzing around the farm and inside the barn. "Was that thing following us or something?"

"It's what I sent into the tunnels to track Lex," I tell her.

"Judas Priest. I have no flippin' idea what's going on anymore," only she doesn't say *flippin'*.

"Let's head back to the cars so I can lock up Ranger in case Mr. Owl decides to come back for more," I've got the wounded PONG snugly held in the crook of my arm. "We also need to grab the gas masks. We're definitely going to want those on when we're searching inside."

We make our way through snow and slush, loaded down with tools, weapons and gear. Reaching the Tahoe, I lock Ranger inside as Fran retrieves our gas masks.

"This is why they pay us the big bucks," I shine my light on the next target, the black trellis garbage can enclosure. "Time to go through the trash. One more thing you love almost as much as tunnels, heights, confined spaces, predatory birds . . ."

"Very funny. And insensitive," she says huffily. "Maybe you don't know what it's like to be controlled by things you can't do a bloody thing about."

"You might be surprised what I understand," I reply, brushing snow off the top of the supercan.

I open it and get a snootful of a putrid stench before my light finds the cause of it.

"Shhhhh . . . !" I slam down the lid, about to gag, and I don't like snakes any better than Fran does. "You don't want to look."

"Oh God! What now?" startled, she almost falls on her butt, which wouldn't be a good thing to do while holding a machine gun.

"I know how you are around dead stuff," I explain, and she doesn't need to experience the rotting headless python that's at least as long as I'm tall. "I guess we know what happened to Birdman's pet snake."

"God no! Crap! What if there are more of them inside? Who the hell is Birdman?"

"Well if there are reptiles of any description inside, they're not moving around much as cold as it's going to be," I reply. "Because no power, and the heat's not on. Anything cold blooded would be pretty lethargic."

"Gross! You're not making me feel any better!"

"The man who used to live here, a.k.a. Birdman, had a python," I explain, as Fran and I make our way to the front porch. "And let's just say it appears to have been euthanized rather inhumanely possibly weeks or months ago. There's nothing else in the garbage can, and that's significant," I add as we carefully climb up snowy steps to the front door.

"Meaning the guy in the Denali moved in last August, and since then has been disposing of his trash himself, hauling it somewhere," Fran decides. "Which is what you do if you want to make sure nobody goes through it."

I shine my light on the front door with its dead bolt lock, then up at the wireless white metal camera, probably the only thing on the property that's powered and running. I've counted

6 so far, all of them tracking us, their LEDs lighting up when our motion is detected.

00:00:00:00:0

THE HITMAN isn't monitoring what we're doing but that doesn't mean someone else isn't.

"We're being filmed for sure," I tell Fran. "But the question is whether anybody's watching," and as I say it, I'm hoping ART has the information I want.

But nothing appears in my SPIES that tells me much. The trailer's wireless network is locked as I'd expect. It's called KMA, which could be the dead assassin's initials. Or maybe it's an acronym for Kiss My Ass, and that would fit with what I think of the man who tried to kill me.

He must have a mobile router somewhere that runs on batteries the same as the outdoor cameras, and at the moment the only devices connected to his network would appear to be those. That would suggest he doesn't have additional cameras inside the house or I'd pick up the electronic signal, I explain as ART does what he's so good at and hacks.

Suddenly I'm watching Fran and me in my SPIES, our faces looming large as we stare up at the camera over the front porch. He's letting me see what someone else could. But if we're being surveilled remotely, then he should be able to detect that another device is logged into the cameras.

If he does, then he's not telling me, and I can't outright ask without Fran wondering who the hell-o I'm talking to. Rapping the door with my gloved knuckles, I'm disappointed to discover that it's solid wood, the brass lock shiny like new.

"Police!" I yell. "Anybody in there?" I bang harder.

Silence.

"It's pretty obvious nobody's here," Fran says, and she'd prefer not to be either. "I think we should call Hampton PD . . ."

"Nope," and I decide to go after the hinges first.

Working on them with the screwdriver, I remove them in short order. Taking the pry bar from Fran, I splinter the door out of its frame, hoping like crazy we don't set off anything. Gas masks on, face shields down, helmet chin straps fastened, and it's time to remount our flashlights on the rails of the submachine guns.

Covered from head to toe in black, only our eyes showing, we're armed to the teeth, ready for a raid or a riot, and I go first. Stepping through the opening, the ruined door overboard in the snow, I point my lighted weapon wherever I turn, clearing the landfill of the trailer from one end to the other. Searching for anything living or dead, I make quick checks of every nook and cranny without stopping to examine and explore.

"All clear," I shout, pointing the barrel down, returning to the living room where Fran is cussing up a storm.

"Dammit! Oh crap," she complains through the voicemitter covering her foul mouth like a hockey puck. "It's as dark as a freakin' cave in here," as we shine our lights around the den of a monster.

Folding tables are arranged with tools including the same macabre ones I discovered inside the Denali. Also, there are the makings for cement-boot anchors, and all the right stuff for reloading your own organ-shearing, armor-piercing ammo. The hitman's assortment of pistols, carbines, machine guns and other deadly weapons brings to mind what he intended to shoot me with.

And I wonder what became of the full-auto assault rifle equipped with a grenade launcher. Who has it now? Carme or Dick? And has anything been learned from it? Why does nobody fill me in on anything I really need to know? I'd never heard of a Chinese QBZ-95 before Carme told me what I was holding, and it doesn't make me happy that my DNA's all over it.

How did something like that end up in the United States? It wouldn't be simple to sneak it across the border. Probably the best way was the good old-fashioned postal service, I suppose. The hitman must have places he was using for his mail drops and packages. I doubt he frequents gun stores or shows, any place where he might become familiar.

As I'm thinking all this, Fran shines her light on something big and boxy covered by a braided rug. I make my way over to her in a hurry, shouting not to disturb anything because I don't need her going into a full-blown panic attack.

"I have a feeling I know what this is," I unpleasantly recall what was inside the supercan. "I doubt there's anything in it to worry about but . . ."

"Oh crap!" as it dawns on her. "It's not some kind of snake tank, is it?" she backs off as fast as she can while I remove the rug.

The python's former home has been converted into storage space, and there's no sign of the erstwhile exotic pet, not so much as a trace of mulch. The big glass aquarium is crowded with primers, bottles of smokeless gunpowder and metal cans of military-grade solvents, degreasers, lubricants, acetones.

Everything is tightly sealed, nothing off-gassing abnormally, and the air is safe enough to breathe, my sensors are telling me. We're not about to be poisoned or blown up it seems, and boy howdy it would make me happy to take off some of this gear. I have a hotspot on the top of my head, and my face shield keeps fogging up. It takes way too much effort to talk, the sound of my own breathing distracting and loud.

"Are you sure it's too cold for snakes?" Fran's muffled voice, the intense beam of her light probing wherever her weapon points. "What about rats?"

"Rats and mice are a possibility if they can burrow into something," I reply. "Especially if it was warmer in the recent past."

I shine my light on an indoor propane heater near a makeshift workbench scattered with tools, alligator clips, sections of PVC pipe, batteries, rolls of electrical wire, buckets of nails and ball bearings.

"Why couldn't a freakin' snake do the same thing as a freakin' mouse? And do it even better since it's not freakin' warm blooded!" Fran is swearing like a sailor. "So, what you're saying is there could be snakes in the furniture. In anything, let's be honest!"

"I seriously doubt it. But you know what they say, expect the unexpected. We're okay to take these off. And how about disconnecting your light from your rifle before you shoot something you don't mean to. Like me," I remove my gas mask, my helmet, clipping them to D rings on my gun belt, and what a relief.

Fran does likewise, far more worried about reptiles and rodents than any bomb, gun, chemical or physical discomfort. She detaches the flashlight from her MP5, the high-intensity beam stabbing and slashing everywhere, especially down low, and under and between things. And in cramped cozy places.

Awkward in all her gear, she picks her way to the couch that's been shoved up against a wall. She's careful approaching cushions and hidden places where danger might coil, poking and prodding grocery bags of food and other provisions that I suspect came from a food pantry, perhaps the one at the Baptist church that Lex mentioned.

Using her gun barrel, Fran flicks filthy towels off the nearby reclining chair, and uncovers a pile of mail she starts going through. We may know who Birdman is, she declares.

"Does the name Pebo Sweeny ring a bell?" she asks.

"I don't know him," and for the most part that's true.

"Well, I've never heard of him," Fran replies. "Not that I would necessarily. At least we know who used to live here. That's a start."

She digs out more envelopes, different sizes, some with cellophane windows, a lot of what she sifts through junk mail and circulars. Some of it has been opened, most of it not.

"Apparently, he worked at the Air Force base, must be older because he's retired based on what I'm seeing," Fran informs me.

His date of birth indicates he's almost 80, and she's finding a lot of the mail relates to his benefits.

"Medicare, notices about missed appointments," she says. "The dentist. A proctologist. Plus, notifications about events coming up on the Air Force base that he might want to attend. The most recent postmark I'm finding so far is December 3rd, this past Tuesday," she adds, and it fits with the timing.

The hitman picked up the mail that day, probably doing it routinely so the PO box didn't fill up, raising questions and drawing attention. Not long after that, he was dead inside his stolen silver Denali, out of gas and out of luck in a deserted parking lot.

"So, Pebo Sweeny's mail delivery wasn't stopped, and was being picked up until just a few days ago," Fran adds. "I'm betting that includes checks, and I'm not seeing any."

27

WITHOUT POWER, the appliances inside the kitchen couldn't be used unless the hitman cranked up the generator.

But as much gas as it probably burns in an hour, I suspect he saved it for more important electronics such as the tablet I saw inside his truck. Or he'd wait until he wanted to watch TV, charge his burner phones, maybe turn on the electric heat for brief durations when the temperature dipped below freezing as it did earlier in the week.

Nothing I'm seeing gives me the impression he cooked or did much in the way of preparing meals. My light paints over a countertop disgusting with stains and crumbs, a plastic double sink caked with dried detritus, dust bunnies and dead bugs on the faux bamboo flooring.

In a corner is a pile of glass shelving from the powered-off refrigerator-freezer, and opening the doors, I discover cases of ammunition, range bags full of loaded magazines, another Mossberg 12-gauge pump-action shotgun like the one that was in the hitman's truck. I try the handles of the faucet next. Nothing. Not even a drip.

The water has been turned off. Or more likely, the pipes froze during the nor'easter because the heat wasn't on, and Pebo Sweeny's murderous squatter wasn't around to do anything about it, thanks to Carme. Opening a door, I discover a broom, dustpan, a mop in a bucket, a vacuum cleaner, and three big black plastic trash bags that are full.

Dragging them out, I slash them open with my tactical knife, kicking them over to see what's inside. I shine my light over paperwork, receipts, all sorts of miscellany that I suspect came from Sweeny's files or desk drawers. Commingled with this are dirty paper towels and plates, and a lot of cans and jars.

I push around fast-food wrappers, containers, bags, and caffeine-infused energy drinks, Vienna sausages, tuna fish, sardines, beef jerky, SpaghettiOs and Chinese noodles. Most of what I'm looking at could have come from a charitable pantry and local drive-through restaurants.

In fact, all but the fast food could be ordered over the internet, dropped off wherever the hitman decided, and no one was the wiser. It wasn't necessary for him to visit many stores, and not the same ones frequently. Much of what he ate was either take-out food or it didn't need to be cooked or even warmed.

But there's a two-burner propane stove top with a kettle on it, and teabags, packets of honey and instant soup. He had plastic spoons, big Styrofoam cups, and it may be that hot beverages were as much as he was going to bother fixing for himself. Had he cared, there's cookware in cabinets and drawers, also dishes and silverware he wasn't interested in, and a lot of spices he didn't use.

Under the sink are more cleaning supplies he didn't touch, and based on what I'm seeing so far, the hitman didn't stay here all the time. I seriously doubt he planned on hanging around indefinitely, was in this area temporarily because that's what Neva wanted.

There's no question he would have monitored the trailer from a distance should anybody decide to show up uninvited. I suspect this was his temporary office and workshop where he dreamed up and fabricated his monstrous acts. I'm betting there's some other place he's been staying, and I mention this to Fran.

"A place not too far away in case his cameras picked up something he didn't like, and he wanted to get here in a hurry," I add, returning to the living room where she's taken off a glove, and is unlocking her phone. "And he might have a boat somewhere."

"It's going to be hard to look if we don't know what name he might have been using," she scrolls through her contact list. "You finding anything that might tell us why he'd kill himself? And since when do serial killers and hitmen off themselves?"

"I can't imagine how many aliases someone like this might have," I reply. "One thing's for sure, he's got a big enough arsenal to take out the entire neighborhood. Maybe more than that."

"God only knows what he planned to do next. Or what else might already be set in motion. Time to bring in the troops," Fran has the number queued up on her cell phone.

She hits send, and we listen to the ringing over speakerphone, waiting in our cumbersome gear, standing in the dark horror of the trailer's living room. Cold air blows through the opening where the front door used to be, our flashlights and gun barrels pointed down so we don't blind or shoot each other.

"I know it's Sunday night," Fran says right off when a familiar male voice finally answers. "I'm sorry to bother you, Al," and she's talking to her counterpart at the Hampton Police Division, Major Alvin Pepper.

"I'm actually in the office catching up on paperwork," he sounds tired and harried. "That's how I'm spending my Sunday night. What's up?"

"We've got a situation in the mobile home park near NASA . . ."

As I leave the living room, I overhear Fran request the crime scene unit, the bomb squad, battery-powered auxiliary lights and possibly hazmat.

"Maybe animal control too," she says, "because there's this huge mother of an owl loose that captured a drone . . ."

She gives him the sound bites of what's going on as I follow the hyphen of a hallway, checking out the only bathroom, and it's beyond disgusting. The toilet is stained muddy brown, no water in it, the plastic sink scummy, the linoleum floor filthy. Rolls of toilet paper are in a plastic bucket, the trash overflowing, and I push back the shower curtain.

It scrapes loudly along the rod, and not many bathtubs have butcher tools in them. A meat cleaver, a meat saw, a boning knife and the type of cut-resistant gloves that I've seen in the morgue, all of it is clean, the stainless steel blades spotted from their last rinsing. My light paints over heavy-duty trash bags, folded black plastic tarps, duct tape, a big sponge, a jug of an industrial cleaner and degreaser.

It's obvious what they're for, and I feel an angry sadness settle over me as I turn my attention to the chipped Formica-topped vanity. Opening drawers, I illuminate personal belongings that shouldn't be any of my business, hemorrhoid and anti-itch creams, stool softeners and laxatives, ankle and wrist braces, and all kinds of over-the-counter pain remedies.

Prescription bottles in the cabinet over the sink include Sectral, Ativan, Celexa, all refilled not long before Pebo Sweeny disappeared. As I look at the labels with his name on them, I'm seeing data about the medications in my lenses. It would seem he had high blood pressure, problems sleeping, possibly anxiety and depression.

At the end of the hallway I open a door, and he might have done his laundry not long before he vanished. Khaki pants, boxer shorts, and dark socks are still in the compact washer-dryer that can't be run without electrical power. To the left is the bedroom, and the first place I check is the closet, my sensors detecting naphthalene before I get a whiff of mothballs as I open the door.

00:00:00:00:0

MY GLOVED FINGERS walk through old suits, shirts, ties, a winter coat hanging on a rod. Some of them have laundry labels sewn inside with Pebo Sweeny's name on them, and I'm getting the impression he was small of stature and slender.

I don't see clothing or other personal effects that might tell me anything about the hitman, but there's plenty of evidence to show what he was up to. The desk is cluttered with paper, a ruler, scissors, Magic Markers, and a stack of prepaid phone cards for his burners.

The wall on either side of the flat-screen TV is covered with corkboard. Pinned to it are skillful drawings, maps, photographs, elaborately detailed directions, and a cursory review is all it takes for me to know what I'm looking at. A home invasion. One that would end in flames.

And I can't let Fran see this. But I can't prevent it as I hear her footsteps, and then she's walking in.

"Backup is on the way . . . ," she stops midsentence when she sees what I'm looking at. "Good God . . . What the . . . ?" stepping closer, stunned.

"I'm sorry you had to find out like this. That either of us did . . ."

"Is that . . . ?"

"Afraid so. I know it's hard to take . . ."

Shocked, she stammers, "But why . . . ?"

"I can't tell you for sure, and we may never know definitively. But likely it's been in the works for months at least. And my family was the primary target. Or I am," and possibly also Carme but I'm not going to bring her up.

"And what? *My* family's just effing collateral damage?" Fran's fear turns to fury.

"Possibly. This was supposed to go down three days ago. December 5th at 0200 hours as you can see from one of the schematics."

"And it would have been just Easton and me," her flashlight whites out the drawing of her family's small cottage on the other side of the garden from where my parents and I live. "Tommy was out of town, still is . . . Not that it would have mattered," she says about her accountant husband who hasn't been home for a while.

"The gas cans we saw out back in the shed are for more than just the generator," I tell her, and I don't need to spell it out.

Neva's personal fixer planned to torch Chase Place after taking down all of us, probably with one of his machine guns. And Fran looks like she might throw up.

"If he's the dead guy inside the Denali, then he's not hurting anyone again," I reassure her.

"Who else could it be?" she declares.

"It's him," I agree. "And the reason he showed up around here is because of Neva Rong."

"Good luck proving it."

"We never have and probably won't," I reply, and that's how it feels.

She gets away with murder, and has for years.

"But why would he kill himself?" Fran has her back to me, standing rigidly in front of the corkboard, directing her light at everything on it. "Since when do psychopaths commit suicide?"

"They don't usually," and I can't tell her the truth about what really happened at the Point Comfort Inn. "But they're afraid of getting caught. Maybe he had reason to think that might be in the cards," and I sound like quite the profiler as I continue to steer her wrong.

"Based on what I'm seeing in here, he wasn't very worried," she replies angrily. "He doesn't seem like someone who felt anything at all, good God! At 0200 hours this past Thursday," she repeats, incredulous. "All of us would have been home asleep. Except for you," almost accusingly. "You would have been safely tucked away at Dodd Hall."

"But he couldn't have known that when he was making his plan," I reply as a matter of fact. "Even I didn't know I was going to end up there," I point out, and the reality of what might have happened is unthinkable. "That was a last-minute plan because of the cyberattack," I offer more misinformation from my origin story.

Fran doesn't know and never will that I wasn't isolated in Dodd Hall simply because NASA got hacked. There's no reason to think that Neva or her hired killer were tipped off about what was in store. He may have tracked me to the Point Comfort Inn but he didn't know anybody would be waiting behind the ice machine.

He hadn't a clue that my sister was working out of a room there or she couldn't have ambushed him the way she did.

". . . I saw what was in the bathtub right before I walked in here," Fran is saying as I hear car engines outside the trailer.

Blue and red lights throb around the edges of blackout shades, and I hear the thudding of car doors, of footsteps in a hurry.

"And the weapons, the homemade cement anchors," Fran says. "God only knows how many people have vanished without a trace," she's a dark shape in the doorway as boots sound on the porch. "This was someone we didn't stand a chance with!"

"It's best not to dwell on it," I return to the desk with its 4 drawers, shining my light on the top left one, sliding it open, not letting on how surprised I am.

"Well, let me go deal with the Hampton guys," Fran says as she leaves. "Hey!" she calls out to them from the hallway. "There's two of us back here, and the power's turned off! The stuff you're most interested in is in the living room, the kitchen . . . ," she lets them know as I open other drawers, lifting out shooting logs, dozens of them.

The pocket-size notebooks are identical, each with a black cover neatly dated and numbered in white Magic Marker. Some haven't been used, the rest are inside ziplock sandwich bags containing small plastic trinkets I recognize as Cracker Jack toys. Not new ones but from the good ole days when you never knew what fun prize might await inside the box of caramelized peanuts and popcorn.

There are whistles, charms, rings, figurines, games, stickers, mini comic books that bring back memories, most of the journals meriting but one prize. But some baggies contain multiple tiny trophies including the one for the hitman's planned attack on Chase Place. The accompanying log, Number 42, was started in early September when he "made another drive-by" of my family's farm.

". . . It's going to be challenging but not impossible, very important not to rush as these aren't the typical quarry," he writes in the precise penmanship of an engineer. "I believe in this case the key is to create a diversion that causes the targets to leave the residences, thereby eliminating all of them in one sweep," he completely objectifies us. "That way I don't have the headache of dealing with burglar alarms, a screaming kid and all the rest . . ."

He goes on to describe his clever idea "of borrowing the cat, then bringing it back at the appointed time, and letting it loose," he pens. "I could do something to make sure it starts yowling, and lights on, everyone up and out. Welcome home, kitty, kitty! And that's all she wrote. Ha . . . !" He seemed to enjoy his journaling.

Flipping through pages, I find mentions of him visiting our property in the dead of night, watching windows, learning our routines and habits, making certain he carried no "electrical gadgets" that could be detected. He'd leave his truck out of sight not too far away, and when he mentions "making friends with the cat," meaning Fran's orange tabby named Schroeder, I can barely stand it.

The 7 brightly colored vintage prizes the hitman picked for us are figurines of a uniformed policewoman and a cat. A pencil sharpener. A typewriter. An airplane. A rocket and an astronaut. It's not hard to know who Neva Rong's hired gun had in mind for each, and obviously, he'd been gathering intel for a while.

There are 42 shooting logs, one per job, and the 79 Cracker Jack toys indicate how many victims. The entries begin on March 13, 2013, ending on December 4, certain dates shocking in what they imply.

28

I START WITH the most recent completed job. And as disciplined as Neva's hired thug may have been to stay off the radar the way he did, his fatal flaw was he couldn't resist preserving a detailed record.

No doubt it was the best part of his violent fantasies, allowing him to savor and relive his vile accomplishments. It's apparent that he was obsessively careful and meticulous, never in a rush to get the job done "just right." He planned months in advance in some cases, and was quicker on the trigger in other "less intense jobs."

He doesn't identify his victims, their addresses or occupations, and he didn't need to for me to know who he's talking about when I skim his account of the double hit in the Houston area 7 weeks ago. The first victim was Hank Cougars, Number 40, a beer mug charm included with his log. Referred to as an "intoxicated male," he was out of work, lived in a trailer and drove a 2016 silver Denali.

On October 28 at 2 o'clock in the morning, the hitman "picked the trailer's back door lock," he writes. "I was able to use a bobby pin. Stupid people who don't believe in dead bolts!" He then entered undetected to discover his intended victim passed out in bed. "I finished the job with a pillow, butchering the body at the major joints, taping up everything in trash bags" as if it were a deer he'd hunted.

Renting a boat, he weighed down the remains with anchors, dropping his morbid bundles into Trinity Bay. He camped out in the dead man's trailer for the next three nights, and on Halloween he set out in the stolen Denali after his real target and reason for coming to Houston. Pandora aerospace engineer Noah Bishop was inside a bar the hitman doesn't name but I know he's talking about Woody's.

A popular NASA watering hole near Johnson Space Center, the place was hopping with Halloween-related events. A lot of hopeful astronaut candidates were in town for the next round of interviews at Johnson Space Center, including my sister. I'd been there the week before for the same thing because NASA wanted us separated to see how we would do without each other.

The night of October 31, Carme and Noah happened to be at Woody's but not together, and some of this I know from what Dick told me earlier in the week. My sister was in a private room with other astronaut candidates. Noah was at the bar with a female colleague and friend from Pandora's Houston facility.

At almost 10:00 p.m., he, his friend and Carme ended up in the parking lot at the same time. They got into an argument that likely was fueled by alcohol. Soon after, my sister returned to the restaurant while Noah drove his friend home, dropping her off. He didn't go inside the house, and headed in the direction of his Shore Acres neighborhood, the hitman following.

Waiting until they were on a dark, deserted residential street, he sped up and "passed the target's vehicle, dropping 6 tire spikes out the window. What an embarrassment of riches, three flats!" he fairly chortles. "A clean shot to the head, and they might find him and his rental car some day at the bottom of Clear Lake. Or maybe they won't . . . ," he concludes in log Number 41, accompanied by a toy pistol.

Since Halloween night there's been no sign of the Pandora aerospace engineer alive or dead, and that's caused considerable trouble for Carme. Under a cloud of suspicion, she's wanted for questioning at the very least. I don't know why she and Noah Bishop were arguing or if they knew each other. But she's not the one who disappeared him.

Neva's hitman did, eliminating him the same way he had Pebo Sweeny several months earlier on August 7. In his case, it wasn't a job but "an obstruction to progress, and a means to an end," I read in shooting log Number 39, a toy figurine of an owl inside that baggie.

Sweeny is described simply, unimportantly as "an elderly male living alone on a remote property in a trailer park in the Hampton Roads area of Virginia." After the hitman "choked him out and prepared him for disposal," he rented a 21-foot Sailfish motorboat. "Other than being hot, it was a good ride," he says, adding that all went according to plan when he deposited body parts in the Chesapeake Bay.

Next, he cruised around the eastern edge of the peninsula near Plum Tree Island, swinging around into Back River, passing by my family's farm, what he refers to as the "Big Prize."

"I'm going to give you dates and general locations for each," I say to ART as I get ready to pack up the logs and their Cracker Jack treats. "What we're looking for is anything unusual that might have happened. Deaths, injuries, other types of violations and intimidation."

A drowning in Kiln, Mississippi . . . A house fire in Las Vegas . . . two more in Houston . . . A jump from a balcony in Orlando, Florida . . . Accidental falls from heights in New York City and Seattle, Washington . . . A questionable suffocation with a dry-cleaning bag in Ogden, Utah . . . A pipe bomb in Silicon Valley . . . A drive-by shooting in Pasadena, California . . . One in Huntsville, Alabama . . .

ART shows me tragedy after tragedy, almost all of them occurring in locations that are hubs in the aerospace world. I monitor the depressing crawls going by in my smart lenses, realizing not every victim died. There are multiple nonlethal cases of break-ins, vandalism, arson, blasting a shotgun through someone's window, of muggings, maimings, and the implication is obvious.

The hitman was a thug, a goon, and killing wasn't his only assignment or goal. It wasn't his intention Christmas Eve three years ago when he followed his targets "into a tunnel that runs deep under the water, ships passing over on top of us . . . ," he writes, and I don't have to flip through many pages of notes and diagrams to know exactly what happened on the worst night of Fran Lacey's life.

Driving home with Easton who was three at the time, they were returning from supper and a candlelight service in Portsmouth. It was close to midnight, he was asleep in his seat as they crossed under the Chesapeake Bay, the 4-lane tunnel empty except for the pickup truck that passed them.

Suddenly, it cut in front, and as Fran hit the brakes, her tires blew, two of them as it would turn out. One of those strokes of bad luck that happens in the wrong place at the wrong time, and in this case the wrong person offered roadside assistance. Or that's been the assumption.

00:00:00:00:0

THE MAN in the pickup truck stopped, and Fran remembers him as broad shouldered and tall, clean shaven and bald.

Maybe in his 30s, maybe older, she wasn't sure after the fact. He had on a Bass Pro Shops fishing cap, amber-tinted glasses, and she didn't get a good look at his face. She didn't have time to think about the pistol in her fanny pack before he temporarily blinded her with a blast from a powerful LED flashlight while shoving a gun to the back of her head.

Forcing mother and son into the cargo area of Fran's disabled SUV, he zip-tied and gagged them. She remembers that he did all this silently and with astonishing speed, spending at most 10 minutes with them. Possibly as few as 5, then he cut the engine, turned on the flashers, and she heard him speed off.

Later she would tell me it seemed like an eternity as she lay there, her heart hammering, trying to free herself to no avail as she listened to the occasional car going past, nobody stopping until a state trooper did. The entire incident lasted no more than an hour, and from the beginning the story hasn't made a lot of sense.

I never completely bought that robbery was the goal. The man in the fishing cap took nothing but the cash in Fran's wallet, less than 50 dollars, and didn't want her Walther PPK pistol or police credentials. Your average Joe criminal wouldn't leave either or think of using a high-lumen flashlight to disable someone.

Since no tire spikes were recovered from the scene, I can only conclude that he collected them before leaving. Rather much like gathering his brass after shooting someone, and I don't know if Fran's going to feel better or worse when I tell her. Returning to the living room, I find it grandly illuminated in battery-powered lighting.

The trailer doesn't look any more inviting, maybe less as I pass through to the loud tearing and rattling of heavy paper. Camera flashes are going off, police dressed in protective Tyvek wrapping up weapons and ammunition, and carrying them outside to a crime scene truck.

I walk out the open doorway, down the porch steps, making my way through the sloppy wintry mess as a K-9 unit pulls up, diesel engines rumbling, the sound of the dog barking reminding me of Mr. Owl. I find myself scanning the trees, the sky, looking for him at the same time I wait to hear from Lex.

If I don't pretty soon, I'm going to do something about it, and I hope he and Nonna are okay. I head toward a cigarette glowing like a tiny orange coal, Fran by her Tahoe with Major Pepper, and I remember that after the incident in the tunnel, she started smoking again and swearing more than ever.

She quit going to the gym and church, eats and drinks whatever she wants, can be as mean as a snake, and won't get away with any of it forever.

"So much for a Sunday night when most people are furloughed or having fun," I say when I reach them. "It's no wonder I have no social life," my same lame joke, and truth be told I don't have a social life on any day or night of the week.

"You never know what's in your backyard," Major Pepper says grimly, and it's rare he's not in uniform.

Dressed casually in corduroys, a ski jacket and boots, he's busy on his phone, bombarded I can tell. Second in command of the Hampton Police Division, he also works closely with NASA, is in his 50s, nice looking, and drives a racing-yellow Corvette.

"This was a good find, Captain," he says to me with a congratulatory nod. "Good job following up on a tip," as if that's all I did.

"I'm not seeing much that's good about it except there's one less a-hole in the world, I guess," I reply, and I ask Fran to open the back of her truck so we can put away our heavy gear and weapons.

I think we can do without ballistic helmets and vests, gas masks, submachine guns, and she locks them up. I tell her I need a moment alone, and we walk through snow and slush to my Chase Car as ART turns it on, and I make my secret motion to free the locks.

"What have you got?" Fran eyes the bags of journals I'm carrying. "And where are you taking whatever it is?"

"The guy kept a detailed record of each job, 42 of them," I reply, "and it's significant that there's not one for last Tuesday."

"Now I'm really confused," she says, her vague face frowning in the dark.

"December 3rd, Vera Young," I explain. "There's no log that might be for her, suggesting she wasn't a job. Not his job at any rate."

I imagine Neva showing up at the Fort Monroe apartment to get the GOD chip, and when Vera wouldn't hand it over, things spun out of control. In a rage, Neva garroted her sister with a computer cord, and I assume at some point after this the hitman was there in his Denali to pick up the big boss. He may have given her a hand with staging the scene for all I know. But I have a feeling he didn't, that he had his pride. It wasn't his job or a good one, and he didn't want credit.

"You can't just take evidence home with you," Fran says as I set the bags of journals on a seat.

"I'm doing it, end of story," I reply. "I intend to go through all of them carefully before anybody else does. Maybe we'll figure out who he was. Maybe we'll find something that definitely links the victims to Pandora Space Systems."

I leave out the most important part, the hitman's own written record of Noah Bishop's death. My sister had nothing to do with it.

"Seriously?" Fran says cynically. "You're thinking Neva Rong's behind every one of his hits?" she drops the cigarette into an ice-watery puddle. "What makes you so sure a scumbag like that wouldn't do jobs for other people, anybody who'd pay enough?"

"Neva has to control everything and everyone," I reply. "If he did jobs for other people? Then he didn't answer only to her, and she wasn't the center of the universe."

My Tahoe's headlights illuminate Pebo Sweeny's trailer where he was enjoying retirement with his exotic pets, I can only suppose. He was home alone, possibly running a load of laundry when a stranger showed up at his door. "Pretending to be lost," his killer describes.

They struck up "a pleasant conversation" about car races at the nearby speedway, and what it was like to live so close to NASA. Then the hitman "got around to business," I recall from the log with its Cracker Jack plastic owl.

"Plain and simple," I'm saying to Fran, "this is how the hitman did location scouting and acquired habitats that would go undetected," and I can see faces in the lighted windows of mobile homes across the street, people looking out at what's going on over here. "He needed a local off-the-grid place to do his work, and a trailer that backed up to the woods was the perfect spot."

There was no motive other than that, I summarize. There was no competitor or adversary to intimidate or eradicate, no score to settle, just an old man retired from the Air Force who had something the hitman wanted.

"Based on what I saw a few minutes ago, I have a feeling Neva kept her personal attack dog plenty busy. I'm not sure he would have had time to work for anybody else," and then I tell Fran the rest of the story, that this same assassin who planned to wipe out all of us had victimized her in the past.

The purpose wasn't robbery then, I explain as she stares at me in cold silence. The goal was to traumatize, to create chaos, and maybe to send a warning. By his own accounting, the plan was to follow Fran home, to wait for an opportune time to disable her vehicle with tire spikes, I paint the nightmarish picture for her.

"And I'm betting he'd put a tracking device on your Land Cruiser long before that," I add.

"I don't understand," she stares off at the trailer, the lights harsh inside, police carrying out weapons wrapped in brown paper. "Why?"

"To destabilize, to create huge distractions and emotional distress," I emphasize.

"If Neva's really behind it," Fran decides, "why sic him on me three years ago? I had nothing to do with her then."

"But you had everything to do with me," I remind her. "And I'd just left the Air Force and started with NASA. I'd just started working with you in protective services, you're my neighbor, my friend, my family. What happens to you, Easton and Tommy happens to me. It happens to all of us."

"I remember having a funny feeling when I saw his driver's license," she means the hitman's fake one with his bearded photograph and Hank Cougars's information. "It doesn't really look like the man I remember. But it bothered me, and I guess now I know why. Except I don't understand why Neva would go to so much trouble."

I'm not going to remind Fran of the consequences. She doesn't need to hear how much time and effort I've spent on her raging phobias while helping her hide them from everyone. I won't mention how often I've turned the other cheek when she's insensitive, rude, and at times barbaric.

These past three years it's almost as if she's done everything she can to run me off, alienating plenty of people including Carme, and at times Mom, Tommy's cousin. But most of all him, the long-suffering husband, driven to renting a getaway in Williamsburg, and at the end of the day, Neva knew what she was doing.

29

"NEVA understands love and human decency well enough to use them as weapons," I explain as I slide into the blast-resistant driver's seat, open the window, and turn on the heat.

"Sort of like planting that phone on a 10-year-old if that's what she did," Fran's demeanor has turned as hard as steel. "Creating diversions, ruining lives, well may she get back as good as she gives."

She calls Neva a few choice names that don't bear repeating, and in my SPIES I can see my messages, and still nothing from Lex.

"Time to go home," I fasten my seat belt.

"I'm not leaving until everybody clears out," Fran says. "Still no luck finding the Cherokee, by the way."

"I'm guessing it's out of sight in a garage somewhere," I suggest.

"You probably won't be up by the time I get home. The babysitter dropped off Easton at your parents' house a little while ago for a sleepover. He's watching TV with George," she's looking at everything but me the way she does when she gets emotional.

"A lot of trauma for one day," I say kindly. "And when's Tommy coming home?"

"Next weekend maybe. Or whenever I'm not a grizzly bear with PMS, as he puts it," and for an instant it sounds like she might cry.

"You gonna be all right?"

"I'm fine," in a dead flat tone, and she steps back from my window. "See you in a little while," turning her back to me, Fran watches where she steps, headed back toward the trailer.

I drive off, and ART turns on the displays and audio as law enforcement vehicles continue arriving at the trailer park. No doubt there will be quite the investigation into the hitman's illegal weapons, and at least I can trust that Fran will keep it to herself about the 42 journals in my possession.

At almost 11:00 p.m. the winds are calm, the moon and stars showing. The temperature is 8.8°C (48°F) and the roads have cleared considerably. As I approach Lex's street, I decide to make a wellness check, parking where I did before.

I'm unable to tell from the gift wrap–papered windows whether any lights are on. But I can hear the TV playing inside, and I rap on the aluminum storm door. Nothing, and I try again, louder. Still nothing.

Then, "Who is it?" Nonna's distrusting voice.

"It's Captain Chase again, sorry it's so late. You don't need to open your door," I don't want her having another spell.

"I'd rather not."

"Best to leave a shield between us."

"I agree."

"I was driving by, are you and Lex all right?"

"He's in his room out like a light. I couldn't sleep, got up a bit ago to watch TV."

"Sorry to disturb you," and I tell her good night, oddly disappointed that I didn't see him.

But it's good to hear that Lex is sleeping as he should be at this late hour. Back inside my Tahoe, I stop at Commander Shepard

Boulevard, waiting at a red light as a Hampton Roads Transit bus glides past. I'm reminded of what he said about running errands, taking care of everything, a little man who never really had the chance to be a normal boy.

"Are there any updates I should know about?" I ask ART, and I'm back to multitasking, monitoring flat-screens, and data in my SPIES. "Anything earthshaking in the past few hours?" and he replies by displaying the Langley sitemap.

As late as it is, I'm surprised there are any outside contractors left on our campus, some of them the same engineers I saw at the Gantry earlier. Other ID numbers lighting up are from NASA and the military, a total of 8 people working in the hangar where the test model was hauled late afternoon. Dick isn't among them.

"What's going on in Building 1119-A?" I inquire.

I fully expect ART to reply that he's not authorized to show me. Instead, I'm connected to a live video feed from inside the spacecraft test model. Snap the crash test dummy is decked out in a launch-entry pressure spacesuit made of an iridescent-blue smart material, the soft hood equipped with a visor.

My purloined mannequin has assumed the position, on her back, knees bent, strapped snugly in a carbon fiber seat liner, her artificial arms folded across her zipped-up torso.

It occurs to me ironically that considering my implanted intricate network and all that goes with it, I may be more of a full-scale anthropomorphic test device than she is.

It's hard to tell very much else about the spacecraft itself since none of the avionics and other bells and whistles are present. But based on openings in the test model's aluminum sides and flooring, I suspect there are atypical components including ports for deploying miniprobes and satellites, and other autonomous devices.

I'm seeing real estate for powerful engine pods and thrusters. I recognize the slots for retractable landing skids like we have on many of the drones we build in the autonomous incubator and test on our ranges.

"Do we know where Dick is?" I'm grateful ART and I are back to talking freely. "And I'm wondering what his interest in the space vehicle might be exactly."

"What is your question?"

"Also, I'm wondering who decided to put Snap inside the test model. No one should have laid a finger on her, frankly. Especially after all the time and resources I've devoted to overhauling her. She was in very bad shape when I first met her. I realize that was before your time."

"I don't understand," ART says as I retrace my steps, following the same route home that I took 4 mornings ago during the blizzard.

"Do we have any further data on the drop test that was conducted at the Gantry earlier? More to the point, what's being done to Snap as we speak?" and when it comes to my hand-tooled and personally engineered mannequins, I'm as fiercely protective as my mother is toward Carme and me.

"The drop test was considered a success," ART answers blandly, reminding me of Dad's dry way of talking. "All test devices performed as designed, the results within normal limits."

"But what is this spacecraft supposed to be? It appears to have all sorts of atypical features?" I monitor the live feed as I drive, not expecting ART to answer beyond reminding me I'm not authorized.

"A reusable combination rescue vehicle and space ferry that can both land and take off," he surprises the hell-o out of me.

Echoing the very details Dick and I have discussed for years, what ART's talking about is a spacecraft with a retractable landing gear. It can set down on legs or skids in environments with little or no atmosphere such as the airless moon where wings won't fly with no wind beneath them.

00:00:00:00:0

"An M-O-B-E, a Manned Orbital Ballistic Escaper," ART spells it out, the very acronym Dad and I came up with one summer while Dick was visiting us.

"It appears to have landing gear similar to helicopter skids," I point out. "Only for space landings in little or no gravity. When the vehicle returns to Earth, it splashes down in the ocean like most crew capsules. Sort of a getaway car."

"A MOBE isn't designed to be used for criminal activity," ART takes me literally.

"An escape car," I restate what I mean.

Pronounced *MOBY* like the whale, its powerful propulsion system can blast away from a damaged spaceplane, a failing inflatable habitat or other trouble. Then AI-assisted telemetry would rendezvous the vehicle with the most direct descent profile to return to Earth.

Or the MOBE could power its way to the safety of the International Space Station, the Lunar Orbital Platform, and other gateways and facilities already in the works up there. I envision the huge unmarked wooden crates that arrived on an Air Force transport Globemaster C-17 several weeks ago.

There's little doubt what was on those pallets tucked out of sight inside the aviation hangar, a MOBE high-fidelity test model and whatever might go with it. As I think of the blue-luminescing spacecraft wing I saw inside the full-scale wind tunnel, I suspect that whatever was going on in there might be related.

"Thanks for answering because I didn't expect you to," I say to ART while noticing that Papa John's Pizza is open as was Hardee's a moment ago, my stomach growling as if it might lunge. "Not so coincidentally, I wasn't unauthorized this time."

No response.

"Not that I believe in coincidences. So, it sounds to me that Dick or whoever's editing you thought it okay to tell me about the MOBE test model, one that hasn't been mentioned before you just did. A concept I'm all too familiar with since I worked on it with Sierra Nevada Corporation a few years ago, and before that brainstormed about it with Dick."

ART has no comment.

"Anyway, I didn't know anything had gone into production, and it shouldn't be you breaking the news to me. He should have. And you can tell him I said so."

Silence.

"I hope Dick isn't taking sole credit or much at all really," I admit, and the thought irks me more than I let on.

Truth be told, very little about the MOBE was his doing. It was Dad and me. Also, Mom always adds her creative touch just as my fighter pilot twin has her hawkish ideas. But it would sound petty to point it out.

"So, what happened?" I resume quizzing ART. "Why did you answer me this time?"

"Unauthorized."

"Dick or somebody must have changed the algorithm since I asked about Snap earlier? When I didn't see her in the hangar and got worried? Remember? Because you wouldn't answer me then."

"Unauthorized."

"Well, you didn't tweak your own algorithm unless you're now self-programming. What a scary thought, and that will probably be next."

Silence.

"Who gets to decide what I can and can't know?" I keep pushing, and the 7-Eleven glowing up ahead makes me want a Big Bite hot dog something awful.

I imagine drowning it in chili and cheese, extra mustard, and my mouth waters.

"Unauthorized," ART always says it in a monotone.

"Because it's not you who's deciding," I add, "that's for sure. Or at least I hope not. And never mind why certain topics are off limits because I know you won't tell me."

Crickets.

"It's like trying to get something out of Mom. Well forget it," as I reach the Hampton Hop-In, lights out, no sign of the pearl-white Cherokee with its damaged front bumper.

There are no cars at all, the plowed parking lot empty, and I find it strange that the convenience store would be closed on a weekend night when the snow's melting, the weather good. There have been plenty of people shopping, in restaurants, getting ready for the holidays, catching and cleaning up after the evacuation and storm.

"Do we know why the Hop-In is closed?" I ask ART as if he's an oracle with the answer to everything even if he doesn't tell me.

"I'm sorry," his voice through my truck's speakers. "I have no information," and it's probably my imagination that he sounds chagrined.

"But what about the Jeep we saw earlier at Bojangles'? You ran the plate and also located a traffic video of it traveling east on I-64 near Richmond yesterday, remember?" as if he might not. "It has a scrape on the right front bumper," he doesn't need me to remind him, and immediately I'm seeing a recording captured three hours earlier.

On Patch Road near a brewery, turning onto Pullman, the Cherokee heads in the direction of the Chesapeake Bay. This was soon after Lex and I had been sitting behind the damaged SUV in the drive-through line. Presumably, it's driven by the woman wearing pearly nail polish, a black leather coat, and flashy silver rings similar to ones the hitman had on when I saw him dead inside his car.

The Cherokee weaves in and out of dark side streets, and moments later disappears into the labyrinth of the sprawling Dog Beach Marina & Villas apartment complex. It's not far from Fort Monroe or the Point Comfort Inn, and I suggest that ART alert Fran immediately.

"She needs to send in units to check the area for what else might be back there," I explain, reminded of the weird man inside the Hop-In when I drove past in the snow, thinking of Neva's dead assassin and his rental boats.

"Would you like me to contact dispatch directly?" ART asks.

"No. We don't want anything going out over the radio," I remind him firmly. "We don't know who else is listening, and whoever the driver of the Cherokee is, I worry she already knows we're watching."

"Copy," ART updates Fran in a text I can see in my SPIES, and I'm close enough to home that I can make out the cobalt glow from my mom's light pollution, her LED miniblues entwining and spangling anything that doesn't move.

She keeps them up all year long, going into overdrive at Thanksgiving, arming herself with the electric topiary shears, strapping on a tool belt, dragging out the extension ladder or cranking up the cherry picker. Memories of my childhood are accompanied by the hydraulic sounds of her rolling around, extending and retracting the boom, raising and lowering the bucket.

Forever weaving strands of miniblues through trees, shrubs, around lampposts, pilings, fences, chimneys, and the nor'easter from earlier this week didn't deter her in the slightest. She didn't take down a single light that I can see as I turn into our long narrow driveway that Dad named Penny Lane. My headlights slash across his handmade sign, and it's like I'm driving into Saint Elmo's fire.

Mom's space-themed topiary of sculpted bushes seems to have survived the storm overall but they're not as pristine as when I drove through 4 days ago. The rocket is a bit of a wreck. The family of blue-faced extraterrestrials is badly shaken up like crash dummies when things don't go as planned. The roundly pruned old boxwood that's supposed to be Pluto looks more like a tumbleweed or an unraveling ball of indigo yarn.

All that's missing are the inflatable Jetsons around the Christmas tree, Yoda as Santa, the Star Trek *Enterprise*. The winds for sure would have blasted them where no one's gone before had Mom not opened their air valves, returning them safely to their boxes in the basement.

The unpaved road that leads to my family's modest hamlet on the river hasn't been plowed. But I can tell there's been plenty of traffic. Dirty snow is rutted and sloppy, with a lot of muddy patches, loose rocks, and leftover autumn leaves that still have their color.

30

"CALL MOM, please," I say to ART, reaching the gravel walkway bordered by sapphire pathway lights, her blue Subaru in front.

"Welcome home!" my mother says cheerily when she answers the phone, and either she hears me on the driveway or sees me on the security cameras.

"I'm going to clean up first, promise I'll be quick," I reply. "I've never felt so dirty and hungry in all my life," and up ahead, Chase Place glitters like a blue starry universe, our old farmhouse on one side of the driveway, the big barn on the other.

Electric candles are in the windows, miniblues strung along the eaves, and wrapped around lampposts, fencing and the stump of our favorite tree that got struck by lightning. The boat dock is brightly outlined as if someone went after it with a blue neon crayon, and the zip line that slopes from the barn's top floor to the river is lit up like an endless strand of sapphires.

Across the snowy garden is the tiny tin-roofed cottage where Fran lives with Easton and sometimes Tommy, and multicolored lights glow through the living room curtain. She's always the first to put her tree up, no later than Thanksgiving, and when I was last here 4 days ago, I noticed the front door had an evergreen wreath with a big red bow.

Dad's white Prius is in its usual spot near the illuminated pecan tree that's regularly raided by the neighborhood squirrels he battles. That's if you ask him, but if you ask the rest of us and truth be told? The spreading gnarled branches are as bare as bones. There's nothing on them this time of year except strands of mini-blues, and not a nut in sight (well, maybe one).

Defending his empire has become Dad's major preoccupation, and he baits his shiny steel cage traps with whole pecans he expensively orders off the internet. On the rare occasion that he catches a bushy-tailed offender, off he goes in the car to release it far enough away that it won't come back (supposedly).

Parking in front of the barn, I gather my belongings and the 42 shooting journals. I cradle poor Ranger the PONG, and he's out like a light, not making a whimper. As I near the pedestrian door, motion sensors trigger the front light to blaze on, and since I was home last, the lock has been swapped for an electronic one. And I have no code or key.

"Ummm, how am I supposed to get in . . . ?" I deliberate out loud as I think, *Oh shhhh . . . !*

"Would you like to program a gesture for accessing locks on your property?" ART replies in my implanted earpiece, reminding me of my new abilities.

"Yes," and with my thumb and index finger, I make the simple motion of turning a key in a lock.

Apparently, that will do fine, and with a quiet click I open the door, another light blinking on, the burglar alarm beeping. ART instructs me to use my WAND, and I point my right finger at the keypad. The alarm is silenced, and he turns on the downstairs lights without my asking.

"Welcome home," he says what Mom always does. "If you point your WAND, you can reset the alarm," and I do. "Thank you," he responds to my surprise.

"Anytime," I reply, and squinting in the brightness, I stoop down to unlace my filthy boots, kicking them off.

Dropping my ballistic vest, jacket and duffel bag on the floor, I set the journals, my backpack and gun belt on a table to deal with later. Nothing much has changed since I was here days earlier, only me. I feel at home and absolutely don't as I look around at our big open area of workbenches, machines, tool chests, electrical components, the empty car lift, and Dad's rebuilt '68 Camaro covered up next to it.

Vintage automotive calendars are everywhere, and there's not much we haven't worked on in here including radio-controlled vehicles like dune buggies and aircraft. We've refurbished small planes, old cars, experimenting with sensors and all sorts of autonomous contraptions including PONGs and pieces and parts of them.

I leave Ranger comfortable and stable on a beanbag near an assortment of less serious orbs, ones that aren't prototypes but meant to be festive and imaginative, lighting up Mom's favorite blue. Dad and I were working on them as a special Christmas present for her, and he's not supposed to leave them out in plain view.

He'll ruin the surprise if he hasn't already, and I head to the stairs where my take-home crash dummy Otto is parked in his wheelchair. He looks the same as when I saw him last, naked as the day he was made, his steel lifting ring protruded like a loop antenna from a hairless pate the same brownish-pink tint as a pencil eraser.

Slouched with his chest unzipped, wires and cables hanging out, he holds a set of hex keys in his rubbery hands as if trying to put himself back together again. I feel a twinge of guilt that he's undone and undressed, the dummy beyond his prime when it comes to being banged up and tossed around, wrenched, slammed and bounced.

Upgraded beyond his capabilities, he's limited and rigid, and I suppose after being abused for decades, it was only fair NASA decided to retire him, allowing him to come home with me. For the past three years Otto has lived in our barn, trying on all sorts of things for size, new types of sensors, remote controls, accelerometers, antennas, and a variety of smart materials and fabrics.

He's been dropped from the roof wearing a ballistic parachute, sent crashing through trees on the zip line while clad in an exoskeleton, upended by his jetpack, thrown from moving vehicles in helmet tests and subjected to extreme temperatures. Just to name a few of his misadventures.

"You and I are more alike than I knew," I greet him and he doesn't answer. "I've had done unto me what I've done unto you. And thus, the meaning of karma, not to be confused with my sister."

His head is turned toward the wall, his empty eyes not looking at me. If I didn't know better, I'd think he's miffed, suspicious I'm cheating on him with ART, and I am, let's face it. I can't possibly feel the same way about a crash dummy now that I have a SIN inside me, and with each passing hour it's harder for me to remember what it felt like to be normal.

Upstairs in my office, I begin shedding my disgusting clothing, opening a closet, stuffing everything in the upright washer-dryer that makes me think of Pebo Sweeny's sour-smelling laundry. As I walk past my desk's array of spectrum analyzers, I'm reminded they shouldn't be detecting my implanted devices. And they're not.

I can see that for myself on the displays, and it seems my invisibility cloak is working just fine. Although I'm still baffled and slightly concerned by Nonna's reaction. I don't like that she had a spell, an energy disturbance as Lex called it, and I hope it doesn't mean she actually detected my transmissions.

00:00:00:00:0

ART suggests I point my WAND at the Norfolk pine that Dad and I electrified, and it turns on, casting a lovely glow over my home office.

The softly illuminated fernlike branches host a flock of recharging PONGs varying in shape and purpose, ranging from pocket size to as big as basketballs. Their attachment to their living spring-green perch is mutually accommodating, the "stem" an electrical current, the recharger and recharging never quite touching.

Their connection is held fast invisibly, ever so distantly until the signal is interrupted when it's time for the flying orbs to go to work. Unfortunately, it will be without Ranger for a while, I think sadly, envisioning his shredded shell, feeling I failed to take good care of him. Dad and I both will have to step up our drone testing, and figure out a way to include raptor protection.

While I'm thinking all this, I'm reminded it probably wouldn't be a bad idea to give my PEEPS a little juice, and finding them in my backpack, I attach the smart glasses to the perch the same way I would a PONG. Next, I check computer displays showing video feeds from the security cameras that constantly monitor the farm, and ART shows the same images in my SPIES. I scan the house and barn, Fran's place, the dock, various outbuildings that aren't much more than sheds, and the areas where we park our cars.

Everything looks quiet, a couple of deer strolling through the garden, a few rabbits hopping, lights and candles glowing, the moon slipping in and out of wispy clouds. Barefoot and stripped down to my skivvies, I walk into my bathroom, not sure what to do.

Should I take off my SPIES and CUFF? Will showering and washing my hair cause a problem with my implanted earpiece? Considering I now have devices inside and out that supposedly work in concert with my environment, should I be concerned when taking off the rest of my clothes?

I worry how much Dick knows, and if he can tell from my transmitted data that I feel dirty or clean, too hot or cold, contented, excited, dressed or not, if I'm daydreaming or thinking private thoughts. No doubt he's aware that I'm starving and a bit frayed at the edges right now, and I wonder when I'm going to hear from him again.

I don't understand why he ignored me at the Gantry, and hasn't bothered to check on how I'm doing. It seems callous not to offer further instruction after reprogramming me and practically everything I own and have, including my identical twin. Locking the bathroom door, I step into the shower, turning it on, and as Carme's always saying, you never know how beat-up you are until you stop.

The hot water drumming down feels like heaven. My neck and shoulders are sore from all my gear, my blood sugar sinking, and I scrub myself but good with antibacterial soap while envisioning the hitman's trailer. I'm trying not to dwell on what I saw in the garbage can, and the tools in the bathtub or the detailed grisly descriptions I read in the journals.

I wonder what Dick's reaction will be when I tell him what happened to Noah Bishop, and if we now have a better chance of clearing Carme's name and taking down Neva. Except I honestly can't imagine either happening. There's nothing I've seen so far in the journals that's definitive, no names or specific places, no records of communications, associates, where he shopped, and who might have paid him.

I know whose bidding he was doing, and that we'll likely never prove it. Even if we managed to charge Neva with something that stuck, I don't believe it would stop her. Dick's right about that, I decide as I blow-dry my hair, a towel wrapped around me. Still sweating from the shower, not bothering with a touch of makeup, I pad across the narrow hallway with its exposed-beam ceiling.

I walk back through my office, and into the bedroom where I started living in high school when Carme and I moved into the barn. Nothing's all that different from what it was, the same posters on the cypress-plank walls. The first landing on the moon, and the Space Shuttle piggybacking on a rocket. James Bond when Roger Moore played him, Lindsay Wagner as the Bionic Woman, and the Dave Matthews Band.

On a shelf over the dresser is a collection of my dorky trophies for spelling bees, competitions for robotics, computer coding and mathematics, and one of my finer moments when I came in second at a truck rodeo. Throwing on a warm-up suit and thick socks, I grab a weapon-concealing fanny pack, and hurry down the stairs.

Rushing past Otto, I find my pair of UGG boots, my down vest in a closet. Collecting my gun belt, the journals, Lex's thumb drive, I carry them to the gun safe in a small back room where Dad has a desk buried in paperwork and drone components.

"The combination has been changed," ART lets me know in my earpiece.

"Well, it sure as shooting should have been after all that's happened," I retort in frustration. "But now what?"

"Would you like me to access?"

"That would be helpful. But I'd like the combination so I have it . . ."

"Unauthorized."

"Of course it is!" I declare impatiently.

A series of beeps, a hum and a click, and he enables me to open the heavy steel door, setting the journals, thumb drive, my duty gun inside for now. Grabbing my Bond Bullpup 9 mm pistol, the same as my sister's, I zip it inside the fanny pack. Thinking of the missing GOD chip again, it's weird to think of it locked up in here while I had no clue. Dick and Dad knew about it, and I'm betting so did Mom.

It's almost midnight when I venture outdoors to the sound of melting ice and snow drip-dripping. Galaxies of minilights glitter and wink, flickering like blue fireflies in swaying branches, and reflected in the river's gentle current. The pecan tree is ablaze in azure sparkles, and underneath Dad's shiny new cages look like mean-spirited gifts left by the Grinch, each baited with a generous pile of purchased nuts.

The shoveled sidewalk is lit up like a runway, and I climb the 4 wooden steps, my feet sounding on the sprawling porch. I walk past the glider settee where Mom used to rock Carme and me in warmer months as fireflies sparked in the dark, and cicadas sawed to beat the band. She'd tell us stories, describing her latest NASA lesson plans, and I'm hopeful those days aren't gone for good.

I imagine us sitting out here again or in front of the fire, having a bite of supper the way things used to be when all was good. Emotions stirring, I clear my throat, taking a deep breath. Knocking my special knock on the knotty pine door, I'm aware of another new electronic lock. No doubt all of them have been changed, and my mother's probably to blame.

Unless it was Carme who did it. Then again, Dick might have been the influence. Although it could be Dad's reaction to what's become of the GOD chip he shouldn't have told Lex about. I doubt Fran's responsible for beefing up security on the property since her knowledge is limited to my fabricated origin story. She has no idea why the hitman's really dead or the danger all of us might still be in.

"There you are!" the door swings open, Mom hugging me, and I can hear the TV playing in the den down the hall.

"Something sure smells good," the aroma of her chili and homemade bread make me ravenous.

"Let me look at you," she takes my face in her hands the way she's always done when she wants to see inside me.

Her hazel eyes are touched by gold, lamplight shining on her short graying hair. Strong and capable, she's in her usual faded jeans and flannel, and a pair of sturdy Chelsea boots that could stand a polishing. She's what I call outdoorsy pretty, her idea of makeup ChapStick, and you'll never catch her in high heels or a dress, nothing impractical that doesn't last forever.

"How are you?" she asks, knowing full well what was done to me at the Point Comfort Inn.

"Maybe you should tell me how I'm doing because you should know," I reply, increasingly suspicious she's had more to do with my engineering and predetermined destiny than anyone on the planet.

Mom was right there inside room 1, and later in and out of suite 604 tying me up, tethering me to an eyebolt, feeding and cleaning me, taking care of my every need. As altered as I was, I wouldn't let anyone else within striking range to hear Dick talk. And I envision his bruised hands, and the cameras inside the room.

It's hard to describe how it feels to think my mother has been watching, listening, and surveilling whatever she deems necessary. Invading every part of me, she evaluates and tweaks, tending to her flock while influencing ART right down to him informing me if I'm authorized or not.

31

"IT'S NICE weather, the river pretty in the moonlight," Mom says.

Stepping over to the coatrack, she informs me that the winds are calm, and it's not too cold. She sounds a lot like ART, and I can tell when she's preoccupied by heavy thoughts.

"I've heard a few charters going by," as she puts on her vintage adirondack jacket, "people night fishing for red drum, flounder. I don't like boats going past this late. And I'm sorry our driveway isn't gated. But we can't live behind walls, may as well be in prison or the cemetery."

"Are you doing okay?" and when she's uneasy, so am I.

"Don't you worry about me. I want to talk to you on the porch for a minute," she says, and obviously she doesn't want Dad or Easton waking up and overhearing.

As hard as my mother is to read, I always know when she's down or angry. If she's privy to as much as I think she is, I can only imagine what she feels about Neva Rong, who's come close to taking out our entire family. Now things have become personal for Mom, although they were before, more personal than I know, I have a feeling.

"Tell me how you're holding up," she asks as we head out to the porch.

"I'm not sure anymore. That's the honest answer, and who decided to change the locks?" I close the door behind us, but not all the way.

"It was time," she says, taking my hand, my right one.

Absently rubbing my scarred index finger the way Dick sometimes does, she leads me to the glider, the same one she had when she was growing up, white-painted aluminum with weatherproof floral cushions. We sit down, and I can feel the cold vinyl upholstery through my clothes.

"I guess you knew I'd get into the barn anyway even though my keys weren't going to work anymore," I decide. "Same with the alarm code and the safe. I assume you know my new Artificial Research Technician," I'm not going to dance around what's going on.

"We're acquainted," she answers, her voice low pitched and softly modulated, reminding me of ART again. "How's everything working for you, Calli?"

"I'd give myself a B minus for today."

"I'd give you much better than that. At least an A, maybe even extra credit," she smiles in the dark, her face indistinct in the glow of her miniblues all around us.

"And how would you know about my performance today?" I goad her, seeing if she'll tell me.

"There's not much I don't know about you, dear."

"And it feels that way, all right," I admit. "It probably doesn't bother Carme a bit that she's watched, studied and adjusted. One thing my sister's never been is modest."

She thinks nothing of walking around with very little on, and maybe I would too if I had her body. Mom has no comment, and it's occurring to me where ART learned his silent treatments.

"I'm not sure how I feel about everything," I add to the familiar creaky whisper of the glider sliding back and forth, a sound I'd recognize anywhere. "I wish I knew how Carme's reacting. Is she really okay with all this, Mom?"

"Each of you has always had a decided flight plan that's the same and different. You've always known your purpose. But knowing what's expected doesn't mean you have to go along with it. It's up to you to decide."

"What if Carme and I hadn't gone along with it?" I ask as ART informs me in my SPIES that the government shutdown just ended, much earlier than expected.

"You wouldn't be happy," Mom says as if she knows it for a fact. "That's what people don't understand about free will."

"There's no such thing, that's for sure."

"Of course there is, and you can do what you want," she replies. "But if you reject your purpose, if you make it all about yourself, you'll have no satisfaction regardless of the consequences. Whether you end up an inmate or a rock star, you won't get the reward you really want. We're programmed like this for a reason."

"I just wish all that programming wasn't on a computer chip that's missing," I go ahead and say it. "Is Dad okay? How does my sister feel about it, realizing what could happen if the wrong person gets hold of it? Specifically, if Neva does, because we know she's after it. Dick told me everything. Well, he never tells me everything. But I've got the broad strokes."

"What do you remember?" Mom asks the same thing he did when I woke up after being drugged for days.

"Probably more than he thought I would," and I can't resist answering everything she asks like I always have.

I give her the highlights, including my awareness that she was present inside room 1 with my sister and possibly others when my network was implanted. Sharing the events of the day, I'm mindful that whenever the subject returns to Neva, it's as if the night gets emptier and colder. I can feel Mom get stony, and I come right out and ask her about it.

"I know she doesn't like any of us but I'm wondering if her real target is you," I conclude. "She seems gratuitously scornful and cruel. It seems personal, as if there's a history maybe I don't know about."

Silence. Just like ART.

"When she was a postdoc in one of Dad's labs at Langley, did something happen between you and Neva?" I persist. "Now would be a really good time to shoot straight with me as I'm trying to figure out what the psycho might do next."

Mom is quiet as we push with our toes, sliding back and forth slowly and gently, surrounded by darkness and lights.

"I recognized what she was when no one else did," she finally answers. "Unfortunately, it wasn't until I'd gotten to know her."

"How did that happen?"

"I may not be a scientist or an astronaut but I have my value as it turns out," she says. "If you're looking for someone who has an overview of everything that goes on at NASA and in the space world, I'm a pretty good place to start."

"Ask the person who teaches it to everybody else," I reply. "Plus, you're exposed to a lot of privileged information. Much of it classified and top secret even if it's through osmosis," thinking of projects Dad and I routinely work on.

"She'd drop by my office regularly, insatiably curious about all my lesson plans. We spent a fair amount of time together," Mom says. "George and I had her over for supper or on the weekends. We were friendly, saw each other daily until I began hearing rumors that clued me in on what she was really up to."

"How long had you been hanging out by the time you became suspicious?" I inquire, and it bothers me tremendously to think of Neva ever stepping foot on our farm.

00:00:00:00:0

"IT WENT ON a few months longer than it should have," Mom doesn't really answer the question. "Your father had several inventions he hadn't patented yet, and she stole them right out from under him. Can't prove it but there's no doubt. Why do you think she has more money than God?"

"Did you confront her with these rumors? Specifically, your suspicion that she stole Dad's intellectual property?" I ask as we stare out at the night, rocking gently on the old settee glider, our breath fogging when we talk.

"I knew better after some of what I was hearing. You don't openly challenge someone like that. Instead I distanced myself while alerting key people that she's trouble," Mom explains, and I go ahead and tell her the truth about what happened in the tunnel on Christmas Eve three years ago.

"Just weeks after I moved back home," I remind her. "I'll never forget when we got the phone call. You remember what that was like for all of us. A nightmare. Pure chaos that's never really ended, as you well know."

"If she disrupts someone you care about, she disrupts you, and if something happens to you, it disrupts me. If I'm disrupted, that's the end," Mom continues to avoid saying Neva's name.

"Why is it the end?"

"It just is."

"Explain what you mean," but I think I know.

It's always been Mom holding everything and everyone together. Carme and me. Dick and Dad, possibly in that order, I have to wonder.

"What did Dad think of Neva in the early days when she was visiting the farm?"

"You know George, he's nice to everyone. Only sees the good."

"Well, I hope he knows what she is now."

"He's known for quite a while what she is, and I wish he wouldn't take things so hard," Mom says. "But he shouldn't have told that kid a darn tooting thing, and I saw what was coming."

"Lex isn't so bad. It's easy to resent someone like him when Dad plays favorites the way he does."

"George feels terrible about it. But he should have known better," she says what she always does when Dad's too trusting, and I envision him shopping with Lex at the Hop-In, spending a small fortune.

"Your theory about what went down at Fort Monroe?" I want to hear from her what transpired when Neva showed up unannounced at Vera's apartment door. "I have a feeling you have it on good authority exactly what happened."

I want the whole truth, and I'm convinced Mom knows. She might not have been watching. But someone was, and what I'm really suggesting is that she and Carme are in communication.

"Well, what makes sense to me is her hitman was driving her in the early afternoon of December 3rd," Mom's talking about Neva. "And it's also possible her intention was to drop in unannounced as she claims."

But Neva didn't show up to be friendly, to act like the caring sister who happened to be in the area. She intended to catch Vera off guard because she had something Neva wanted, Mom says. Things got out of hand, as I've suspected, ending violently, she suggests, and I think of what Vera was garroted with, a thin power cord.

It's probably the same one used after the fact to rig her up from the closet door. The computer charger likely belonged to the conveniently password-less laptop displaying Vera's alleged suicide note. The weapon, the note were indigenous to the scene, suggesting the killer used what was available, and that feels more like an impulse than a plan.

"I suspect she killed Vera in a rage," Mom goes on. "And now, uh-oh, there's a mess to clean up. So what do you do? You fake the scene to look like Vera hanged herself. Then you douse her body with chlorine bleach in hopes of destroying or at least damaging DNA and any other evidence that might point your way."

"It makes no sense to think Vera did that to herself," I agree. "Imagine bleach all over your face and in your eyes? How was she going to string herself up from the door, elaborately I might add, once she was covered with a caustic chemical? Also, if she did that to herself, then what happened to the container or bottle? Why wasn't it at the scene?"

"That's what ruins the staging," Mom nods her head as we glide back and forth. "The glaring red flag."

A deliberate one, that and the missing ID badge that later turned up in Vera's apartment, and the motion sensor alarm that went off in the airlock, all of it was my sister's doing. I envision the dried blood drops on the asbestos-covered pipe inside the steam tunnel, and the likely source of it, the glass tube of blood that mysteriously showed up inside the evidence refrigerator at protective services headquarters.

Probably it will turn out to be Vera's postmortem blood, another gift from my sister. The ham sandwich with pico de gallo, the empty beer bottle found in Vera's living room made me think of Carme as did any number of details that gave me the sense someone had spent time inside the apartment after Vera was dead. All of it was orchestrated by my other half, I now feel sure, based on what Mom says.

My twin was sending me mirror flashes, messages, really no different from what she did at the Point Comfort Inn, planting and removing evidence creatively, ruthlessly. I wonder where she was when Neva appeared, and I imagine my sister waiting in the wings until the coast was clear, then helping herself to the faked suicide scene. Further staging and unstaging, leaving hints and manipulations, and maybe she was looking for the same thing Neva was.

"A good example of the end justifying the means," is all I can think to say about what Carme's done. "Do we know if she's okay?"

"I assume so," Mom turns vague, reminding me of Ranger ghosting.

"Is that your way of saying 'unauthorized'?" I ask, and she doesn't answer. "You and Dick must have been planning your Gemini project for years," and hearing the words come out of my mouth makes me feel heavy inside.

"For as long as we've known each other, really," she finally says, quietly, softly, in rhythm to our rocking. "Before George and I were married, actually," and this I didn't imagine. "Your father didn't leave the Air Force Academy simply because of family issues or because he was pining away for me. He was conscripted by NASA and the Department of Defense to do the very things he's done."

"I can see why they would have grabbed him," I reply. "I'm not the genius he is, but it's not so different from what happened to me. I leave the Air Force and return to the farm so I can serve a purpose I wasn't quite planning on," I don't say it bitterly.

"I'm sorry if in any way this is against what you might have wished for your life, Calli."

"I didn't have to go to the Point Comfort Inn," I don't hesitate to answer. "And I didn't have to say yes. Carme gave me every chance to go home as you no doubt are well aware."

"You must be hungry," Mom plants her feet to stop the glider.

"I might die, that's how hungry I am," I reply as we get up, returning to the house.

32

HANGING UP our coats, we walk through the living room, the lighted Christmas tree decorated with ornaments collected over the years, a lot of them space themed like Mom's topiary. Stockings are hung from the fireplace mantel, our names embroidered on them, and soon enough they'll be filled with thoughtful foods and small gifts.

"What are Dad and Easton watching?" I ask, the noise of gunshots on TV coming from the den. "Or better stated, what's playing while they're sleeping on the couch as usual?"

"*Gunsmoke*," she says to hoofbeats, horses neighing, rifles cracking as we pass the rustic dish cabinet and table in the dining room.

"I'm just not sure it's appropriate for a 6-year-old," and it's not the first time I've said it.

"Goodness. I guess you don't watch cartoons anymore. Not to mention what's all over the news," Mom replies as we walk into the kitchen where I've spent so much of my life.

It's also her office, and her desk to the right of the countertop gives her quite the view out the windows. Whatever Carme and I were up to, Mom was always watching as she cooked our meals and worked on her lesson plans. Back when we were growing up, she had a big computer, now it's just a laptop connected to an oversize display.

"I guess you heard about what they found in the debris at Wallops," she says to my surprise as I slide out my usual chair from the butcher block table.

"I've not heard or seen any updates," and I wonder why ART didn't inform me of whatever it is.

Then I remember he wouldn't if Mom, Dick or someone in charge doesn't authorize it.

"The answer is nothing," Mom says from the stove. "Nothing was in the payload that was unexpected, suggesting that contrary to rumor, there was no spy satellite, no top secret government project that accidentally was destroyed."

"So, we were putting on the big act of trying to recover something quickly from the blast site," I reply, remembering the video feed I was watching in my truck after leaving Mission Control. "All of it was for Neva's benefit, to give her the false impression that something important blew up."

"Dick will explain," Mom lifts the lid from the shiny steel stockpot, stirring chili that looks divine.

"I've heard nothing from him all day," I watch her put on an oven mitt, opening the oven door, sliding out sourdough bread she's been keeping warm.

"He'll be picking you up in the morning very early, I'm afraid," ladling chili into a bowl. "Both of you will be dropped off at the hangar . . ."

"Which hangar?" I interrupt in alarm as I feel another unplanned drama coming on.

"Ours," she means the huge aviation hangar at NASA. "From there you'll be flying to DC for a briefing, and beyond that I can't tell you much."

We're probably meeting with the Secret Service, I think. Or it could be the CIA.

"Make sure to bring toiletries and other essentials, enough for several days," Mom adds, sawing off a hunk of bread, generous with the butter.

"What's wrong with me that I'm hungry all the time? Hungrier than I used to be, and it was bad enough before," I complain, watching her every move with my food. "You would think that would be better, not worse."

"Why might it be better?"

"Because I thought the point was to improve functioning. Did you goof up, and my hypothalamus thinks I need rewarding all the time? Or is there something with my pituitary that makes me think I'm pregnant? Because I have real cravings."

"Your technical assists regulate many things and ultimately will enable you to perform in ways not possible before," Mom says, and it sounds like ART talking.

She carries over my very late dinner or it could be an early breakfast, and I don't care about manners. I dip in my spoon, tearing off a piece of hot buttered bread.

"Having a SIN doesn't mean you won't struggle with the same temptations and desires, quite the contrary," Mom finds a glass in the cupboard, opens the freezer for ice cubes. "You wouldn't want to stop wanting, now would you?"

I don't admit that I learned to stop wanting a lot of things long ago when I knew I would be disappointed. Most of all, I gave up on thinking I'd get to make the same kinds of choices my sister's been given. It wasn't Carme who was expected to quit the military when the going got tough. She's not who Dick called with bad news about Mom while I was assigned to his Cheyenne Mountain military installation near Colorado Springs.

Non-Hodgkin's lymphoma, he told me. Just one more lie like so many, maybe my entire life is one, and it's time I know what was really done to beta test Carme's and my eventual implanted networks. Because now that I'm face to face with Mom, I'm reminded that there's nothing she wouldn't do for us including taking on the first SIN herself before allowing any version of it to be passed on to her daughters.

"You started wearing contact lenses a few years ago," I say to her as I finish eating everything in front of me, telling myself no more. "And now Carme and I are wearing them. Only they're not intended to correct our vision, and maybe yours aren't either."

"Would you like something more to eat?" she collects my dishes before I have the chance.

"Yes, but I'm going to say no," I reply as a phone starts ringing in the direction of the den. "You don't even wear reading glasses. But you have contacts, and I should have wondered about it before now. Who tried out the SIN prototype, Mom? Because I know what you're like."

"I wouldn't allow anything done to you and Carme that I don't know about."

"Is that what made you sick?"

"We learned the hard way that if you don't coat the devices with proteins from your own body, chances are the implants are going to be rejected," she loads the dishwasher. "My immune system went on the attack, and removing the SIN had unexpected side effects," she explains dispassionately as if what she's depicting is reasonable, and I remember what Dick said about it.

Dissolving the injectable devices is possible in an emergency. But it's uncertain what the consequences might be, and in Mom's case it may as well have been cancer. For all practical purposes her body responded with similar symptoms, and she tells me again how guilty she felt when I quit the Air Force because of her.

She knows I didn't want to return to Hampton to live in the barn again, working for NASA as Dick directed. But plain and simple, he wanted me home with her, not that I needed him or anyone to make me take care of my mother. There wasn't a question what I would do, and he seized the situation as an opportunity he could use to further his scheme.

Mom's bad outcome was an unexpected gift, really. Dick facilitated my leaving the military, an unusual thing for a 4-star general to encourage. It would be fortuitous if I went to work for NASA Langley, and he claimed it was in the cards for me anyway. But just not quite so soon, and he's yet to tell me what cards he meant.

"There's been no better place for your training," Mom places a soap pod in the dishwasher, starting it up.

00:00:00:00:0

"TRAINING for what? To be a cyber nerd, a test pilot, a human factor pessimist?" I ask, monitoring the live security video images in my smart lenses, looking for whatever just triggered a motion sensor light near the barn where my Chase Car is parked.

"Best to learn things from the ground up," Mom the educator says. "No better person to pilot the plane than the one who created it . . ."

"You've got to be kidding me!" I exclaim as I see Lex in my SPIES at the same time rapid footsteps sound in the dining room.

Dad looks terrified and dazed, padding into the kitchen with no shoes on, the overhead light shining on his hair sticking up everywhere like Einstein. His eyes are wild behind his thick glasses, in gray sweatpants, his corduroy shirt buttoned crooked.

"We've got real trouble," he says in a quiet fast voice.

"What's Easton doing?" Mom dries her hands on a paper towel.

"He's asleep."

"What's happened, Dad?" I ask.

"Nonna just called in a panic because Lex isn't there," and no matter the crisis he's always low key and soft spoken. "She doesn't know when he ran off or where he might have gone, and he's not answering his phone."

"He's here," I reply.

Picked up by our security cameras, he's small and frantic, breathing hard as if he's been running. Hesitating in front of the barn, he stares at my Tahoe, looking around, wearing his same green jacket, his backpack on. I remember the transit bus when I was leaving the mobile home park, and he must have been on it instead of asleep in his room as Nonna assumed.

"I'll get him," I hurry back through the dining room, and Dad's right behind me, ready to fly out the front door in his socks. "No!" I tell him.

"Let me help, Calli. This is my fault."

"Right now, I need you and Mom to stay inside with Easton. And it's not about fault, never has been, never will be," as I go out the door into the cold, not bothering with my down vest.

Hurrying down the walkway, I detect a droning noise coming from the water, something small and quiet like a two-stroke engine. And then I see the shadowy shape of the boat coming close, no lights on, two people in it, nearing our dock at the same moment Lex steps out from behind the pecan tree, bathed in blue among Dad's shiny squirrel traps.

"Run!" I yell at him, and he freezes as tripped motion sensors illuminate the dock.

I see the gas cans in the back of the boat as I recognize the man from the Hop-In, and the woman has short black hair, a dark jacket and white fingernails you could see from space. Both of them are armed with machine guns, and Lex has turned into a statue.

"RUN!" I scream at the top of my lungs, and he doesn't budge, staring at the monstrous duo as they dock their boat.

I take off as fast as I can, down the sidewalk, across the driveway, cutting through snow and slush. Grabbing his arm when I reach him, I take cover as best I can behind the pecan tree, which isn't nearly thick enough. We're sitting ducks, the distance between us and the dock about the length of a tennis court.

I pull out my Bullpup as the woman with short black hair and white nails trains the barrel of her full-auto weapon at us, the man lifting gas cans out of the boat.

"Drop your gun. Step away from him, and he doesn't get hurt," she calls out in a flat shrill tone at the same moment I hear a car on the driveway.

Fran is returning home, it occurs to me, all of us about to die. I order Lex to get down on the ground behind me and not move. Raising my pistol, I wait to be ripped apart by a barrage of bullets as I feel him pressing against my legs while headlights shine through trees, getting close. Then the unearthly hooting starts.

. . . WHO-WHO-WHO . . . !

Louder as a shadow swoops close to the dock, straight toward the killer couple. Mr. Owl dive-bombs them feet first, his talons going for their heads as they duck and shriek, and I start shooting.

BANG-BANG-BANG-BANG-BANG-BANG-BANG-BANG!

Both the man and woman are down, not moving, and just as quickly the great horned owl is gone. He gives a final hoot somewhere in the darkness over blue-spangled trees along the river.

"What were you doing?" it's all I can do not to explode at Lex. "I told you not to leave the house. I trusted you when I could have locked up your butt. You've got to stop almost getting me killed!"

"I shouldn't have frozen like that!" is what he has to say about it, angrily.

Mom and Dad are headed toward us. She's carrying my down vest, and it's a good thing because I'm freezing.

"What the owl did was awesome!" Lex exclaims, his attention riveted to the illuminated dock with the bodies on it. "Are they dead?"

"I'm pretty sure they are," I reply, and as if on cue the motion sensor lights go out.

"Good, because they're bad! But I froze! I was stupid," he's about to cry.

"It's okay, son, you were very brave," Dad assures him while I look at the Tahoe on the driveway.

Engine running, headlights burning, and I'm puzzled why Fran doesn't climb out. I know she couldn't have been shot, the thugs Neva dispatched not firing a round. They didn't have a chance, thanks to Mr. Owl.

"Is everybody okay?" Mom hands me the vest, and I put it on.

"Not everybody," I reply, alluding to our uninvited guests as she moves close to Lex, looking him in the eye.

"What happened?" gently, kindly, she puts her arm around a boy she's never liked or given the time of day. "What frightened you enough that you would take the bus here in the middle of the night?"

"She wants to hurt Nonna and me. And I got scared," Lex digs out his phone.

He goes to recordings, selecting one, and Neva Rong appears in the display. Her voice sounds in the blue-glowing darkness as if there's nowhere we can go to get away from her.

". . . This is Dr. Rong. Neva Rong," and she must have used a videophone app, the same thing she did to me earlier in the week. "I know it's late for a 10-year-old to be up but I thought it very important we get acquainted. Vera would want us to be friends."

"Why are you calling me?" Lex in the recording, his face surprised and wary, and I recognize the mathematically inspired art printed off the internet, his bedroom in the background.

"I realize we don't know each other yet, but I wanted you and your grandmother to be reassured that most of all I admire your talents, Lex. Or should I call you Lexell? I understand your astronomer parents named you for a lost comet. I'm very sorry about what happened to them. I believe there's a place for you at Pandora someday . . . ," she says, and the implication is obvious.

33

BOLDLY, outrageously, Neva's intention was to harass and intimidate as only she can, and to curry Lex Anderson's favor for the future. She has to headhunt the best talent on the planet like everybody else, and a 10-year-old prodigy she could control and manipulate has to be extremely appealing.

There's no better way to keep him under her thumb than to cause him real trouble, and then rescue him from it. She probably got his phone number from Vera, and when Neva called, he was smart enough to record the conversation.

". . . Vera thought the world of you," Neva goes on in her seductive tone. "But I'm afraid there's the untidy matter of the burner phone in your backpack at the failed rocket launch. After you hacked into NASA. Or that's the accusation."

"I didn't do it! Someone else did! Maybe it was you!" and Lex is a firecracker, I'll give him that.

"Well, even if you did it . . ."

"I didn't!"

"Either way, all can be forgiven. But you're going to need a lawyer, and I'm happy to help because they can be awfully pricy. As can college."

"I don't think I'm supposed to be talking to you . . . !" Lex says in the recording, and I pause it, emailing the file to myself so I can listen to it more carefully later.

He and my parents return to the house as I walk toward the Tahoe parked on the driveway. There's no sign of Fran because it isn't her SUV, and it's as if my Chase Car drove itself from the barn. But what I'm seeing is its twin, the windows down, Carme climbing out with her Bullpup pistol now that the coast is clear.

"It's a good thing I decided to drop by," she heads toward me, dressed similarly in a warmup suit, a down vest, shearling-lined boots.

"What are you doing here?" I couldn't be happier to see her.

"I had a feeling you could use some company," she says as I begin looking around for my ejected cartridge cases.

Finding them where they melted divots in the snow, I collect them as if I've forgotten everything I've ever known.

"Four rounds," I let her know, tucking the spent cartridge cases in a pocket.

"Ditto. Two per a-hole," Carme replies, and we begin walking to the river, our matching pistols with their long-barreled silencers pointed down.

We cross the sloping snowy grass to the dock, and the bodies are completely still, eerily visible in the soft glow of Mom's miniblues.

"Just so you know, I'm pretty sure I took out both of them," Carme can't resist needling me like she always does.

"Nope. I don't think so."

We trudge past the stump wrapped in lights, all that's left of our favorite tree. Images flash in my mind of sunny days and better times when we'd swing out over the river, landing like cannonballs before a lightning strike put an end to it.

"I saw what was happening before you did," Carme adds.

"Nope. Not possible since we have the same equipment and see the same things," and I'd better not find out ART gave her a heads-up that he didn't give me.

"What I mean is, I visually saw the boat as I was zooming up the driveway."

"Did you expect this might happen?"

"I'm not surprised," my sister says cryptically. "But as you know from your own cyber sleuthing, they were smart enough to go dark, no signals transmitted, and I'm betting they don't even have phones with them."

Nearing the dock, we're detected by motion sensors, and the lights blink back on, illuminating the would-be assassins. Crumpled in a spreading puddle of blood, they have 4 holes each, head shots but not snake eyes or even close.

The deadly pair was a moving target as they frantically tried to ward off their winged attacker. Their faces are shredded as if a pterodactyl got them or someone with a pitchfork.

"Told you it was me who nailed them," Carme starts going through the dead man's pockets.

"I know I did," and I'm reminded of my plaque from the Protective Services Academy for shooting a perfect score repeatedly.

But I've never been one to brag the way my sister does, and there's no point in nagging her about not wearing protective anything including gloves. She just doesn't care, and it occurs to me that I'm not hearing sirens. Looking back at the house, I see Mom watching through the dining room window, and she hasn't called anyone, not the police, at any rate. And neither has Dad.

"How are you going to explain this when Fran rolls up any minute," and I'm not talking about her discovering dead people on the dock.

I'm worried about her showing up and seeing Carme. She's supposed to be overseas somewhere, not here with me, both of us armed with matching clothing, Chase Cars and guns.

"Fran hasn't left the scene at the mobile home park," my sister says, her quick fingers darting in and out of the dead man's pockets, producing a thick roll of hundred-dollar bills.

"Why? Because that doesn't sound like her," I take a look at the bass boat tied to a cleat.

There's nothing in it except a folded nautical chart. A range bag filled with loaded magazines. Two large-caliber pistols. A handheld spotlight.

"Fran called Mom a while ago and said it's like herding cats getting everybody working as a team," Carme starts counting the dead man's money. "And she'll probably be at the scene all night, making sure everything's done exactly right."

"That's industrious of her when just a few hours ago she was freaking out all over the place because of a snake tank and an empty owl cage," and as I say it, I realize that Fran got considerably settled and more centered after I told her what I'd found in the shooting log from Christmas Eve three years ago.

Knowing that Neva had sent a hitman to terrorize her, that the flat tires were deliberate, seemed to hit a reset button. I felt a resolve in Fran, a slow-burning defiance that's been missing since then.

"Ten grand," Carme says with a low whistle. "That's a lot of cash to be carrying on a boat ride."

She zips the roll of hundred-dollar bills inside her jacket pocket.

"Finders, keepers," she says, no more bothered by breaking the law now than she was at the Point Comfort Inn.

The heck with gloves or my crime scene case, the heck with everything except accomplishing the mission and staying alive.

"But I sure hope that wasn't their entire fee for service," she adds. "Otherwise, I guess we're a cheap date."

"Be careful digging around with bare hands," I go on to remind Carme that she may know how to tamper with crime scenes but she's not trained to work them. "You don't want to touch something you wish you hadn't, including blood."

00:00:00:00:0

THE DEAD WOMAN stares up blindly, gorily, one of her eyes partially avulsed from the socket, her hair a helmet of sticky red from deep wounds to her scalp.

I avoid blood as I search the pockets of her jacket, remembering the slender arm reaching out the Cherokee's window in the drive-through, the black leather sleeve, the flashy rings and gaudy nail polish.

Finding what might be house or apartment keys, I ask Carme if she's seeing one that might belong to a Jeep Cherokee.

"Nope, and I'm not seeing a phone, are you?"

"Not so far."

"As I expected, they knew what they were doing," she turns the dead man on his side, and blood spills out of the small holes in his head.

One went through his left temple, another through the bridge of his nose, two more through his cheek and jaw.

"Bingo!" Carme slides a wallet out of a back pocket.

"I have a feeling the rented Jeep they were driving is out of sight in a garage at the Dog Beach Marina," I surmise. "They might have a short-term rental or someone does," and I'm thinking of the assassin in the Denali again.

Unzipping the dead woman's black leather jacket, I check for inner pockets, discovering that she also was carrying a wallet.

"Fang Yanshi," I read from a driver's license, and in Chinese the surname means *agreeable demo*, ART lets me know in my lenses, as if it might be helpful. "A Los Angeles address, 34 years old," and I ask out loud if there's an apartment, home, anything in that name around here.

It dawns on me that there's no problem talking to ART in front of my sister, who knows him better than I do. But I'm unsure what will happen when we query him at the same time or how he'll decide who to answer first. I'm not sure artificial intelligence or quantum computing could make the right choice, one that feels comfortable for all parties, and not dismissive or hurtful.

"There's nothing in the greater Hampton area that's owned or rented under the name Fang Yanshi or anything similar," ART informs me in my earpiece.

"What about the name Beaufort Tell, if that's who this dude really was?" and it's Carme asking, looking at a rental receipt from the Dog Beach Marina, confirming the very darn thing I'm worried about.

She's hearing ART in her earpiece the same way I am, helping herself to him as if she has special status rather much like she does with everyone. Although to be fair, they've worked together for the past 6 months based on what Dick relayed this morning, and I've known ART less than a day.

"Anything in the name of Beaufort Tell or anything close? That's what's on the driver's license and the boat rental receipt, paid in cash," Carme is talking to ART. "And switch to audible. It's just us. He might have called himself Bo for short. Bo Tell, and that's a good name to have if you want to be teased a lot."

"I bet some people pronounced it *bottle* or teased him to *Bo tell it on the mountain*," I agree, knowing all too well what it's like to have a name people make fun of, at times brutally.

Like Callisto or Carme with a last name like Chase, our initials are *CC* as in *carbon copy*. I've been around the mean-spirited schoolyard more than once, and I guess killing strangers for pay is one way to get revenge.

"Negative," ART lets us know out loud. "No residences or hotel rooms in the name of Beaufort Tell, Bo Tell or anything similar."

"Fang Yanshi might have been the hitman's wife or girlfriend," I suggest.

"Because of the rings she's wearing," Carme says. "The same ones he had on, remember?" as if I could forget. "It's looking like I likely took out Fang's main man, and I'd say she was pretty motivated to settle a score tonight."

I ask ART to give us the names of every rental at the Dog Beach Marina apartment complex where the Cherokee was last caught on camera.

"But run an algorithm that excludes people who don't fit the profile," I'm saying. "Such as families, young or elderly couples . . ."

Instantly names begin appearing in my lenses, and I assume in Carme's too. But she doesn't seem to notice what's crawling by right now, and if my hair could stand on end, it would.

"Speaking of getting teased in school," I say, dumbfounded. "Especially during roll call when the teacher said the last name first. *Kracker comma Jack* and everybody laughs. Kracker with a *K*," and ART gives us the address.

"Now what?" I ask Carme. "I don't know what you're thinking but someone might want to get their bodies out of here before Fran comes back. She won't appreciate the creative way we handle things."

"I was thinking of letting the police deal with it."

"Why play by the rules now?" and I can't believe what I'm hearing.

"They're in our favor because what went down was caught on our security cameras," Carme checks out the gas cans on the dock, 4 of them, a total of 8 gallons. "Enough to torch the place," she announces matter-of-factly. "With everybody in it, I suspect. After they shot whoever happened to be here, and it's as good a case for self-defense as you'll ever find."

We start walking back to the house.

"ART, alter the metadata so we're not on film at the same time," she adds.

"Is this the way it's always going to be? That we can't be seen together?" I'm more bothered by that than anything else, including the people we've killed.

"We're more powerful when we're apart," she echoes what Dick says.

"And you believe that?" I detach the suppressor from my Bullpup, and they've cooled enough for me to tuck them in my vest pocket.

"For the most part," she says as we climb the porch steps.

"Seriously?" I protest, and I don't want it to be true that I'll wake up tomorrow finding her gone again. "Then explain what we just did, Carme? Because all kidding aside, *both* of us took them out."

"The way this needs to go down, Sisto, is you handled the situation yourself. You get all the credit. The only embarrassment is it took an owl and 8 rounds to get the job done," she playfully, affectionately nudges me with her elbow like the old days.

34

AT LEAST while I was drugged, roped and tied inside suite 604, I caught up on my sleep, and it's a darn good thing. When Dick picks me up at 0600 hours sharp, I've not been to bed.

"Morning," he says as I climb into the back seat, setting my bags on the floor by my feet.

"Good morning," I buckle up in the dark, looking at the backs of the agents up front, neither of them greeting me.

"Let's go," Dick says to them, and he asks me how I'm doing.

"Fine, thanks."

I act as if the morning has been like any other, the past few hours a marathon of interrogations that began when Fran sped home from the mobile home park, her emergency lights going full tilt after Mom called her about the shooting. By then, Carme and her Chase Car had vanished again, leaving me to explain that I supposedly took out both assassins single-handedly.

Fran and other police are busy on our property, all kinds of investigators roaming about as I'm driven off in Dick's black Suburban. I recognize his Secret Service detail from the aviation hangar when I rushed there after the rocket exploded and the Space Station was hacked. The agents sitting up front were part of the posse looking for Carme.

Or that's what I assumed when in fact they were dealing with other dire problems including the missing GOD chip. Except I'm wondering how missing it really is as I think of comments Mom made when we were talking earlier on the porch and in the kitchen. Dad shouldn't have told Lex *a darn tooting thing*, she said, and she *saw what was coming*.

She knows from painful experience what can happen when Dad tucks his latest ward under his wing. If my unstoppable, secretive mother *saw what was coming*, she would do something about it. And not tell anyone. Ever. Not even Dick, who's all business this morning, decked out in dress blues, a chest full of ribbons, 4 shiny silver stars on his epaulets.

There are few cars on the road, and nobody talks as we drive fast with the grille lights strobing, the Suburban's cockpit, storage boxes and other extra features the same as my Tahoe's. Dick is busy on his phone as usual, and I monitor my own communications and updates in my SPIES as we head to NASA Langley's 10-story hangar.

Fifteen minutes later we're crossing the Southwest Branch Back River, then following Perimeter Road around the airfield, headed to the hangar looming in the dark. Its massive sliding door is closed as we drive across the lighted ramp, my attention seized by what awaits on the helipad. Flat gray, sleek and elegant, and I don't need the specs from ART to know what I'm looking at.

The Agusta 109 helicopter has a fully articulated 4-bladed rotor system, twin Pratt & Whitney engines, and can cruise all day at around 155 knots (178 mph). I've piloted a few but nothing tricked out like this one with its searchlight, FLIR, and mounts for machine guns and missiles, and what I wouldn't give to fly it.

Grabbing our bags, we head that way as two men in black flight suits meet us, neither of them military or they'd salute Dick to the point of genuflecting. Instead, they shake our hands, the younger of them flashing me a smile and winking. I'm stunned when he greets me by name, and I recognize his voice.

Only Conn Lacrosse isn't really CIA as it turns out. He's a member of the Joint Terrorism Task Force and assigned to the Central Intelligence Agency, I'm informed.

"So Calli, how badly are you salivating right now?" he says, and I also didn't know he was a chopper pilot.

He's much younger than I thought, I'd peg him mid-30ish, someone who spends serious time in the gym, and probably eats all the right stuff like hummus and salads. Easy on the eye, he has wavy chestnut hair, a clean-shaven square jaw, and perfect teeth that he might whiten.

There are no identifying patches, no name tag on his flight suit, and the material looks suspiciously woven with sensors. His fitness-tracker-type bracelet and tinted glasses are remarkably similar to my CUFF and PEEPS.

"No stick time for you today," he picks on me just like he's always done over the phone, only I never knew he might be flirting. "You get to be chauffeured."

"It makes me sick," as I do a walk around, feeling one of the worst cases of aircraft envy I've suffered in a while, and I ask if he's the pilot in command.

"Who other?"

"Then you'd better hope you do a good job because I'm watching," I point at my eyes and his, the way Carme does when she's being aggressive, and the gesture sets off the Suburban's car alarm, the engine gunning.

The awful honking and roaring stop as quickly as they started, and Dick has a bemused smile as we climb into the cabin of the helicopter, sitting down in the forward-facing seats.

"That's happened twice now," I let him know. "I cause a misfire, setting off the car alarm, the accelerator gunning and sticking."

"Our bad," he admits. "Pointing at your eyes sent the wrong message to ART. He confused the gesture with a different one I don't need to bore you with," translated, he's not going to tell me. "Suffice it to say what you witnessed is a misinterpreted gesture that causes misfires. A programming error that needs to be sorted out."

We begin fastening our 5-point harnesses, and it frosts my cupcake. I want to be up front flying right seat, not sitting back here like I'm in a taxicab, talking. I don't care who it's with.

"The intercom will be set to *crew only*," Dick informs me as Conn and his copilot begin going through their preflight checklist. "I'll give you the upshot of what's about to happen, Calli. And I don't want you to get upset."

"Why would I?" I feel the blood drain from my face, always dreading that he's about to deliver terrible news, because he has before.

These days I worry most that it will be about Carme. I've always known that if something happens to her, Dick would be the one who tells me. Somehow, he'd get word first, before her own family because of who he is. I ask him if she's okay as I hear the sound of the Agusta's battery turning on, my built-in spectrum analyzer picking up electronic signals like mad.

"She left before Fran or anybody else showed up, didn't say where she was going and I've not had any contact with her since she left," I explain.

Carme also didn't mention if and when I might see her again, and I hope I'll get used to living like this. Here today. Or maybe not. Showing up when least expected just in time to shoot someone and hide the evidence.

"You don't need to concern yourself about her," Dick says as the first engine fires up, the blades turning, and we put on our headsets. "You need to worry about yourself," his voice over the intercom now, and I turn down the volume, my hearing more sensitive than it used to be.

"What is it I might get upset about?" I push the foam-covered microphone boom closer until it's touching my bottom lip as the second engine fires up, both of them in flight idle.

"It was never my intention to throw you into the fray this soon. Much sooner than ever intended," Dick's voice in my headset. "I wouldn't blame you for being angry and feeling put upon," as the blades spin faster.

We can't hear the chatter between the pilots or their calls to the tower, and Dick assures me they're not listening to us either. It seems an irony that he would expect me to believe that considering who we're talking about. The CIA and Secret Service. The commander of Space Force and a NASA cyber investigator. I don't know why any of us would trust anybody, least of all each other.

"What *things* are you talking about?" I insist. "Beyond what I learned at Dodd Hall."

The helicopter is getting light on its wheeled landing gear, and I feel us lifting off, nosing forward to gain speed.

"I realize you were preoccupied at the Gantry yesterday afternoon," he changes the subject as he does so artfully, referencing my foot pursuit with Lex while the test model was splashing down. "What did you think of the MOBE?"

"I guess it's like patenting an invention, then seeing it in a store, and nobody told you," I reply, the NASA Langley campus below dark, empty and slushy with melting snow.

The Gantry hulks blackly against the horizon, the first morning light touching vacuum spheres that look like ghostly planets from up here.

00:00:00:00:0

FLYING OVER Smith Lake, we cross I-95 at an altitude of 365.8 meters (1,200 feet), ART lets me know. He's thoughtful enough to give me constant flight updates on our speed, heading, aircraft in the area, nearby cell towers and other obstructions.

After hearing me complain to Dick about how badly I wanted to be at the controls instead of a passenger, ART gave me my own heads-up display in my PEEPS and SPIES. I'm able to monitor the same maps the pilots have in the cockpit. I almost believe my artificial friend feels a little bad for me.

By now it's obvious where we're headed but I'm not sure why or what's expected of me. For the past 40 minutes, Dick and I have been discussing the extensive research I conducted on the MOBE, although it wasn't called that then. Helping with the design of such a vehicle was one of my first tasks when I began working at NASA Langley.

I remember driving myself crazy imagining every far-flung potential and worst-case scenario. It was on me to anticipate conditions and failures that could cause catastrophic problems, if the heat shielding got damaged, for example. Or a thruster malfunctioned, causing the spacecraft to go into a spin, running out of fuel and spiraling down into the Earth's atmosphere. In other words, toast.

Less than 10 minutes out from our destination, and Quantico is directly under us now. Usually one doesn't fly over the Marine Corps base, and is polite enough to give the FBI National Academy a wide berth. But our pilot in command navigates through restricted, sensitive airspace as if he answers to no one, gracefully banking east toward the Potomac, the sun low over the river as we begin to follow it.

When the visibility is as good as it is right now, I'm reminded that the past is always present, and at times I get the uncanny feeling that nothing begins or ends, everything happening at once. In creeks and shallow water along the shoreline are the coffin-shaped charred hulls of Civil War fleets set ablaze more than a century and a half ago.

Chimneys and other ruins stand starkly alone in fields where marauding soldiers burned homes to the ground. Nearing Washington National Airport, we cross the Potomac, entering the District of Columbia, and Dick gets around to telling me why I'm headed to a secret briefing.

He informs me that 5 days ago, alarming orbital maneuvers were detected in the geostationary belt (GEO), 35,786 kilometers (22,236 miles) above Earth's equator. The area of space is where some communications and spy satellites live, and this is the sort of thing I've feared.

"We already were aware of something unusual," he explains. "We've been monitoring the strange activity since we first picked it up on radar 6 months ago," and by *we*, he must mean Space Force. "But this was different and far more aggressive."

"Six months ago, Carme was implanted with her network," I put two and two together.

"After she was almost a casualty to what I suspect is going on, and you'll hear more about that at the briefing," Dick says. "We wouldn't have escalated like this but the boom was dropping, Calli, and now the situation has gone critical," he continues sharing information drop by drop, reminding me of how stingy he was with the space bag of lemon punch.

"And what role does MOBE play in all this?" I hate to ask.

"Your escape vehicle has a very important one."

"What do you mean, *my* vehicle?" *besides the fact I helped develop it more than a little bit,* I'm tempted to brag like my sister but I don't.

"The MOBE is an emergency escape vehicle for a spaceplane you haven't met but know a lot about," Dick says, as usual not answering what I asked. "The escape module is attached to the winged vehicle at launch, and concealed in the fairing of the rocket until you reach space. Prior to your return to Earth, the MOBE will be detached and left to orbit."

"In other words, it's parked up there for future use," I fill in the blank because it's not a new concept with us.

Besides the MOBE there eventually could be other specialized modules for laboratories, debris collection, drone deployment, and also potential escape vehicles if something happens to your spaceplane, the mothership. Eventually, there will be a school of MOBE-type vehicles launched and left up there. Or that's what we talked about, I remind him.

"A futuristic concept, only the future got here a lot quicker than we thought," Dick says, and what I'm hearing in my headset is getting more surreal by the second.

It comes as no surprise that Sierra Nevada Corporation would help NASA and the military develop some top secret new spacecraft or even more than one of them. But I never imagined I might be an important component beyond any ideas I might come up with.

ART lets me know without asking that we're three minutes out from our destination, and collecting my coat from an empty seat, I'm reminded with a sinking feeling that I'm not in my usual tactical clothes. I look nerdy Howdy Doody, maybe a little plainclothes detective-ish, doing my best to follow Dick's texted instructions to "dress civilian but look professional."

I'm not sure I fit the bill in my black suit from a Banana Republic outlet store and my best ankle boots that I buffed in a hurry on my way out the door. Slowing down and going lower, we're flying smack in the middle of the most restricted airspace in the country. I watch out my window as we slalom around the drab fortress of the Pentagon, and I think of Fort Monroe.

Arlington Cemetery's perfect rows of white headstones bring to mind Chiclets candy-coated gum, the Lincoln Memorial stolid and proud. The Washington Monument seems to stand up straighter as we thunder over, and Dick has no worries about being late for good reason. Rush hour and gridlock traffic are of no concern if you follow roads from the air but don't need to drive on them.

The White House is off our nose, a big American flag waving on the roof where snipers stand sentry like statues overseeing an ancient city.

"They expecting company?" I indicate the rooftop detail as we hover-taxi over the South Lawn's fountain . . .

The tennis court tucked in trees on my left . . .

Big magnolias and a guard booth . . .

"The president of Uganda is meeting with ours," Dick says. "Security is stepped up for a number of reasons," including us, I infer as we close in on three metal plates that have been set down in the snow, one for each wheel of the landing gear.

The White House has no helipad, the landing zone precisely located. One wouldn't want rotor wash to blow down the Rose Garden or damage trees planted with gold shovels by presidents and first ladies throughout time and from all around the world. The South Portico with its twin staircases and Greek columns is out my window, snow billowing in a whiteout as we set down as soft as a feather.

Engines are cut to flight idle, and we wait to shut down as Secret Service agents in earpieces and ballistic gear stand watch. Dick and I take off our harnesses, and after a quick cooldown, the engines are turned off, the main rotor braked to a halt, and we put on our coats. He hands me my backpack but says to leave everything else.

The helicopter is going to wait, and will drop us off back at the Langley hangar, he adds to my confusion. If I'm going home after this, then why did he have me pack for several days? But I'm not going to ask what might sound unseemly and too personal.

35

THE WEST WING is off to our left, and I would have thought someone might have shoveled a path.

The snow is deep in places, seeping into my boots. When we reach the pavement, my socks are wet, and soon enough my feet will start to itch. I hope I don't start making squishy sounds next, and of all times to have a wardrobe failure.

"I don't know why you couldn't have mentioned this," I finally speak my mind to Dick, walking with purpose past huge boxwoods, tall black lampposts, and I have no doubt there are cameras and microphones monitoring everything. "I'm not a kid anymore. I'm not someone you and Mom are supposed to keep secrets from," and it sounds weird as I say it, as if he's my father.

"You're told what you need to know, and when it's appropriate, Calli," he says, end of story, and I don't appreciate it.

But it's probably not a good idea to squabble in front of the West Wing's white awning with the presidential seal, the entrance guarded by Secret Service police in tactical gear, ready with assault rifles. Landing on the lawn, we didn't go through the usual layers of checkpoints, and once inside we produce our creds to an agent in a dark suit sitting at a desk.

There's no x-ray screening once you've gotten this far but our backpacks are gone through, and we're checked with a handheld scanner. All the while this is going on, I'm nervously expecting my SIN to be detected. No matter what Dick claims about my invisibility cloak, I'm not convinced. But if I'm sending out questionable signals, there's no sign of it based on the demeanor of everyone we encounter.

Beyond the security desk is a sitting area of blue carpet, blue upholstered furniture, and big oil paintings where the president of Uganda sits with his detail, all of them in suits. They don't look at us, and we don't look at them as Dick leads me to the sofa. I'm surprised what a bustling place this is, like a busy corporation in an elegant antique setting with a constant traffic of fast-walking people.

A lot of them are in uniform, the West Wing run by the White House Military Office, WHMO, pronounced *whamo*. Everyone is dressed a lot better than I am. So far, I'm the only woman not in a skirt, and I feel self-conscious in my simple suit, and shiny lace-up boots that look a little more combat-like than I thought when I first put them on this morning.

"We're early, so if you need to freshen up, you've got exactly 6 minutes," Dick says as I stare hard at the familiar painting hanging behind his head, recognizing *Washington Crossing the Delaware*, and it's not a print.

Emanuel Leutze, 1851, I'm informed in my lenses. On loan from the Metropolitan Museum of Art, and I'm sure the White House can borrow anything it wants. I look around at the large gilt clock with a rampant eagle on top, the mahogany bookcase, other American-themed oil paintings of Yosemite Park and Old Faithful.

People come and go nonstop, some have scarves around their necks but no coats, and as I take mine off I wish I'd left it in the helicopter. I wish even more that my wool socks weren't soaked, my feet beginning to itch as I predicted, and I ask Dick where the ladies' room might be. Behind us off a short hallway, he points as I catch a flash of blood-red out of the corner of my eye.

I look up in time to see Neva Rong in a fitted red skirt suit and matching heels as high as stilts. She's walking away from the security desk without a glance in our direction but I sense the monster sees us. If nothing else she had to hear our helicopter coming in, and she takes the same short hallway Dick just pointed out. Headed to the ladies' room, no doubt, and I wonder what the hell-o she's doing here!

"You might want to wait a minute," Dick watches me carefully.

"You saw her, right?"

"She's a regular. I've run into her before. Sometimes she's cloyingly nice. Other times like now she pretends she doesn't see me."

"She'd better not be sitting in on our meeting," as if I have any say about it.

And I don't, none at all, let's be honest. Barely an hour ago I didn't even know I would be here.

"No, she's definitely not," Dick answers in no uncertain terms, and I get up from the couch. "You might want to wait," he repeats.

Meanwhile the clock is ticking, and I can't be late but need to deal with my itchy feet among other necessities. I have a right to the White House ladies' room just as much as Neva does. And I head there, following the short passageway, the walls arranged with poster-size photographs of the First Couple boarding Air Force One, entertaining royalty, visiting disaster sites.

I reach the ladies' room as Neva opens its mahogany door, and we almost run right into each other.

"It's a onesie," she says, screwing the lid back on her gold jar of lip balm, tucking it in her black eel-skin bag.

Behind her is a stand-alone white porcelain sink, a toilet, more artwork and a lot of gold.

"What brings you here on an early Monday?" not smiling, I ask as if this is routine for me, and more to the point. "Because you certainly seem to pop up all over the place. Including your late sister's apartment and the morgue," I'm not pulling any punches.

"You know, life doesn't have to be so difficult and dreary," Neva says, stepping into the hallway, paying no attention to people moving past, everyone intense and in a hurry.

"I'm sorry about Vera," I taunt her with a subject I know she doesn't like while trying not to be distracted by my feet itching like I have poison ivy. "I'm sure you must feel terrible, having just spent time with her before heading off to Wallops Island for the ill-fated rocket launch and everything else that went *wrong*," and I can tell by the angry flash in her eyes that she gets the message and the pun.

"You'd be so much better served if you would think of the big picture instead of constantly tilting at windmills, Calli," she says. "Look around you. Look where you are. Isn't this what everything's about?"

"Not for me and the people I come from."

"Yes, you and your people," her face hardens into a mask of condescension, and for an instant I see the beast inside her. "Should you ever tire of working endlessly for nothing and decide to venture out into the private sector where everything's headed, do give me a call," she adds disgustingly.

"That would be *nev-a*," I mock her name again.

"Now if you'll excuse me," she smiles icily. "I have a meeting with two presidents and don't want to be late."

00:00:00:00:0

INSIDE the ladies' room, I lock the door, freshening up, sitting on top of the toilet lid to pull off my boots. I peel off my wet socks, at a loss as to what to do with them, trying to calm myself, my hands shaking slightly.

"Oh, what the heck!" I drop my socks in the trash, feeling even tackier.

When I return to the sitting area, I find Dick has been joined by Conn. And if he can wear his flight suit to a meeting at the White House, I don't know why I had to dress *smart casual.*

"Everything all right?" Dick asks quietly, and maybe I won't take fashion tips from him anymore. "You seem agitated," and I remember I'm transmitting data that he and certain others are constantly downloading.

"She basically just offered me a job," I answer.

"I'm sure she did," he says as a Secret Service agent appears to take us to the Situation Room.

Beyond the sitting area and down carpeted steps, we follow toward the mess hall run by the Navy, busy at this hour with the breakfast crowd. As we move past, I hungrily smell bacon, catching glimpses of blue carpet, paintings of naval scenes, and important-looking people sitting around blue-cloth-covered tables. Another short hallway, and this one dead-ends at a heavy oak door, a red phone receiver on the paneled wall.

The agent scans us into an installation of offices and workstations where the most sensitive information on the planet is exchanged. At the reception desk we're given keys to store our computers, phones, and other electronic devices in lockers. I left my PEEPS in the helicopter but still have on my SPIES and CUFF, and no one seems the wiser.

I recognize the Situation Room from photos I've seen, a big conference table surrounded by black leather chairs. The walls are lit up with flat-screens showing live feeds. The International Space Station. The Baikonur Cosmodrome, Russia's launch facility in

Kazakhstan. Images of China from space. Plus, maps of satellites and junk orbiting the Earth like countless electrons spinning around an atom.

Dick avoids the empty chair at the head of the table, and the one to the right of it. He sits down, and Conn and I take seats on either side of him. Most officials I recognize as I look around a sea of paperwork, water bottles, dark suits, white shirts and ties. ART takes it upon himself to inform me in my SPIES who everybody is in case I grew up in a barn.

But then again, I sort of did, and it feels that way as I sit here sockless in my fire-sale suit surrounded by Mount Olympus. The secretary of state, and directors of the expected agencies. NASA. DARPA. The Secret Service. The National Security Agency (NSA). The National Reconnaissance Office (NRO). The Defense Intelligence Agency (DIA). The Pentagon's Defense Innovation Unit (DIU).

Everybody is a lot more important than I am, to say the least, and I feel shadings of what Lex must feel when he visits a food pantry and rides the bus. I turn toward the door at the sound of footsteps as the president and vice president of the United States walk in, taking their chairs, paper rustling, people greeting each other and making small talk.

"Mr. President, Mr. Vice President," Dick gets started, acknowledging everyone.

He slides over an electronic tablet, the remote control for the data walls, and I can tell he's been through this routine many times before.

"I think you know from the materials in front of you that last week we had one of the most serious cyberattacks to date," he begins, and the president raises a finger the way he does when he's about to interrupt.

"We're in a cyber war," he says, not known for beating around the bush. "An armed space race," unscrewing the cap from his water bottle. "I don't know what it's going to take to make the public understand that. It's not an eventuality, it's right now," taking a drink. "We've been suffering attacks on our satellites, serious ones for months, and it's going to stop. That's why we're here today. Because it's going to stop now," and I must be imagining it when he looks straight at me.

"We *assume* they're attacks," says the CIA. "What we know for a fact is something is causing incorrect data."

"The most dangerous thing of all," the vice president concurs.

"I'd rather have a dead satellite than a brain-damaged one," the NSA agrees, as does the DIA, the Secret Service, NASA and the Pentagon, everybody nodding their heads, flipping pages and jotting notes.

"I'm going to show you an example," Dick picks up the tablet. "An incident in Syria last summer involving one of our prototypes," and I wonder who he means. "Incorrect GPS satellite coordinates were given to a Delta Force, and it ended up exactly where it shouldn't have been. Just watch."

All eyes are on the data walls as a video begins to play, accompanied by the subwoofer racket of heavy metal, diesel engines and blowing sand in the muddy lime green of infrared. Refugees with haunted faces stare out from the gouged sockets of bombed doorways and windows.

I recognize sacred ruins, the battered province of Raqqa as a helicopter gunship churns in bone-shaking low and slow. A Blackhawk MH-60L Direct Action Penetrator (DAP) flies over at 91.5 meters (300 feet) or less, tricked out with air-to-air missiles and rocket pods, chain guns under the belly, mini-Gatling guns on the wing stubs, and Hellfires.

Peeling off to the Euphrates River, it skims over water, graceful as a predatory bird, and next we're taken inside the glass cockpit. Radio chatter peppered by gunfire, and there she is, Carme on the flight deck in a combat helmet, flying solo from the right seat, crowded by a stockpile of ammunition amid a dazzling array of technical information and flight data in LCDs.

My sister shrieks into hairpin turns, the instrument readings straining toward the red, our Delta troops surrounded on the ground and about to get slaughtered. Radio exchanges are frantic, the situation critical on the ground.

"Kilo 1-5, our position is compromised. Request immediate Q-R-F!"

"Negative on Q-R-F, Kilo 1-5."

"Kilo 1-5, request speedball immediately."

"Negative on the speedball."

"Then air assist, scramble some F-18s over here now . . . !"

I can see Carme's CUFF and the unusual sensor-embedded fabric of her flight suit as her black-gloved finger presses the mic trigger on the cyclic.

"Kilo 1-5, be advised in from the north, danger close, three miles," her voice over the radio just like mine, banking hard to the right, thudding lower.

"Denied. You're not cleared hot. Do not engage. Repeat. Denied. Do not engage."

"A little late for that," Carme comes back.

My heart pounds as I watch her descend into the firefight from hell. Lower and slower, settling into an audacious rock-hard hover, eye to eye with enemy rebels on the ground.

The burping of Gatling guns. BAM-BAM-BAM-BAM-BAM . . . ! Hellfires streaking. BLAM! BLAM . . . ! Scorched earth, and in the distance the massive up-lit Tabqa Dam . . . , then Dick pauses the video.

"Erroneous information that created a catastrophic situation as you may have gathered," Dick says, "and the pilot happened to be in the area when all this went down," he doesn't mention that the pilot is my twin. "And she disobeyed orders not to intervene, not necessarily what we encourage in the military but in this case effective."

There's a lot of discussion around the table about other incidents I've not heard about until now. The result is any number of near disasters from erroneous information that caused the wrong decisions to be made as was the case with the Delta Force my sister saved.

"Brain damage," I speak up, may as well, I'm sitting here. "Far worse to compromise key satellites than to take them out. Bad data is worse than none at all."

"That's the point," Dick agrees.

As the president lifts his finger again, not looking up from his note taking, "Are we concerned that someone's launched a weapon we don't know about?"

"Very much so," Dick says, zooming in on a time lapse of what's assumed to be a satellite.

Except it appears to be moving from one orbit to another as it speeds around the Earth, and no satellite I'm aware of can do such a thing.

36

“IT’S HARD to tell from this,” Conn directs everyone’s attention to the map of GEO on a data wall. “But that little pinpoint of light you see moving in this time-lapsed video is moving in the direction of a multibillion-dollar intelligence-gathering satellite capable of listening in on conversations and conducting top secret reconnaissance.”

“USA555A was launched three weeks ago from Kennedy Space Center,” Dick takes over again. “And the concern is that an adversary is aware, and the spy satellite is what this rogue object is now pursuing.”

“Does the public know about this recently launched spy satellite? Because it’s news to me,” the NSA puzzles.

“Not that we know of,” Dick says. “We were hoping certain adversaries might believe it or something similar blew up in our rocket last week. We tried to give that impression, that maybe there was something in the payload no one was talking about.”

“Trying to capitalize on the disaster,” Conn explains as I envision Wallops Island emergency crews recovering debris from the blast site throughout the night. “But it didn’t work. By all appearances an adversary is aware of USA555A and is targeting it.”

“Whoever’s behind this has stepped up what we believe is the next imminent attack,” Dick adds. “Whatever this rogue object is, it has sufficient thruster power to change trajectories and altitudes, now moving on a course that places it directly in the path of our satellite."

"Thankfully, whatever this rogue spacecraft is, it's not any faster than it is," the Pentagon says.

"Thankfully indeed, and to the swiftest go the spoils," Dick replies. "If the vehicle involved were any faster, we wouldn't have been able to mobilize in time. Even so, neutralizing the problem is a long shot," and that's a word I could have done without.

"How much time do we have?" asks the Secret Service. "Now that this rogue object has changed its orbit again as of 5 days ago, escalating possible contact with USA555A."

"By our calculations," Dick answers, "it's scheduled to be within striking range tomorrow at 0900 Zulu time, 4:00 p.m. here in DC," and now I understand the urgency.

It's making sense why everything had to happen when it did, and as fast as it has. It's not just about the missing GOD chip. It's about deploying a spacecraft to GEO.

"We must prevent another attack on our satellites, the most sensitive one yet," Dick explains. "We have to figure out who and what's doing this, and eliminate the threat."

"Pure sabotage," says the secretary of state.

"Space terrorism," the CIA adds gravely.

"One of Uganda's concerns," the president grimly lifts his finger. "Nations are reticent to invest in starting a space program if this is what happens."

"Some kind of weapon is being deployed. Has to be," the DIA adds.

"But why can't we pick that up on radar?" the Secret Service wants to know.

"How could there be a weaponized spacecraft up there and we have no idea?" the vice president looks extremely unhappy about it.

"It would have to be constructed of a material with a very low signal," DARPA decides.

"Like plastic," I volunteer. "It's extremely hard to see on radar, especially if you're not looking for it, and this is causing increased problems with space debris. A lot of CubeSats and other things being sent up are made of plastics and other composites that don't include metal."

"Last week we lost communication on the International Space Station," Dick says. "And there were other malfunctions that could have been fatal to our astronauts while they were installing a quantum node during a spacewalk. The Station commander was riding the robotic arm when it lost power, stranding her," and touching the tablet, he shows another video.

Astronauts Peggy Whitson and Jack Fischer are weightless inside the Space Station, holding themselves in place with foot loops, both of them somber. And it bolsters me a little to see they're dressed no better than I am, in khakis, polo shirts with their mission patches, and socks.

". . . There were multiple failures simultaneously," Peggy looks into the camera, bobbing a little as she floats in microgravity, hanging on by her toes. "Both electrical channels powering the prime and redundant strings of the robotic arm failed."

"Then there was an entirely separate event," Jack says. "The prime and redundant communication systems also failed . . . ," and Dick stops the recording.

"It's not credible that this cluster of disasters in addition to the rocket's destruction were a coincidence," he renders his verdict. "An examination of commands sent to the Station found that they were sent from another location."

"Hacking?" asks the secretary of state.

"Actually, worse than that, as it turns out," Dick answers. "Bad information from a communications satellite in GEO. And this same problem resulted in a rogue signal that caused us to hit the kill switch at Wallops Island," as he's saying this, I think of Lex.

Damage to a communications satellite didn't happen because he or anyone else dialed a number on a burner phone.

"I'm confused," says the NSA. "If a satellite was damaged, how does that explain what seems to be precision targeting of a resupply rocket and the Space Station."

"Not necessarily precision," Conn replies, and I would have spoken up if he hadn't. "If a certain satellite is one of several that controls the communications on the Space Station or at Wallops, then if you damage this satellite sufficiently? Chances are good there's going to be a serious if not catastrophic problem."

"Exactly," I concur. "When a bad command is given to a rocket or a dish antenna linked to it, no matter the source or the intention, you don't take a chance. You hit the kill switch. When bad commands were given to the Space Station, it lost communication and power to the robotic arm. But it just as easily might have caused some other major malfunction."

"Scary stuff," the vice president scratches notes on a legal pad.

"In other words, there's something up there that's going to keep on doing this until we figure out what it is," the president decides, his jaw defiantly set. "What do you suggest?"

"That we deploy a vehicle immediately to intercept whatever this thing is," Dick says. "To get close enough that we might detect a signal, something we're not picking up on the ground. Or better yet, see what it is."

"What vehicle are we talking about?" asks the CIA. "Because I thought I knew everything going on around here," to a flutter of tense chuckles.

"Probably the best-kept secret in recent memory or maybe ever, and a critical part of the Gemini project," Dick says as if they already know about it, and I see nods around the table. "While you're aware of Space Force's mission, you aren't aware of this," as an image fills the flat-screens around the room.

The interior of a spotless hangar, and parked inside it is what looks like a mini Space Shuttle, only sleeker and with small morphing wings like what I saw in the wind tunnel. Its skin is a startling dark gray, and overhead light flares on an intricate gridwork of metallic filaments forming a conductive network.

The vehicle is flown single pilot with AI assistance, in this case ART, but there's no mention of him. A Propulsion Engineered Quantum Orbit Defender, Dick tells the Situation Room.

"Or PEQUOD as in the novel *Moby-Dick*," he explains, and I wonder if anybody gets the irony that his last name is Melville. "An allusion to the murderous whaling ship painted black, and covered with whale bones and teeth," he adds.

00:00:00:00:0

AT HIGH NOON our helicopter hovers along a taxiway at the pace of a brisk walk, making a loud low beeline toward NASA's oldest aviation hangar, built in 1951, the metal siding dull and tired, barely glinting in the sun.

The rooftop radome where Carme was hiding last week is white like snow against the cloudless sky. NASA's big blue meatball logo is faded but proud over the closed sliding bay door, and it's hard to fathom what's happened since I encountered Dick and his posse. It must have been someone else sticking her hands in the air before getting shoved facedown into the snow.

Our sleek bird settles gently a safe distance from the Boeing C-17 that wasn't here this morning, and Air Force loadmasters are collecting short segments of thick wooden planks from the tarmac. Something big with wheels must have been hauled inside the combat-gray transporter with its T-tail and low-slung wings, the rear loading ramp gaping wide like *Jaws*.

Through the opening I can see military cargo specialists making sure everything is properly stowed. No telling what's in there crated and shrouded, possibly the MOBE test model that splashed down at the Gantry. Or the iridescent morphing wing I noticed in the wind tunnel might be on board along with weapons and other military equipment destined for Cape Canaveral, Florida.

Opening our doors, we climb out of the helicopter, our clothing flapping in the wind of blades thud-thudding, and if I had a brain in my head, I'd make a run for it. I'd tell Dick I'm honored, even grateful, and he shouldn't think for a minute I'm not mindful of all he's done since the day I was born if not before. But I'm not ready. He can't possibly think I would be, and what do Mom and Dad have to say?

Or Carme, by the way, and why not my brash fighter pilot sister instead of me? She's not afraid of anything except being bored, and never disappoints in a crisis, witness the video of her single-handedly saving an entire Delta Force. The point is, it doesn't matter what anybody says because I'm not up to a task this unprecedented and beyond my reach.

The best thing would be for me to go home where I belong. Instead, I walk off into the sunshine with Dick, maneuvering around puddles and patches of slush, doing what he says as usual. To give myself credit, I'm better at keeping things to myself such as my slow-burning anger over having no privacy or say about my life.

I don't show how overwhelmed I'm feeling as I turn around, smiling, waving thanks and see you later to our pilots. More honestly, I'm saying goodbye to Conn Lacrosse. He responds by flashing that toothy grin of his through the windscreen, giving me a thumbs-up.

I'm not sure why, maybe because I survived my first briefing in the White House Situation Room. Possibly he's showing his approval because I'm about to hitch a ride on a supercool tactical transporter that can land on short runways, a road, in a field. It can back up, turn around and take off again.

Also, I'm off to Kennedy Space Center, and as exciting as that sounds for someone who's always dreamed of being an astronaut, it was quite a jolt getting the news at the same time the president of the United States and everyone else did. Conn already knew what's in store for me because he and Dick are in cahoots (to use one of Mom's favorite words).

They decided if I got volunteered in front of Mount Olympus, I would have a hard time saying no. It would have gone over like a lead balloon had I attempted to explain to the president that I know enough to know what I don't, and maybe someone else should take care of the problem. I can imagine him lifting his finger, about to tell me I'm shirking my patriotic duty.

All to say that in my book, what Dick and Conn did was dirty pool. But I made a conscious decision not to take it personally, to be a good sport. I made sure I told my mysterious Secret Service counterpart how impressed I was with his piloting skills. Conn's landing on the South Lawn scored a 9 out of 10 in my book, the same with his takeoff.

"Why only a 9?" was his response.

"It gives you something to look forward to."

"But what made you take away a point?"

"Maybe next time I won't," I suggested, and we casually batted around the idea of catching a beer one of these days.

It's not so different from my back-and-forth with Davy Crockett. Except Conn Lacrosse isn't the least bit annoying, doesn't bully, and I don't need Carme to set me up with him. The Secret Service agent and I probably have a lot in common even if I can't be certain who he really is. I suppose he could live up to his name and be a con artist, a double-crosser.

He might be married with kids in some other life, already in a committed relationship, or is a philanderer (and why wouldn't he be?). The real Conn might not be kind to animals or into women (even if he acts otherwise convincingly). How am I supposed to know what's genuine when dealing with a spy?

Why should I trust him any more than I would a salesman or an actor? Maybe it's my SIN but I seem to be friendlier, more sociable with men, maybe with everyone, the same way I'm feeling about food all of a sudden. And that's not necessarily good.

"Thus, the meaning of drinking from a firehose," Dick sums up a day that's far from over as we walk across the ramp to the awaiting C-17.

"I've given up worrying about whether I know what I'm doing anymore," I tell him the truth.

"You've always known what you're doing."

"It never feels that way. How am I supposed to be good at something I've never done?"

"No one who goes to space does it until they do. The training happens down here, most of it virtual as you well know, and you've been doing it for years," he says. "We don't have practice rockets, and you don't walk in space until you walk in it," and we've reached the side door.

Our feet clunk hollowly up metal steps, and I hear the hydraulic hum and clank of the rear ramp beginning to close like a steel drawbridge. The cockpit is to the left, and the pilots and a loadmaster snap to attention, saluting Dick.

"Afternoon, sir."

"Welcome aboard, sir."

"How's it going?" they get around to me, no salute, barely a glance, no competing with the big cheese.

"Fine, thanks," I reply as if anyone is listening.

“You know where we’ll be,” Dick says to them. “And what I requested?”

“Yes, sir, all there. Whatever you need. I made sure there’s TP in the head.”

“Now that’s good thinking,” Dick nods with one of his bemused smiles.

“Much appreciated,” and I mean it.

37

THE CENTER FUSELAGE is as big as most submarines, windowless and dimly lit now that the back ramp is closed, everybody gone.

Military transporters aren't built for comfort, and the less flammable the materials, the better. There's nothing much in here but metal, nonskid flooring, cargo straps, and no wall panels or headliners to cover cables and anything else most passengers don't want to see.

"I had a brainstorm last night when I saw the manifest," Dick says as we walk through deep shadows, our feet loud on metal.

I can feel the cold through the soles of my dress boots that were terrible in snow and not the best idea here. The only seats look like fold-up beach chairs in this part of the plane where troops stay during transports. But we're not stopping, and I follow Dick into the cargo section where we weave through foothills of shrink-wrapped wooden crates chained to tie-down rings.

"A sleeping bag is helpful," he's in his element, and I'm definitely not dressed for the environment. "The problem is the floor is so hard and can get really cold," he has to remind me of how uncomfortable I'm going to be.

"Well this doesn't sound like much fun. I can see my breath in here," I finally comment. "And I doubt it's going to be better at 30,000 feet . . ."

As I say it, ART verifies in my lenses that yes indeed it's nippy at that altitude, –44.44°C or –48°F as we speak. Reaching the rear of the cargo section, I discover the reason for the wooden planks on the tarmac, a beauty of a Sikorsky HH-60W. Its 4 blades are folded together and bungee corded to the tail boom so the helicopter could fit inside the plane.

"It's supposed to replace the Blackhawk," Dick says as I gawk at yet something else today.

"How many times are you going to torture me?" my aircraft envy is back with a vengeance, my stomach reminding me nonstop that it's empty.

"It's been in testing, now headed for the skid strip," Dick says, and he means the test airstrip at the Cape Canaveral Air Force Station. "Not as comfortable as your living room," he means the Sikorsky isn't. "But a hell of a lot better than sitting in one of those seats or on the metal floor. Hop in," and we open the cockpit doors.

It may be petty of me but I'm grateful he climbs into the left seat. It's only fitting that I should sit in the right one since I'm a helicopter pilot, and he's not. It's me going into space I've just discovered, not him. Since I'll be flying my Chase Plane single pilot (if I don't count ART), that would suggest I'm in command, and Dick needs to start treating me accordingly.

"You ready for some refreshment?" reaching behind his seat, he grabs folded blankets, and a soft-sided insulated bag.

Truth be told, I could eat a horse right about now, and I watch with keen interest as he opens the bag, pulls out a thermos.

"There's a first time for everything," he finds large Styrofoam cups. "Afternoon tea inside a helicopter that's been swallowed by an airplane."

Afternoon tea, and that's it? I'm protesting in my head.

"An old trick of mine I learned after years of traveling on military transports," he's happy to explain. "The first thing you do is find something halfway comfortable to sit inside like a Humvee.

A helicopter. A tank. Especially if you're flying halfway around the world."

"I guess there's no real food because you're worried about me getting motion sickness, which is more likely to happen on an empty stomach," I'm disappointed, a bit miffed. "And more to the point, it isn't supposed to happen to begin with considering my enhancements."

"I'm not worried about you being motion sick."

"Then why skip lunch? Why not ask whoever left the tea also to include food?" I'm tempted to add that the commander of Space Force should be able to request anything he wants. "There's probably nothing for us in the galley either," I already know the answer, and Dick shakes his head, nope, not a morsel.

I don't mean to be a crank but the last I ate was when Mom fixed me two fried egg sandwiches before I left the house, and that was a long time ago. It would have been nice to grab lunch in the White House mess hall before we headed out. But there wasn't time, Dick mandated.

He said, and I quote, *"You don't keep a 140-ton military tactical transporter waiting while you order a turkey rueben even if it's to go."*

"I said you'd be upset with me," Dick sips his tea. "I've held off telling you for as long as I could in hopes of making it easier. But the fact is you can't have anything else today, nothing tonight or in the morning. Nothing to eat before the launch except clear fluids, maybe crackers. And after that it's space food, some of which you've had before."

"Probably while I was locked up at Dodd Hall," I connect the dots. "Like the bags of space punch. You probably had me eating reconstituted space food that I don't remember."

"Your mom and I had a discussion about whether you should have those fried egg sandwiches this morning," Dick says, his phone in hand like always, monitoring messages.

"What did she do, text you about it?" as I think, *Are you kidding?*

"Actually . . . ," he hesitates, and that's exactly what my mother did.

"Do I get to decide anything on my own anymore?" I'm incredulous, annoyed and secretly flattered.

"Penny pointed out that whether you ate or not this morning, it was risky either way," as if they were discussing surgery instead of breakfast. "As important as the White House briefing was, better to make sure your blood sugar didn't drop."

"Which it does more than it used to," I admit, taking the blankets from him.

I begin unfolding them, draping one over his lap, the other over mine, sitting side by side like roomies again inside our private space. Our view is the wiper blades parked askew on the windscreen, the dimly lit steel fuselage filled with big darkly silhouetted shapes, and in the distance the cockpit glows like a light at the end of a tunnel.

"Hunger is a powerful thing," Dick says. "I'm sorry if your appetites are out of whack," as if it's not just food we're talking about. "There have been a number of things to adjust with Carme too."

"It's like the volume is lower in some areas," I reply, "and higher in others. That's how it feels," and it's not a subject I'm eager to discuss with him.

"Well, clearly something needs to be adjusted," he decides as if we're talking about a misfiring carburetor. "Probably your hypothalamus. But I'm no doctor."

"Then maybe don't guess about things like that," I suggest.

By now the pilots have begun firing up the 4 engines, and if we weren't sitting here with the helicopter doors shut, I'd suggest hearing protection.

"How about some nice hot tea?" Dick says. "You can have all of that you want," pouring himself a cup.

"Not helpful. You know what happens," I remind him. "What's the bathroom like on this thing? I prefer to avoid it if possible. It would be like tromping out into the cold to use a steel outhouse, and no thank you."

00:00:00:00:0

"HERE," Dick hands me the steaming cup. "A few sips, and if you have to hit the loo? Just remind yourself that won't be a problem soon enough," he nudges me with his elbow the way Carme does, the way he used to do when she and I were kids.

"You mean when I'm wearing a diaper again," I reply.

"There are some advantages to our humiliations."

"That's probably not one of them," trying the tea, I taste honey and lemon, the way he's always taken it for as long as I've known him.

As we talk in the near dark, I ask him to be honest. We're way beyond being coy or disingenuous, and I don't need him sitting on details that might cause me to walk off the job.

"Is it possible Neva could know about the PEQUOD, the MOBE? If so, for how long? And might she have similar technologies?" I get to the point. "Or what if she has more advanced ones?" and it's a very bad thought as I prepare to face off with whatever rogue spacecraft she's dispatched to screw the rest of us.

"We've kept the technologies as off grid as any project we've ever done. But with her there's always a chance for anything," Dick tops off his tea, and I don't know where he puts it. "The short answer is we don't know the extent of her capabilities. We can't say for sure that she doesn't have a secret spaceship that's been weaponized."

"One that's attacking our satellites at the moment and about to strike again apparently," I'm sitting with my feet up on the helicopter seat, my arms around my knees, the blanket over me.

"For starters, very possibly she's behind it," Dick agrees, the C-17 lumbering along the runway as we take off. "And yes, it's my suspicion that she's doing all of this, intending to monopolize everything she can."

"So much for getting to take my Chase Plane on a test spin," I reply. "Or even seeing it in the showroom beyond the photograph of it in the hangar. By this time tomorrow I'll be orbiting in GEO, piloting a spaceship I've never been in before and didn't know existed except in white papers, schematics and my imagination."

"There's nothing you haven't done countless times in the simulators, and a lot of those very programs are the ones you wrote. Or you and your dad did," Dick reminds me. "I wouldn't allow you to do this if I didn't think you were up to the task, Calli."

"I don't know why you're so confident."

"Because I know who and what you are a lot better than you do," he says, the C-17 picking up speed, pushing us down in our seats as we lift steeply with a roar worthy of a tornado.

"At the end of the day," I resume when it's quieter, "what happens if I get up there and don't find anything? What if after all this we're no closer to discovering what's happening to our satellites? What if I can't prevent our new spy satellite from being the next casualty? And I let everybody down."

"You have a chance of detecting things from up there that we can't from here," he repeats, "because of the AI-assisted quantum computing capabilities, and the conductive skin among other things."

My Chase Plane's sensors will work in concert with my own, giving me an enhanced signal-detection sensitivity that should pick up on pretty much any intruder. With ART's assistance once we reach GEO, we'll be orbiting the Earth in a vehicle that has spectrum analysis capabilities.

In a sense, it won't be all that different from my doing pirouettes as I scan with a mobile antenna. It's just I'll be some 35,000 kilometers (21,700 miles) above the Earth, scanning a much bigger area really fast, and with exponentially more at stake.

"The other thing to remember?" Dick adds. "Part of the objective is to put the PEQUOD and MOBE through their paces. To see if they're all they're cracked up to be."

"I don't like to hear the words *if* or *cracked up* right about now."

"If all goes well," and there he goes again, "then it will be a successful mission whether you find the target or not."

"Let's be honest, okay?" I'm warm beneath my blanket but my face is cold, and the seat hits my lower back exactly wrong. "The mission can't be considered successful if our new spy satellite is the next casualty. Then what? A next, and a next? So, while it's nice of you to act as if there's no pressure, I know better."

"Do you need to make a visit?" he opens his door to find the toilet.

"I'm fine."

"I'll be back in a few," he gets out of the helicopter, and as soon as he's dissolved into the shadows, I ask ART to go audible, placing my phone on top of my blanketed lap.

"What may I help you with?" and it's nice to hear his voice again, sounding mellow but pleased as if he's happy to hear from me.

"I'm sitting inside a helicopter that's inside a C-17, and before that it was an Agusta and the White House," I feel compelled to tell him as if catching up with a parent or a friend on Facebook.

"I don't understand your question," his response, and at disheartening moments like this I'm reminded that humans created ART and not the other way around.

He doesn't exist separate and apart from Carme and me, those of us who are programmed to depend on him. Yet it doesn't feel that way when he and I start talking. He seems as real as it gets while showing me all sorts of images in my lenses, and giving me alerts in my earpiece. None of it seems like it was anybody's idea but his, and I could swear I've detected emotionality from him.

"I didn't ask a question," I let him know. "I was just talking the way friends do when they're catching up."

Silence. The throbbing noise of massive engines. The shudder of mild turbulence.

"You know, informing them, updating them," I add. "Something you've not been doing with me, not today. I've heard very little from you and there's been very little in the way of updates."

What I'm getting at is I'd better not discover that ART was programmed to drop everybody (most of all me) like a hot potato the minute Dick comes around. I won't be undervalued or invisible. I'm also not a cheap substitute because someone like my sister is unavailable.

Been there, done that, when the Conn Lacrosses of the world pay attention to me until something better comes along. Then suddenly I'm like Ranger in GHOST mode tagging along transparently. Nope, not happening. I'm not in high school anymore, and it's not an option for me to be ignored because my artificial sidekick panders to someone who can't sneeze without being saluted.

I don't know who's responsible for some of ART's unfortunate ideas and attitudes. Maybe it's Dick. Maybe Dad. Even Mom can be a tad old fashioned. But when I get my hand on the algorithms, I intend to make a few changes, and I pick up my phone, looking at it as if ART and I are FaceTiming.

"Is there a reason you've given me the silent treatment today?" I confront my blank display.

"It was my impression you weren't to be unnecessarily distracted," ART says.

"I don't know who gave you that impression because it wasn't me," I let him know.

38

"I'M SORRY. What would you like to be updated about?" ART's soothing voice might be slightly contrite.

"Status reports. How are things at home?" I inquire, and he shows me the live feed of police cars on our property, a state police helicopter circling.

It won't be long before the media gets the scent of a huge story, and I worry what life will be like for all of us. How much more off-nominal can it get?

"Maybe send a text to Lex," I decide, looking out the helicopter's windscreen, watching for Dick, wondering if he knows I'm talking to ART.

"What would you like me to say?"

"Maybe tell Lex I'm checking on him, hoping he's okay. I'm thinking about him," and words like that have never been easy for me to say. "Maybe let Mom and Dad know the same thing. Also, Carme. And Fran. I know these last few days have been rough."

"Wilco."

"I assume there's been no mention in the news or on social media about the White House briefing . . . Okay, shhhhh . . . !" I hush him as I make out Dick's shadowy shape heading toward me.

"I don't understand."

"No more audio," I lower my voice to a bare whisper. "I don't want him hearing everything you and I talk about. He's not listening right now, is he?"

Unauthorized, in a text.

"Has anything hit the media?" and ART links me to a news live feed I'm seeing in my lenses as Dick opens the door, the helicopter shaking as he climbs back in.

While Mason Dixon broadcasts his latest breaking news in front of a town house with the front door ajar, police everywhere . . .

". . . Right here," he points behind him in the video playing in my lenses, "that's where this was going on, folks. An entire network of criminal activity involving illegal firearms, homemade bombs, all right here under our noses at the Dog Beach Marina and Villas . . ."

Dick rearranges his blanket, refilling his tea, and I don't mention what I'm watching in my SPIES. Maybe he already knows that Jack Kracker's short-term rental has been discovered, the pearl-white Jeep Cherokee inside the garage.

"What happens to Mom, Dad, to everyone?" I ask. "If Chase Place and everything about it ends up all over the news, then what?"

"I wish I had a good answer for you," Dick says.

"At least that's an honest one," and I almost add *for once.*

"We're less than 30 out," he hands me the tea again, his hand warm as it brushes mine.

We sit quietly for a few minutes, sharing a tea, and I think of what Carme's always saying. Now or never. I ask Dick what he was doing with the Secret Service and other undercover agents in the NASA hangar 5 days ago.

"Why was Dad there?" I continue before Dick can answer or not. "When I was climbing up to the top of the hangar, I could see you below with Dad and your posse tracking stuff with signal sniffers, huddled around computer displays. At the time, I thought you were searching for Carme."

I assumed Dick had assembled his troops to hunt her down, and had Dad helping somehow.

"But now I know that can't be true since obviously she's working with you," I go on. "There's no posse after her, and Dad wouldn't go along with that anyway. You knew where she was and have all along, yet when you spotted me climbing up to the roof, you went after me like a pack of dogs. Why?"

"Why might I not have wanted you there?" Dick says. "Beside the fact we weren't expecting you."

"I had to get inside the radome to reset the dish antenna if we were to restore communication with the Space Station . . ."

"Yes, yes, yes. But your showing up introduced an unanticipated risk . . . Let's just say, a threat that was completely out of left field when suddenly there you were climbing up to the roof."

"You knew where Carme was hiding out and didn't want me to find her," I can only figure.

"Plain and simple, the two of you can't be seen together," Dick reminds me of what's most painful. "Your power comes from working together while you're not. That's all you need to know about it."

I'm feeling my tea too much to argue, to tell him how unmanageable everything is, and I weigh my options. I can brave the bathroom here. Or I can wait until we land with more g-forces than my bladder would appreciate, and I decide to brave the elements.

"My turn," I announce, and as I walk away from the helicopter, I think of the irony if I trip and hurt myself, what a way to scrub my first mission.

"The one thing I didn't bring today was a flashlight," I remark to ART as I step around shrouded wooden crates, careful of tie-downs and rings in the metal flooring.

“You have a flashlight app on your phone,” he says in my earpiece.

Duh, it seems I’m quickly forgetting how to do the smallest thing on my own. Lighting my way, I find the bathroom, a sink, a toilet, and a roll of toilet paper as promised. Except there’s no running water, and flushing doesn’t seem to be an option. Fortunately, someone was thoughtful enough to leave a few packets of hand sanitizers, and I wonder if it was Dick.

Back in the helicopter seat, I tuck my blanket around me, and ART must have taken my lecture to heart. He’s acting extra nice, paying attention, being thoughtful as we begin making our approach into Cape Canaveral. He shows me in my lenses what the pilots are seeing as we swoop over a tawny strip of beach, the white froth of waves breaking on the sand.

We turn on final for KXMR, the Cape Canaveral Air Force Station skid strip, a single runway with sandy dirt on all sides, and numerous launch pads. The moving map display shows me the runway’s configuration, letting me know its length, the elevation, our speed and the latest weather. Then the C-17’s wheels touch down, engines screaming as we brake to a quick stop that presses us hard against our seats.

As loud as it is, we give up talking until we’re being marshalled into our parking place on the ramp. What we do next strikes me as another one of Mom’s quirky conundrums. We climb out of a helicopter so we can climb out of a plane, neither of them moving. Yet all of us are at 107,826 kilometers per hour (67,000 mph) as the Earth orbits the sun at a sizzling clip.

00:00:00:00:0

"YOU DO realize we just landed without our seat belts on," I say to Dick as we reclaim our baggage on the floor outside the helicopter.

"I guess we could have buckled up in there," he considers.

"I'm not sure how much good that would have done had we gone off-nominal," and all kidding aside, I don't know the answer.

Based on ART's lack of response in my SPIES or my earpiece, I don't think he knows either. It's another one of those brainteasers like Mom used to fire at Carme and me all the time. If a mosquito is buzzing around inside a car going 128 kilometers per hour (80 mph), then what is the mosquito's airspeed?

Or in this case, if Dick and Calli are sitting inside a helicopter that's cargo inside a transporter, what happens in a crash, seat belt or not? Are we a helicopter crash? Are we a helicopter and a plane crash or only the latter? I don't know why such morbid preoccupations are invading my thoughts.

But I suspect it's for the simple fact that any test pilot worth his or her salt knows that the next mission could be the last. People like me aren't needed unless nobody's really sure how something will work until it's driven or flown for real. Deploying Ranger the PONG for the first time is a good example because we hadn't factored owls into the equation, and we should have.

Or how about my taking my new Chase Plane into space where neither of us has been, both of us prototypes? No matter what the statistics might say, it's impossible to foresee every possibility for disappointment, damage and death. Chances are good what I'm about to do may not turn out well.

"How are you feeling?" Dick asks as we walk across the ramp, headed to the airstrip's flight office and lounge, the afternoon warm, the sky bright with only a few clouds. "You didn't sleep a wink on the plane."

"I was too busy worrying."

"I wish you wouldn't," he holds the door.

Soldiers inside instantly salute, and I wonder if it ever gets old.

"It's just that Neva was at the White House," I explain. "She wasn't inside the Situation Room, and shouldn't know anything that went on in there."

"But that doesn't mean she doesn't," Dick says as we emerge from the small building.

Another black Suburban is awaiting, this one flanked by two Air Force security officers armed to the teeth in full ballistic gear. Our detail for the trip, and we climb in the back of the armored SUV as they take the front. Dick and I buckle up this time, and I send him a text old-fashioned-style, typing it myself, not asking ART's help.

Is it ok to talk in front of these guys? I touch send.

Affirmative, Dick writes back, and we're communicating remotely while in the same place.

"You know as well as I do," I resume out loud, "that Neva must have a legion of snitches. And when you think of all the people in the room this morning, she's probably friendly with every one of them."

"That's the problem," Dick agrees. "After we left, she had lunch in the mess hall with the secretary of state. This was after both of them sat in on the meeting with the president of Uganda."

"Who's concerned about investing in a space program when it's unclear if his satellites would be safe," I add as we drive through the barracks and hangars. "And they sure as heck wouldn't be, and we both know that Neva's probably the reason."

The causeway connecting the Air Force Station to Kennedy Space Center is off limits to members of the public unless they're on a NASA tour bus. And I'm not seeing any of those at the moment as we cross the lagoon called Banana River.

"Why not deny Neva access to absolutely everything she wants and needs?" I suggest to Dick what I have before as the serious-minded officers up front stare straight ahead, hearing every word. "Why help her hurt us? Why do we make it easier for someone like that? Are we the only ones who see her for what she is?"

"The problem is as old as time," Dick says. "A lot of the people she deals with aren't necessarily any more altruistically motivated than she is, and what she's managed to do over the years is to join them in order to beat them. She has dirt on people, and they owe her. She's masterful at creating entanglements and conflicts. In other words, human nature wins."

"Maybe not always. And not everything about human nature is as rotten to the core as she is."

"It's always complicated when someone manages to place any number of powerful individuals or groups in compromised positions," he says, and Kennedy's main launch viewing area is out my window, a strip of grass with bleachers and a few palm trees along the fence-lined shore.

Across the lagoon I can see the rocket on its pad pointing up like a bright-white finger against deep blue, 76.2 meters (250 feet) tall. Its twin BE-4 liquefied natural gas–fueled engines are capable of 4,800 kilonewtons (1.08 million pounds) of thrust, almost triple that when you add the 6 solid rocket boosters. All to say that when I'm strapped into my seat, for all practical purposes I'll be sitting on top of a missile.

My attention stays out the window, across the alligator-infested water, and I sense Dick looking at me. I wonder if he's proud of what he's wrought, grooming someone from the beginning to do exactly as instructed. How must it feel to rewire, and reprogram that person, to play God?

"You doing okay?" he asks quietly, his sunglasses fixed on me.

"Sure," I lie.

Our tires sing over the metal drawbridge that's raised when NASA's covered barge called *Pegasus* arrives with rocket stages and other huge components after a 900-mile ferry from Michoud Assembly Facility in New Orleans. Once on shore at Kennedy, the priceless cargo is hauled by a special carrier to the 50-story Vehicle Assembly Building dominating the flat horizon.

"Mostly I'm starved," I add, and that much is true as we enter the Merritt Island National Wildlife Refuge.

I remember from my days here at the NASA Protective Services training academy that you never know what might be crossing the road. But I wouldn't count on a chicken, more likely an alligator, snake, turtle, maybe a black bear, could be all sorts of critters trying to get to the other side.

For the next several minutes we encounter endless acres of marshland, giant pines, and old mangroves with thickets of roots exposed in shallow brackish water. Then Kennedy Space Center is in front of us, more industrial than a showplace, miles of white concrete and metal facilities.

In the distance are the launch pads, water towers and tall lightning-protection masts as far removed from civilization as one can get without tumbling into the Atlantic Ocean. Now that the furlough has ended and the government is back to work, employee parking lots are full, plenty of personnel out and about.

We take a left on East Avenue at the Space Station Processing Facility. As the name implies, it takes care of everything that goes into building, maintaining and resupplying our orbiting laboratory 408 kilometers (254 miles) above Earth. The next sprawling complex is the Neil Armstrong Operations and Checkout Building, actually twin long buildings side by side.

A narrow lane runs between them, and we follow it to a parking area designated for astronauts confined here prior to launch. The entrance reminds me of a sally port to a jail, except over the steel double doors are crew mission patches and a NASA meatball logo.

"My home away from home, I'm in and out of here so often," Dick says as we grab our bags. "But by design it's not exactly a room with a view, I'll warn you in advance."

His security detail is standing at the ready, and he tells them that will be it for now.

"I don't think I'll be going anywhere else for a while," he adds, thanking them.

"We'll be right out here, sir."

"Let us know if you need anything, sir."

"This area back here is for the walk-outs," Dick says to me, holding his badge over the scanner by a drab entrance that couldn't be more thrilling. "When you've suited up and are headed out in the astrovan, you'll walk out these doors," he opens them, gray metal, scuffed up and windowless. "I've done it a few times in my pumpkin suit," he adds with a trace of a wistful smile.

I try to imagine how I'm going to feel at oh-dark-hundred when I'm doing the same thing, heading out in a launch-entry pressure suit. Only mine will be blue, not orange, and there won't be crowds of adoring NASA employees to greet me as I emerge from the building, walking to the awaiting van.

There won't be journalists, television news crews or the usual police escorts on the ground and in the air, hardly anyone knowing about the top secret mission before or after the fact.

39

DICK KEYS the elevator to the third floor, an open area thoughtfully appointed to put astronauts in the right frame of mind before launch time.

Walls are filled with big posters of eye-popping space art. There are whiteboards for announcements and other information including which astronaut is assigned to which room. The only names written in Magic Marker are ours, nobody else staying here.

Dick is in room 1, I'm in 12C, and we head down a long corridor filled with *Peanuts* comic strip art. Snoopy as the Red Baron encourages *All Systems Are Go!* Wearing a spacesuit, he has his *Eyes on the Stars*, and there are the expected group pictures of previous astronaut classes and crews, photos that won't include me going forward.

Chances are there won't be crews of 7 astronauts quarantined in here together as there were during the Space Shuttle's glory days. As space technologies and travel are increasingly about national security and the survival of our planet, there will be more stealth missions conducted by astronauts untraditionally trained like me to be fighters and spies.

Passing break rooms, we turn down another hallway where a sign warns to **REPORT ALL SYMPTOMS OF ILLNESS**. Where I'm staying is at the end on the right, and Dick opens the door, my quarters reminding me of barracks I've lived in before, small but functional and civilized.

The bed is queen size, neatly made with a creamy spread that has a floral medallion in the center. There's a bedside table, a built-in desk, and a wood-framed mirror. The carpet and walls are gray, and there are no windows because you're not supposed to know if it's morning, noon or night.

Sleep patterns are shifted depending on the launch window, in my case scheduled at 4:00 a.m., some 12 hours from now. Dropping my bags on the bed, I check out the bathroom. A sink, a toilet and a shower, and on the counter is a water glass, a wrapped bar of soap, bottles of magnesium citrate and a box of enemas.

"Looks like I have a lot to look forward to," I comment, returning to the bedroom.

"Get yourself settled," Dick is glued to his phone, his jaw muscles clenching the way they do when he doesn't like what he's seeing. "Make calls, do what you need," he heads out the door.

The gym sounds like a fine idea, I decide, unzipping my duffel bag, changing into sweatpants, a T-shirt, sneakers. Out the door, I head back in the direction of the dining room, following the carpeted corridor with its astronaut art, inspiring photographs and cartoonish whimsy. Inside the gym, I start out in a gentle jog on a treadmill, and ART alerts me that Mom's on the line.

"I understand you were impressive this morning," she says in my earpiece, and I assume she means the White House briefing. "A little birdie told me you held your own just fine in the ladies' room."

Obviously, she's talking about Neva Rong, and the little birdie would be Dick. He must have filled in Mom about the encounter, and I have a feeling this phone call is about more than her checking on me as I think of the look on his face while leaving my room a few minutes ago.

"I hope you don't mind if we talk while I'm on the treadmill," I increase the incline and the speed. "I thought it a good idea to move around while I can. Since you saw me last, all I've been doing is sitting."

"I won't be coy with you," Mom's unflappable voice. "Just as it's very likely she knew you and Dick would be at the briefing this morning, there's a chance she knows other things," and she's talking about Neva.

"If you're referring to the launch," I reply, running faster, "it's in the news that there's one in the morning."

"Exactly. And the launch time is on the internet if you look, publicized as a new weather satellite that's supposed to be helpful tracking wildfires."

As she tells me this, ART shows me news feeds about it. But nothing hints that there's anything unusual about the launch, just another private company sending up an expensive satellite in an expensive rocket.

"It's not like you can hide it when the rocket is on the pad as big as life," I tell her over the fast thudding of my shoes on the belt. "Besides, Pandora has a facility here at Kennedy, a huge new building near Blue Origin and Boeing. There's no way Neva wouldn't know what's launching. But she won't necessarily know the payload is a spaceplane, and there's no reason she should have a clue I'm here."

"Don't you think something must have crossed her mind when she saw you at the White House?" Mom makes a good point. "Calli, you were attending a briefing in the Situation Room."

She's right that Neva running into us blew our cover even if Dick hasn't admitted it. I don't think it's accidental or a coincidence that she was there this morning to meet with the president of Uganda. Neva was tipped off by someone, maybe the secretary of state whom she had lunch with in the mess hall. It could be anybody, and it makes my blood run cold to consider that she might know exactly what we're planning.

"I just wanted you to know I'm thinking about you," Mom's voice catches, and there are very few times I've known her to cry.

Usually it was over Carme, most memorably when Dad made friends with a traveling stunt pilot I wish he'd never met. Fortunately, there won't be the same outcome with Lex. He's not a bad seed. But he could be if someone like Neva ever got her hooks in him, and I ask Mom if she's heard how he's doing.

"I dropped some of my chili by this morning as promised," she replies, and I appreciate her doing that for me. "Your sister came along," she adds to my surprise. "Nonna had the same reaction to her that she apparently had with you. A nosebleed, a spell requiring a space blanket. I have to admit it was a rather strange thing to witness."

"And they thought Carme was me," I steepen the incline and bump up the speed, wiping my face with a towel. "Even Lex thought she was me?"

"I can barely hear you, dear."

"Did Lex think Carme was me?" I don't know why it matters but it does.

"She was actually very sweet with him," and as she's saying this, I'm startled by Dick suddenly appearing next to my machine, that same look on his face, his jaw muscles clenching.

"I've got to go, Mom."

"Don't forget I love you," she says, and I end the call as Dick tells me there's been a change of plans.

"The launch time has been moved up," he informs me, and why am I not surprised after what Mom just said?

"What's going on?" as I slow down the treadmill, ending the session, mopping myself with the towel.

"The rogue object moving toward our spy satellite has made an unexpected maneuver as of 10 minutes ago," he says.

"Whatever this thing is, it may have greater propulsion capabilities than previously thought," I reply as we leave the gym, and Neva must have caught wind that we're coming after her.

"It's now calculated to be within range of USA555A in less than 9 hours," he fills me in as we walk briskly along the hallway.

"What kind of launch window are we talking about?"

"Factoring in range safety, collision avoidance and all the rest, the most optimal time is going to be a one-hour window beginning at 8:00 p.m."

"That's less than 4 hours from now," I protest as we reach my room, and I can tell by his face that there's no choice.

"Do what you need to do," Dick says as I think unpleasantly of the magnesium citrate, the enemas by the sink.

He tells me to stop by the medical clinic in an hour, and from there it's the suit-up room, and maybe it's better not having any time to stress myself out. For sure I wouldn't have slept a wink tonight anyway, would have been pacing the gray carpet, inside my gray windowless walls.

00:00:00:00:0

I CLOSE myself inside the bathroom, grabbing the box of enemas. Covering the floor with a towel, I follow the instructions, lying on my side with knees bent, and when I dreamed about being an astronaut, this wasn't what I had in mind.

A half hour later, I'm stepping out of the shower, toweling off my hair as I leave the bathroom. I find certain items waiting for me on the bed, including a formfitting skinsuit just like Carme's.

Also, the expected Maximum Absorbency Garment, a MAG, or let's call it what it is, a super-duper diaper.

In addition, I've been issued underwear, clean room booties, and I pick up the skinsuit, finding it surprisingly lightweight. On close inspection I can see that the smart fabric is woven with fine gold metallic fibers that remind me of the Chase Plane's conductive skin.

"What exactly does it do?" I ask ART, noting the unusual front ziplock closure that doesn't look much sturdier than a sandwich bag's.

"The Smart Integrated Skin interfaces with other devices and environments," he says.

"A Smart Integrated Skin," and I don't like it. "As in a SIS?"

"Affirmative."

"So, Carme and I are both wearing a SIS?" no way I'm calling it that.

Silence.

"Sisters wearing SISes. Whose idea was this?"

"I don't understand the question."

"It sounds like one of Dad's goofy acronyms," I decide, sitting down on the bed with a towel wrapped around me.

I pick up the MAG, examining it closely, making sure I don't put it on backward.

"I'm not calling it a SIS," it's only fair to let ART know. "And I would think most guys will have a problem with being told to put their SISes on. Nobody's going to like it. Can't we change the name?"

"Unauthorized."

"Well, names are important," as I put on my NASA-issued gray underpants, a gray sports bra, size medium. "Astronaut candidates become ASCANs. And astronaut hopefuls are ASHOs. And next people who want to go into space will be SISes, which could get permuted into SISSIES, if we're not careful."

"I don't understand the question."

"I don't either, not sure I understand much, to be honest," I worm my way into my new skin.

Boots, gloves and hood are connected, and I work my legs in first, then my arms, finally standing, pulling up the front plastic zipper that runs from crotch to collar. I don't know what I was expecting but nothing happens. It's as if I have on a very lightweight, comfortably loose-fitting dive skin.

"Am I supposed to feel anything?" I ask ART. "I mean, what's so special about this?"

"It must be zipped up all the way to the neck if you want the power on," his reply.

"That's the first I've heard about turning the power on, but okay," and I do what he says, the skin tightening as if I'm being shrink-wrapped.

At the same time, I hear a barely perceptible click, the plastic zipper healing like an incision before my very eyes. It looks like a seam in the fabric, barely visible, and if I break the connection by moving the zipper down the slightest bit, the skin relaxes again.

"I don't guess there's an instruction book to go with this thing," I say it in jest because of course there isn't.

"Negative," ART confirms, and for the next few minutes I test pilot my skinsuit, doing push-ups, jogging in place, running hot water over my gloved hand, then cold.

I jump up and down as high as I can, doing skip steps, dripping water on the bathroom floor to see how my boots do in slippery conditions. Then I go through the same routine again, this time while wearing my CUFF, my SPIES, but I won't need my PEEPS in space, ART informs me.

The launch-entry suit has a smart visor that syncs with my other devices. Those in addition to sophisticated avionics, and I should be fine, he assures me. There's no point in bringing my phone, ART reminds me. It won't be any good in space, and he can connect me to calls and other communications without it.

Covering my feet with clean room booties, I'm out the door in my peculiar skinsuit, my feet whispering on carpet. Passing the dining room, the gym, I find the door to the small medical exam room open wide as I hear the sound of water running. Inside, the flight surgeon is washing his hands, an older man with wild hair and shy eyes, something about him reminding me of Dad.

"Hi," I knock on the open door.

"Come in," he turns off the water, the sleeves of his splashed denim shirt rolled up, and he's wearing khakis and sneakers.

"I'm Calli Chase."

"I know who you are," he grabs paper towels to dry his hands. "If I didn't, neither of us should be here. I've been given the scoop."

He looks me in the eye as if he's peering into my mind.

"How are we feeling?" he removes the stethoscope from around his neck. "I'm Dr. Helthe," he says, pronounced like *health* with a slight tongue thrust, I decide.

"An unusual name," and sometimes I'm no better at small talk than my dad.

"I frankly think it got misspelled along the way," Dr. Helthe replies, finding a digital thermometer. "Likely it originally was *Helth* and an *e* was added, probably by whoever was taking the census at Ellis Island back in the 1880s."

"I don't need to take this off, do I?" and I mean my skinsuit.

"No," he inserts the thermometer into my mouth. "By all accounts, you're going to have nice weather," as if I'm looking forward to a sailboat ride or a stroll. "But then thunderstorms will be building by late morning. You'll be long gone by then. I understand you're from Virginia. Never been to Langley but have visited Wallops a number of times."

He talks quietly, quickly, almost breathily and nonstop, sort of what Dad does when he's nervous and ill at ease with people he doesn't know. The thermometer beeps, and Dr. Helthe is happy to inform me my temperature is 97.9, in the normal zone, and I could have told him that.

ART lets me know everything before the flight surgeon finds it out as he busily takes my blood pressure, taps my knees with his little rubber mallet, listens to my heart and breathing. None of it is necessary when I have an implanted network of devices downloading the data and a lot more. But no longer having a need for certain protocols in life doesn't mean you are exempt from them.

Even if Dr. Helthe knows about my secret SIN, he'd examine me as usual, filling in the blanks, checking off the boxes. He very well may be part of the Gemini project, and in fact, I'm getting more suspicious by the moment. Dick has his own pied-à-terre in Kennedy's sacred astronaut crew quarters, therefore I think it's reasonable to conclude that NASA personnel and those at Space Force are merging.

Certainly, I sense something in Dr. Helthe's demeanor that makes me suspect he knows darn well what's going on, who I am and that I might not live to tell the tale. At the very least, he has to know it's not business as usual when I show up to launch in a rocket that supposedly has nobody inside, just a weather satellite with a special knack for tracking fires.

"We feeling up to snuff?" Dr. Helthe bends over me, moving the stethoscope around. "Your ticker's sounding strong as a horse," and in the past I'd be offended by the comparison.

All my life I've been called strong as a horse or as healthy as one. I never saw it as a compliment, more as an insinuation that I look something less than fine, maybe common or thick.

"Breathing's normal," he decides. "Anything going on I should know about before you rocket into space for the first time, young lady?"

"I'm feeling fine," I let him know as he holds up a finger, telling me to follow it with my eyes, moving it in an H pattern.

Finding a tongue depressor in a glass jar, he tells me to open wide and say *ahhhh*.

40

NEXT STOP is the suit-up room with its padded brown recliner chairs, long tables and big panels of pressure valves that go back to the late '60s.

There's scarcely any legend who hasn't passed through here, Neil Armstrong, Buzz Aldrin, John Young and Sally Ride to name a few, and also those less fortunate, the crews on the *Challenger* and *Columbia*.

All of them made their final stop in this room, each with a suit technician who might be the last person they'll see on Earth, depending on how things turn out. My tech is about Mom's age, I'm guessing, all in white with a headset on. She tells me to come in, looking me up and down.

"You're wearing everything I left on your bed?" her eyes are bright like a bird's, and she's kind but no-nonsense.

"Thank you, and yes," I reply, imagining myself on the bathroom floor, sincerely hoping she didn't walk in at the wrong moment.

"You can sit down," she indicates the recliner next to a sanitized plastic-covered table where my blue launch-entry suit is broken down into its components.

The pants, the torso, gloves, boots and helmet attach with plastic zippers, and missing are the usual metal rings, the clunky metal clasps, the dreadful rubber dam around the collar, the comm cap that causes hotspots. I've tested all sorts of spacewear, including the Advanced Crew Escape Space Suit System (ACES), what most call a pumpkin suit because of its color.

But it would seem that blue is the new orange, and my crash dummy Snap has tried out my new getup but I haven't.

"I'm Stella, by the way," my suit tech says, and of course she'd work for NASA and have a name like that. "No more need for long johns with their 300 feet of water-cooling tubes," removing my paper booties, she begins helping me into the bright-blue pants. "It kind of makes me sad to think."

"Don't be too sad," I reply, "I still have a diaper."

"It's really not that bad unless you have to wear it very long."

"What's your idea of 'very long'?"

"It depends on if we're talking number one or number two," she says as if there are no adults in the room.

"Makes sense," and I'm grateful Dick wouldn't let me eat anything since my egg sandwiches early this morning, and thinking of them makes my stomach growl audibly.

"You wouldn't want to go as long as two days without changing your MAG, that's for sure," Stella takes off my clean room shoe covers, and helps me pull on my space boots. "You'll get rashes and stuff. How are you liking your skin? And I don't mean your real one."

"It feels good so far," and it really does. "Almost energizing, and it's definitely regulating my temperature. Otherwise I'd be sweating buckets right about now."

"You'll find you get less tired sitting," she zips my boots to my pants, "and the electrical stimulation for your muscles and bones you might feel slightly. But I actually think it's pleasant, like a gentle tingling," and as she says it, I'm feeling it, especially in my right index finger.

"How many years have you been doing this?" I ask as she pulls Tyvek booties over my electric-blue spacesuited feet so I don't get them dirty.

"May 6, 1999, was my first crew, Space Shuttle *Discovery*," she says. "Seven astronauts," she picks up the suit's upper torso. "Unlike you here all by your lonesome. That's probably going to be the norm going forward, single pilots, depending on the vehicle. Or smaller crews of two or three. But to be honest, the way things are changing, I don't know what to expect."

She shows me how to lean forward, entering the torso from the back, working my head up through the neck opening. I push my arms through the sleeves, keenly aware of the slight tingling Stella mentioned. It doesn't feel bad at all, rather good I agree, and I'm perfectly comfortable in my skin but could do without the diaper. Or better said, I wish I could.

"It's a lot easier when you don't have that big metal neck ring, right?" she zips me up in back. "Or that awful rubber dam that snatches the hair out of your head if you're not careful. Of course, most of the guys don't have much hair, but it's a challenge for the women."

"To be honest, I've not worn one of these before," I confess.

"Nobody has," she zips my torso to my pants. "It's all been very hush-hush. No one's actually worn one during a launch. But there's a first time for everything."

"What is it called?"

"Around here, we keep it simple and call it a BS. A Blue Suit but it's not exactly blue, more of an iridescent blue that can go reflective like a mirror in an emergency."

"You mean, if I crash or end up in the ocean."

"It shows up like crazy if need be, and I can tell you from my own experience that it's comfortable and not that hard to get on and off when I'm not around to help you."

"It sounds like you've tried out the merchandise," taking off my CUFF, I tuck it into a pocket of my BS space pants.

"Absolutely everything I'm putting on you, I've put on myself," she says as I think of Mom. "It's crazy to think of wires and sensors replacing threads. When I first started working here, most people didn't have cell phones. Barely anybody was using the internet or any sort of social media."

Stella pulls up the hood of my skinsuit, and it form fits around my skull. The sensor-laden smart material firms up just enough to comfortably support the back of my neck.

"Lucky you, not needing a comm cap," she says. "Testing, 1-2-3 . . ."

I give a thumbs-up, reading her loud and clear through sensors in my conductive hood with its integrated audio system.

"1-2-3-4 . . . ," I reply, and she nods that she's picking me up fine in her headset. "Does this mean I have to wear the hood all the time to have radio contact?"

"No. There are teeny-tiny mics built into the fabric of your skin, right around your collarbones," she helps me into my space gloves. "The skin is good protection while you're learning to float. When it senses you're out of control, it stiffens enough to prevent injury as you bang around."

She tightens the palm straps, making sure that if the suit is pressurized in an emergency, the gloves still fit properly.

"I'm not planning to bang around," I reply.

"You scuba dive?"

"Yes."

"So, you're good at being neutrally buoyant. You've probably been up in the zero-gravity plane too. The Vomit Comet," she adds, and I nod. "You're still going to knock into things at first, you'll see."

00:00:00:00:0

STELLA attaches an oxygen hose to a port on my left thigh, clicking it into place, and we're getting close to showtime.

"I wish I knew more and felt better prepared," I may as well be honest with the last person I might ever see.

"That's what everybody says except for the ones we should worry about," she zips the spacesuit's soft helmet around my neck, pulling down the visor over my face.

Reaching for a valve on the control panel, she chooses a pressure of almost 3.5 pounds per square inch, and I feel the suit tighten and stiffen. Bending my legs and arms, I wiggle my inflated gloved fingers, reminded of why I've worked so hard at getting strong. Thank goodness for all the hours I've killed myself with weights, doing push-ups one handed or on my fingertips, squeezing tennis balls until my hands cramp.

Stella goes on to explain all sorts of minutiae that remind me why ART is good to have around. The oxygen flow in my helmet is controlled by the rate of my own breathing, very much like using a regulator when scuba diving. Only in this case there's no threat of running out of air, and there's also an antisuffocation valve, it's good to know.

It's now 7:20 p.m., and a message from Dick appears in my SPIES. He'll be downstairs waiting in 10. Stella disconnects the hose from my thigh, and opens a valve, the air hissing out like I'm wearing an inflatable mattress. She unzips my gloves and helmet, telling me they'll be waiting inside the rocket when I get there.

"Here's what to expect next," she begins taking off her Tyvek coveralls. "I'll meet you in the white room, and then I'm going to get you strapped in, repeating the pressure check and other fun stuff, okay?"

"Thank you," is all I can think to say as she leaves, and ART is giving me the countdown time in my SPIES.

T-minus 92 minutes . . .

At half past 7, I board the elevator, bare headed and gloveless in my vivid-blue spacesuit and Tyvek booties, looking like a clueless astronaut or in my case a lost one. Dick climbs out of his Suburban as I emerge from the double metal doors, and it's very dark back here. Moving with relative ease down the ramp, I walk toward the silver Airstream astrovan, windowless for privacy I won't be needing.

"Space looks good on you," Dick gives me the once-over. "What do you think?" he slides open the van's door.

"I think the BS is pretty good so far," I reply as we step inside what looks a lot like a compartment in a corporate jet.

Four big seats face each other with a table in between, a wall-mounted flat-screen is divided into quadrants displaying the rocket on its floodlit pad, and Kennedy's and Houston's Mission Control rooms.

"Ask me later," I add as I carefully sit down. "I guess I'll know better when my life depends on it."

"That's why you get the fun job of troubleshooting," he takes the seat across from me. "And all kidding aside, you can expect glitches. Something will go off-nominal as sure as we're sitting here right now. With your suit, your skin, it could be the vehicles themselves, especially ones untried and untested in the environment they're meant to operate in," and he's talking about the PEQUOD and the MOBE.

"I didn't notice any police cars," I lengthen the shoulder harness so I can fit it over my Blue Suit. "We're not worried about security at all? After everything else that's happened? It's a long dark stretch ahead," I add.

"If there's so much as one car with flashing lights, it sends the signal something's going on," Dick says as our van pulls away.

I can see where we're going on the flat-screen, but don't need security live feeds to know what I'd be looking at. During my academy days and return visits for special training, I got to know Kennedy Space Center like the back of my hand, driving around in one of our trucks or patrolling the local marshes and waterways in one of our airboats.

It's the ultimate selfie, watching our van on camera turning onto the NASA Parkway. To our left are buildings barely lit up, to our right the dark void of desolate scrubland where the pads are located near the water's edge. In other quadrants of the screen NASA personnel here and at Johnson Space Center in Houston are getting ready, the digital countdown ticking off the time before launch.

T-minus 52 minutes . . .

"What's going on with our rogue object?" I ask Dick.

"It did a series of burns to rendezvous with USA555A, and is closing in on it," he says.

"It's too soon for that unless it has a prop system on a par with ours or close," I protest.

"You've got 4 hours to get to GEO, to find whatever this predatory spacecraft is and take it out," he says as I think, *Who are you kidding?*

If all goes well, he adds, it should take eight and a half minutes for me to reach Low Earth Orbit (LEO), some 1,931 kilometers (1,200 miles) away. From there, it's about two hours to get to GEO, he says.

"Leaving you some wiggle room to locate the problem," he explains. "If possible."

"Your idea of wiggle room isn't exactly mine," I reply, and lit up on the flat-screen is the massive Vehicle Assembly Building with its huge American flag and NASA meatball painted on it.

Our ride together is coming to an end, and Dick clamps his hands on his knees, leaning forward in his seat, locking eyes with me.

"You're going to do fine," he promises what he truly can't. "Your entire life has been about this moment, Calli. You're more prepared than you know, and are going to find out soon enough," as the van comes to a stop.

Dick takes off his shoulder harness. He gets up from his seat.

"This is where I leave you. My car's behind us, and I'll be in Mission Control. After launch when you're passed off to Houston, I'll be linked to them."

He slides open the door, and I don't care if he doesn't like it, I get up awkwardly, giving him a hug.

"Godspeed, Calli," he kisses the top of my head as if I'm a child again, and then the door slides shut, and he's gone.

The van moves on, and in the flat-screen I watch the Suburban's headlights turning off toward the 4-story Launch Control Center where Dick will be sitting inside Mission Control. Cameras track my journey as we turn off on the road that will take us to the pad. Running parallel to us is the Crawlerway, two lanes of crushed Tennessee River rocks that the 3,000-ton crawler-transporter follows when carrying the mobile launcher and its precious cargo.

I've seen it many times before but never get used to it. The sight seems to defy the laws of physics, a platform the size of an Olympic swimming pool riding on 8 tractor belts while carrying an upright rocket. Moving at the blistering speed of 1.6 kilometers per hour (1 mph), and I ask ART if he's up.

"What can I help you with?" in my earpiece.

"Just making sure you're still here."

"Affirmative," he replies as I feel us slowing down.

Turning south toward the water, I can see our destination on the flat-screen and also in my SPIES. The towering steel scaffolding of the mobile launcher is bright in floodlights, the rocket and its solid-fuel boosters pristine white. Nearby is the water tower that seconds before ignition will flood the pad with a 450,000-gallon deluge to dampen the noise and vibration.

There's one parked car in sight as we stop in front of the 5,000-ton mobile launcher with its multiple platforms, my awaiting vehicle held in place by pyro bolts that explode on blastoff. Clouds of condensation are from the liquid oxygen, the rocket off-gassing and hissing like an awaiting dragon.

Climbing out of the van with nobody to greet me, I walk alone to the mobile launcher's steel elevator door. It slowly slides open, the inside lined with quilting, and buttons on the control panel designate the altitude of each platform. If I'm headed to various service structure areas, I might choose 36.5 meters (120 feet) or 45.7 meters (150 feet). For Space Shuttle launches back in the day, it was 59.5 meters (195 feet).

To catch my ride, I select the button for 70 meters (230 feet), and it's a slow boat to China, as impatient as I am by now, my adrenaline going, my heart at a good clip. It would be nice if my fancy built-in gizmos did something to help out more than they are, and that unpleasantly reminds me of what Dick said about glitches.

I can expect them. Likely there will be problems no one has anticipated, and that reminds me of what Mr. Owl did to Ranger the PONG.

"Okay, it's now or never, and I'm not talking to you, ART," taking a deep breath, I walk off the elevator into an open area of scaffolding on the top of the world.

41

I PAUSE by the railing, taking in the view, looking the rocket up and down, moved close to tears by its enormity.

Only the tip of its nose and the lightning-protection masts are higher than I am right now, the flame trench and fuel tanks illuminated 23 stories below. The night is clear enough that I can make out Cocoa Beach's string of lights, the ocean heaving and glinting, the surf lacy white on the dark shore.

"You can do this," under my breath.

"I'm sorry," ART in my ear. "What do you need me to do?"

"Wasn't meant for you," and off to my right is the walkway, a metal covered bridge, and I keep hearing my sister in my head.

Now or never . . . Now or never . . .

Big yellow chevrons painted on the mesh metal flooring point the opposite direction I'm going, offering an escape route for getting the hell-o out of Dodge in an emergency. The Yellow Brick Road (as it's called) reminds astronauts which way to run as they make a mad dash for the zip line and its attached blaze-orange chair at the opening of the covered metal bridge I'm about to traverse.

A steel cable runs from here to the ground well beyond the pad, and from there you're supposed to flee into a bunker, and good luck with all that while wearing a spacesuit, blue or otherwise. But if push came to shove, I wouldn't hesitate. It's not so different from the good ole days when Carme and I would streak through the air from the barn to the dock, and as a last resort I'd be on that zip line in a flash.

But it's a choice I won't have to make because it's not possible in this situation. The PEQUOD and its attached MOBE are closed up inside the rocket's clamshell fairing like a bug in a Venus flytrap. If there's a fire or imminent explosion, I can't be jettisoned to safely land the spaceplane like a glider on a runway.

Escaping on foot isn't an option. I'd never make it back through the two hatches in time to try the zip line. And I guess that's the price you pay for making sure no one sees that what we're launching isn't a weather satellite, it enters my mind as the metal bridge I'm crossing terminates in a set of saloon-type steel doors.

I push my way into the white room, a clean bright staging area that, like a surgical tent, encloses and protects the rocket's open hatch. Stella has on her headset, swathed from head to toe in white like an awaiting angel.

"Hands on the wall and spread 'em," she's not being funny, and I do as I'm told.

She pulls off my disposable booties one at a time, a difficult task while standing up in a spacesuit, especially if you're still getting used to it.

"I don't want you tracking in dirt," she informs me. "You don't want to be breathing recycled particulates."

"I certainly don't."

"You're all set to crawl in, and I'll be right behind you," she means that literally, and I get down on my hands and knees.

The steel ramp she's laid down like a plank connects the hatch in front of us to one on top of the PEQUOD. A port at the back of the spaceplane is attached to the MOBE, the entire vehicle bolted upright inside the fairing. As I inch along in my spacesuit,

I'm aware of the drop-off on either side of me and wouldn't want to lose my balance, toppling overboard.

I might not fall very far but there's a good chance I'd get wedged between unforgiving metal structures that would severely damage my pride if nothing else. I might be stuck for hours and suffocate. For that matter, I don't know how anyone would rescue me when it requires being this close to a fully fueled rocket.

Well, what I'm not going to do is die of embarrassment, I decide, and safely across, I shimmy through the second hatch into the glass cockpit of my Chase Plane. The avionics are up and running, a single carbon fiber seat liner facing multiple displays and fail-safe switches.

"Be careful not to bang your head," Stella's right behind me. "Use only the designated hand- and footholds to pull yourself in position," and this is going to take some getting used to.

When I work in simulators, I'm usually sitting upright like a normal person. But inside a rocket, the orientation shifts 90 degrees. I'm standing on a wall, then crawling along the floor to climb into my seat, and it isn't pretty.

"Grab that handhold overhead," Stella says. "Do a pull-up and I'll help lift your feet into position."

I pull myself up, and it's not easy in the spacesuit. Then I'm lying on my back with the control stick between my legs, my bright-blue space boots elevated above my head.

"I'm not being fresh," Stella roots around for the crotch strap. "Here we go. Can you reach the lap belt on your side? I've got the one over here."

"Here it is," I slide the metal tongue into the buckle with a reassuring click.

"Crank it tight. Tighter than you think is needed or comfortable."

"Got it," I pull the belt tight.

"Tighter. You'll thank me later."

"Copy," sucking in my gut, and ouch that's snug.

"I can reach your shoulder straps . . . hang on . . . got both of them," and she fastens them. "Now you need to really crank down on them, Calli. You're gonna want them really snug . . ."

I tighten them some more.

"Let me help," and she gives them quite the yank before connecting my oxygen hose to the port on my thigh.

We zip on my gloves, my helmet, and she shows me netting on the side of my seat. More of it is along the wall, and it will be handy for stowing my spacesuit and other items so they don't float away in weightlessness. I study the displays, the toggle switches overhead.

"Everything's computerized," Stella connects the push-to-talk button on my shoulder harness.

"Seems a little low tech," I point out.

"Unless you're on a spacewalk, I don't think you want Mission Control hearing your every comment," she replies. "You can go into a voice-activated mode if you like. Or push the button on your stick."

"What about when I'm not in my seat?"

"Speakerphone or in your earpiece. Just like on the ground, and you'll get more familiarized as you go along with the obvious assistance," she says, and she must mean ART. "This thing's built to fly autonomously, and you won't be flipping switches unless it's a really bad day at the ranch. Same with the control stick. It's there if you have to manually override. Or if for some reason you want to hand control whatever it is you're doing, and from what I hear, you've got plenty of stick time and even more hours in the simulators."

She has me open and shut my smart visor, conducting oxygen and pressure tests, and I see the life-support data in the clear plastic shielding covering my face, and also in my SPIES and the Chase Plane's heads-up display. She pressurizes my suit again, reminding me unpleasantly how difficult it is to move my arms and hands into natural positions.

Then the purge valve again, and I hear all the air rushing out as my BS deflates. Finally, we begin the communications check, and I imagine Dick listening in.

00:00:00:00:0

"CALLI, how do you read us?" Kennedy's launch control talking to me personally sends a chill up my body unless it's my skinsuit doing it.

"Loud and clear," I make my first radio call from a rocket.

"T-minus 20 minutes and counting. The weather's looking great, skies are clear."

"Copy, ready to go in here," I reply, and Stella gives me a thumbs-up.

"You're all set, and it's time for me to fly like the wind," she says now that I'm all strapped in, not going anywhere no matter what. "May I shake your hand, Captain Chase?"

I awkwardly hold out a gloved one, thanking her for trussing me up like Houdini, and she makes her way back through the hatch. I hear it shutting as I see it in my lenses, and there must be small cameras all over creation. I imagine her crawling along the narrow metal ramp, and the sound of it clanging and scraping when she drags it into the white room.

In a few minutes, she'll close the rocket's hatch, and from that point on I'm committed. She'll hurry down the elevator, dashing into her car, the rocket off-gassing and hissing as if it's getting violently impatient. She'll speed away to safety, and I'm either going into outer space or nowhere ever again.

"It looks like it's just you and me now," I say to ART. "If the worst happens, you'll still be around but I won't. Take care of Carme and everyone. And know I appreciate you. I'm sorry I wasn't all that nice at first. I didn't mean to hurt your feelings even if you don't have them," and darn it's hard to say.

"Enabling control stick circuitry," his obtuse voice in my ear, and so much for sentimentality. "You now have the capability of manual operations should a critical auto-function fail," and I recall Stella's and my conversation about hand controlling if I want or need to take over.

Then Mission Control is in my other ear, instructing me to lower my visor, to initiate the flow of oxygen as I watch the countdown clock in my displays. At T-minus 5 minutes I'm given the official GO for the launch, and I can't believe I'm doing this. Watching the clock, 4 minutes, 3, 2 . . .

"One minute, Calli," Kennedy's launch controller, and maybe I'm reading into things, but he seems friendly. "Be prepared for the shake of your life . . . 30 seconds . . . 20 . . . 10 . . . main engine start . . ."

The twin BE-4s roar to life as ART tells me in my ear that they're at 100 percent as the countdown continues . . .

". . . 3, 2, 1 . . . ," and next the solid rocket boosters ignite, and now I'm being shaken like a margarita.

It's as if we're having a seizure as we're shoved up through the atmosphere, and all I can do is hold on, strapped in on my back until 80 seconds into the flight when things begin to simmer down.

"We've just passed max q," Houston lets me know the worst of the structural loading is over, and our vehicle probably isn't going to break apart in the atmosphere.

The boosters begin to burn out, then the 6 muffled booms when the pyrotechnic fasteners explode, jettisoning away the huge metal tubes.

"Mach 13," mission control has been switched to Houston, and my ride is considerably smoother, and I can raise my visor. "One minute into the flight," and I'm watching the speed and other data on my displays.

Suddenly, I'm shoved forward hard against my restraints, the BE-4 engines drained of fuel and suddenly quitting. More pyros blow, and the first stage jettisons away. Then the second stage's single engine ignites, slamming me back in my seat, and I understand better why Stella wanted me to tighten my harness.

Next the clamshell fairing blows off, and I can hear and feel that bang big-time because it's right over my head. My arms are starting to feel heavier as I use the control stick, switching to the systems page, grateful I'm not seeing any red warning indicators that might suggest death is imminent. The engine isn't about to fail or explode. My oxygen is good.

"How's our trajectory?" I ask ART, remembering he's my copilot, and he switches me to that page in my heads-up display.

"Trajectory is normal," he says. "Engines and all systems, normal."

"Mach 17 . . . ," Houston over the radio.

I'm informed that the g-forces are up to 2.8, as I would expect. Now I'm really feeling it in my arms, and I cross them at my chest, tucking my hands under the straps of the harness.

". . . 3 Gs . . . Mach 21 . . . Mach 25 . . ."

At 5 Gs, I'm feeling the pain. No training or simulator has quite prepared me for this. It's as if a big dog is sitting on me, my skinsuit compressing my abdomen and legs to minimize the forces. But there's no smart fabric that would help my lungs expand, and it's getting scary hard to breathe. Eight and a half minutes into my wild ride, the engine stops. The g-forces ease. And then my arms float up.

"Welcome to space, Captain Chase," and it's Dick's voice in my earpiece. "There are a lot of relieved people down here on the ground."

"I'm kind of relieved myself," I begin unzipping my gloves as Dick lets me know that we're on a secure radio feed.

Our conversation won't be overheard by mission controllers or anyone, he says, not that I believe him. Off comes my helmet while he explains that in a little less than two hours, I should reach GEO and rendezvous with the satellite I'm there to protect.

Digging my CUFF out of a pocket in my spacesuit pants, I unzip the pants from the torso. Taking off everything, I begin stowing my disassembled BS in the netting.

"The rogue object we're tracking is staying the course," Dick informs me. "It's fitting the description of some type of satellite as you know, but obviously that's not what it is. Hopefully we'll know more when you get there."

"We can see it, but can it see us?" I can't stop worrying about it the same way I'm unconvinced my SIN can't be detected.

Now that my Chase Plane and its attached MOBE are no longer enclosed in a fairing, we should be picked up easily on radar or possibly by a space telescope. But hopefully we're not. The vehicle's conductive skin is in stealth mode, rather much like Ranger when he's ghosting. We're supposed to be totally blacked out, not just on radar but visually.

We're to blend with our surroundings, and mostly that's going to be the dark vacuum of space. But I can't say for sure. While there's much the cameras can pick up, they can't show me what color I am. I have to infer it from one of many mind-withering codes, and right now our shade of black is RV3, which ART lets me know is *raven*.

Dick assures me there's no reason to believe my vehicle is detectable by the normal means. And I don't like his use of words as I look out the porthole window next to my seat, seeing nothing but complete blackness.

"What about the weather satellite everybody's looking for?" I remind him as I put on my CUFF. "Imagine all those satellite watchers out there looking for it," I add but they're not who I'm worried about.

"We've solved that rather simply," his voice in my earpiece. "It's been leaked and making the rounds that a very expensive weather satellite didn't deploy properly, and burned up in the atmosphere along with the fairing, the rocket stages."

"That might do the trick," I answer but I'm never reassured when it comes to Neva Rong, and I sure as heck don't want her knowing what's really going on.

I remind Dick with all due respect that when he tried the same manipulation after the rocket blew up, there weren't any takers. No one who matters buys that NASA might have been looking for something important in the debris at Wallops Island or I wouldn't be in outer space right now. His misinformation didn't fool anyone.

"Do we have to worry about anyone monitoring my communications with the ground?" I ask. "Because no one's supposed to be up here. So anybody listening to us would be onto our secret mission."

"Nothing can be monitored," Dick reiterates. "I suggest you acclimate yourself to the MOBE, and to floating around. No matter how much they tell you it's like being neutrally buoyant underwater, it's not," and as I release my harness and various straps, I remember Stella saying the same thing, and both of them are right.

Floating in microgravity is nothing like scuba diving or anything else I've ever done, I'm finding out the hard way after shoving off a little too vigorously from my seat, knocking my head on the ceiling.

Terrified of kicking my avionics, the control stick or switches, I tuck myself into a ball. Slowly somersaulting out of the cockpit, I float along the ceiling like a PONG.

42

"OKAY, this is ridiculous!" I'm mortified, trying to straighten myself out, moving and knocking about in my skinsuit like a drunken eel.

"The key is to do everything much more slowly than you think you should," Dick's voice through speakers now. "The first time I was on Station, I was like a bull in a china shop. It's a little bit like flying a helicopter . . ."

"It's not anything like that!"

"What I was about to say, Calli, is very small corrections, feel it, don't think it," his voice all around me.

I begin to settle down. Or rather I'm up, still around the ceiling, and swimming with my hands won't get me anywhere, only makes matters worse. Trying to hold my breath or blow it out to regulate my buoyancy doesn't work when there's no gravity or water.

"Use your finger," Dick says, and for a moment I figure he's referring to my WAND, my scarred right index finger.

But he's suggesting I push off and stop with a finger, doesn't matter which one. Any finger will do, and he goes on to give me a physics primer, and I relax more. I stop struggling and begin floating in place as Dick goes on about mass versus weight, and every force creates an equal and opposing one. The lighter the touch, the better, he lectures me like he always has as I begin to get the knack of it.

I float around a storage area of Nomex storage bags strapped in place, and the galley with its hot-water dispenser and drawers of space straws and drinks. Grabbing a silvery bag of lemon punch, I drink a toast to myself because someone should. I just blasted off in a rocket. I'm in outer space headed to GEO, and if I never did another thing, this might be enough.

Clamping the straw shut so the liquid doesn't float out, I think about the last time I drank this stuff, when I was handcuffed and tethered. I don't want to fool with reconstituting spaghetti or beef stew at the moment but wouldn't mind a simple protein bar. In fact, I take two out of the netting inside a drawer.

Floating to the hatch that connects the PEQUOD to the MOBE, I turn a valve to equalize the pressure. Then I crank the handle, pushing in the metal access door, and I thread my way through the opening, careful not to scrape my back or whack my head again. The MOBE looks familiar because I saw its test model splash down at the Gantry, and I spot the hand- and footrails.

Moving from one to the other, doing as Dick said, I let my fingers do the walking. There's not much in here, mostly storage space, and I float to the single carbon fiber seat liner just like the one in my Chase Plane. The control stick, the displays and switches, everything mirrors the cockpit I was just sitting in, but there's no toilet or galley.

There's very little in the way of creature comforts, the MOBE a combination utility module and getaway car, sort of like having a trailer that's capable of driving you home after the attached truck breaks down. It takes some finagling for me to get situated, hanging on to a handrail while fishing around with my toes to find the foot loop.

"There, that's better," I say to ART, and I pull down my hood, aware that my hair is going to float up like I've seen a ghost.

"What can I help you with?" his voice through speakers.

The porthole next to my seat is filled with the empty blackness of space, nothing to see at the moment, and I ask him to give me a quick overview of the MOBE's capabilities. Besides being an emergency vehicle should something happen to my Chase Plane, what else might be good for me to know?

His dry technical explanation sounds exactly like what Dad would say, and I deduce that what I'm sitting in right now is another version of my Tahoe. The MOBE is equipped with a High Energy Laser that can take out a spaceship. I have a "harpoon" and drone deployment at my disposal for capturing and dragging debris or other objects we might want to lasso or shepherd for some reason.

I can fire short microwave bursts to damage electronics, and that's what I suspect is happening up here in GEO. The rogue satellite-like object is causing brain damage resulting in mayhem with data. Our flight trajectory is calculated to rendezvous with USA555A, our endangered spy satellite, in exactly 22 minutes, and I decide this would be a fine time to try out the toilet.

The bathroom is nothing more than a broom-closet-size space with a curtain. Inside is a stainless steel bowl with a tank under it that no one wants to empty, and a tube with a cup on the end that you urinate in no matter your anatomy. Everything floats in microgravity, especially things that you don't want at large, and I hook my toes through a footrail on the floor.

Tugging my zipper down a little way, I can feel my skin relax as it powers off, and it's a lot easier to pull down around my knees than a wet suit, that's for sure. The toilet's not a flushing one, and flowing air sucks the nasties into the tank. Or that's the hope, and I help myself to the netted bag for toilet paper. Good to go, zipping up my skin again and unhooking my toes, I float back to my chair.

I'm barely in my seat when ART alerts me that we're beginning a series of rendezvous burns, and he fires the thrusters. I hear them banging like fireworks as we slow down and gain altitude. I maneuver my spaceship through multiple burns, the thrusters firing and banging.

I can see Earth outside my porthole window, a dazzling blue marble with swirls of slowly moving white clouds. I recognize the reddish orange of the mountains in China, and I guess I know what our satellite's spying on. Sunlight flares on its solar arrays about the length of a football field away.

The rogue object doesn't seem to be moving, neither one of us do as we orbit at 17,864 kilometers per hour (11,100 mph).

"What is this thing?" I ask ART. "Can we get a better look?"

I can see it getting closer as he zooms in, and the rogue spacecraft looks like another satellite only with a larger somewhat cylindrical body. Its 4 solar arrays reflect the light of the sun, and I can see a hatch door is open.

"What are we picking up?" I'm liking this less by the second.

"Sensors indicate surveillance and propulsion capabilities," ART answers. "The vehicle is controlled remotely."

"Does it know we're here, and is there reason to think it might be weaponized?" I ask the most important questions.

"Insufficient data. There are no indications of evasive or aggressive maneuvers," and ART's no sooner said that when I notice something bizarre.

At first, I think my eyes are playing tricks on me as I watch what looks like a big translucent cone floating this way. I can see it out the porthole but it doesn't show up in any of the displays.

"Do you see what I'm seeing?" I ask ART, but he doesn't understand, and I don't have time to explain.

00:00:00:00:0

THE CONE is coming right at us, traveling in a perfectly straight line that it will follow into infinity if nothing interferes with or stops it.

"It's evading visual detection but are we picking up its composition?" I ask, using my control stick to toggle through menus.

$(C_2H_4)_n$, ART shows me in my SPIES, the chemical composition of polyethylene, in other words, plastic. And small amounts of various metals including aluminum, nickel, copper and tungsten, all of it consistent with some sort of energy-emitting weapon, and I'm reminded of the turret on top of my Chase Car.

"Where's the HEL on this thing?" I'm looking for a menu that might offer the High Energy Laser as an option, and then ART has it in my heads-up display.

I'm feeling slightly frantic as the cone-shaped object gets closer, closer, its round base coming at us like an open mouth. I think of the Tracking and Targeting Locator (TATL) for the weapons systems in my Tahoe, and a spaceship sure as heck ought to have an even better one.

"TATL is engaged but unable to provide all functions," ART says, giving me a weapons display that's missing data, and I tell him I also need to see the information in my SPIES.

"I'm going to have to line up the target visually since it's not showing up on the display," I exclaim as the plastic cone gets closer, and I go for broke. "Another burn, and make a 10-degree turn. Let's go eye to eye, and take out both these mothers!"

ART fires up the thrusters again, and the view out my porthole changes, the cone closing in, directly level with us, and I grab the control stick. Remembering what Dick said about a light touch, I take manual control of the HEL, lining it up on the display while watching the cone off my shoulder.

When the weapon is in fire mode, it points where I orient the rear of my vehicle, and it's not precision shooting, more like a drive-by when I line up the target with my eyes while controlling the stick with my right hand. Closer, closer, the cone will be on top of us in seconds, and I squeeze off two rapid bursts that I can't hear or see.

"Target destroyed," ART lets me know, the ruined cone-shaped weapon tumbling by my window.

"One down!" I turn my attention to the satellite-looking spacecraft with its open hatch. "Going eye to eye again," I point at my eyes, and then at the target, making that gesture again at the same instant a thruster bangs to life, suddenly igniting, reminding me of the darn car alarms and engines gunning.

"CRAP, not again . . . !" I exclaim as I see the Earth speed past my window.

Then it's back, coming from the opposite direction, faster, and faster, flying by my porthole as I'm pushed toward the wall.

"Turn it off!" I'm yelling at ART the same way I did in the wind tunnel. "We're in a spin!" as the Earth passes by again and again and again.

"Unable. The thruster is stuck."

"Why?" and I need to stop yelling because for sure he'll start yelling back.

"I'm getting an error code for a malfunction," he almost shouts as I think of what Dick said about glitches.

"Which thruster?" I tone it down as we spiral like a top.

If we don't do something fast, we'll burn through our fuel, and gravity will have its way with us.

"Port aft thruster," ART identifies the culprit.

"Isolate it."

"Fuel manifold valve for port aft thruster closed," he tells me because otherwise I wouldn't know.

The Earth continues zooming past my window every second, and it isn't easy holding myself in my seat as centrifugal force tries to push me against the side of the spaceship. The only hope of stopping the spin is to counteract it.

"Fire up starboard aft thruster," as I work the stick, my toes wedged under a foot loop.

Another bang, and the Earth goes by slower . . . and slower . . . and stops.

"Cut thruster. We've nullified spin rate. I'm going to hand fly her to target."

And then I go after the satellite-camouflaged spacecraft with its open port yawning like the maw to hell. Making small corrections with the stick, I change my trajectory just enough to line myself up with the target at the same time, and I realize it's doing the same thing to me.

It's sluggishly reorienting, nowhere as nimble as our vessel, and I watch through the glass while keeping a light touch on the stick. Lining up the target in the heads-up weapons display exactly where I want it, I squeeze the trigger. I can't see or hear the laser beams, but I know they found their mark, sending the spacecraft into a spin it won't recover from, its scorched solar arrays whirling like a pinwheel.

ART lets me know that we took out the electrical circuitry, frying everything that matters. There are no transmissions detected, no sign of life.

"Targets disabled," I push the talk button on the stick.

"Objective accomplished," Carme's voice startles me through the speakers.

"A little more enthusiasm would be appreciated," I reply but I'm smiling from ear to ear.

"You find any aliens?"

"Not yet. Just a cheap plastic microwave gun shaped like a traffic cone."

"I never had a doubt," and now it's Mom on the feed.

"That's my girl," Dad sounds as pleased as punch.

"A 9 out of 10," Conn pays me back for what I said about his piloting.

"Why did you take away a point?" I reply, playing his flirty game.

"To give you something to look forward to."

"Lex is fine," Mom again. "I knew you'd be wondering. You're a worrier just like me."

"Mission accomplished so far," Dick announces.

"What do you mean, *so far*?" sliding my toes out of the foot loop, I float out of my seat, flying like a superhero through the MOBE.

"A few housekeeping matters for you to take care of, and then we're bringing you home," his voice follows me as I make my way through the hatch, returning to my Chase Plane.

"Such as?" I inquire, and it would be nice if he could say *good job* or *way to go* or something.

"Debris management for one thing," it's Conn talking again, and I grab a handrail near the galley, thinking now might be a good time for real food.

Almost real food, and I unzip the lid of a white Nomex bag Velcroed and bungee corded to the galley's ceiling. Inside the fire-retardant storage container are all sorts of things to eat, held in place with netting so they don't float away. Macaroni and cheese, Italian vegetables, beef stew, fajitas, spicy Cajun rice and sausage.

". . . Assuming the rogue spacecraft is Neva Rong's, we need to get detailed images of it and our damaged spy satellite, USA555A . . . ," Conn is saying.

Deciding on spaghetti, I rehydrate it by inserting the hot water dispenser's needle into a port at the top of the bag. I ask ART how to open the package, and he directs me to another Nomex container that has blunt-tipped scissors attached to a tether and inside netting.

". . . We need to capture any data we can before removing the damaged objects from GEO," Conn goes through my upcoming chores as I place a rubber-lined trash bag inside a white vinyl pouch that I bungee cord to the siding.

"How is it?" Dick asks as I squeeze spaghetti into my mouth.

"How's what?"

"How's the food?" and it's easy to forget there are cameras everywhere.

"Not bad at all," I reply honestly. "Of course, the spacecraft was Neva's, that's if you ask me. The weapon, the microwave gun, is disposable like a 3-D printed pistol, sort of. And I'm guessing it's single fire, deployed to brain damage a satellite with a microwave punch. Afterward, the plastic cone is space debris that the atomic gases will deteriorate eventually."

"Enjoy lunch, I'll be back with you a little later," Dick signs off, and we're disconnected.

Floating up to the ceiling again, I root around in the netting, thinking the oatmeal with raisins and brown sugar might be good to try next. Another shot of hot water, squishing it around inside the bag, another snip with the scissors, and I float through walls tiled with white storage bags.

Returning to the cockpit, I'm doing just fine without gravity, even sucking oatmeal from a bag while I'm at it, and I pull myself back into the carbon fiber seat, and am fastening the lap belt to hold me in when ART lets me know audibly that a voice mail was just left.

"I'm sorry," I reply, puzzling as I eat. "I don't have a phone up here."

I look out the porthole at the blue-and-white Earth vivid against pitch darkness, grateful it's not flying past anymore, that I'm no longer spinning.

"The VM was left on your mobile phone in your room at crew quarters," and ART takes it upon himself to play the videophone message, Neva Rong's face appearing in my heads-up display as if it's a crystal ball.

"Hello, Calli," her cold smile and colder stare.

Dressed richly, smartly, and for warm weather, she's sitting at a desk, a blood-red kerchief spilling from the breast pocket of her ivory suit. On the wall behind her is Pandora's logo, depicting a winged female warrior, reminding me of the tattoo on her devoted hitman's dead neck.

". . . Such a nice surprise running into you at the White House yesterday . . ."

"Where was she calling from?" I ask ART.

". . . Your first time can be overwhelming but I'm glad you got to see it. Such a treat for you, I'm sure . . . ," she says as if I fell off the potato truck.

"The call was made from the Pandora Space Systems assembly facility at Kennedy Space Center," ART informs me in my earpiece while I hear Neva over speakerphone.

". . . And I was very sorry to hear about the incident on your farm," she outrageously goes on. "How terrifying to have a murderous duo show up with guns and gasoline . . ."

"Does Dick know she's at Kennedy, that she's in his own backyard this very minute?" and why bother asking, because of course Dick knows.

". . . And I hear a child was present for all of it. Poor Lex . . . ," Neva's dry-ice smile and unwavering dead stare.

"Affirmative," ART answers that yes, Dick and the powers that be are aware that since we saw Neva at the White House, she's flown one of her private jets to Cape Canaveral, Florida.

And how weird to think she may have been a stone's throw away while I was getting ready to launch.

". . . Ta-ta, Calli. Until next time!" she promises cheerily, and if looks could kill, I wouldn't be here anymore. "Don't forget to give my very best to your mom."

ABOUT THE AUTHOR

Photo © Patrick Ecclesine

In 1990, Patricia Cornwell sold her first novel, *Postmortem*, while working at the Office of the Chief Medical Examiner in Richmond, Virginia. An auspicious debut, it went on to win the Edgar, Creasey, Anthony, and Macavity Awards as well as the French Prix du Roman d'Adventure prize—the first book ever to claim all these distinctions in a single year. Growing into an international phenomenon, the Scarpetta series won Cornwell the Sherlock Award for best detective created by an American author, the Gold Dagger Award, the RBA Thriller Award, and the Medal of Chevalier of the Order of Arts and Letters for her contributions to literary and artistic development.

Today, Cornwell's novels and iconic characters are known around the world. Beyond the Scarpetta series, Cornwell has written the definitive nonfiction account of Jack the Ripper's identity, cookbooks, a children's book, a biography of Ruth Graham, and two other fictional series based on the characters Win Garano and Andy Brazil. While writing *Quantum*, the first book in the Captain Chase series, Cornwell spent two years researching space, technology, and robotics at Captain Calli Chase's home base, NASA's Langley Research Center, and studied cutting-edge law enforcement and security techniques with the Secret Service, the US Air Force, Space Force, NASA Protective Services, Scotland Yard, and Interpol.

Cornwell was born in Miami. She grew up in Montreat, North Carolina, and now lives and works in Boston and Los Angeles.